10/25

Under Cloak of Darkness:

The Story of John Apparite

Under Cloak of Darkness:

The Story of John Apparite

I. Michael Koontz

Five Star • Waterville, Maine

First Edition
First Printing: July 2006

Published in 2006 in conjunction with Tekno Books and Ed Gorman.

Set in 11 pt. Plantin.

Printed in the United States on permanent paper.

Library of Congress Cataloging-in-Publication Data

Koontz, I. Michael, 1963–
    Under cloak of darkness : the story of John Apparite / by
I. Michael Koontz.—1st ed.
      p. cm.
    ISBN 1-59414-431-1 (hc : alk. paper)
    I. Title.
PS3611.O625U53 2006
813'.6—dc22   2006002674

To my ever-patient wife,
and my two young daughters.
Hang in there—I'll be off the computer in a minute.

Duty violated is still with us,
for our happiness or our misery.
If we say the darkness shall cover us,
in the darkness as in the light
our obligations are yet with us.

—Daniel Webster, 1830

Introduction

The world political climate after World War II was one of acute tension and uncertainty. The communist Soviet Union, under the iron fist of Dictator Josef Stalin, had oppressively brought East Germany and Poland to bear, and had Greece, Yugoslavia, and Czechoslovakia in its sights. Overtly, the USSR used military force and repression to further its aims, as witnessed by its eventual invasion of Czechoslovakia in 1948; covertly, it used an extensive program of espionage and counter-espionage aimed at the Western Allies—chiefly the United States and Great Britain—for the expansion of Soviet-style communism around the globe.

The Soviets were expert in intelligence; its military branch, known as GRU, was so effective in World War II that they not only served as Stalin's personal security team at the Yalta Conference, but they also took the opportunity to eavesdrop on President Franklin Roosevelt during that event. After the war, an off-shoot agency, then called KI, consolidated Soviet intelligence and extended its espionage net around the globe with devastating results; in 1954, it was renamed to the more famous and feared acronym, KGB.

For the Western intelligence agent, a subdivision of the KGB was even more terrifying in its reputation and ruthlessness: SMERSH, short for *"Smert Shpionam,"* or "Death to Spies." It was thought by some to have been dissolved in 1946, but in truth continued to secretly operate with impunity, and many valuable Western agents would indeed suffer at their hands in the years following the Second World War.

The West responded in kind. In 1947, the United States formed the Division of Central Intelligence, also known as the CIA, to counter the international communist espionage threat. In 1952, a second agency was formed which in some ways was even more secretive and powerful than the CIA: the National Security Agency, commonly called the NSA. Even today, most of what the NSA does remains undisclosed to the public.

The United States' closest ally, Great Britain, ramped up its intelligence services as well, bolstering their internal division, known as MI5, as well as their more famous international agency (as the employer of the fictional agent James Bond), known as MI6. And, in an effort to solidify worldwide Western intelligence gathering, a secret but highly effective intelligence network between five nations (the United States, Great Britain, Canada, Australia, and New Zealand) was created with the signing of the "UK-USA Agreement" in 1947.

By the mid-1950s, the game was afoot. All around the globe, Soviet and Western intelligence agents bought and sold military, political, and scientific secrets, and murdered, kidnapped, and generally crossed and double-crossed each other in a covert though very real and deadly war. The American public, however, remained blissfully unaware of nearly all of it.

For the United States and Great Britain, the most feared Soviet tactic in this war was communist infiltration; double-agents and spies littered the Western intelligence and scientific communities. After the United States was dealt a blow with the Alger Hiss and Harry Dexter White affairs in 1948, it became clear in the upper levels of the United States Government that secrecy was the first and most important order of business. As potentially every level of security had been compromised, drastic measures needed to be taken.

In 1950, the United States created an agency which would be small, secret, and elite, yet have the power to effectively fight this new kind of war. It had no official name, and was so secretive that its existence was unknown to the FBI. Its mission was to conduct worldwide espionage in the interest of the United States using whatever means necessary; assassination and murder were routine. As no permanent records were kept, its files cannot be found in any U.S. Government office; not even at CIA headquarters in Langley, Virginia, nor at the National Security Agency at Fort George G. Meade, Maryland. As a counter to the KGB and SMERSH, it was unparalleled in its successes, despite the fact that nearly sixty percent of its agents died performing their duties.

Its founder was rumored to be a uniquely impressive, ruthless, and powerful (though enigmatic) figure; his true name remains unknown. Its most successful agent was as talented and nearly as enigmatic, and until recently, only this was known about him: his code name was Agent E; his assumed name was John Apparite; and the rumors of his exploits defied imagination. What follows is a part of his tale.

As no evidence exists that this secretive agency has been disbanded, the sources for this story cannot be revealed, though fifty years have elapsed since the events described in this book. For the same reason, some of the names have been changed or are incomplete.

One
"Your new name
is John Apparite"

The *Times*, London, 29 May 1955:

> *Body of Unidentified Man Found in St. James's Park: The*
> *unclothed body of a man was discovered yesterday morning*
> *near the Royal Artillery Memorial in St. James's Park. Two*
> *small-caliber bullet wounds have been identified in the chest of*
> *the victim, who has been described by Scotland Yard officials*
> *as a Caucasian male between the ages of thirty and forty, of*
> *athletic build, with brown hair and blue eyes. He is thought*
> *possibly to have been an American. All attempts to identify the*
> *victim have been unsuccessful, and Scotland Yard officials are*
> *requesting the public contact them with any information about*
> *the victim or the murder, believed to have taken place during*
> *the night of the twenty-seventh.*

What the brief story in the *Times* could not say was this:
the man indeed was an American, age thirty-four, who could
never be identified as his name was not listed in any official
registry in any nation in the world. He was an operative in
the most powerful and clandestine espionage agency in
United States history—the "Superagent" program—and
had been working covertly in the United Kingdom. His contacts, agents from the MI5 and MI6 British intelligence services, knew him only by the code name "Agent G." They
had been led to believe he was working for the United States

11

Agency of Central Intelligence.

At 0100 on the morning of the twenty-eighth, Agent G had been awaiting a rendezvous with an English agent behind the Royal Artillery Memorial in St. James's Park; each man was to carry a jagged portion of an English five-pound note they were to match together to insure each other's identity. They were meeting to discuss the assassination of a top-level Soviet SMERSH operative known as "Viktor" who had recently arrived in the United Kingdom.

Agent G was waiting in a break in the shrubs behind the large memorial; its bulk, and the trees and bushes behind it, shielded him from the traffic and lights of the Mall to the front and Horse Guards Road to the side, although both streets were practically deserted at this time of the early morning. Despite its central London location, the area behind the memorial was well situated for a covert meeting.

At 0102, Agent G saw a man walking purposefully around the memorial toward him; he assumed it was the English agent, although he had not yet met him in person. The Superagent held out his portion of the five-pound note, as did the Englishman: the serial number and cut edges were a match, confirming each man's identity to the other. Agent G was the first to speak.

"You're late, but it's good you've come. I've confirmed that Viktor is near, probably in London itself."

"Yes," said the English agent, "intelligence we have from our man in the KGB has confirmed that Viktor arrived last month."

"I believe he will begin assassination operations; probably of Western agents, or even British Cabinet members. He may also attempt to 'turn' agents that may be disgruntled or under financial strain given the present British economy."

"Agreed," the Englishman replied. "Do you have colleagues in the United Kingdom that I should put on alert? If so, tell me their locations and my people can warn them—with extreme discretion, naturally," he added.

"I work alone," said Agent G. "Can your KGB mole pinpoint Viktor's exact location?"

"There's no need. He's right here." Before Agent G could answer or reach for his weapon, the Englishman had a semi-automatic pistol pointed at the American, a silencer threaded on the end.

"Pheeewt! Pheeewt!" The pistol fired two bullets, each entering Agent G's heart and tearing open the thick, muscular left ventricle. The blood poured out of it, gushing with each contraction as the heart rhythm accelerated to over two hundred beats per minute in a vain attempt to keep him alive, and rapidly filled his thorax. He gasped, collapsed onto his knees, and then fell over onto the ground as his heart fibrillated. A moment later it stopped.

A tall, pale man walked around the corner of the memorial.

"It is finished?" he said in a thick, Slav accent.

"Yes. Perhaps we should have taken him, Viktor; made him talk," answered the English agent.

"Nyet," said the pale man, "The American had nothing to tell; it is better he is dead. I *enjoy* watching him die."

Agent G's assassination would go nearly unnoticed in Great Britain, aside from the brief commotion that an unsolved murder would naturally excite in that country. Five weeks later, on July 2nd, 1955, and 3,185 miles away, however, his death resulted in a very curious meeting that would prove crucial to the future security of the United States of America.

"This will be the only personal conversation you and I will

ever have, Mr. K————, and that will be the last time I will call you by your given name. Your new name is John Apparite."

The man now called John Apparite found it difficult to meet the gaze of the hard-looking character speaking so imperiously to him; a gaze so focused and intense it seemed there must be a well of white-hot fire burning behind the man's eyes to give it such power, reminding Apparite of the LASER prototype he had seen the month before. Averting his own eyes from that discomforting, piercing gaze, Apparite took a moment to size up the rest of the man who was glaring at him so intently.

The Director, as Apparite would call him, looked like most men somewhere in their middle ages; he had some gray at the temples of his thinning black hair, and the wrinkles about his blue eyes were deep and hard. But the numbers Apparite tried to attach onto that cruel face didn't want to stick; he had to place him in the unsatisfying and broad category of "over fifty," and leave it at that.

And there was something about the man's face that was very curious, Apparite thought; something that made it seem like it had *always* looked this way. For one thing, the Director had prominent wrinkles around his eyes, but the skin on the rest of his face was absolutely smooth, without any trace of sun exposure—it didn't seem likely it could have attained this appearance through the natural process of aging. Had the skin on his face been purposefully stretched to alter his appearance? Were those unusually deep furrows around his eyes *really* the result of the wear and tear of a hard life, or had they been chiseled there with intent? And the thought that this dour man had once been a baby who had parents that held him or made him laugh; well, that seemed *absurd*. This man was never born; he just *was*, and exactly as

14

John Apparite was seeing him now.

The two men were sitting in a small room in a non-descript building somewhere in a run-down section of Washington, D.C.; no surprise, given the need for absolute discretion. On entering, Apparite, using his automatic powers of observation, estimated the room to be nine feet square and, despite the stifle that had come with this hot July day, he saw the sole window was closed airtight. The only exit was through the same door through which he had entered a minute before, leaving the man who had driven him to the tiny office sitting outside the room reading an issue of *Life* magazine from April (Apparite had noted the glamorous picture of Grace Kelly on its cover). The door to the little room was wooden and thick, without a window or transom, and there were no locks on it of any kind; a fact which struck him as being oddly out of place for a secret meeting.

The room was old and unkempt; a quick glance at the ceiling revealed the plaster had cracked considerably, leaving little dust trails on the faded wooden floor where it had fallen, piece by piece—someone had picked up the larger chunks, but no one had swept the room in months, or maybe years, Apparite thought. The wallpaper, a fading, nicotine-stain yellow, had a light blue floral pattern (violas, he remarked to himself—what an odd place for a meeting of this importance!), and the edges of it were freely peeling away from the wall, exposing the crumbling, light-brown wallpaper paste that had been applied, oh, about thirty years ago, he estimated. Apparite had noted all of this in the time most persons take to glance at a passing car; it was one of his greatest talents, the instructors at the FBI Academy had told him.

The man facing Apparite did not appear to be sweating or even put out one iota by the swelter in this hot-box of a room, despite the heavy, dull, black suit he was wearing—definitely not Italian, Apparite thought, and probably not even custommade, judging from the slightly differing lengths of the sleeves. He sat behind one of those cheap, metal governmentissue desks that populated governmental offices like the lower level bureaucrats enslaved behind them. The Director, however, was certainly no lower level bureaucrat, and this was certainly no lower level governmental office—it was much, much too shabby.

That was all there was to take note of, thought Apparite; there was no one else, and literally nothing else, in the little room. The closed window in the face of this ungodly heat, he mused, added a final touch of absurdity to the situation.

"As you have accepted our offer, you must now know it is irrevocable," the Director said.

Apparite recalled the meeting he had a little over one week ago with another powerful man, Allen Dulles, the head of Central Intelligence, when he had been unexpectedly offered a "most secret and dangerous long-term assignment." He was promised "global travel, high pay, and higher stakes; just what a young man in your position should be looking for." Behind the salesman-like banter, however, Apparite had detected nervousness and suppressed excitement. Strange, he had thought at the time, that a man of such untouchable importance as Allen Dulles would betray his emotions (or even *have* such emotions) during a meeting with a new agent—and an agent who believed he was being summoned for dismissal, at that. The whole situation smacked of improbability if not impossibility, yet here Apparite was, about to be initiated into the absolute upper echelon of secret agency.

"Think about it," Dulles had told him in a business-like manner, "and let me know if you will accept this challenge." Dressed in a black suit, wearing frameless spectacles and taking leisurely puffs from a pipe filled with richly aromatic tobacco, the head of CI exuded competence and authority, and Apparite did not have to think long on the offer. He had already drawn in breath to answer in the affirmative, but his intentions were suddenly cut short by the unexpected interjection of words he would never forget. "If you tell *anyone*, I cannot protect your life," Dulles had quickly added.

The phrase had come out in an alarming change of tone, strained and cutting; a warning not unlike a snake's hiss which, for most people, would have chilled them to their core—but not for John Apparite. Rather than being frightened of it, *he* had felt curiously drawn to it, like a pathologist who unexpectedly stumbles upon a bloody corpse and pauses to examine it before summoning aid.

It was a phrase that would forever echo in his head, along with the words a Major Appleby had nervously stuttered on a frigid January day in 1945 ("The United States Government r-regrets to inform you that your father, Private Edwin K——
—, was k-killed in combat with the enemy), and Assistant Deputy Charlie Bennett tearfully choked out on a dewy autumn morning in 1947 ("I'm so sorry but, your ma; she was killed in a wreck, out on Highway Thirty-six"). Those deaths, and the words that heralded them, had carried him ever deeper into a world hidden from most ordinary persons; a world that had no limits in its cruelty, and was merciless in its finality. Apparite began to believe himself meant for that world, apparently being driven into it by fate.

The Director spoke, jarring Apparite back to the present day.

"When you walked through that door, you forfeited your previous life. I see you have questions—do not bother asking them. I already know what they are." He stared at Apparite, gauging his reaction to this declaration. Apparite tried to intensify his own gaze back at the man and meet this unspoken

17

challenge: *of course* he wasn't going to ask questions; *of course* he knew there was no turning back. And yet he was horrified to discover that he was unable to silence that inner voice which kept running queries through his mind: How long, how secret, how dangerous, and finally, one directed at the mysterious Director himself: Who *are* you?

"You do not need to tell me about yourself, Apparite—there is nothing you can tell me that I do not already know. You are twenty-five years and one hundred twenty-two days old; you were born at ten-thirteen a.m. You were raised in Eckhart Springs, Maryland; a small town just west of Cumberland. Your upbringing was marked by an often-absent father, and an industrious, though caring mother. Although your family was one of meager means and possessions, your childhood was not overly marked by deprivation.

"Your father was killed in the Battle of the Bulge; your mother was killed in an automobile accident when you were seventeen; you have no living relatives. You graduated from the University of Maryland at College Park in nineteen fifty-two; though you majored in Biological Science, you mastered the Romance Languages as well, and were elected Phi Kappa Phi. You began Special Agent FBI training after reaching the minimum age of twenty-three, graduating first in your class from the Academy. After serving with the Bureau for approximately one year, you were earmarked for Central Intelligence, where you completed the Espionage Operations course at Camp Peary with the highest recommendation. You are fluent in six languages, including German and Russian, both of which you mastered during the E.O. course in record time. When approached about our opportunity by the Director of Central Intelligence, Mr. Dulles, you accepted the challenge without hesitation.

"You have had three lovers: two while in college and one

while at the Federal Bureau of Investigation; their names were Betty, Rose, and, most recently, Margaret—who was the most attractive of the three, a slim brunette—though you were unable to form any lasting emotional attachment to any of them. They have been thoroughly investigated and cleared. You have established no close friendships these past eight years, and all of your childhood friends are scattered, or killed in the war. You have no homosexual tendencies. You do not smoke, and have never used marihuana or cocaine. You prefer beer to wine or distilled liquors. You have a tendency to drink to occasional excess, but it is not thought to be a risk. You are proficient in many athletic endeavors, including gymnastics and boxing—your favorite boxer is welterweight champion Carmen Basilio—and, since childhood, you have been an avid fan of the Washington Senators, attending many of their games despite their dismal record. You are left-handed."

This rattle of information, given without emphasis on any one particular, was, to Apparite, thorough though admittedly idiosyncratic—it seemed strange that the Director would lend equal weight to his education and the deaths of his parents as he would his old girlfriends and the baseball club he followed. Yet it was all absolutely true; every little detail had been accurate, right up to the color of his last girlfriend's hair. And, he noted with chagrin, the Director had been correct on another point: Apparite *hadn't* formed much of an attachment to any of his steadies. Even Margaret, a vivacious Jeanne Crain look-alike who indeed *had* been the sharpest-looking of the three (was there anything the Director *didn't* know?) could not make Apparite love her as she loved him; could not make him tremble if she held his hand, kissed him softly, or stroked his hair. In his heart, John Apparite had long been well fortified against such emotional attacks, and it

19

would take more than a mere college coed like Margaret to pierce his defenses.

Apparite had no idea where this strange interview was leading, but he was beginning to feel slightly disoriented, and increasingly naked and uncomfortable. During his interrogation training, he remembered being told to keep his subjects off-balance, to never let them get emotional control of the situation; never let them predict the questions, or understand the motives of their questioner. The Director, Apparite noted, could have written the book on the subject.

"I am well aware of the unfortunate incident that prompted the Director of Central Intelligence to make final his recommendation of you for our program. In the E.O. hand-to-hand combat course, the instructor, a man called Bullard, took an immediate and inexplicable dislike to you. For the entire course he rode you mercilessly, yet you never responded in anger or defense. At one point, he even dared insult your dead mother; still, you did not respond. However," and the Director leaned forward, pointedly, "at the immediate completion of the course, you strode to the instructor's office at CIA headquarters and challenged him to a fight, despite the fact he was six inches taller and forty pounds heavier than you, plus infinitely more experienced in karate and street fighting. He accepted, and the fight commenced in the hall outside his office in full view of seven individuals, including Mr. Dulles."

Apparite tensed slightly in remembrance: yes, he had chanced dismissal, but day after day of that SOB Bullard taunting him, berating him, had pushed him over the edge. And then there had been the long months of waiting, waiting, waiting for the right time to do it; let him think you're a coward, but when no longer under the constraints of his orders, teach the brute a lesson—he was certain that his instructor, like all bullies, was over-confident and would underestimate a smaller opponent. Apparite had walked right into Bullard's office, and to issue his challenge, he hadn't even had to speak—he simply nodded to him with a look of defiance and anger, and they had walked out into the hall.

Apparite had assumed his karate fighting stance; his instructor had then come at him with a textbook karate kick aimed for the neck; to Apparite, the kick had seemed unusually slowed and distant, as if viewed through a gel. He had easily side-stepped it and unleashed a wicked, lightning thrust of the side of his outstretched left hand, fingers and thumb extended, to the tender space between the man's fourth and fifth ribs.

The instructor had clutched his right flank, howling, backed up a step or two, and then come at Apparite again. A series of rapid, short jabs—all misses—then a round-house kick; again, for Apparite, time had slowed, and when the man's leg was fully extended with the kick, Apparite had dropped to the ground, one leg splayed, and swept it under the larger man's planted foot; the instructor had hit the ground hard, the air leaving him like a deflating ball.

Apparite had sprung to his feet and waited for the instructor to rise, reassuming his stance. The instructor had come at him again, hands and feet thrusting and kicking, hoping to overwhelm Apparite in a flurry of blows, but none would connect. After one particularly lunging, over-reaching thrust had missed, Apparite had grabbed the instructor's outstretched arm and savagely kicked him between his vulnerable ribs; he had felt them yield and break, as easily as a wafer in a hungry child's hand. The man had fallen like a shot facedown onto the unyielding tile floor, his breaths gasping and spasmodic. Apparite had then leapt upon him, straddling him; right leg digging into those broken ribs, left hand on his neck, with his right hand evilly bending the man's right arm back, back.

"Submit," Apparite had growled.

"Go to hell!"

"Submit!"

"Go f— yourself!"

Apparite had felt the man's arm start to yield; the torque he was applying had begun to bend the humerus and stretch the shoulder joint beyond anything God or man had designed. At any moment, he had expected it to snap, dislocate.

"All right!" A new voice; an angry voice, had spoken. "Let him up!"

Apparite had then heard the unmistakable click of a revolver cocking, and had let loose his victim's arm. A senior agent had his .45 trained on him.

"Mr. Dulles wants to see you. *Now.*"

Ten minutes later, Apparite was in Allen Dulles' office, and the "most secret and dangerous assignment" was his. Ten days later, he was in this curious meeting with the mysterious Director.

"You put one of the toughest men at CI in the hospital for a week with a punctured lung and multiple rib fractures. *Good:* CI instructors have a tendency to become cocky, and every so often one needs to be taken down a peg. You might be interested to hear that the instructor, now that he has left the infirmary, has been reassigned to Alaska in punishment for his humiliation.

"The incident demonstrated that you have exceptional physical conditioning, reflexes, and fighting skills—you handled him quite easily despite the fact you were considerably smaller than he. Your speed and quickness has been noted to be of the highest caliber, and the ophthalmologists tell me your eyesight is particularly exceptional: twenty-ten left eye;

twenty-oh-eight right eye. Your medical history includes an aortic heart murmur, but it is not thought to be a risk at this time. You have had no surgical procedures. You had mumps at age five—sparing your testicles—and chicken pox at age nine, but no serious medical illnesses. You have no uniquely identifying marks: unusual. I note that you are five feet six inches tall and weigh one hundred forty-one pounds."

There was a prolonged, purposeful pause: why? Apparite wondered if he should speak, but then thought better of the idea—maybe he was being tested in some way.

"I repeat: you are five feet six inches tall and weigh one hundred forty-one pounds. As you well know, the minimum height for the Academy of the Federal Bureau of Investigation is five feet *seven* inches tall with a weight of *one hundred forty-five* pounds. I know, of course, how you managed to slip through on this matter during your FBI training, even if the fools at the FBI do not."

Yes, the FBI had never caught on to his little ruse, those tricks that had kept him in the Academy, but it had been worth it. After college, Apparite had hated the idea of having a "normal" job like his mother, who had been a biology teacher in a dull secondary school in the Allegheny Mountains. He detested even more the idea of working in sales like his father, traveling the length of the Atlantic Coast trying to get people with no money to buy insurance. Insurance! For what—their property? In the thirties and forties most had none; it had been swallowed up in the Great Depression. Their lives? Worthless without jobs, decent homes, clothes—hell, without decent *anything*.

Most of the able-bodied men in his quiet, mountainside Maryland town had joined the Army right out of high school—if they had even *made* it through high school—for the proverbial "three hots and a cot" and warm clothes on their backs. Apparite, however, had always been more ambitious than his peers. He had longed for something he could not get in sleepy Eckhart Springs, and which definitely did not come in the U.S. Army uniform that had forever marked his last memory of his father (even after his father's death there had been unhappy reminders: in 1945 the Army had sent him his father's dog-tags and a letter of condolence in the mail; Apparite refused to read it, and threw the dog tags on the scrap heap).

So as a boy he had lost his father in the war, and as a young man he had lost his mother in a wreck and, soon after, John Apparite had lost himself; had lost his connection with the rest of humanity. Sure, he had had some buddies at College Park, but he'd never really let anyone get to *know* him, and he hadn't wanted to get to know anyone *else*, either—not after the pain of losing his parents, not to mention half the young men from his hometown who'd joined the 29th Division and got shot-up before they took even one step out of their Higgins Boats at Omaha Beach. After all of the pain and death in his life, Apparite's girlfriends and college buddies never stood much of a chance: he was a hopeless case.

After Apparite had graduated from college, about all anyone seemed to remember of him was that he was easily the most rabid Washington Senators fan they had ever met. The "Nats" had been such an intense obsession for Apparite that he seemed incapable of sharing it with anyone who had a lesser passion for the club; which was, of course, just about everybody. All of his attempts to find a comrade-in-arms therefore proved spectacularly unsuccessful, although he never minded showing even a complete stranger his most prized possession: a Walter Johnson tobacco card, signed by the Senators Hall of Famer himself. Apparite always carried it with him like a talisman against ill fortune. As far as his life had gone so far, it had not been a rousing success.

With his university degree and "lucky" baseball card in hand, Apparite had joined the FBI to satisfy his craving for something new, something exciting—*anything* to keep his mind off the tragedies of his past. How appealing the lifestyle, the extreme responsibility, and even the danger of being a FBI agent had seemed to him at the time! And he had indeed gone through FBI training and even the quiet intensity of CI espionage training without connecting with anyone, just as he had wanted, spending all of his time and energy training as hard as he could, and doing what he was supposed to do. Who cares if he was too short for FBI standards? Who cares if he only weighed 141 pounds? That had never mattered a *whit* to Apparite—all that had mattered was that he did his exercises and his duties better than anyone else. So far, he had not let himself down.

Apparite looked at the Director in surprise and embarrassment—his FBI ruse had finally been exposed. He sat up a bit more in his chair—unconsciously, perhaps, in an effort to make up that inch and those pounds—and waited to be dismissed. *Why bring me here,* he wondered, *only to be humiliated?* The Director broke the uncomfortable silence.

"I believe you are *ideal* for our purposes."

Apparite breathed a quiet sigh of relief, though his inner voice broke through his defenses and asked one last unanswerable question: What the *hell* have you gotten yourself into?

The Director spoke again; loudly, authoritatively.

"Directive number one: *Maintenance of Secrecy.* Directive number two: *Mission Completion.* Directive number three: *Minimization of Civilian Casualties.* Directive number four: *Minimization of Property Destruction.* The directives are nonnegotiable and are in absolute order of importance. You will not forget them.

"You will be joining the most covert espionage program in existence. Not only is it entirely unknown to your old colleagues at the FBI, there are just three officials in the United States Government—other than myself—who are aware of it, and only because their resources are required for it to function: the Secretary of Defense, the Director of Central Intelligence, and the Director of the National Security Agency. Significant exposure of the program's nature or existence might result in the public humiliation—or even the assassination—of any of these persons. Secrecy, therefore, is of the utmost importance."

The Director again paused; what Apparite could not know was that, for the first time as director of his unique program, he was taking a chance on an agent. Apparite was unproven in the field, but had the skills and potential to be the greatest intelligence agent the United States had ever seen—*that* had been obvious to all at the FBI and CIA. The only unknown was the level of commitment of this capable young man, which the Director thought might be found in the answer to this question: Just how far would the newly christened John Apparite go to protect his program?

The Director resumed speaking, a knowing look on his face.

"You are wondering about the President. The President is not, and *cannot* be made aware of this program for his own protection and in the interests of national security. Final authority rests with me: in the event of catastrophic mission failure, I will be assassinated and the program disbanded. You will be in the program for no less than four years, and no more than eight years, pursuant to a suitable replacement being found when you have fulfilled your duties. At program completion, you will be given a new identity, passport, and five million U.S. dollars deposited into a Swiss bank account."

Another pause; Apparite felt his face warming, as though he was actually being touched by the Director's continually probing eyes. The Director held the silence a beat longer than seemed natural and spoke again.

"Your old life has ended. Your colleagues at the FBI and CIA believe you are dead."

The Director glanced at his watch and fixed those burning eyes back on Apparite, to the young man's continued discomfort.

"You died seventeen minutes ago in an automobile accident. Your charred corpse will be discovered in the wreckage of your black nineteen forty-eight Studebaker; the dental records will match, and the appropriate identification documents will be found. Your funeral will be next Tuesday near your hometown of Eckhart Springs."

Apparite found that his mouth had slowly fallen open, his eyes widening with the realization that he had passed a failsafe point he had not seen coming: he had expected to be "sheep-dipped," of course, and leave his old life behind him, but he had *not* expected it would be unceremoniously snuffed-out in this manner. And what's more, though he realized the ridiculous nature of the complaint, they had destroyed his car! A fine used car he had paid nearly two hundred dollars for! Curiously, *that* rankled him more than anything else; even his supposed demise.

And yet, he could not help but chuckle inwardly at the gross absurdity of it: everyone in his family had now died a tragic, untimely death. Apparite privately wished the Director would "bury" him next to his mother in that beautiful mountaintop cemetery in the Alleghenies, where the unceasing wind would whip off everyone's hats during the funeral, mussing the hair of those few townsfolk who would show up for it. Their main reason for coming, Apparite figured, would probably be for the fried chicken and potato salad at the luncheon afterwards, but that was all right by him.

He could hardly believe it, but he was genuinely *amused* at the thought; he almost wished he could be there for the burial. Looking at the Director, and guessing how his diabolical mind worked, Apparite was certain that next Tuesday a lovely walnut coffin would be lowered into the last of his family's plots, the headstone reading, *F—— K———, 1930–1955, beloved son of*. . . et cetera. Damn, but he was sure of it. Slowly, in the vain hope that the Director would not notice his reaction, he closed his still half-opened mouth and refocused his gaze. The Director, having briefly paused to read the curious look which had appeared on Apparite's face, then continued.

"There have been a total of five Superagents since program inception; two are active at any given time. You will be pleased to hear that one has lived to complete his program and is now living comfortably abroad. As for the others, three have been killed in the line of duty and another is on active duty. You will be replacing Agent G, who was recently murdered in the United Kingdom; we are still gathering information on this matter. I do not want you to view his death as a bad omen; the perception of luck—good or bad—should not enter into the performance of your duties.

"The two active Superagents do not work together and are assigned to different parts of the globe. The other agent is presently operating in Eastern Europe; your responsibilities will primarily be in the United States and Western Europe. You will have absolute power and discretion to complete your missions. You will have inexhaustible financial and technological resources to complete your missions. You will therefore have no excuses if you are unsuccessful.

"You wonder how we maintain secrecy, and yet have access to such resources—it is surprisingly simple. The bureaucracy of the United States Government is the largest in the world; within its bloat of paperwork and offices hundreds faithfully serve us, yet none have any awareness of whom they actually work for, duped into believing they serve Central Intelligence, the FBI, or the National Security Agency, among others. We hide in the cracks and crevices of this bureaucracy, using its resources and feeding on its infinite intelligence gathering capabilities—as invisible as the microscopic insects that live in our eyebrows and scavenge dead skin for food.

"We have used these tools to effectively infiltrate the bureaucracies of other nations, friendly or not (we have found the communists and socialists to be particularly accommodating). As a result, our intelligence exceeds not only that of the vaunted FBI, but also Central Intelligence, Interpol, MI Six, the KGB, and even the secret alliances within the NSA. Do you understand?"

Apparite nodded; speaking would have been too difficult, and betrayed his awe at what he was being told. He had served in the FBI himself, and had never heard even one faint rumor about the Director's agency—to think that all of this was going on right under the noses of the famous J. Edgar Hoover and his "G-Men"! And at CI, well, there were always rumors about "splinter-cells" and rogue agents, but no one took them seriously—and now he was the most rogue of agents in the most splintered of cells in the world! To be able to operate at will in the Director's agency, using every resource of the most powerful government in the history of the world, was alluring—almost *intoxicating*—to him.

"For official program purposes, you will be known only as Agent E; for security reasons, the name John Apparite will be unknown in any file. The other active Superagent, in case you are wondering, is known as Agent B; it is imperative that you never be told *his* true name or meet him, again for security purposes. For reasons of program secrecy, I am not assigned any name or title whatsoever. My assistant, whom you will call 'J,' will be your liaison in the field, as I seldom travel outside of the District of Columbia. You will remain in close contact with J or, at the beginning of each mission, be given a telephone number or address where you may contact him. If so, you will memorize the information, then burn or eat the paper before leaving the room in which you receive it."

This was a bit much, thought Apparite—actually *eat* the paper? It sounded like something from a bad radio play—surely he wouldn't have to *do* that sort of thing! It seemed quite out of place for the Director to talk about unlimited resources and power in one sentence, and eating a secret phone number in the next. Apparite feared the situation was becoming comical, and he was having a much more difficult time holding his steely countenance. A look of bemusement—or was it confusion?—had started to creep onto his face.

"I see you are amused by some of our practices. You consider them quaint, but you do not know the danger you create when you think so. A Superagent must be protected twenty-four hours a day; protected from the enemy *and* protected from himself. The greatest danger of exposure is from *within* the program—it cannot occur. Each Superagent therefore has a companion agent—a 'Shadow-agent'—who is instructed to kill him if the program is significantly and irrevocably breached during the course of a mission. The Shadow will remain no more than two hours automobile travel from the Superagent at any time: *you* will not know who your Shadow is, but *he* will know who you are."

The Director stopped talking once again. Apparite said nothing; he was unwilling or perhaps unable to break the claustrophobic silence in the hot little room. After another very long, discomforting silence, the Director resumed speaking.

"The United States has many enemies. Some are obvious—the KGB and SMERSH, the Red Chinese, the East German HVA—while others are not; some are even from within. Those who wish to harm the interests of the United States must be defeated; we must protect those interests using whatever means are necessary: *period*." The Director's voice was rising in intensity, and a slight tremble began to emanate from his hands.

Finally, Apparite thought, some emotion from this automaton, although the obvious explanation for it disturbed him: was the Director some sort of secret agent version of communist-baiter Joe McCarthy, meting out his own brand of vicious and radical justice, oblivious to the world outside him? This strangely intense man struck Apparite as the type who didn't enjoy doing *anything* other than, say, killing Red spies, or destroying East German listening posts, or shooting down Chinese spy planes, and the like. Obviously, the man was not the type to joke or kid around with, or relax and have a beer with, or even, thought Apparite as he swatted away a pesky fly, find a decent place to sit and interrogate a potential colleague. What kind of man would take a job where he worked in a hellhole like *this?* What kind of man would take a job that would never allow him any real human contact? The answer came to him immediately: a dangerous man, that's who. And then another thought struck Apparite: maybe he, too, was that kind of man. Maybe that was the reason he'd been chosen.

The Director, wiping his sweaty brow and rearranging his face into its previously rigid incarnation, opened the left-side drawer from the sickly green desk. He removed a semi-automatic pistol, a Beretta 1951, which he placed on the aluminum top. He then opened the right-side drawer of the desk, removing a clip and a silencer from it. With that familiar, deep, metallic click, the Director thrust the clip into the Beretta, and then, in a smooth single movement, threaded the silencer onto the protruding end of the weapon. Quietly, and in his usual emotionless monotone, he spoke again.

"The man who drove you here is waiting outside this room, correct?"

Apparite nodded. The driver, a quiet, bearded man who appeared to be in his mid-thirties, wearing dirty dungarees, a stained yellow shirt, glasses, and a Senators baseball cap, had picked him up from his apartment at ten a.m. sharp. As Apparite had entered the car, the driver had given him a typed note: "Do not speak to the driver." The journey, a disorienting array of U-turns, cut corners, and back alleys, was done in a complete and eventually stifling silence. On arrival, the driver had gotten out, opened Apparite's door, tipped his cap to him, and handed him a second note: "The driver will accompany you. He will wait outside the meeting room."

The Director spoke again.

"You do not need to worry about the driver overhearing us; he is deaf and mute, and I have often used him in these situations, although to my knowledge we have never met in person. I am, however, displeased to point out that when you entered this room, he had a brief, unfortunate glimpse of my unshielded face, and appeared to recognize me. You will therefore take the pistol from on top of the desk, open the door, motion for him to come in, and shoot him through the heart."

Apparite tried against all his instincts not to feel the impact of this command, but had to ask himself, *was the Director serious?* Or was this some sort of perverse test? He studied the expression on the Director's face, but saw only the same emotionless stare that had been burning a hole through him these last ten minutes. Apparite then realized that this was no exercise—he was going to have to shoot the unlucky SOB.

But he had never killed a man before—what would it be like? he wondered. He had talked to men back home who had shot and killed Germans in the war, but this was different—unlike the driver, the Germans had not been innocent, unsuspecting, and unarmed.

Regardless, the distinction didn't matter much to him, once he had given it some thought. The driver looked like a nice enough guy, but Apparite didn't know or care much about him—he didn't even know his name. The only thing Apparite cared for at the moment was the doing of his duty, and if it took the killing of the man wearing the Senators cap to fulfill it, then so be it. Killing the driver wouldn't feel much different than shooting that twelve-point buck he had bagged back home last fall, he surmised; crouched in a tree, he had seen it searching for some berries and felled it with a single, skilled rifle shot through the heart. The driver might be a different kind of prey, but if Apparite was there to do it then he would get it done, and the result would be the same. His only regret was that it would be a shame to kill a fellow "Nats" fan—as far as he was concerned, they could use all the support they could get. *Well, too bad,* he concluded; *I can't let that stop me.*

Apparite reached over, silently picked up the pistol in his right hand, and slowly walked over to the door. He opened it a few inches and motioned with his free hand for the unsuspecting driver to come in the room. He then stepped back from the doorway, smoothly transferred the weapon back into his left hand, assumed his firing stance, and waited.

Slowly, as Apparite forced away the foreknowledge he was going to kill in cold blood, he saw the driver coming through the doorway in a prolonged reveal of dungarees, grease-stained yellow shirtsleeve, and Senators baseball cap. He counted down the targets as they appeared in apparent slow motion: right lung, aorta, left lung, pericardium of the heart, and then he squeezed the trigger. Apparite might have been interested to know that his heart rate had remained a cool and unaffected fifty-two beats per minute and, despite the heat, he had not broken into a sweat.

"Click. Click-click-click-click": a dummy clip. The driver stopped, grinned slightly, took out a cigarette, and lit it with a silver Zippo. The Director spoke.

"What were you thinking, Apparite? You may speak."

"I thought nothing," he said.

It was true. When Apparite had seen his target, he had pictured the twelve-point buck and then simply done what he had to do: the man had become just another trophy to bag in the hunt; the task just another to be checked off the list. It had been much easier than he had thought it would be, too. Emptying his mind of the significance of pulling that trigger and killing a fellow human had been disturbingly easy to him.

"Good," the Director said. "It is not your duty to think when commanded. You acted without hesitation, as I expected."

The Director paused briefly to lend his next statement the impact it deserved.

"If you had not, the driver had been instructed to terminate you immediately."

As the deadly nature of the test sunk in, Apparite slowly let out the breath he had not realized he had been holding.

The Director motioned to the driver to leave, Apparite noting that the man did so with unusual stealth and quiet. And as the driver passed through the doorway, Apparite caught a brief flash of silver metal under his untucked shirt-tail: a pistol. Was he a Shadow-agent? No, Apparite concluded, and even if he were, he would not have been his own; they'd never let him meet his own. The other Superagent, perhaps? Apparite wished he had studied the bearded face under that ball-cap more closely.

"You have questions," the Director said, surprising Apparite with his prescience. "You want to know whether that man is in my employ. He is, although, like so many others, he does not know for whom he is working. You also wish to know whether this is a standard situation for a potential agent in my program—it is. But I sense you have one more question you need to ask. You may ask it."

Apparite could feel the sweat rising on his brow and his heart beating slightly faster. There *was* one thing he had to know, and it was the only part of the test that was still eating at him.

Would the Director *really* have done it? Would he have actually killed him if he hadn't pulled that trigger? After all the testing and probing and mind-games, Apparite had to know if this one thing was true. He felt the question both men knew was coming suddenly leap out of his throat.

"Has anyone ever hesitated? And been—?"

"No, not yet."

"But if they did, would you—?"

"Yes. Without hesitation, Apparite."

To his surprise, Apparite was relieved to hear this. He thought that someday he might even know the reason why.

Two
The Warehouse

Apparite awoke in unfamiliar surroundings the next morning; after the interview, he had been taken to a large red brick warehouse in one of the worst sections of D.C. Initially, he had been struck by the striking Victorian features of the building's impressive exterior—the turrets, curved windows, and stone friezes common to the period—and yet on closer inspection, the bulk of it had proved to be run-down and neglected. Lying on the decrepit, WWI-era Army cot he had found placed in the middle of the building's otherwise empty main room, Apparite wondered how many others—probably just innocent and frightened "doughboys"—had slept uncasily on it that first night, as he had. It must have been thousands, he concluded, which explained why every inch of it smelled of sweat, urine, mold—and fear.

Apparite heard a door open. He turned his head toward the sound and saw the Director walk into the warehouse; he was holding a white robe and a thick, dog-eared notebook. With him was a slight man whose ancestry Apparite found intriguing and surprisingly difficult to pin-down. He looked somewhat Oriental with his thin brown eyes (slanted only slightly) and flat nose but, strikingly, also had an absolutely white skin tone that seemed out of touch with the rest of his body. The man was barefoot, but even wearing shoes would have been significantly shorter than Apparite, and at least twenty pounds lighter. Apparite figured he must be a sparring partner or even his combat instructor, but the man's small stature seemed unsuited for the job. The Superagent was doubtful he could learn very much by fighting this little wisp of a man.

"Take the notebook," the Director said to Apparite. "I expect you to have it memorized in eight weeks. The robe you will receive when your training begins. This man will be your combat instructor, to whom I do not wish you to speak. He will speak to you plenty, however, and I expect you to listen, and listen well—every word is precious. In the future, what he says will save your life, many times over."

The man in question, whom Apparite nicknamed the "White Oriental"—not out of disrespect for the man's unusual ancestry, but for an utter lack of a more definitive term at the time—smiled and bowed, hand and fist together, head slightly extended. He then unbent and unleashed the fastest and most accurate karate thrust Apparite had ever seen, stopping only millimeters from the Superagent's solar plexus. Apparite did not jump or stir noticeably to outward appearances, but on the inside he was fighting an innate urge to strike back at his "attacker"; his heart rate had risen and his breathing had significantly and unconsciously accelerated.

I never saw anyone that fast or accurate with a thrust at CI, Apparite said to himself.

The Director, who had seen this demonstration play out before (each time to his silent amusement), spoke again.

"I understand you learn *Ryukyu* karate at CI; it's a good beginning, but against SMERSH it would be ineffective. The KGB fighting technique, "SAMBO," *Samozaschita bez orujiya,* is brutal and merciless; a SMERSH agent using it would easily kill a new graduate of the CI combat course. Learning one technique will *not* be enough if you wish to fight

38

the KGB and SMERSH; for that purpose, you will need to learn *three*.

"In addition to combat SAMBO, you will become expert in *Krav Maga*, the defense and fighting art of the new State of Israel. Unlike Eastern techniques, which rely on postures and fanciful names for their blows, this discipline concentrates only on your survival and your enemy's death, by any means. Most importantly, you will learn a new Okinawan form of karate, *Isshin-Ryu*, which we have adapted into a fast and deadly fighting technique—as you have already become expert in *Ryukyu*, I feel you will master it quickly. It is a discipline to which you are uniquely suited, relying on quickness and a lowered center of gravity, turning your diminutive size to your advantage.

"When you have completed your training, you will have learned to kill your enemy with your hands, your feet, and any objects within reach. You will have learned to fight in close quarters, while on your back, and while pinned to the ground. You will not waste time on useless meditations or the teachings of the ways of the old masters. Simply put, you will have learned to kill, and kill well. Do not be intimidated by the fact you will need to learn these methods in a short period of time; your instructor is expert in every technique and is an unsurpassed teacher—if you fail, I will attribute it to incompetence and laziness on *your* part. I will return to assess you in eight weeks; until then, you will be wholly immersed in your training."

It was then that Apparite realized he would not be allowed out of the building for the next two months, and although he knew this time of intense training and isolation would stretch him to the limit physically and mentally, the only part he truly minded was this: he would miss eight weeks of the heart of the baseball season, and would have no news of the "Nats." But as long as the strange little man who was to instruct him knew his stuff, Apparite figured it would be worth the effort, if not the sacrifice.

"I have the highest expectations of you, Apparite; do not disappoint me," the Director said; he then turned toward the White Oriental, bowed slightly, and said one word.

"Begin."

The Director left the warehouse, a hint of a smile slowly emerging on his face. The moment he was gone, the White Oriental leapt at Apparite, using small but very rapid steps. Apparite tried to side-step him, but the White Oriental had surreptitiously grabbed the robe the Director had held, and rapidly wrapped it around Apparite's head as he passed to the agent's left. Apparite back-flipped, jerking the robe from the White Oriental's hands, but before he could free it from his head, he found himself lying on his back with what he guessed was a board pressed tight across his neck.

Apparite felt the robe being removed from his head. He saw the White Oriental's face break into a grin, and—could it be?—a giggle was coming from the small man's throat. Apparite tried to get up, but found his neck was firmly being held to the floor by the spine of the Director's combat manual. *How the hell did he get a hold of that?* Apparite wondered.

The White Oriental removed the book from Apparite's neck, leaving a distinct red impression, but Apparite *still* could not rise; his opponent had somehow got hold of the Director's ball-point pen and had it pressed against Apparite's left carotid artery. Not only that, but Apparite's left leg was going numb; the White Oriental was firmly compressing the Superagent's left femoral artery with his right knee.

"*Holy smokes,*" Apparite mumbled to himself, "*this guy could have killed me three times over.*"

The White Oriental let him up, grinning from ear to ear. He told Apparite, in extremely broken English, "Do you as I do, please. Then, you fight as I do." This would be the only time in the next eight weeks Apparite would hear him string more than two words together in a sentence—the rest of their time together would be filled with monosyllabic commands, the next of which was one Apparite would hear over and over again, like an echo that would not fade.

"Fight!"

Apparite struck a traditional fighting pose; the White Oriental did not bother to do so, using that time and energy to strike, and nearly land, his outstretched foot to Apparite's exposed midsection just below the navel. Apparite jumped back, but found he had been cornered; thrusting with his right hand—Apparite was a southpaw and led with his right, saving his left for the coup de grace—he moved his smaller opponent backwards, nearer the middle of the room. But the White Oriental was quicker; he ducked low and swept Apparite with his leg, knocking him to the ground. He then grabbed an old shoe that had been inconspicuously lying nearby, and pressed the heel of it into Apparite's right eye socket before the agent could even contemplate his next move.

"Blind," said the White Oriental. He pointed at Apparite. "Slow." He took the shoe and placed it over Apparite's throat. "Crush." The man assumed Apparite's traditional fighting stance; he began waving at his feet and shaking his head from side to side. "No," he said. He demonstrated a few short, rapid thrusts, saying, "Like."

Good grief, thought Apparite, the Director was right: every word *is* precious, particularly when they're let out but one at a God damn time! How in the world am I going to learn anything if all I hear are one word sentences for the next eight weeks? Nevertheless, the White Oriental *had* given him some swell ideas on how to blind and kill a man with a shoe, and had taught him not to bother with a fighting stance—at least, that's what Apparite *thought* he was supposed to have learned.

He also noted that his instructor never used a full punch. Keeping his arms slightly drawn-in, the White Oriental had used short bursts of quarter or half-punches that were lightning-quick, did not expose his chest, and were difficult for Apparite to fend off. He had also tensed his entire body as each punch reached its zenith, almost "snapping" them off at the point where they would connect. Apparite would try that, too; he was willing to try just about *anything* to get an advantage over this miniature comet.

"Fight."

Apparite rushed at his opponent. Using the short, quick bursts of hand thrusts that the White Oriental had demonstrated, Apparite found he was able to keep his instructor on the defensive, his body blows exposing his opponent's thighs and knees for downward, maiming kicks. Seeing an opening, Apparite unleashed a kick directly at the White Oriental's left knee; the smaller man jumped back, and the kick—which would have certainly torn up his knee at the angle Apparite had chosen—harmlessly missed, but had been razor-close. The instructor held up his hand and smiled.

"*Good.* Fight!"

The White Oriental now went on the offensive. He advanced rapidly on Apparite, using those pesky little thrusts and rapid, low kicks, the defense of which occupied nearly all of Apparite's concentration and effort. Out of the corner of his eye, Apparite spied a broom resting against the wall—*I might find a use for that,* he said to himself. Luring his opponent near it, Apparite suddenly kicked it up into his hands, spun it around, and thrust the sharp bristles dangerously close to the White Oriental's eyes. The White Oriental again held up his hand. *"Good!"* Pause. "Fight!"

And so it went. Every day, all day—and sometimes all night—the two men fought until Apparite's training had become an obsession for them both. And every evening before he dropped off to sleep, Apparite would read the thick combat manual, ready to apply its diabolical teachings during the long training sessions the next day: the fighting grips that would best maim an opponent; the forceful blows that would kill a man; and the use of every conceivable kind of weapon and the defenses against them—all in countless, grimly detailed scenarios.

The White Oriental and Apparite would then test each one with a real-life proof, guided uncannily by the White Oriental's one-word lessons: how to disarm a man holding a gun on you within reach, and now from two paces away, and then from five paces away; how to throw a knife and hit the gun-hand, and now the knife-hand, and then the upper arm, the chest, the thigh, and the neck (good for severing a carotid, or puncturing the wind-pipe, if silence is desired); how to break a man's knife-wielding arm four ways (Apparite's favorite: pinning the assailant's hand against a firm surface and striking the forearm sharply with the *Isshin-Ryu* thumb-on-top vertical fist, breaking the radius and ulna); and endless ways of killing a man by piercing the heart or brain, crushing the skull, or lacerating the liver (a hopeless wound leading to death in thirty minutes, unless in an operating room in twenty).

Every combat scenario was undertaken: fighting on a staircase, fighting in the dark, fighting while drunk (Apparite's favorite session, he admitted to himself as he polished off his last bottle of Schlitz), fighting on one leg, with

43

one hand, on no sleep, with one eye covered, blindfolded (not recommended, Apparite discovered), and lying on the floor. He learned how to receive a thrown-knife wound and keep fighting (take it in your non-dominant upper extremity, or even the lateral right chest, but *never* pull it back out of that location); how to dodge a gunshot by guessing the gunman's reflexes and timing (only fifty percent effective), and then disarming and killing him (one hundred percent effective).

Apparite quickly became expert in the art of knife-wielding and throwing, and when he had mastered that, the White Oriental taught him the Okinawan art of *Kobudo*—"weapons fighting"—using ordinary, everyday objects. A pool cue, a broom, or even a floor lamp could become a lethal weapon by a man using *bo*-fighting techniques; silverware, a sharpened stick, or a fireplace poker could kill when used by a *sai* expert. The White Oriental was particularly pleased with Apparite's makeshift *nunchuaku*—two steel-toed boots connected by their heavy laces—when the little man was knocked unconscious during one heated dual.

In Apparite, the White Oriental saw a mind that derived more cunningly evil uses for ordinary objects than he could ever have imagined himself: many of their battles ended with the Superagent holding a seemingly innocent household object poised to slit his instructor's throat, crush his trachea, sever a femoral artery, gouge out an eye, pierce the ventricles of his heart, or scramble the frontal lobes of his brain (Apparite thought a pencil thrust up the nose at a sixty degree angle would about do the trick; the White Oriental, flat on his back and nervously laughing, did not disagree).

Apparite's reactions to surprise situations were tested by having the White Oriental unexpectedly ambush him while reading, relaxing, or sleeping. The first few times, Apparite awoke with the White Oriental holding a blade to his throat or a gun to his temple, grinning and saying *"Surprise!"* in that odd little voice of his. (How Apparite had nearly crapped his skivvies the first night his instructor had pulled that stunt!). By the sixth week, however, Apparite could sense the White Oriental coming at him even while sleeping and in pitch-blackness, having developed that enviable but necessary animal-sense which awoke him at even the slightest hint of a threat.

His instructor knew Apparite had caught on when, having crept up on the sleeping agent, he found himself holding a gun to Apparite's pillow. Just as he recognized his error, the White Oriental felt a pair of hands slip around his neck— Apparite had silently gotten behind him and had his hands around his throat, ready to asphyxiate him. *"Surprise!"* Apparite had said lustily, and then let loose his grip. Both men had burst out laughing as the White Oriental pumped Apparite's right hand up and down in a congratulatory gesture. "Good! Good fight!" he had told him.

But life in the warehouse was difficult; the accommodations were a combination of American sweatshop and Soviet *Gulag*, Apparite decided. The toilet was a thirty-year-old, inferiorly designed, pull-chain gravity-flush model, lending each flush a comic suspense (Apparite could never be sure whether things were going to creep downward slowly or shoot up and *out* quickly; he usually just pulled the chain and *ran*). There was a shower, but it expelled a bare trickle of a rust-colored liquid with questionable cleaning properties, and the tap water tasted strongly of iron. The many cartons of K-rations that Apparite ate four times a day were just barely edible, leaving him frequently unsatiated. Looking around this virtual prison, he had to wonder, couldn't the Director shell out a few bucks to install a decent crapper? Couldn't such an important agency with unlimited resources afford better food?

The chow may have been barely enough to sustain his extreme caloric expenditure each day, but by God he slept well on that disgusting, lumpy, musty Army cot; he had never appreciated the wonders of a good night's sleep as much as he did in that warehouse. On awakening each morning, he hardly ever remembered dreaming, but even when he had, his dreams somehow didn't seem like they could have belonged to *him*, the man who had been named John Apparite; the nothing-man.

Many of his dreams seemed to be from those innocent days of his childhood—catching craw-dads in a creek, playing sandlot baseball, or hunting squirrels with his father—but the emotions they recalled felt too foreign and distant for him to identify as his own; like whispers that contained words which were beyond his understanding. But the elusive dreams remained a welcome relief; a brief respite from the rigors and dangers of his waking life, even if their meaning, and often their content, remained a mystery to him.

Apparite often wondered where the Director had found his unique instructor, and what circumstances might have possibly brought the little man to this old warehouse in D.C. Was he Mongolian? Siberian? Filipino? And what in the world was he thinking about all of this? Here he was, stuck in this old warehouse; charged with training a man with no name; supervised and, presumably, paid by someone else with no name; and all for a secret agency with no name. What did he believe was going *on* in here? And yet what a swell guy he was, ever-patient with his young pupil, never tiring, and always cheerful (especially when he's got me in a death-hold, thought Apparite). The White Oriental, despite his reticence, was the greatest teacher Apparite had ever had—so much so, that by the end of the eight weeks of training sessions, the two men had become so symbiotic that even those cryptic one-word commands were no longer needed; not once during the course of a long, sixteen-hour day of fighting and teaching. It had been, Apparite admitted to himself, the most rewarding time in his life.

Oh, how he wished he could arrange a fight between the White Oriental and that SOB Bullard who supposedly had trained him in karate at CI! As much as Apparite had enjoyed nearly breaking the bully's arm, watching the even more under-sized White Oriental do the same—or worse—would have been doubly satisfying.

As for the White Oriental, who had easily handled Apparite that first day, indulging him with a few confidence-building "victories" that no longer were necessary, he had found his most willing and able pupil in all his years of working for; well, he did not know either, but whoever he was, he was going to be impressed. He had demonstrated holds and Apparite had improved them; he had demon-strated lethal blows, which Apparite had done with increas-ingly greater force and finesse; he had demonstrated quickness of movement, which Apparite had exceeded. He was pleased, and not just a little proud, of his young protégé.

"Good. Very good," the White Oriental said on the last day of training, after Apparite made him submit with a nearly arm-breaking high elbow-hold that forced him to the ground. The White Oriental stood, placed his hand warmly on Apparite's shoulder, and then looked him directly in the eyes.

"Good student. Good-bye."

He patted Apparite's shoulder softly and, slowly and si-lently, shuffled toward the door, but before stepping out into the cool humidity of the late summer's night, he turned and faced Apparite one final time. He bowed, slowly and deferen-tially, a slight smile breaking across his face as he honored his greatest student.

Apparite was profoundly, surprisingly touched by the gesture. He had felt deepening feelings of respect and friendship for this unusual man these last eight weeks, but had buried them to maintain the cold demeanor he would need to carry out his deadly missions; however, he could do so no longer. His breaths were beginning to come out in little chokes and spasms and his throat was feeling tight, and all he could do was ask himself, *what the hell is happening to me?*

Apparite bowed slowly and deeply as well—partly in answer to the White Oriental's gesture, and partly to hide his impending emotional outburst—when he felt his lower lip start twitching and his eyes mist over. He unbent only when he heard his instructor leave the building, and then his composure crumbled: putting his head in his hands, he began to weep. He tried to stop himself; to consciously will his body to cease jerking and stop the gathering of tears in his eyes, but the sobs and tears kept coming and coming as if propelled by an irresistible force. He was helpless and he hated it.

After a few more moments of weeping, the chokes and tears eventually faded and Apparite was back to normal, except for the disturbing knowledge that the episode had actually *happened*. Suddenly drained of all his energy, he lay down on his Army cot and fell fast asleep.

When Apparite awoke, he expected to see the sun breaking over the eastern horizon but, to his chagrin, his watch read eleven-ten a.m.—he had slept nearly fourteen hours. Had he been drugged? Or was this disturbingly long sleep the cost of spending days and weeks of exhaustion, finally come for payment? Either way, Apparite figured, he felt terrific; like a tightly wound spring whose energy sits ready to be unleashed when the mechanism is finally tripped. It was then that he noticed the Director standing in a doorway, eyeing him with a strange look.

Apparite had to wonder how long the man had been staring at him like that, but it didn't matter, he figured: the Director's intentions must have been non-threatening. Otherwise he would have awakened, and besides, he felt all aces today; nothing could faze him right now. Something seemed different for him since he had awoken from that long sleep; he had only the faintest hint of his dreams, as was his usual, but beyond that hint there was now a little hum in his head—like an echo of what he had dreamt that had not yet disappeared—and he found it energized him. Apparite wished he could go back to sleep and find the source of that humming so he might know more, but then the Director sharply spoke and the hypnotic humming ceased.

"You will fight today, Apparite. Your instructor has kept me apprised of your progress, and I am pleased to report he considered you his finest pupil. It is now time for you to put your studies to practical use, so I may see if you are ready for the final phase of your training. You should know that my training philosophy is based on the fact we live and work and fight and die in the real world, so your 'final exam,' if you will, will also take place in the real world. Today we will drive to Butch's Place, a tavern in one of the most notorious sections of D.C., and a meeting place for petty thieves and unsavory characters. You will enter the tavern—unarmed—and demonstrate what you have learned on each and every one of the patrons."

"You want me to fight everyone in the bar?" Apparite said, disbelieving this strange order.

"No; the word 'fight' implies they will be fighting *back*, which I hope you will not give them the opportunity to do. You will enter the tavern and create a situation where multiple persons will rush you in a futile attempt to harm you.

You will then disarm any that are armed, and will leave the tavern only after everyone has been rendered unconscious, or in no position to harm you. How you do this is your business; I will wait outside and give you your evaluation when you return."

Apparite would have been lying if he had said he hadn't felt a bit of a thrill at the chance to put his teachings to practical use, but the idea of brawling with civilians who were innocent bystanders in a highly illegal test was—to his chagrin—bothering him a little. However, he quickly remonstrated himself for these feelings: why the hell should *he* care about beating up a few low-lifes in a seedy bar? For the life of him, he could not understand why he suddenly *did*. The Director seemed to sense Apparite's fleeting hesitancy.

"Do not concern yourself with harming men who have not harmed you; men who do not even know you. You need to dispel those feelings, as you did in the exercise with the driver. As a part of your training, you must learn to be unaffected by such moral issues. The test is before you; I do *not* want you to question the appropriateness of it, only to succeed in the performance of it.

"I should also tell you—though this is really a minor point—that these are not innocent men and this is *not* an innocent tavern; the injuries they will receive are only what their many helpless victims have been unable to give them. But, as I say, the moral justification is minimally important, if applicable at all. What *is* important is this: you must not be taken. The police must not be involved. The security of the entire program is at risk if this occurs and, by extension, your very life is then at risk. Do not think your Shadow-agent is inactive simply because you are in training; he will not be in the tavern, but will be nearby to clean up any messes if you fail, in which he knows only one method. I do not believe I need to spell this out any further."

"I understand," Apparite said, meeting the Director's eyes, trying to project some measure of confidence, trying to reassure him. "When I leave the tavern, there will not be a man standing."

"Get dressed and meet me outside by my automobile. Do not bring any weapons; do not bring your wallet. I will provide you with alternate identification when the time comes; the name John Apparite must not be known to any law enforcement agency, or where anyone may connect your face with it in the United States."

Apparite nodded in silent agreement and began to dress for what he would always remember as his "Final Exam in Ass-Whipping 101."

Three
Ass-Whipping 101

When Apparite met the Director outside the warehouse, he found him standing at the curb, holding open the door to a black four-door sedan; a 1952 De Soto Firedome that looked like it had seen better days, although it was only three years old. Apparite climbed in the passenger seat and sat down; the car was more comfortable than he had guessed it would be, but it absolutely reeked of cigarettes—a smell that had always repulsed him. Apparite assumed the Director must be a smoker, which surprised him—the man did not seem the type to do anything as undisciplined as chain-smoking. Then again, thought Apparite, Eisenhower is a three-pack-per-day man, so what the hell do *I* know?

He glanced at the Director's watch, noting that it was noon. *High noon,* Apparite said to himself, reminding him of the Western of the same name starring Gary Cooper. He'd seen it a couple of years before, but the parallel seemingly ended with the time of day: town sheriff Cooper had fought a gang of men who were coming to kill him, whereas Apparite would fight men who did not know his name. Most tellingly, Cooper's gunfight was a Hollywood movie fight, and did anyone in the audience think *Gary Cooper* was going to bite the dust? Apparite, in contrast, would have no one who could stop the action simply by yelling, "Cut!"

He knew—as any sane man would—that the situation dictated he have a healthy element of fear for his safety; it only stood to reason that one man can't fight half a dozen or more without getting maimed or killed. And yet Apparite remained strangely calm, as if he knew the outcome was preordained. Just like the crowd that filled the Strand Theater knew Gary Cooper wasn't going to bite the dust in *High Noon*, John Apparite knew he wasn't going to bite it at a shit-hole called Butch's Place.

The Director drove along Alabama Avenue, the white brick office buildings passing steadily by as he turned right on Suitland Road, and then left onto Pennsylvania Avenue. Gliding along one of the most famous streets in the world, Apparite watched with some measure of irony as the neoclassical buildings that were the foundation of the government he was serving came into view: the Supreme Court, the Capitol, the National Archives, and then finally the White House itself.

The most powerful man in the world lived in that stately mansion, Apparite thought, but despite the President's influence and strength he would remain completely ignorant, by absolute necessity, of the most secret and powerful of agencies at his nation's disposal. Apparite thought it probable that he would someday give his life to serve that man, President Dwight David Eisenhower, but the President himself would never know it, *could* never know it.

"There is a reason why I chose this particular route," the Director said, motioning around him. "This is the center of the greatest society and government in the history of the civilized world, and you have the opportunity to be one of its greatest servants. Do not wonder at what I am saying, thinking me naïve or a blind and misguided idealist—I know how the world works; better than you likely ever will. I am aware the United States has made many enemies around the globe; powerful enemies that wish to destroy her, and not always without good reason or justification, I might add. The defense of our nation against these enemies is of paramount importance, of course, but unfortunately this has led to a paralyzing paranoia on the part of our government's politicians and intelligence officials, who too often see enemies around every corner.

"The United States Government's entire mission has become corrupted by an obsession with these 'enemies'; often referred to as 'Commies' or 'Left-Wingers' by those who stand to benefit by the witch-hunts that inevitably follow: you only had to watch the Committee for Un-American Activities and McCarthy hearings to be convinced of that. Valuable men and resources are squandered in these useless chases while the real culprits, the true enemies of the United States, operate freely in our midst.

"Our government has also become corrupted by the protection of personal monetary interests of those in power; a force that has begun to cripple our intelligence services abroad. I would like to give you a very illuminating Civics lesson to better illustrate this point. Do you know the true story of the Guatemalan revolt last year?" He looked straight at Apparite, gauging his interest, and then back at the road as he continued to drive.

Apparite shook his head *no* in response to the question. "Only what was in the *Post*." The Director glanced at Apparite and then spoke in a forceful tone.

"When Guatemalan officials centralized United Fruit's land, the elected government—which was communist-leaning, though not yet 'red'—was overthrown. It was no mere coincidence. United Fruit is a powerful company on whose board has sat such men as John Foster Dulles, John Moors Cabot, and one you know personally, Allen Dulles, the Director of Central Intelligence. The revolt was fomented by CI chiefly to protect the monetary interests of United Fruit and American investors in Guatemala; protecting the world from communism was only part of the story; the final justification for the coup that followed.

"Do not look so shocked; such episodes have happened not infrequently in our nation's checkered past, and I consider them a great distraction from the real issues at hand; yet, they occur. Allen Dulles has done much in the loyal service of the United States—you would be hard-pressed to find someone more highly regarded—yet even a man such as he is not immune from influence and temptation. Few men are, I have discovered.

"So you see, even the great and powerful masters at CI have their measure of official corruption, as do those in the Cabinet and at the FBI, and in most governors' offices as well. Is it any wonder that the true interests of the United States might be pushed aside when the personal and financial interests of such men exceed those of our nation?

"You and I *must* be different: we must remain pure to our mission, uninfluenced by personal gain or feelings. Our agency is small but powerful; our targets limited but critical; our immediate rewards non-existent; and our legacy anonymous. No, the Government of the United States is not perfect—it is at best a flawed organism fraught with good intentions—but the United States herself is great, and I will not allow the failings of our government to hinder what I, and you, must do for her."

Apparite was astonished to hear the Director say such things: the man had made some odd statements in that first interview, he recalled, but had said nothing that had hinted at *this* degree of extreme patriotism! At the FBI and at CI, people sometimes talked about the importance of doing one's duty and defending one's nation, but no one had ever spoken of God and Country with such pride and purpose as the Director, and in such an unadulterated and pure form—ninety-nine and forty-four-one hundredth percent pure, thought Apparite, like God damn Ivory Soap!

He had also been astonished by the revelation that Allen Dulles—CI Director Allen Dulles!—might have overthrown the Guatemalan government for the sake of a fruit corporation. He felt relief he was no longer slaving away at Central Intelligence, working for those apparently impure demagogues who'd been pulling the wool over the public's and maybe their own agents' eyes for years. The Director's lesson had cast a shadow over his tenure at CI, and it would be some time before Apparite would look at that agency with his former pride again.

But strangely, after the unusual sermon had unfolded, Apparite discovered a newfound and growing respect for the Director's philosophy and beliefs. In fact, the Director had been so persuasive that Apparite thought it quite possible that the man was, indeed, correct: perhaps the two of them *had* been predestined to serve their country with a higher purpose.

Could it be, Apparite asked himself, *that the only way to be true to his duty to the United States was to trust this enigmatic man and embrace his brand of holy patriotism, disregarding everything else he had ever known? Did that sound so crazy?*

Yes, he concluded, maybe it *did.*

The Director had stopped talking for a moment to resume his concentration on the road, guiding the De Soto on its way. Apparite sat quietly, sifting through the Director's odd lecture of morality and patriotism when a familiar sight came into view and disrupted his thoughts: Griffith Stadium, corner of Georgia Avenue and U Street. For an instant, all he wished was to get out of this car, forget the past eight weeks, and sit and watch a ballgame for a few hours while he sorted out his head.

Good old Griffith Stadium, home of the Washington Senators, Apparite's ball club since he knew what a baseball was—oh, how that team had alternately infuriated and thrilled him in that wonderful ballpark! The unique rhythm of a ballgame had spoken to Apparite in a way that nothing else had—even after his parents had been killed, and he had had no connection with anyone or anything else, he had found an escape in his beloved "Nats." For years, Apparite's only lasting human connection had been with the guys on that team, despite the fact he'd never spoken with a single one.

But what terrific players they were, even if they lost more than they won! There was Mickey Vernon, the great two-time batting champion who was President Eisenhower's favorite; Eddie Yost, a third-baseman who seemingly drew walks at will, usually coming around to score; ace pitcher (and twenty-game winner) Bob Porterfield; and hard-hitting young outfielder Jim Busby.

For years, they had seemed just a player or two away from giving New York and Cleveland a run for the pennant, but instead had remained a team that hadn't taken one since 1933, and had won only a single World Series in all their long history, back in 1924. "First in War, First in Peace, and Last in the American League," was the taunt traditionally aimed at the fans of the "Nats" down the years, and every time Apparite heard it, it was like a dagger. It stung all the more so since it was so often true: the Senators had gone 66-88 in 1954, with no reversal of that losing trend in sight after the first few months of the '55 season.

He had seen over a hundred games in that ballpark with its huge, oddly asymmetrical outfield (the right field foul-line was inconceivably long at 406 feet, but the left was just a cozy 320, though crowned by a thirty-one foot wall), and he had remembered every one, wins and losses alike. And although Griffith Stadium may have had an unusually large playing field, it held only 29,000 people, so the majority of fans sat quite close to the players, creating a setting so intimate that you could tell if a player had shaved on game day! Apparite wondered if he would ever sit in those uncomfortable wooden seats again, drinking a cold beer and listening to the chatter of Yost and shortstop Pete Runnells—a real pleasure for him, even if the team was on the losing end of the score, which was the usual.

Seeing the stadium brought back memories of the last game he had watched there. It had been three days before his interview with the Director, on a clear, blue-skied eighty-degree afternoon with a little breeze to help keep the flies and sweat down. What a gorgeous day for a ballgame, he had thought, as he sipped a beer while sitting in his usual spot behind the Senators dugout. Camilo Pascual had pitched—"Little Potato" he was called, in contrast to his elder and rounder brother, "Big Potato"—and the Cuban fastballer had given the "Nats" a rare win, pitching a beautiful three-hitter as they beat the Boston Red Sox, 3-2. Mickey Vernon had gone 2 for 4, Eddie Yost had made an amazing diving stop, and the beer was crisp and cold. It had been a great day all around, even though it had only brought the Senators' record to 24-46.

"We're here."

As if in a slide show, the picture of idyllic Griffith Stadium was replaced abruptly by the ratty, red-painted wood façade of Butch's Place, and the task was upon him. Suddenly, Apparite couldn't recall the stats of a single Senators player; instead, a dozen ways to kill a man with his bare hands had automatically sprung to mind. The White Oriental had trained him well: the sight of the battlefield had automatically thrust his fighting instincts to the fore; he had become that coiled spring waiting to be tripped.

"I'm ready," he said in anticipation.

"I will wait for you here," the Director answered. "Here is a wallet with new identification cards; the name on them is 'Joseph Judge.' I cannot emphasize strongly enough that the police must not be involved, and you must not be taken: if you are, I cannot guarantee your safety. And remember, your Shadow-agent is always near."

"I understand." He took the weathered, brown leather wallet containing the documents that renamed him Joseph Judge—the spring was being wound tighter still, he thought. The Director spoke, giving one final instruction, though in a tone of voice that was unfamiliar to Apparite.

"Oh, one last thing: *try* not to kill anyone. It makes for a lot of paperwork."

For the first time in Apparite's experience, the Director let a smile form across his face. *Can it be possible*, Apparite asked himself, *that the Director actually made a joke?* What could have prompted this little touch of humanity? And why is it coming out of him *now*, right before his big test? Realizing he had no time to ponder such questions, Apparite responded with force.

"With all due respect, I'm going to do what it takes." He would never know it, but it was exactly what the Director had wanted to hear. Apparite opened the De Soto's front passenger door, stepped over a pungent slop of vomit in the gutter, and began to walk down the street to the tavern. After a few steps, he paused, turned, and faced the Director, a smile now forming on *his* face.

"Besides," Apparite added, "we don't *have* any paperwork."

He turned and walked briskly to the entrance of the tavern, opened the door, and slipped inside. The Director guessed he'd be back in about five minutes, noting the time on his Hamilton. He would be wrong.

As soon as Apparite had walked through the door, he could tell that the Director had been right on the money about Butch's Place: it was a real rat-hole; a classic haven for petty thieves, thugs, unrepentant wife-beaters, inveterate gamblers, and everyday scum-of-the-earth. In anticipation of the challenge ahead, Apparite's powers of observation were more revved-up than he had ever known before, and he took a quick inventory of the place.

The dark walnut bar, peppered with knife-scrawled initials and obscene words, was on the left, and a few feet behind it, against the wall, was a large, long sideboard topped by a dusty old mirror. The crowded sideboard held the usual assortment of tavern bric-a-brac: large two-gallon jugs in which pickled eggs and chicken gizzards floated unappetizingly; half-empty bottles of liquor (not the good stuff, either; possibly even hooch); sheets of horse races and tallies from the local D.C. numbers rackets; random groupings of beer bottles (some full, most empty); a well-worn cash register (empty, probably, the cash going somewhere less conspicuous); and bottles of after-shave (usual punk stinkola-brand).

There were brewery signs, too, of course—National Bohemian and Old German beer were well represented in this department—as well as a 1955 girlie calendar showing May (the name of the month and *not* of the half-naked girl holding a can of Texas Gold 30-Weight Oil in her hands—*her* name was "Daisy"). Apparite surmised it was the nakedness of the girl and not the actual date that had determined which month the calendar was opened to, since it was August of 1955 and *not* May.

The room's hideously green-brown embossed tin ceiling was at least ten feet high, in the middle of which was a large fan whose blades turned too slowly to move even one molecule of the heavy, hot air in this oven of a tavern. Directly across from the bar and against the opposite wall were five thickly painted red booths; in the back of the tavern was a door labeled "men," but tellingly, there was none marked "women," and looking around, Apparite understood why: he doubted that any sane, sober, or possibly even live woman had ever dared step in here (about the dead or drugged kind, he was afraid to even ponder). There was, as far as he could tell, no exit in the rear of the place—good, he thought; I don't need anyone suddenly running in or out of here.

Moving on to his opponents, Apparite counted seven persons in the establishment; all male, of course, and all between the heights of five feet seven inches and six feet two inches tall, he estimated. Three looked quite obese, two were merely heavy, and two others he deemed rail-thin. The bartender—who was the shortest, at five-seven—had a bar-rag slung over his right shoulder; a southpaw, Apparite figured, since a lefty would reach up to his right shoulder to grab the towel. The barkeep had the usual drawn face of a coward, and wore a very sour expression—it struck Apparite as that of a man who'd spent a lifetime sucking lemons—with, he guessed, an equally unpleasant disposition to match: he surmised that this man would have a knife, if not a revolver, hidden behind the very solid-appearing bar. Looking at him, Apparite also guessed that this barkeep—whom he had immediately nicknamed "Lemon Face"—would go for the phone or a revolver rather than duke it out or take his chances with a knife. The other men, he noted, were seated at the near end of the fifteen-foot bar (two), or clustered around one of the heavily painted red booths (four), and all had hard and unshaven faces.

Stupid men carrying guns had always fascinated Apparite, as they had invariably never been formally or even adequately trained to carry or conceal firearms, and he could almost always pick them out of a crowd. Like little children with a new toy, these types could never resist playing with their weapons; touching them, placing and replacing the clips in an automatic, or messing around with the bullets in a drum-loading revolver.

He observed that two of the men—Cheek Scar and Greasy Hair, both at the bar—were playing with the insides of their jackets which, he also noted with interest, they wore despite the heat (approaching ninety degrees outside, and at least eighty in this dump, thought Apparite). They were both right-handed, so the butts of their weapons would be logically just inside the left side of those well-worn jackets about heart-high. He noticed that their right hands were constantly flitting about in that very spot; like bees circling an enticing flower, just itching to touch down.

The four men in the booth appeared more obsessed with the card game they were playing than with anyone or anything else in the bar, and had taken no notice of his presence so far. Apparite guessed that they were either unarmed or, more likely, carrying some type of knife or stabbing instrument rather than guns. Serious card players, he knew, often had a rule banning firearms (in the interests of impulsive-murder prevention), but knives were commonplace. He figured that the men at the bar would be easy to take down in a fight—if he was fast enough—but he was worried about the four in the booth. Big Britches and Toothless were on the left side and Bad Moustache and Tobacco Stain were on the right, and they were practically unreachable from where he stood just a couple of feet inside the doorway. He noticed that, like their counterparts sitting at the bar, they, too, were all right-handed, which he could tell from the way they held and played their cards—good, he thought; better to keep things simple.

Well, time to get cracking, Apparite said to himself. First, he had to find out where the telephone was, and then disable it. He cleared his throat a few times—no reaction from the barkeep—but then a moment later, he briefly caught the man's eye.

"Are you Butch?" he asked.

"No," Lemon Face answered roughly, looking away from Apparite in indifference. "He ain't here." He continued wiping down the bar with a dirty rag.

"Oh. Where's your phone?"

The bartender, with a face now as sour as a lemon soaked in vinegar, jerked his thumb in the direction of a pile of newspapers at Apparite's end of the bar; the Superagent presumed the phone was buried somewhere under them.

"Thanks; I gotta call a cab. I'm kinda lost," Apparite said as meekly as possible. He started to walk toward the pile of newspapers, but was interrupted by the barkeep's harsh voice.

"Ya can't use it, bud. It's only for bookies."

"Boy, I sure wish I could use that phone," Apparite responded, still trying to reason out his plan. Four things were certain: *one,* he had to get rid of the phone; *two,* he had to take out the gun-toters at the bar; *three,* he had to find a way to keep the guys in the booth bunched up so they couldn't get to him all at once; and *four,* he had to wipe the dirty floor with that barkeep's sour puss.

Okay, Apparite said to himself, having settled on his plan, *here we go.*

He slowly walked over to the untidy pile of newspapers at

the end of the bar, found a black telephone underneath them, took the receiver off the hook, and held it out of sight. The Director had told him to initiate a brawl and, looking at his intended victims, Apparite figured he knew just what to say to get things started.

"All right," he loudly intoned, turning every head in the place. "I just got done layin' all your mothers—and let me tell ya, they sure know how to please a guy!"

He figured that would probably about do it, given the limited brainpower and sophistication of the intended audience.

But his bizarre declaration was met with absolute silence. It struck Apparite that maybe he'd stunned them a bit *too* much with the brazen outrageousness of his pronouncement—he couldn't imagine they'd ever had a runty-looking fellow like him waltz in and insult their mothers before. Maybe the message would take longer to penetrate their thick skulls than he'd expected.

But a tick or two later, his doubts that the challenge would go unanswered were dispelled—he saw Cheek Scar and Greasy Hair at the bar reach deeply into the left sides of their jackets, and with more conscious intent than they had before. He turned his head and saw the four men in the booth put down their cards; they began to draw their elbows back in order to place their hands on the table and push themselves up and out of the booth. It was all going to happen, and in about two seconds.

He glanced at the barkeep, and saw that he was in the act of ducking down behind the bar—well, Apparite thought, at least *he* won't put up much of a fight. Turning his head once again to face his targets, Apparite caught a glimpse of a National Bohemian beer sign. He paused briefly to glance on the round face of "Bo," the brewery's cartoon mascot, whose trademark was that he was always drawn with only one eye (on this particular sign, the left one was missing). For some reason, this made it look to Apparite as if Bo was *winking* at him—like the little beer mascot knew what was about to happen and heartily approved. Apparite smiled at the absurd, comical thought, and then sprang into action.

First, he grabbed an Iron City beer bottle from the end of the sideboard, and with a lightning-quick flick of his wrist sent it crashing into the forehead of Cheek Scar seated furthest from him at the bar. It shattered, the shards cutting Cheek Scar deeply about the face and disfiguring his ugly mug even further, and blood streamed down his face in thin ribbons, blinding him. Too stunned to even utter a groan, he crashed to the ground and knocked himself unconscious, the revolver he had been reaching for dropping onto the crumb and peanut shell-encrusted floor along with its owner.

By the time the bottle had been done rearranging Cheek Scar's face, Apparite had ripped the heavy telephone receiver from its base, swung it on its cord once over his head, and then with a downward motion smashed it against Greasy Hair's right wrist as it appeared from the inside of his jacket, jarring the drum-loading revolver from the thug's hand. Apparite then swung the phone receiver on its cord *nunchuaku*-style, sending it crashing into Greasy Hair's thick skull, stunning him; a quick, snapping punch to the throat and Greasy Hair was on the floor in agony; helpless.

During this time—about two and a half seconds—the four men in the booth had risen to a nearly standing position but, as Apparite had hoped, two of them were too large to move quickly and were having quite a sweaty struggle getting their pendulous abdomens out of the confines of the booth. Apparite saw the two revolvers lying close together on the floor; he kicked them a safe distance from the melee and, swinging the telephone receiver on its cord, hit Big Britches hard, deadeye in the temple as the large man squeezed himself out of the booth. With a sickening dull thud, offset by a slight, barely discernible crunch that heralded a skull fracture, Big Britches seemed to nearly dive face-first onto the floor; unconscious.

Five seconds had now elapsed. Freed by the fall of Big Britches, the smaller Toothless had made it nearly to the edge of the booth, switch-blade knife in hand, before Apparite grabbed a nearby bar stool and swung it like a baseball bat, smashing the metal seat into the side of Toothless' face, and hard enough to knock him completely off his feet. Toothless dropped his knife and fell in a crumpled heap onto the floor; Apparite kicked the knife safely away.

Meanwhile, Bad Moustache, holding a grimy "pig-sticker" in a shaky straight grip, had finally worked his bulk out of the other side of the booth. He lunged forward at Apparite, a sickly grin crossing his greasy, red, and fat moon-face. Apparite leapt back a step, easily avoiding the clumsily wielded blade, and brought the phone receiver around into Bad Moustache's knife hand, flinging the arm away from him and onto the edge of the booth's tabletop. Apparite then thrust his right hand, which he had clenched in a firm *Isshin-Ryu* karate fist, and tensed his muscles as it smashed into Bad Moustache's forearm, breaking it—and the edge of the table—in one whip-like motion. Bad Moustache fell to the floor, vomiting in his pain.

Eight seconds had now elapsed. Tobacco Stain appeared in the space where Bad Moustache's hulking figure had been a second before; he had *two* short switch-blade knives—one in a straight grip, the other in an "ice-pick" hold—and a look of utter disgust on his face as he spewed profanities, spitting and snarling like a cur as he lunged at Apparite with his right hand. Wasting no time, Apparite grabbed Bad Moustache's jacket—which had been resting on the post of the booth—and with a flick he wrapped it quickly around Tobacco Stain's right arm, swinging the thug around. A couple of quick, devastating kicks to Tobacco Stain's right flank, punctuated by the sound of cracking ribs, and the man was down.

Apparite looked around the bar and saw that none of the toughs remained in any condition to fight; every one of them was lying on the ground and gasping in pain, either unwilling or unable to get up and scrap further. *Good. Now for Lemon Face,* he thought.

He picked up one of the revolvers lying on the floor and walked over to the bar. He tapped on it with the weapon, positioning it so the barkeep could clearly see its business end even while cowering.

"Alright, Lemon Face, *get up.*"

Lemon Face's head slowly appeared from behind the bar; his face had a deathly, white pallor and he was shaking.

"Lock your hands behind your neck and turn around," Apparite said, motioning with the barrel of the revolver. "Don't worry: I'm not going to kill you. It makes for a *lot* of paperwork."

Lemon Face complied and turned around slowly, his hands locked behind his neck. Apparite saw that the barkeep's sour mug looked even more miserable than usual: he was showing the excessive salivation and cold sweating of someone who was nauseated and about to puke. Well, he won't have to be miserable for long, thought Apparite.

"Ya know, Lemon Face, you really should let your customers use the phone."

Apparite rapped him sharply on the back of his skull with the butt of the revolver, and Lemon Face disappeared behind the bar with a thud, knocked into an unwilling sleep. The barkeep would awaken, however, about an hour later, though with a tremendous headache, a huge "goose-egg" on the back of his thick skull, and a much more liberal policy about letting customers use the telephone as a result.

Apparite opened the door and stepped out into the bright sunlight of the cloudless afternoon, quite pleased with himself: he couldn't wait to tell the Director how well the task had gone. He bounded up to the De Soto, but his face quickly assumed a look of shock at not what he saw, but what he *didn't* see: the driver's-side door of the car was ajar, and the Director was nowhere to be found.

Four
The "Feds"

Apparite had no inkling where the Director had gone, but he knew the reason for his sudden disappearance—he'd been in the De Soto only a couple of minutes ago!—couldn't be good. The Director, he thought, would *never* have left the car except under the direst of circumstances: if he'd told Apparite that's where he'd be waiting, then that's where he should be right now—only he wasn't. Apparite had to assume the worst: the Director had been kidnapped or killed by a hostile power—probably KGB or SMERSH—although he believed there were other possibilities as well; for one, perhaps the FBI had found out about his little program and decided to terminate it, and him.

Or, wondered Apparite, maybe it was of his doing: if he failed the test, could *that* explain the Director's sudden disappearance? But how could that be? Surely he'd exceeded the Director's expectations: he'd put down the seven toughs in less than thirty seconds! And he hadn't killed anyone or attracted any outside attention doing it, either. Could this all be a part of yet *another* test? Apparite asked himself. He wouldn't put it past the Director to mess with him twice in one day.

No matter what the reason for the Director's disappearance, Apparite knew he had to remain open to every possibility and plan his actions with care. If this was *not* a test, and the worst was occurring, it would be up to him to find the Director, or find out what had happened to him, before the "catastrophic failure" scenario—the fatal implosion that would occur if the program were compromised—became a grim reality for all of them.

And regardless of what was happening, he knew that he could not linger here for long: sooner or later, the police would make their way to the tavern. He quickly climbed into the De Soto and pulled away from the curb: he had decided to drive back to the warehouse; the only place he knew he could go at the moment. Perhaps another agent, or the White Oriental, or the Director's liaison might be there and have some explanation for him, but the thought that this could all be a part of the Director's fiendish suicide plan continued to chill him. Could this event really be unfolding? Would Apparite be next? If so, he figured he would not survive the night.

Driving as rapidly as he safely could, he retraced the route the Director had taken with him earlier. His mind was a jumble of confusion, but amongst these random, unhelpful thoughts there was one thing that Apparite knew was certain: he had no real plan. Go to the warehouse, and that was it. It wasn't comforting.

After a few minutes drive, Apparite arrived at the decaying, gothic-accented brick warehouse. The sun was at its zenith in the clear, blue sky, but it felt like the middle of the darkest night in the worst section of town, given the potentially deadly nature of the situation. Looking around him while still seated in the De Soto, Apparite saw—nothing. *Good*. No cars, no passersby, and his innate danger-sense told him he was not being watched. He took the key out of the ignition and slid it under the floor mat; *if they search me*, he thought, *there's no need to give away the key to the only source of transport I have.* He stepped out of the car and walked up to the double delivery doors that led into the warehouse: cautiously, attentively.

He put his ear to them, trying to pick up any sound that might tell him someone was waiting for him inside, but there was still nothing. He cracked the doors open slightly, peering through a miniscule crack—still nothing. Opening them a bit more, he was able to scan around the large room: he saw the stairs that led to the second floor; the doorways leading to the numerous other, smaller rooms; the winches and large hooks that dangled from heavy iron chains from the ceiling; and the dirty floor where Apparite had spent so much time grappling with the White Oriental. Everything checked out clear. He dared take some careful, silent steps inside the room, noiselessly opening the doors just far enough for him to slip through.

Nothing at all seemed amiss; there was no one in sight. Everything is just as I'd left it, he thought. His danger-sense, though, was now pricking up his ears—was it just paranoia, or his lack of a plan manifesting itself as a brief free-floating anxiety?

No! He dove under a heavy table, a second before two men wearing long trench coats appeared from a doorway about fifteen feet from him, guns pulled. Their skillful silence gave them away as fellow agents, but friend or foe he could not yet tell.

Caught like a rat in a trap, he thought; well, at least *this* rat will soon learn what's going on before the trap closes and snuffs it out. He clambered out from under the table and stood, arms raised above his head.

"I'm unarmed."

The two men slowly moved toward him, pistols held steadily in front of them, gradually advancing on him with hyper vigilance apparent in their unblinking eyes and their dilated pupils, obviously hostile to Apparite from their aggressive body language. Apparite wondered who they were: the

"Feds" perhaps? He saw their Colt M1911 semi-automatics and thought it a possibility. Or could they be some of the Director's men, coming to inflict punishment for a failed test? He could waste no more time; he had to try and learn something about them. He spoke, though his voice sounded small and weak in the large, empty warehouse.

"Why are you here? This is private property and you are trespassing."

The lead gunman, a tall, well-built man who was walking about a step ahead of the other, answered him.

"Why are *you* here? This building is used for illegal and dangerous purposes, and there is no reason for you to be in it, unless you are a part of those activities. Strip off your clothing, please, using only one arm at a time. I advise you not to make any sudden movements."

Apparite was smart enough to see he had no choice in the matter: no one, not even the White Oriental, would be able to disarm and neutralize two trained persons holding pistols on him at five paces. He lowered his left arm, unbuttoned his shirt, and with a quick shake of his shoulders it fell off him and onto the floor. Unbuttoning his pants at the waist, and then undoing the fly, he pulled them down until they fell about his ankles, his right arm remaining straight up in the air in a sort of humiliating salute to the men who were controlling his actions.

"That's enough; keep your pants around your ankles. Hop over to the chair," the gunman said, motioning with his pistol and kicking a chair toward Apparite; it slid with an irritating screech, stopping a foot away from him.

"What do you want?" Apparite said, sitting back in the chair, trying to keep one eye on his interrogator and the other on the gunman's younger partner, an intense appearing man with a look of unnatural concentration on his face.

The interrogator looked over at his partner. "Keep him covered," he said, pointing at Apparite with his pistol. He began walking in his direction, eyeing Apparite intently. Apparite hoped that his captor would pat him down to check for weapons; if so, he might get close enough for the Superagent to make a grab for him.

Yes, yes, Apparite said to himself as his interrogator came closer and closer, *put down your weapon and check me out.* Apparite would fling his legs up, grasping the gunman between his pants-bound ankles, and then throw him to the ground. Using him as a shield—the other gunman might hesitate to shoot for fear of injuring his partner—Apparite might then be able to make a dive for the table and improvise a weapon, or perhaps even get his interrogator's pistol away from him. The gunman walked closer indeed, raising Apparite's hopes of escape, until he stopped only two paces away.

"I think that's as close as I want to get to you, *Agent E.*"

Apparite stiffened at the sound of his seldom-spoken code-name and knew that his life would soon be over. If they know *that,* he figured, then they know *everything:* the Director, the agency, the White Oriental, and possibly even the name John Apparite. Whether they were the Feds, the KGB, or even the Director's men didn't make much difference now—he knew that if he did not escape, he would not be leaving the room alive. Apparite settled on a plan that had served him well in the past: he would be faithful to his duty and his agency, regardless of the consequences. He had always been much less afraid of dying than of being a failure, and today would be no different.

"I have no idea what you are talking about," Apparite said in defiance. "My name is Joseph Judge; I have never heard of an 'Agent E.' Here," he motioned with his head toward the wallet-side of his pants, "look in my wallet. My name is Joe Judge!"

"You have had a few names, even in your short career so far: Agent E, Joseph Judge, plus the name you had before you joined the agency; perhaps others." The man continued to eye Apparite as he spoke, his pistol carefully aimed at Apparite's heart as if at any moment his prisoner might make a leap for him.

Giving up his earlier tack, Apparite tried another in an effort to get them talking, keep them talking, and buy a bit of time to figure something out.

"What to you want with me? I haven't done anything." Apparite's head ached and he felt like the room was spinning as he concentrated intensely on finding some means of escape—his stalling tactics, he knew, would not last much longer. But Apparite soon realized that things were quickly coming to a head when his interrogator flew into a sudden rage, an almost religious fervor permeating his angry voice.

"Haven't *done* anything? What do you call half-killing seven men in a bar? Or have you already forgotten what transpired at a tavern called Butch's Place less than fifteen minutes ago?"

I know what he's doing, thought Apparite: he's trying to provoke a reaction from me; keep me off balance. Apparite's eyes felt warm and his temples throbbed as the blood rushed to his head. *Think,* Apparite! he said to himself. *Think of something!* But the ideas just wouldn't come.

"So what?" was all Apparite could come up with in response. "Unless you're the D.C. P.D., it's none of your damn business."

"You'll pay for that remark when the time comes; I'll see to that personally," the gunman said with relish.

The interrogator began circling his prisoner slowly,

forcing Apparite to look left, then follow the man to the right, and then look left again to pick him back up again. Realizing he was being "played," Apparite stopped moving his head and stared straight into space: his mind was a blank and he knew that further talking would only enrage his captors. He made a decision; the only one worth making given his helpless position and lack of options.

"I'm done talking, boys," intoned Apparite. Who knows? he thought. Maybe if I shut up, *they'll* start talking.

The interrogator smiled.

"Done talking?" he said, addressing Apparite in a much calmer voice that, in its careful and calculated manner, the Superagent found more compelling than the abrasive version. "Fine," he continued, "I'll do the talking, and we'll see how much you like what I have to say. First of all, your boss is dead. He's a difficult man to find, so when we saw him sitting in his car in front of Butch's Place, we took our opportunity when it presented itself. He was very foolish to expose himself like that; even for five minutes.

"Second, we have had *you* under surveillance, Agent E, since the day you were given this assignment. We know much about you and your program; certainly all we need to know to kill you without regret. Third, you have a choice before you and this is it: you can answer our questions, right here, right now, or you can die, right here, right now."

Apparite remained silent, staring off into space, trying not to think about the conclusion he had just made: these men, he guessed, were elite FBI agents, sent to eliminate a rogue, rival agency by J. Edgar Hoover. The bitter irony of it! Ex-FBI agent John Apparite was going to be killed by a man he would have gladly called a colleague just a few months earlier, and it galled him.

The interrogator spoke again, his voice softening into an

almost gentle tone as if he were speaking to a child.

"You have a chance to be a hero, Agent E, by exposing all of this," he said, motioning around the building with his pistol. "Did you know that your program has never received approval of any kind from the United States Government? Did you know that it was behind the assassination attempt of President Truman in nineteen-fifty? Did you know that the head of your agency has been embezzling and misusing funds for years from the Department of Defense and the CIA, getting fat on the blood of his so-called Superagents?"

Apparite's head began shaking ever so slightly with each beat of his heart, so heavily was it hammering. He was on the verge of saying, "CI Director Allen Dulles was the one who recommended me, you fool!" but had thought better of it: he knew that regardless of who the man was or what his purpose proved to be, it was best to remain mute.

So he continued to stare dumbly ahead, uncaring and unmoved by all appearances, but fuming inside. As he struggled to hold his emotions in check, his headache increased and his pulse continued to pound in his temples like a jackhammer. His "fight or flight" response was reaching its breaking point, and when it did, Apparite knew that something was going to happen, although even he could not yet say for certain what form that "something" was going to take.

The interrogator spoke again but the softness was gone from his voice: it had been replaced by anger at Apparite's lack of cooperation.

"I'm going to count backwards from five. You had better start answering my questions, because if I reach one before you start talking, I will blow your f——g brains out."

Apparite stared straight ahead. Fine, blow my brains out, you SOB.

"Five. What is your real name, Agent E?"

Apparite knew this was one question he could never answer: with that knowledge, it would be simple for Hoover to follow the trail of deception right up to the doorsteps of the Director and CI chief Allen Dulles; maybe even all the way to the Secretary of Defense and the head of the NSA. If Hoover ever got the missing piece to this puzzle, the FBI director would have the power-play opportunity of a lifetime. *And the missing piece,* Apparite said to himself, *is me.*

Apparite looked up and spit at his tormentor, hitting him flush in the eye; the interrogator took out his handkerchief and wiped it away. The man moved back a step, out of expectoration range, and purposefully cocked his pistol. He then aimed it directly at Apparite's forehead.

"Four. What is your real name?" the interrogator said, each word more distinct than the last.

Apparite looked at him with hate dripping from his eyes like tears.

"Three. What is your real name?" The phrase was coming out very slowly now, with a full emphasis on each word.

Apparite held up his left hand, his middle finger dramatically extended.

"Two. What. Is. Your. Real. Name?" The interrogator raised the pistol slightly, and then re-aimed it at Apparite's forehead in a gesture that said, "I can't miss, buster, so you'd better start talking."

But Apparite remained silent and rigid; he was going to die but he would do so with honor. He would not betray the Director for any price.

The gunman re-aimed the pistol yet again, and Apparite guessed what he was thinking: *when the countdown ends, I want to make sure the bullet hits this stubborn asshole right in the middle of his forehead.*

Apparite knew he was finished, and as his headache

reached its crescendo and his vision began to blur, he prepared what he believed might be his final thoughts on this
earth. But just as he completed them, and just as his interrogator's mouth began to form an "O" to start the word "one,"
something happened that interrupted the proceedings:
Apparite's eyes rolled back into his head, his thick tongue
stuck itself clumsily out of his mouth, and suddenly his body
was thrown to the floor by an invisible assailant. He was in the
throes of a grand-mal seizure.

The convulsing Apparite fell at the feet of his interrogator,
his mouth frothing and torso contorted into a "U." His arms
and legs were flailing wildly about him in jerking spasms, and
he was growling like a beast.

The interrogator, who had not yet got the word "one" out
of his mouth, instinctively leaned over toward the helpless
man at his feet.

With lighting quickness, Apparite grabbed the weapon in
the man's right hand by the barrel and gave it a wrenching
twist to the left, freeing it; he then swept the man's left leg
with his right, throwing him to the ground. Flipping himself
prone, Apparite put a choke-hold on him with his right hand,
the interrogator's face turning red in the process, his pistol
now firmly in Apparite's grip. It had taken less than two seconds.

"Click. Click-click-click-click-click-click" went the seven-
shot pistol in Apparite's hand. The barrel had been pointed
directly at the heart of the other agent, who had been tempo-
rarily stunned and distracted by the shock of Apparite's "seizure."

Another dummy clip!

Apparite heard a laugh coming from across the room; a
loud, roaring laugh in a voice that was familiar, though not
fully recognizable in its current timbre of hilarity. For his

part, Apparite had no idea what was so funny.

"*Well done,* Agent E!" said the voice, as its owner began to walk across the room toward the still prone Superagent. It was the Director, and Apparite realized the whole agonizing episode was, indeed, another one of his repellant and ghoulish tests.

The Director turned toward the two men Apparite had "killed," his voice changing into the more familiar, serious monotone that Apparite knew so well (and, until he had heard him laughing, had practically defined the man for him).

"Gentlemen, you have been made fools of. Please put down your weapons—those of you who still have one—and wait outside."

The interrogator arose from the floor, coughing and rubbing his sore neck, his face gradually returning to its usual color. The other agent, who had remained mute during the entire episode, had a very ill look to him, as if he'd just eaten bad fish. The two men reflexively straightened out their trench coats and began to walk toward the double delivery doors, though slowly and without much confidence.

"Wait," the Director said, motioning to the man who had interrogated Apparite, as the other passed through the exit. "I suppose an introduction is in order. Apparite, meet J, my liaison, whose next title might be that of 'Corpse John Doe' if he does not learn to show more caution."

J held out his hand; he was much taller than Apparite and more sturdily built, but had a warm face and a confident shake. His looks reminded Apparite remarkably of Montgomery Clift: J had the same dark eyes and hair, although his manner seemed one of an easy, relaxed affability, as opposed to Clift's quiet intensity. Although Apparite usually kept his emotional distance from new acquaintances, his connection with him was automatic, and he liked J immediately—he seemed like the kind of guy you'd want to be your Best Man, or your "second" in the olden days of dueling. Looking at J's now-smiling face, Apparite couldn't believe that this was the same man who had tortured him into thinking he was going to blow his brains out a scant few seconds earlier.

"Good to meet you. I've heard some fine things about you—now I know why," J said.

"You really had me going there," replied Apparite, who had transformed back into his usual, steady self. "I'm sorry if I hurt you in that hold." The apology made J's face redden in embarrassment.

"No, I'm fine," he said in a voice that seemed unusually weak and hesitant, showing his humiliation. The Director interrupted their exchange.

"Alright, that's enough. J, go outside and prepare yourself for a refresher course in contact fighting and tactics. I would not make any plans for about four weeks if I were you."

J left through the double doors; as they opened, Apparite saw the other man outside, pacing anxiously and muttering to himself, obviously terrified of the Director's impending reprisal.

"Who's the other guy?" Apparite ventured to ask.

"You don't need to know," the Director said quietly, though with a sharp tone.

Apparite figured it might have been a Shadow-agent, or a lower-level agent in training—CI maybe, duped into it by the Director. But the Director was right; he *didn't* need to know.

"By the way, Apparite, you passed both tests, as I am sure you have figured out by now. I have yet to have an agent actually succeed in overpowering his armed and usually vigilant interrogators, but to do so by feigning a seizure, well . . ." His voice trailed off, as if the completion of this thought might cause another outburst of inappropriate mirth on his part.

Apparite sensed the Director softening toward him, that he had been genuinely proud of him and his effort. And, of all things, he had been laughing! When Apparite had "killed" the two agents, he had laughed his ass off! *I wonder how many years it's been since* that's *happened?* Apparite asked himself. There was much more to the enigmatic Director than the hard-ass he had become accustomed to, he decided.

"As is now obvious, this test was not designed solely to evaluate your ability to overwhelm seven men in a tavern; it was also given to assess your behavior under extreme pressure and duress. The situation presented to you is one of the most dangerous a Superagent can face: your capture and interrogation at gunpoint in a hopeless situation; your life bartered against information that might betray the program. The combat test, while important and a good assessment of your fighting skills, was, in some ways, merely the prelude to a more critical and realistic examination of your mettle and commitment."

"What if I'd been arrested outside of Butch's Place?" Apparite asked. "What if the police had come?"

"It would have been an easy matter to clear up; one phone call and you would have been released, with no questions asked. Of course, I could not have let you know that before the task."

"It might have taken all the fun out of it," responded Apparite, a bit irritated with the Director's never-ending string of "kickers."

"Your having fun is the farthest thing from my mind when I take the trouble to plan these exercises—I do not appreciate the sarcasm." The Director was glowering at him and Apparite was feeling very uncomfortable as a result.

"Sorry; I didn't really mean it."

"I'm sure you *did*," the Director said with a slight smile. "However, it is plain the combat test held no small importance for you, so you might be interested to know that the time from when you entered the bar until you returned was less than two minutes—impressive. During the course of those two minutes you caused five concussions, three fractures, two episodes of vomiting, and the destruction of a telephone: not a bad afternoon's work, don't you agree?" The Director's expression had warmed considerably; Apparite noted that a little grin was even showing through the man's usually inscrutable demeanor.

"Get some rest and relax for the rest of the day," the Director added. "You might be interested to hear that the 'Nats' are playing Detroit at twenty-hundred tonight, in case you wish to listen to the ballgame. I have had the radio tuned to the correct frequency."

Apparite could have leapt up and embraced him, for all the man's bluster and bombast—an evening listening to the "Nats" would be a tonic to him. But then—in typical fashion, he thought—the Director followed it with a dram of bitter reality.

"Enjoy the ballgame tonight, but rest well; tomorrow will be the day of your first mission. I will be straight with you at the risk of compromising your morale: for many men, even highly trained agents, this mission would pose great personal risk. It has been in the planning stages for some weeks and its timing cannot be altered, but I believe you are as ready for it as is reasonably possible. You may also find it comforting to know that I have great faith in your abilities. I will be back to brief you in the morning at 0700. Goodbye."

Apparite lived the rest of this grueling but satisfying day as if it were his last—at least, as much as a man held virtual prisoner in an abandoned warehouse, eating dehydrated K-rations, sleeping on a musty rag of a cot, and listening to his favorite ball club getting shut out 4-0 by Detroit possibly could.

Five
J. Edgar Hoover
and the Mafia

Apparite met the Director outside the warehouse at 0700 the next morning. The rehydrated eggs and burnt coffee were battling in Apparite's stomach for attention, but they would receive none. His mind was focused solely on staying alive through the end of this day, his first as a "licensed" Superagent (if that term was not too much of a stretch, he added to himself). But he remained confident and calm despite the difficult mission ahead; after his eight weeks of intense training, and the exercises at Butch's and back at the warehouse, Apparite felt prepared for anything.

The Director was driving a new car to Apparite's eye: a black, 1953 Nash Rambler, which Apparite figured was the unofficial color of the unnamed agency. Inside it was, of all people, J, whose re-initiation into combat and tactics training had apparently been postponed. The Director rolled down his window.

"Get in, Apparite; sit up front."

J got out of the car, leaving the front passenger door ajar. The young agent climbed into the front seat next to the Director, awaiting his instructions, but no matter what they were he was prepared to follow them to the letter.

"I will brief you as we drive to a safe location where I can be dropped off," the Director said. "You two will then take the vehicle and proceed."

Apparite looked back briefly at J; the liaison was sitting

quietly in the back seat, staring at the scenery as the car sped westward, looking quite bored. His blank expression, though, only served to add to Apparite's comfort: "I've done this so much, it doesn't faze me at all, anymore," it seemed to be saying. After another block of driving, the Director broke the prolonged silence.

"Apparite, tell me about the American Mafia from what you learned at the FBI. You may be brief, and speak in generalities if you wish."

Apparite, not wishing to look hesitant or unsure of himself, answered the Director immediately.

"Well, there are many at the FBI who have minimized the existence of the American Mafia as an organized-crime syndicate, but I believe evidence proves otherwise: the Kefauver Hearings in fifty and fifty-one showed as much. My understanding is that the Mafia is centralized in New York City through the 'Five Families,' but has branches in many major cities in the U.S. The members of the Mafia consist primarily of Sicilians and Italians, usually with a measure of blood-linkage between members of each clan. They refer to their crime-family higher-ups as *'Capos,'* with various underlings and lieutenants doing the actual dirty work. These men send the money, which they call a 'tribute,' up the chain to their *Capo*. Avenues of revenue include loan-sharking, prostitution and gambling; the numbers rackets; the illegal sale of drugs, mainly heroin and marihuana; unlicensed cigarettes and liquor; and kickbacks for civic and construction projects."

"What about organized crime activity in D.C.?" asked the Director. "Tell me about that."

"There's not a large population of Sicilians or Italians in central D.C., so the traditional Sicilian-style Mafia isn't very prominent; crime activities are sometimes scavenged by members of the New York and Philadelphia families, however. There's a man by the name of Joseph Nesline who has control of most of the gambling and prostitution rackets in D.C., but he keeps things pretty quiet around here," Apparite concluded.

"I agree with your assessment, except for one point you have overlooked: in addition to the vices and loan-sharking, which have always been money-makers for the Mafia, there is another important revenue stream that you have not mentioned."

"I don't think they are good counterfeiters," Apparite responded, "lacking the technical expertise and patience that requires. They have some legitimate investments, of course, and are backers of Vegas casinos; beyond that, aside from petty theft, hijackings, and such, I'm not sure what you're getting at—sorry."

"How about blackmail; extortion?

"I'm sure they are proficient in that as well, but I can't name any specific cases," Apparite said, working his memory for anything in that line and feeling not a little uninformed coming up empty-handed.

"Do you think the FBI has done a thorough job in investigating and prosecuting *Mafiosi?* Do you think they do so with *zeal?*"

Apparite could see the Director was driving at something, but did not wish to speak ill of his old FBI colleagues.

"They seem to do okay."

"Please speak freely, Apparite; I will give you credit for your honesty and insight, if I see any forthcoming." The Director had been glancing over at the young agent from time to time as he drove, and had read Apparite's facial expressions and seen resistance and hesitancy in them.

"No," Apparite said firmly. "Higher level FBI officials seemed to do a lot of foot-dragging. Agents told me their

Mafia investigations had been slowed, or thwarted by paperwork, or required resources that had disappeared."

"Exactly. Do you know why?"

"No," Apparite answered, shaking his head. He hated not having the answers to the Director's questions.

The Director raised his voice audibly.

"Because J. Edgar Hoover, the Director of the Federal Bureau of Investigation, is being blackmailed by the Mafia. Does that surprise you?"

Surprised? Apparite could not have been more stunned if the Director had told him that he was, in reality, head of the KGB.

"But how is that possible? What could they have on him?"

"Tell me, Apparite: how did Hoover feel about homosexuals?"

"He despised them; everyone at the agency knew that."

"What is your posture towards them?"

"They don't bother me; I don't think I've even met one."

"Well, you have; in fact, you have almost certainly shaken the hand of the most notorious homosexual in this country."

Apparite ran through his memory banks once again, but could not recall ever having met a homosexual, not to mention shaking one's hand.

"Who?" Apparite asked. "Not *you!*" he added impulsively.

"No; not me, Apparite. I bear no malice towards homosexuals or any harmless sexual deviant. I *do* bear malice towards men who allow their sexual proclivities to compromise the safety and security of the United States, however."

"I'm not sure what you're getting at," Apparite said.

"What if I told you that J. Edgar Hoover, who shook your hand at your FBI Academy graduation, has deliberately slowed the investigation and prosecution of the American Mafia because he is homosexual."

Apparite was stunned to near-immobility, like a man whose muscles are held captive by an electric current.

"Hoover—a homosexual? That's unbelievable! How . . . why . . . ?"

"He hides it behind a cloak of paranoia: by persecuting homosexuals, Hoover deflects any thought that he might be one. Knowing that his greatest chance of public exposure is by one of his own kind—whether by accident or design—his true passion has become keeping his agency spot-clear of homosexuals, to the recent exclusion of most anything else."

"How do they know? How do *you* know?" Apparite was still hoping this was one of the Director's perverted tests, or a hoax. He looked back at J to gauge his reaction, but the liaison continued to stare at the scenery with a blank look on his face; apparently, thought Apparite, this wasn't news to *him*.

"There are photographs, taken surreptitiously, of Hoover engaging in homosexual activities while on vacation in Florida. He was careless, and is now paying for it; we're *all* paying for it. These inflammatory photographs and their negatives are in the possession of the Casarano crime family of New York. They have been using them as blackmail against Hoover these past three years."

"That's the most unbelievable story I've ever heard," Apparite said, his voice rising in pitch and intensity. "It's beyond comprehension."

"I assure you it is true, and it has placed our nation at great risk. I cannot say if the Mafia would ever expose him, but the fact remains that they have great leverage over him as long as these pictures are in their possession. It is not just Hoover, or the reputation of the FBI that is at risk, Apparite. The Mafia could use these photographs to potentially blackmail Hoover into doing nearly anything: betraying government secrets, giving up FBI agents, or even," he said, looking over at the young agent, "investigating certain secret agencies that have no name, if he ever finds evidence of one. Our existence and ability to function may someday depend on the fate of these photographs. We cannot let this situation stand any longer."

Having worked his way through the shock wave of the emotional blast that had hit him so suddenly, Apparite was now ready to get to it.

"What do you want me to do?"

"First, you and J will perform surveillance at Dolci's Butcher Shop and Market; a hangout for Casarano's men when they are operating in D.C. I have had a listening device and transmitter planted into the ceiling of the shop; the most advanced 'bug' in existence—smaller than a cigarette lighter—with a range of one hundred feet and eighty-percent comprehension on a clear day."

"*Wheeew,*" whistled Apparite, pleased to finally hear something technically advanced being used, in contrast to his own unusually cheap and low-tech training to date. "Impressive. What will we be listening for?"

"We need to know how many men will be in the shop at eighteen-hundred this evening, and we need to confirm they will have the negatives and photographs in their possession. We also need to know if they will accept my offer to purchase those negatives and photographs."

Apparite, who had thought he could not be stunned again so much, so soon, found himself once again struggling to understand what he had just heard.

"You've been in contact with these men?" he asked. "Have you met with them?"

"Of course not!" the Director answered. "I never personally meet with anyone except my agents and associates—I approached them through intermediaries. But they know that I am prepared to pay one million dollars in untraceable cash for those pictures. Look behind you; it is in the satchel in the back seat."

Apparite, eyes widening in disbelief, turned his head toward the rear of the car: sitting in the back seat next to J was a sixteen-inch high, twenty-four-inch wide heavy leather satchel. A moment later, the Director pulled the car to a stop on a quiet street in southwest D.C. Turning it off, he took the key out of the ignition and handed it to J.

"The Mafia loves many things," the Director said, "like women, horse races, and good *spaghetti puttanesca,* but they love one thing above all: *money,* especially the ill-gotten kind. They have become greedy and foolhardy—having a tough time with their bookmaking businesses recently and needing quick cash—and are now willing to part with the pictures for the sum I named. It is foolish, of course, on their part—the negatives are priceless in what they might gain from them in the years ahead—but I have found that you can get anything for a buck. The other Mob bosses in New York City would have their heads if they knew of this deal, because Hoover's blackmailing benefits them all, but the carrot I'm dangling is especially large, and they will not want to let it dangle for long."

"Will they do it?" Apparite asked.

"I believe they will do one of two things: one, they make the deal, take the million dollars, and give you the pictures; or two, they shoot you dead, take the million dollars, keep the pictures, and dump your lifeless body in the Potomac in a canvas duffel bag weighed down by cement blocks."

"I'm betting on number two," Apparite said.

"Correct. They know how desperate we are to get those pictures—which we are, of course—but they do not realize that we, unlike them, have only *one* option in this deal and that is this: you will walk in the butcher shop and kill every mobster in it. You will then return with the money, the photographs, the negatives, and any other papers or photographs they have on hand. They might normally expect a double-cross, but as the engagement is on their turf and you will be greatly out-numbered, I do not believe the possibility that one man could kill them all has even entered their minds. Nevertheless, that is what you must do."

"I figured as much," Apparite said, having gotten the hang of the Director's *modus operandi*. "Will I be able to use weapons this time? Or will I have to kill them all with the telephone receiver from Butch's Place?"

The Director smiled at the quip, much to Apparite's surprise and delight.

"That's the tricky part," he said. "They will almost certainly pat you down for weapons. But we should be able to conceal a few of them on you."

"That explains why you sent me to Butch's Place; for practice."

"Yes. That was only a dress rehearsal; tonight is the performance. It is imperative for the security of our country that you not fail."

"I won't." Apparite responded, warming to the task.

"We have one very real advantage: you are not handicapped by whimsy, quirks, or *machismo* while doing your duty; if you were, I might have already disposed of you. But *Mafiosi* are funny types, not overly prone to reasoning things out, relying more on brawn than intellect, and constrained by ego. Their balls are big, but their big balls will get in the way and make them vulnerable.

"For example, they will pat you down for guns and knives, but will not strip-search you, for fear it might make them look like 'queers,' although they do not have insight into the psychology of this themselves. They will post men directly outside the shop, but none will be positioned across or down the street. They will have guns, but Mafiosi usually are formally untrained in hand-to-hand combat. If they bring the negatives and photographs—and I believe they will, if only to brag about them and humiliate you with them, as they think you are an FBI agent—they will do so in a big box filled with stacks of papers and notebooks containing their illegal schemes, making no effort to separate them or keep them in a more secure location. They will do all of this in their overconfidence and, as is always the case, it will lead to their undoing."

"I understand," Apparite said. "I won't let you down."

"I expect as much. In the trunk of the car is an assortment of weapons that you may conceal on yourself. I will be leaving you now; J will give you further instructions when you arrive at your surveillance point. We will rendezvous at the warehouse at nineteen-hundred tonight; if you are not there, I will presume you are dead."

The Director got out of the car and spoke to Apparite.

"I would wish you good luck, but I know you will not have to rely on it," he said abruptly. He then walked away, looking as ordinary to Apparite as any of the other dozen persons in view. *You'd never know he was one of the most powerful men in America,* Apparite said to himself as the man turned a corner at the end of the block and disappeared from sight.

After having remained silent for the entire drive, J finally spoke.

"Stay in the passenger's seat; I'll drive. We'll go to a quiet place where you can arm yourself, and then we'll do the surveillance." J got out of the rear seat of the car, opened the driver's-side door, and got behind the wheel. He started the car and began driving, smoothly and effortlessly: Apparite could tell that he had been well trained in that regard, although he could not guess by whom.

"We're about five blocks from Dolci's shop," J said. "I think it's safe for us to get out now."

The two men climbed out of the Rambler and walked around to the rear of the car. J opened the trunk, and he and Apparite peered inside.

"We can conceal at least three lethal weapons on you without detection; we'll also hide a semi-automatic pistol in a compartment in the satchel."

"Good," Apparite said as he picked through the trunk's bounty of weapons and lethal devices. He was pleased to find a .38 caliber Colt Super Automatic pistol; he took it out of the trunk, slipped a full nine-shot clip into it, and held it in his left hand, feeling its weight and balance. It was a well-crafted weapon, complete with the latest Clark modification, though Apparite did not need much convincing of its formidability or usefulness: he had always loved the feel of a Colt pistol, especially when it was such an accurate and advanced model as a modified Super Automatic. He figured he'd find a use for every one of those nine bullets.

Looking further in the trunk, Apparite saw a large assortment of garrote wires, clubs, and knives. He was particularly attracted to some switchblades he had found; they were small but of fine make, with blades composed of steel, or possibly even titanium, he guessed. He flipped open one of the smallest ones; the mechanism operated effortlessly and smoothly as he felt the blade click firmly into place. It was an exceptionally sharp, two-sided blade with a fine, tapered tip effective at creating puncture wounds. Holding it in his hands, Apparite thought it could be thrown as well, as its balance was excellent. Such an unusual style for a switchblade, he said to himself; he had never seen a more intelligently crafted knife.

J removed a pair of shoes from the trunk; he held them up for Apparite to see.

"Gangsters never check shoes like they should," he said. "These are heavy, but not too heavy to prove clumsy; a kick to an adversary would be understandably devastating. Given your karate skills, I think they'd be perfect for you. You wear a size eight and a half, medium-width, correct?"

Apparite nodded and took the pair of black shoes in his hands, feeling them for balance and firmness; each weighed about two pounds, he estimated, with the bulk of the weight near the toe but not so far in the tip as to unbalance them.

"Put them on; see how they feel," J said.

"Let me get these old ones off first." Apparite placed his new shoes on the trunk of the car and then removed the well-worn brown pair he had been wearing.

"Special shoes like these are *very* expensive, so take good care of them," J said, handing the stocking-footed Apparite one of the new black shoes to try on.

"I will," Apparite answered as he slipped it on his foot and laced it. "It feels like a good fit." An amused grin crossed J's face as he handed Apparite the right one.

"I'll admit that black is a little plain, and you were probably hoping for something in a 'pump' to give you more height. But here's some exciting news, Apparite: next year's spy-shoes are going to be all about *color!*" He laughed loudly and with enthusiasm; he seemed to be having a pretty good time at the young agent's expense.

Apparite glanced up at his colleague with an annoyed look on his face: was this *really* the time to be cracking jokes? Apparite's irritated expression only served to add to the hilarity of the situation for the liaison, who laughed even harder.

Is he always going to press my buttons like that? Apparite said to himself, although he had to admit the comment was sort of amusing. He thought it might take him a while to get used to J's sense of humor, however—no one at the FBI had ever said anything funny. Come to think of it, no one at CI ever had, either.

"Wait a minute," J said, getting back to business as Apparite laced up the right shoe, "there's more to them than you know. Under the right heel there is a small hook—see it? Pull on it."

Apparite pulled on the hook and a very thin wire concealed within the heel began to unspool. It proved to be about eighteen inches long.

"It can be connected to another small hook on the left heel to create a garrote wire, or even a crude swinging weapon."

"Kind of like *nunchuaku*," Apparite replied. "I could have used these in Butch's Place; they would have been much easier to handle than a telephone receiver."

"Also," J said, pointing to the bottom of the right shoe, "there's a small throwing knife in each sole that you access from the toe—right here." J pulled on another very tiny hook at the toe and a four-inch long all-metal throwing knife appeared in his hand. "You could do a lot of damage with this," he added.

"Good," Apparite answered. "I can also use objects in the shop itself—should be no problem." His confidence was rising: he figured he could easily take out six *Mafiosi*, even if they all had guns; he had no worries there. "No problem," he repeated.

J firmly slammed the trunk door shut. "I think that should be enough weapons for you to do the job. The satchel has a false side that may be accessed by a hidden pocket from its exterior; we'll stash the Colt in there. We can also hide the switchblade in the handle, where there's another small compartment. After we do that, we'll drive to our surveillance point."

"Right."

They climbed back into the car and J took the satchel from the back seat. He placed the semi-automatic pistol in the hidden pocket, demonstrating to Apparite its simple operation, and then slipped the switchblade into the handle of the satchel as well. Apparite, for his part, wanted to open the satchel and take a look at the million bucks, but did not want to betray his fascination with that aspect of the mission to a veteran like J. He took one last, good look at the satchel as J placed it on the back seat, although he admittedly had a difficult time not peeking at it as they drove to the surveillance point.

Truth be told, the million dollars was the only aspect of the mission that was worrying him. The fact that he would be facing many armed gangsters by himself did not much bother Apparite—he had already done that back at Butch's Place, and everything had turned out fine—and even the pressure to impress the Director and his quirky liaison wasn't much of a concern. No, this was something more homegrown; one of those little hitches from his distant past that was creeping into the present.

As someone who grew up with very little money during the Depression, sometimes resorting to eating game or searching in the woods for mushrooms or berries to stretch his family's food (especially when his father was away), Apparite had always been acutely aware of money or, more accurately, his continual *lack* of it. He may not have been deprived as a youth, but there had been some close calls for him and his family regarding rent, gas, and electric bills. Apparite had not forgotten what it was like to live day to day with only a few cents change in his pocket.

And now he had this satchel *stuffed* with bills in his possession. Apparite had never even been in the same room as a *thousand* dollars in cash, not to mention a *million,* and he found it terribly intimidating. It dawned on him that maybe he was more comfortable doing things on the cheap, like sleeping on a moldy cot, eating vile K-rations, and training in a dilapidated warehouse, as opposed to being entrusted with a million dollars cash he might lose, or using expensive equipment he might break.

A million bucks, Apparite said to himself, *and it all depends on me.*

J slowed the car: across the street was the market.

"I'll park here for a few seconds so you can get a quick peek at the layout of the shop," the liaison said.

J pulled the car to a halt and Apparite took a quick glance through the Nash's side window. The single room of the market was about fifteen feet wide and twenty-five feet long; on the right side of it sat the meat counter, which appeared to be very well built and sturdy. The top half of it was in the form of a typical butcher's display case, and was filled with meats and cheeses; the bottom half was about thirty inches high and looked unusually substantial—probably a refrigerated area for drinks, pasta salads, and such, thought Apparite. Good: that means it's well insulated and many-layered—it could probably stop a small caliber bullet.

The left side of the shop was the market section; Apparite could see shelf after shelf of canned goods, boxes of pasta, soups, loaves of breads, and the like. There were also a couple of small cocktail tables at the rear of the shop—for eating sandwiches, he figured. There was no rear exit visible, but he could see a painted wooden door on the left side; he surmised it probably led down into the cellar where the mobsters would gamble and carouse with their mistresses. Poor Dolci, thought Apparite, getting stuck with these brutes and all their crap. Well, he won't be stuck with them for much longer, he added to himself.

"Okay, that's long enough; we don't want to draw any attention," J said, pulling the car away from the curb. He drove around the block again, pulling the car to a halt when the butcher shop's green, red, and white sign came into view a short way down the street. "Take the satchel, and keep it close to you. We'll start our surveillance in a few minutes when I've tuned in the 'bug.'"

Apparite reached into the back seat and took the leather satchel, cradling it in his lap; it was heavier than he had expected.

"A million bucks," he said out loud, feeling the weight of the bills inside the satchel as he held it in his outstretched hands.

"*Heavy* isn't it?" J said with a grin, detecting Apparite's anxiety about the vast sum of cash and playing on it.

"A million bucks kind of heavy," answered Apparite, still staring at the case—he couldn't take his eyes off of it. *Man, I'd better not f— this up*, he said to himself, using a word he reserved for only the most serious of situations.

Six
The Waiting

Apparite and J readied themselves for their day of surveillance: resting between them on the front seat of the Rambler was a thermos of coffee, a pile of Berg's Kosher Deli sandwiches (pastrami on rye; smoked turkey on wheat), and the latest in covert listening devices. J hooked up the small, military-style headphones—two uncomfortable-looking earpieces on a metal connecting rod—to a small battery-powered receiver, put them on his head, closed his eyes for a moment in concentration, and then smiled.

"It's coming in pretty clear." He made a few more adjustments to the dials. "There we go: *perfect*. It's amazing what fifty grand can get you, huh?"

Apparite was unsure if J was putting him on with the cost of the apparatus, or whether he had detected Apparite's little obsession with money and was playing on it, but the device impressed him, nonetheless. Although Apparite could not hear the transmission himself, he could tell by J's intense expression that the liaison was picking up something quite important. Suddenly, J's face became very animated and he frantically motioned to Apparite, waving his right hand wildly in circles.

"Quick! Quick! Start taking this down; I think it's important—a new job."

Apparite anxiously searched for pen and paper; he opened the glove box and, to his relief, found a composition notebook and a pen. Smudging the ink—as lefties always do when they write—he tested the pen on the paper and made himself ready.

"Okay, fire away," Apparite said urgently.

J made a face of concentration and then began speaking in a rapid-fire cadence.

"Fanucci needs some specialty work done; be careful, it didn't turn out so good last time. Don't use the new guy; he botched it all up. He'll pay whatever it takes; it has to be done by five tomorrow night."

Apparite was writing rapidly in his admittedly horrid scrawl, the fresh ink smearing all over the side of his left hand and across the paper. He hoped he was getting it all down like J wanted.

"He's talking about cutting and blood," J added. "Wait, wait . . ."

Apparite was still scribbling madly.

"I have it!" J exclaimed.

"Fanucci wants five pounds of blood sausage, personally made by Mr. Dolci!"

Apparite put down the pen and looked over at his colleague with extreme displeasure. J saw the irked expression on Apparite's face and let out a loud laugh.

"Does the FBI have a blood sausage task-force, Apparite? Maybe we should *alert* them!" He laughed again, evidently pleased with himself.

Despite Apparite's initial displeasure at this very stale prank, he too broke out laughing. He had to admit that J's jovial personality certainly was refreshing: the liaison was the exact personality polar-opposite of the Director.

But was there more to it than that? he asked himself. Apparite, who had always relieved his pain and stress through his obsession with the Senators, wondered if these little jokes were, perhaps, the liaison's efforts to relieve *his*. And, if so, what troubles was that man hiding under his amicable exterior? Had a tragedy driven him, too, into the Director's agency? Apparite knew, however, that such questions were immaterial—they would, by necessity, forever go unanswered. So rather than continue to ponder the imponderable, Apparite thought he would play along and prove that he could hold his own in the joke department.

"This is what I've taken down so far," Apparite said, showing J something he had just written. Despite Apparite's liberal use of certain four letter words in reference to J's character and intelligence, plus a reference to something that was not even anatomically possible, the liaison laughed even harder.

"Aw hell, don't take it so hard. Get the 'binocs,' " he said, gesturing toward a small wooden box in the rear seat of the Rambler, "and let's see if we can't figure out what's going on in there."

Apparite reached into the back seat, grabbed the case, and opened it. The binoculars were sitting in a custom-made depression lined with red-velvet—*very* classy, he thought—and he took them out and held them in his hands. They were an unusually heavy pair and of an apparently advanced military make, though he had never seen such a complicated design before: the binoculars had multiple sets of lenses that could be interchanged, or rotated; many, many dials; and no identifying markings whatsoever.

"We had those made special by the Zeiss Company in Germany," said J. "They cost ten thousand dollars, so be *careful*," he added with a grin, again playing on Apparite's money obsession.

Apparite gingerly held them up to his eyes—nostalgic for those warehouse days when he wasn't entrusted with anything worth a plug-nickel—and began moving the many focus dials; after a few seconds of fiddling, Dolci's shop finally came into view. As it was a cloudy day and the light was dim Apparite had expected a grainy field of vision, but what he saw was absolutely crystal clear; he was surprised to find that he could even read some of the signs on the walls of the shop: Ground Chuck 60¢ per lb; *Prosciutto* $3.10 per lb.; Fresh Hot Sausage $1.10 per lb.

"Damn," was all he could think of saying.

"Yes, they *are* good, and quite handy. Like at the Municipal Pool for instance; you can really take in the 'cheesecake,' if you know what I mean," J said with a wink. "It'll be a few hours before the mobsters arrive—probably after the late afternoon rush—and then it'll be post-time for us. Until then, you take the 'bug'; let me know if you hear anything interesting. Since I'm more familiar with the names and faces of the mobsters, I'll take the 'binocs.' I'll let you know if anyone I recognize walks in."

Apparite nodded, took a sandwich out of the bag, and had a sip of coffee from the thermos. The minutes and then hours passed as dozens of customers came and went, although Apparite became expert in the purveyance of Italian meats and cheeses in the process: *capocollo* was a big-seller, as was *Parma prosciutto;* the *Locatelli romano* wasn't as good as last month's (although the shipment of *crotonese* that had just come in was fine), and Dolci's home-made hot sausage was the best anyone had ever tasted. No, no one had seen Mrs. Longo for a while—had she gone back to *Napoli* to see her mother? Oh, poor Mrs. Longo, with a sick mother and a no-good husband in that ratfink Joey, and those two darling children, Maria and Gian. Thanks for the *capocollo. Ciao!*

"The closed sign's been put up," said J, "so they'll start coming soon. Listen carefully and write down any names you hear—guess about them if you have to, and we'll figure 'em out later—and don't worry about the spelling."

Apparite closed his eyes in concentration. He could hear the sound of the freezer door closing and locking; the *clink* and *clank* of canned goods—probably stewed tomatoes—and the *chop, chop* of meats being cut by a cleaver. A musical hum began, as the remaining man (the butcher, Apparite guessed) began to tidy-up. Verdi? Puccini? No, and no, Apparite deduced, and then he had it: Sinatra, "Luck Be a Lady."

J broke Apparite's concentration.

"Here comes one." The liaison expertly focused the binoculars on the man entering the shop: "Franco Calabrese; 'muscle' for the Casarano family. Big, dumb, and mean as a wolverine; he'll probably be the one in charge."

Apparite heard the tinkle of a bell as the front door opened and closed.

"Calabrese's being followed inside by two more men. I don't recognize them, but they seem to know him; I'm guessing they're lower level thugs."

Apparite heard the sound of laughter and the *thump, thump* of the men as they embraced and slapped each other's backs. "Franco! Hey, Petie! Hey, Marco! How ya' doin' Frankie? This gonna be some party, huh? A million bucks!"

Apparite relayed the men's words as soon as he heard them, speaking them out loud, giving the impression of a radio-play. J interrupted him.

"All three are armed, from the look of those bulges under their shirts. But you won't have to worry about weapons other than those they'll bring in themselves; Dolci's not a gang member and he doesn't keep firearms in the shop. In fact, he hates havin' these guys around—they help themselves to his best meat, and they've made him hire some of their thugs as butchers. When they're here, Dolci makes himself pretty scarce: as soon as he found out they were meeting today, he took off for Baltimore. If he had his way they'd all be out of there, but he's stuck: his brother, before he got killed, was a *Capo* in Philly, and now he can't get rid of them."

Apparite mimicked some of the small talk coming from the mobsters; nothing of consequence yet to report.

"Here comes two more," said J. "Bruno Maltese, and another one I don't recognize. Maltese always carries a weapon; the other looks like a knife-man."

That makes six, thought Apparite—fine. Six is about what he expected—not a problem.

He heard another round of slaps and introductions. "Bruno 'Malt,' meet my cousin Petie; Petie, this is Angelo," *slap, slap; laugh, laugh.*

"I think that's all," said J.

Apparite felt a sense of relief; six mobsters he could handle. Not a problem, he repeated to himself; heck, he'd handled *seven* at Butch's Place without breaking a sweat.

"Wait—here comes one more," J added. "He doesn't look professional; never seen him before; an overweight guy and probably just in it for 'kicks'—hanging around mobsters makes some guys feel tough. Oh, we forgot to count the butcher, didn't we? He's still in the shop, remember."

And the butcher makes eight. Eight is okay, thought Apparite, although the talk in the shop had become so boisterous he couldn't catch the name of the new addition.

"Hold on—there's one more going in."

"Nine. I can do nine," Apparite said out loud, though with perhaps less conviction. More back-slapping, more laughing, and now there were so many voices intermingling that Apparite could hardly pick out any distinct words at all until one voice rose above the others.

"Alright, let's get started," it said; Apparite guessed it was Franco.

"Franco's talking—he's starting the meeting," Apparite said.

"Right: I can see him. He's holding a meat cleaver—these guys are always *sooo* dramatic," J added, affecting a bit of a lilt in his voice.

"They're sayin' this is gonna be easy; how stupid are we to send one guy to *their* turf with a million bucks?" Apparite relayed, in his best mobster imitation.

"They'll find out soon enough," said J.

"They've brought the photos and negatives. I hear the rustling of files; maybe a box. Now laughter and shouts; they must be showing each other the pictures. "Oh my God! I can't believe it's actually in his *mouth!* Jeez, that Hoover's one sick *f——!*"

Apparite suddenly stopped speaking: hearing the foul debasement of a man he had once respected and pledged to serve gave him a marked feeling of sadness, filling him with embarrassment for his former FBI Director. No matter what Hoover was, or what he had done, he didn't deserve this and it sickened him.

"You get the idea," Apparite added, glancing at the liaison.

"Don't worry; you'll make 'em pay," J said. "I'm not a big fan of Mr. Hoover myself, but you've gotta draw the line somewhere."

Damn right I'll draw the line somewhere, Apparite thought. He narrowed his eyes in concentration as he listened to more of the gang's talk.

"They're planning on letting me into the shop after they frisk me outside," he continued. "Three men will be in the shop, two will be out front on the walk, and four are going to hang out in the cellar and play craps." He began drawing out the shop as he imagined it with the figures appropriately placed inside. "The negatives and photographs will be put in the case, like they're meat for sale; laughter."

"Oh, these guys are *hilarious*," J said, his voice dripping with sarcasm. "They're just showing off; mobsters always do that sort of thing."

"When I go up to the case to 'buy' them, they're going to throttle me from behind with a garrote wire; then, they'll—" Apparite stopped; he had been taken aback for a moment.

"What, Apparite?"

"Sorry. Then they'll cut me up, put my meat through the grinder, package it, and send it to the FBI."

"Sick bastards—don't they know Hoover's on a diet?" J said, grinning once again.

Apparite managed a weak smile at the quip, and said to himself, *I won't mind killing these SOBs; I won't mind it at all.*

"They're going to hang out and have a few beers until the fun begins," said Apparite.

"Good," answered J. "With a few drinks in them, they'll get more and more over-confident and less and less capable. You can take the headphones off now; we've got all we need to know. Besides, they'll spend the rest of the time 'ball-breaking' and swapping stories I've already heard—I don't think we'd learn much more from them at this point."

"Right," said Apparite. He took off the headset while J put the binoculars back into their case.

"Looks like there will be at least nine guys for you to take care of," J said with concern. "Even though we've been planning this for weeks, I don't think any of us thought you'd have to take on more than five or six at a time. And it's too late for us to arrange any back-up for you in the shop: we can't put two of our people at risk in there at the same time—if anything went wrong, someone might connect the dots."

"I understand. I can do it by myself." Apparite was not going to back out or ask for help; not at this point—what happened in the shop would happen to him alone. And if he got himself killed? Hell, he thought, no one my age worries about getting himself killed: how do you think the Army got all those guys to land on Omaha Beach? The ignorance of youth has its advantages, he mused.

"I just want you to be aware of the risks," said J. "I'm worried they might overwhelm you after you make your move."

"Frankly, J, I'm a lot more worried about the million bucks!" Apparite responded, and not without some measure of truthfulness.

"Don't worry; we can always print more," J said in reassurance—and Apparite had the idea that he wasn't exactly *kidding*. "Take care of yourself, and remember: it's the negatives we need the most."

"Right," agreed Apparite. "I have one question for you, though."

"What's that?"

"Did you listen to the 'Nats' game last night? Detroit shelled Ramos something awful, huh?"

"I don't follow baseball, Apparite," J said in an unusually serious tone. "But even if I did, I could never comment on it. If I told you I was a White Sox fan, for example, you might assume that I come from the south side of Chicago or northern Indiana, and that knowledge could be dangerous: we can never discuss anything which might betray our origins or past lives. I should not even have told you my opinion of Mr. Hoover, if you want to know the truth. I must ask you to forget that remark."

Apparite had not seen this side of J before—the liaison had always been such a jokester until this moment. The sharp retort made Apparite realize that, despite all appearances, J was just as dire in his attitude toward program exposure as the Director.

"Sure, I understand; you're right about that," said Apparite, a bit embarrassed, though intrigued by J's little slip-up of his own.

"We're never supposed to reveal anything about ourselves. You should know that."

"Right; what do we do next?" Apparite asked, trying to change the subject, but what he was thinking was this: *If we're not supposed to betray our origins or have outside interests, why did the Director let me listen to the "Nats" on the radio? Why is he allowing me to keep that part of my old life?* Sometime, when he had the Director all to himself, he would find out more.

"Here's my plan," J said, his voice reassuming its warmer, more informal tone. "You go up to the shop without the case; let the guards frisk and clear you. Tell them to step away from the door or the deal's off, and then I'll drive by and drop the case off at the curb. You take it and go straight into the shop; that way they won't get any ideas about taking the case off you while you're still outside. I've made arrangements to take them out from a distance if they rush you, but you'll have to take care of them yourself if they follow you inside. Remember, we can't take a chance on sending anyone else in there, so once you're inside the shop, you're on your own."

"Are they going to want to see the cash?" Apparite asked.

"I doubt it; I bet they'll kill you first and open the case later. They know the FBI doesn't fool around when it comes to Hoover, so I think they're pretty confident we'll bring the cash; if not a million, then at least enough to make it worth their while. If they ask then show it to them, but don't offer to do it."

"Right," Apparite replied, relieved to hear that he

wouldn't have to open the case; the thought of all that money in plain sight would only make him more nervous about it.

"I have one last question for you," said J.

"What's that?"

"You've never killed anyone before—is that going to be a problem?"

"No," Apparite said without hesitation. "Not with these guys it won't." And it wouldn't. Unlike the gang at Butch's Place, or the driver at that first meeting with the Director, these guys deserved it—they really God damn deserved it—and Apparite was ready to give it to them: they'd gotten his ire up. He was beginning to view the mission as his own personal war to save the reputation of the FBI.

"I'll drop you off a minute or two early," J said. "Mobsters hate it when people show up early; it really puts them off."

"Fine. Not a problem."

The next hour went slowly, and neither man spoke. Apparite took his pulse a couple of times: fifty-eight, fifty-six. Good: his mind and body were as calm as he could make them. He went over the plethora of weapons he would have at his disposal: the Colt Super Automatic in the satchel—check; the switch-blade hidden inside the satchel handle—check; the throwing-knives in the front of his shoes—check; the garrote wire in his shoes—check. He made an *Isshin-Ryu* fist—*check*.

"Alright, Apparite; time to go. When they're done frisking you, I'll drive up to the curb in front of the shop to drop off the bag."

"No problem."

"Oh, one last thing; maybe the most important part of the mission," J said, with some urgency leaking into his voice.

"What's that?" asked Apparite, wondering what vital component might have been overlooked.

"This mission had better go as planned, because *one minute* after we rendezvous tonight, *I'll* be in combat training for the next four weeks thanks to you, and I don't want to have to think about your bloody corpse being ground into hamburger the whole month I'm in that f——g warehouse!"

Apparite laughed heartily at the unexpected but welcome jest.

"You won't, don't worry. By the way, enjoy your four weeks of K-rations, J—I'll be having a swell steak at the May-flower tonight."

J laughed in return. He gripped Apparite firmly on the shoulder and gave him a smile, but his anxiety about Apparite's chances could not be so easily disguised.

"Don't worry about me," Apparite said, sensing J's apprehension. He opened the door and stepped out onto the curb. "I'll see you in a few minutes."

Seven
The Butcher's Bill

Apparite approached the shop at a brisk pace; reaching the two men standing on either side of the doorway, he nodded to them as if to say, "It's me." Looking distinctly unimpressed at the young agent, the heavier of the two mobsters stepped forward, his oversized abdomen spilling out of the bottom of his untucked plaid shirt.

"Where's the money, small-fry?" he asked, though with a slight slurring of his words.

"When I'm convinced the deal is on, an associate will bring it to me," replied Apparite, ignoring the insult. He took note of the mobster's impaired speech and the alcohol on his breath, both of which gave Apparite confidence; hopefully, they've all had as many drinks as this guy and their reflexes will be slowed.

"Oh, it's *on,* all right," the drunken mobster said. "Frisk him, Lou."

The other man stepped forward. Apparite tensed slightly in anticipation of this gorilla's paws being all over him, anxious to see if his hidden weapons would go undetected. The man's rough hands, with thick fingers like baby Genoa sausages, ran up and down Apparite's arms, chest, outer thighs, and inner thighs—but not *too* inner, Apparite noted—and then down his legs (but stopping before the shoes). Just as J had said, they *always* overlook the shoes.

"He's clean," Lou said.

J drove the Rambler up Apparite's side of the street. He stopped for the briefest of moments, deftly opened the passenger's side door, tossed the satchel onto the curb near Apparite, and drove off. Apparite quickly retrieved the satchel, holding it up for the mobsters to see.

"Here's the money: a million bucks in untraceable cash. But I'm not walking one more foot towards the shop until you get two steps away from the door."

"Alright, buddy; keep your pants on," Lou said. He took two steps down the street.

Holding the case firmly in his hands, Apparite rapidly walked over to the shop's entrance. Using only his fingertips so he did not have to let go of the case with either hand, he opened the door and walked inside the shop. He glanced behind him for a moment to ensure he was not being followed, and was relieved to see the two men still standing on the sidewalk, flanking the door like sentries.

Apparite looked around the room and was struck by the contrast of the pristine, lovingly maintained butcher shop—the spotless display case, the shining aluminum of the meat freezer, and the orderly, soldier-like lines of canned goods on the shelves—with the slovenly, unkempt mobsters he now saw before him. There were certainly no "Dapper Dan"-type mobsters with expensive Italian suits and perfectly slicked-back haircuts in *this* joint, he thought.

Apparite counted three men in the shop: one standing a few feet before him, one at a small cocktail table in the back, and one behind the meat counter. They were dressed in loose and ill-fitting shirts with unbuttoned collars, and Apparite surmised that their long shirt-tails had been left untucked to conceal the pistols stuck into the back of their pants. The largest of the men—at least six-four and 240 pounds—walked up to Apparite and held out his hand.

"Hey, good to see ya," he said, with what Apparite could tell was a false and forced gregariousness. "The name's Franco, 'G-Man'; *some deal* we're makin' today, huh?"

"Let's get it over with," Apparite said, in no mood for pleasantries.

"Sure, sure," Franco replied. "Good thing we're meetin' at a butcher's—looks like you could use some fattenin' up, little G-man! Don't Hoover feed you guys decent?"

The other mobsters laughed, their loud guffaws echoing in the little shop, but Apparite continued to ignore them, awaiting the time when he'd wipe those greasy smiles off their ugly mugs. Franco led him to the meat counter; behind it was a skinny mobster with straight, oily hair wearing a butcher's smock and an evil grin.

"What'll ya have today, mister?" the butcher said in a reedy little voice. "We got great *capocollo* for three-fifty a pound, or we got Hoover wrestlin' naked with another man for a million."

The mobsters *roared* at the jest: the guy at the cocktail table pounded on it with his fist in a literal fit of laughter; Franco's bulk shook with each loud guffaw until tears ran out of his eyes; and the butcher, whose quip had started this eruption, laughed in little silent jerks until he had to lean against the case with his forehead resting on the top.

"You know what I'm here for," said Apparite, trying to keep his emotions in check, looking around as he made his silent, deadly plans.

"Yeah, we know. You gotta get the great and powerful J. Edgar Hoover out of a bind. Look at the 'pics,' bud—are you sure he's worth it?"

Apparite took only a passing glance at the filth of which they were so proud—the photographs they were using to humiliate Apparite and the entire FBI—and what he saw repulsed him. Hoover had his faults, thought Apparite, but he had built a great agency—no matter what these punks believed—and seeing the pleasure they were getting from the photographs only increased his desire to see them all dead. His only regret about the carnage to come was that none of them would live to tell about the undersized FBI agent who had gone berserk and single-handedly destroyed their gang.

"I'm only here to make the deal."

"Alright; suit yourself, little G-Man," said Franco.

The butcher grabbed a piece of paper with a black number on it from on top of the case. Holding it up, he said, "Eighteen. Number eighteen!"

The gangsters burst into further spasms of hilarity. For his part, Apparite remained stone-faced; his inner spring was coiling even tighter, if that were possible.

"Eighteen! That's *you*, little G-Man!" Franco said, laughing out loud. "Give the case to the butcher and you'll get the goods."

The mobsters seemed to be having a pretty good time of it, but Apparite knew that all good times must end, and theirs would end all too soon. The first order of business, he figured, was to create a diversion.

"Oh, one last thing before we make the deal, Franco," Apparite said.

"What's that, little G-Man?"

"Did you listen to the 'Nats' game last night?"

Franco laughed. "The 'Nats'? Why would I care about *them?* They *stink!*" The other mobsters joined him in laughter. "They lost four-zip! Now the Yanks, *there's* a sweet ball club. With Mantle's hittin' and Ford's pitchin'—"

Apparite never had a chance to hear Franco's full impression of the Yankees, and neither did anyone else, either. In mid-sentence, Apparite whipped out the switchblade he had surreptitiously slipped into his left hand from its place in the satchel's handle, engaged the blade and swung himself around. In a single smooth, rapid motion, he buried it deep into the right side of Franco's neck.

"Garrrrgh! Garrrrgh!" was the only sound Franco could make as his hands whipped up to his neck and he began staggering about. The blade had entered his right carotid artery and penetrated the trachea, robbing him of speech, the sharp tip having been thrust all the way through to the opposite side of his neck. In the second it took to do this, Apparite had already spun back around and thrown the heavy satchel full-force into the face of the butcher behind the counter, knocking him to the ground.

"You son of a bitch!" the man at the cocktail table cried, pulling out the revolver he had hidden under his shirttail.

Apparite jumped over the meat counter, knowing that in about two seconds there would be a hail of bullets headed his direction. He hit the floor, trapping the butcher under him; although the mobster had been stunned by the force of the heavy satchel hitting him flush in the forehead, he was coming to and beginning to struggle. Apparite reached down to the tip of his right shoe; he pulled out its hidden knife as bullets began whizzing over his head and through the display case, sending shards of glass and hunks of meat everywhere. A slug hit the refrigerated lower section, apparently finding a victim; an orange liquid began leaking out from the bottom of the case. Orange juice, thought Apparite, as he made a quick slash at the butcher's throat and the man's life-blood poured out onto the floor; the red mixing with the orange like a sunset.

Apparite moved onto his next victim; the man at the cocktail table. He's closest, Apparite figured, so he'll try and rush me or run around the case to get at me. He then heard the shop door open—heralded by the tinkle of the bell in quaint contrast to the sounds of chaos and murder in the shop—and knew he had but a short time to act. The guards outside the shop had heard the commotion and would soon be on him as well.

The gunman at the cocktail table began rushing at him, pistol ready—Apparite could see the man's reflection in the shiny metallic freezer door getting bigger and bigger as he closed in on the case—and Apparite knew he would have to make his knife-throw count. He quickly stood up, and with one whip of his left wrist the throwing-knife rocketed into the man's chest just as the mobster fired another bullet. The force of the knife-throw turned the gunman slightly, spoiling his aim, and the shot whizzed harmlessly past Apparite's head. Despite his chest wound the mobster did not fall; he kept coming, face reddened with anger, his rage overcoming the morbid effects of the knife still sticking out of him as he staggered toward the display case.

Apparite reached to get his pistol from the satchel, but the hidden pocket was on the side away from him: when the case had fallen, it had landed face down onto the floor. Apparite rapidly flipped it over and whipped the Colt Super Automatic from its hiding place; the gunman was nearly on top of him now, and couldn't possibly miss if he got off another shot. Apparite lightning-quick raised the Colt and put a bullet through the man's heart, a mere inch away from the steel knife protruding from his chest. The mobster fell forward against the remnants of the case, his body making a dull thud as he flattened the piles of beef and ground chuck under him: dead.

"Franco!" shouted one of the guards who had entered the shop; he had just seen his leader staggering around with the knife sticking out of his neck, and a second later, Franco made the mistake of pulling it out. The blade had been giving tamponage to the wound and stemming the flow of blood, but when Franco removed it there was nothing holding it back and it began to gush out of his neck in torrents, cascading rhythmically into the air like a grotesque red fountain.

The guard panicked at the horrific sight; rather than seeking out Apparite, he rushed to the now-prostrate Franco and tried in vain to stem the flow of blood with his hands. The heavily waxed floor, slick with at least a quart of Franco's blood, claimed its own victim when the other guard rushed in and, in his haste, overlooked the slippery fluid, lost his feet, and fell to the ground.

Apparite smiled: he had a real weapon in his Super Automatic and it was time to get cracking. He raised himself up a foot or so, taking cover behind the dead man resting on the piles of meat in the shattered display case. The guard who had fallen had regained his balance, and was pointing his weapon directly at him; Apparite ducked just as the mobster fired, and suddenly the dead man leaning against the case had a new hole in his back, the slug coming out the front to bury itself into the T-bones. Apparite raised his Colt and coolly put a bullet into the chest of the guard, throwing him back; the guard slipped once again on the bloody floor and fell down onto it: dead.

The second guard, who had remained in a kneeling position over Franco's now-dead body, looked Apparite's way and began to raise his weapon; eyes wide open in a look of shock. Apparite wiped the look off the guard's face as he put a bullet into his forehead, causing the man to topple over: dead.

The cellar door burst open and the four mobsters who had been downstairs flew into the room, roused by the shots and the sound of bodies hitting the floor. All had revolvers drawn;

Apparite put a bullet into the chest of the first one—a smallish man with a rough, heavily scarred face, and a look of extreme determination—but he kept coming. Apparite fired again, and the second bullet felled him: dead. Four bullets left in the nine shot clip, Apparite noted.

The three remaining mobsters started shooting and countless bullets plowed into the case, splattering meat everywhere and increasing the already considerable gore; the body resting on the case shook and shook, repeatedly defiled by slug after slug belting it. The bottom of the case had been shot full of holes, and the floor began to swim in orange and tomato juices, lemonade and blood; all mixing together in a multi-colored puddle.

Apparite peeked around the corpse resting on the case, taking just a fraction of a second to draw a bead on one of the remaining mobsters; he fired and hit one in his gun-arm, the man's revolver dropping to the ground as he clutched his wounded arm in pain. Apparite quickly ducked behind the counter as a new hail of bullets from the other two gunmen imbedded themselves in the wall behind him, right where his head had been a moment before.

He crawled on the floor toward the end of the case: maybe the mobsters would believe him hit if he didn't fire for a few seconds, he thought, and they would relax their concentration. The firing indeed did pause for one moment, and Apparite took the opportunity to slide out from behind the case and put down the gunman closest to him with two shots to the chest: dead. The remaining gunman fired at him, but Apparite had already darted behind the case again, disappearing from view.

One bullet left, when the last armed mobster suddenly appeared at the side of the case, revolver pointed at him, ready to fire. *He's a ballsy one,* Apparite thought, but unfortunately the Superagent was in a precarious spot, nearly recumbent on the ground and with his gun-arm behind him. Just as the mobster fired his pistol, Apparite quickly swept his leg under the gunman's ankles, knocking the man over and causing the bullet to speed harmlessly into the wall. Apparite brought his arm around and aimed his own weapon, but as the gunman fell from Apparite's foot-sweep he kicked-out and hit Apparite's pistol as it fired its last bullet: a miss. The force of the blow wrenched Apparite's pistol from his hand, sending it flying into the air, and it landed on the other side of the case. He would have no chance to retrieve it; no bullets to fire even if he could.

Apparite leapt to his feet, as did the mobster. Seeing metallic signs reading, "Rib-eye $2.25 per lb." and "New York Strip $1.75 per lb." which had been stuck into a pile of steaks, Apparite grabbed them by their tops, holding them in his palms, the pointed, six-inch steel stems protruding from between the first and second fingers of both hands. He swung his hands across the man's face and neck; long, deep gashes appeared, and the blood ran out of them in countless rivulets. The mobster swung a fist at him, but was no match for Apparite, who connected a savage kick to the man's groin, causing the mobster to double over in pain. Another quick upward kick to the solar plexus put the man down, and Apparite was on top of him. He plunged the points of the signs deep into the mobster's chest almost to the hilt, forcing out the man's last breath: dead.

Just then, a bullet hit him; Apparite felt a hard shove to his right. In the chaos, he had forgotten about the man whose gun-arm he'd hit; the mobster had regained his senses, his composure, and his revolver, and had shakily aimed it with his left hand and put a bullet into Apparite's left arm. *God, how it hurts,* he thought, his face contorting with pain.

119

Apparite threw himself onto the ground, his left arm throbbing and burning, and barely usable. He crawled to the other end of the case, expecting to take another slug at any second, knowing he had to find a weapon, and quick. He instantly ran through the possibilities. The pistol? On the other side of the display case, clip empty. The switchblade? He had stuck it into Franco's neck. The throwing knives? Yes, he thought: the throwing-knives.

He reached down to his left shoe and took out his remaining throwing knife; he would have one chance to fell this last mobster, throwing with his non-dominant, right hand. He jumped to his feet, throwing knife in hand, and let it fly. The mobster hadn't expected Apparite at this end of the case and took the knife in the left side of his chest, dropping his revolver and crumpling to the ground with a thud: dead. Apparite let out a sigh of relief: it was finally over.

"Tinkle-tinkle-tinkle," went the door as it opened. A husky voice cried out in alarm.

"Holy Christ!"

Apparite whipped his head around to see what he could not possibly handle at that moment: two more armed mobsters had unexpectedly entered the shop, their fingers squeezing the triggers of their revolvers from the moment they had seen the massacre. They might have been a little late to the party, but they had showed, and at exactly the wrong time for Apparite to deal with them.

Apparite threw himself to the floor, but not soon enough; a slug plowed into his right chest, cracking two of the ribs in its path. It tore through the lining of the right lung, deflating it, then into the lung itself, tunneling deep into the tissue, sending out a shock wave of destruction that ruptured countless capillaries and venules. The air was ripped from Apparite's lungs as he hit the ground, and with each labored breath, an odd sucking sound came from the wound.

Funny, but the arm hurts a helluva' lot more, he said to himself. A ricochet, guided by ill chance, then hit him in the left thigh, forcing out a groan. Although Apparite knew he could no longer stand and fight, he would not lie there and wait for the end. Bending at the waist in spite of his injuries and pain, he took his shoes off. He pulled the garrote wire from the right shoe and hooked it to the left, and then fell exhausted onto his back once again, panting as he struggled to move air into his lungs.

When the first SOB's face appears over the counter, he said to himself, *he'll get this around his neck.* He guessed he could throw it hard enough to strangle a man, if the shoes and connecting wire wrapped tightly enough around the throat.

But then it happened: Apparite heard the shop door burst open, followed by the sounds of crashing and smashing amongst various harsh yells and cries. He picked out the sound of the heavy revolvers hitting the floor, and then of—bones breaking? Tables being smashed? Cans spilling onto the floor? After a moment Apparite was beyond guessing; the world around him was becoming increasingly distant. He heard the yells of the mobsters turn to shrieks, and then two gunshots, and then—nothing.

Apparite was bleeding like mad—his arm and leg were sending streams of blood across the floor—but the real danger was in his lung. As he struggled to breathe, he was drawing air into the space between his lung and chest cavity through the bullet-hole, but it was not being expelled by the same route. The pressure was building up in Apparite's right chest, compressing his lung and the vessels leading to his heart. He knew what was happening—it was called a tension pneumothorax—and having taken Human Physiology in college, he knew it would be fatal; there was nothing he could do about it in his current position. As the world slipped away and Apparite's mental state became unfocused and more dream-like, he thought he heard familiar, soft footsteps coming toward him, if that were possible.

No longer with the will or strength to use his garrote wire, he let it fall to the floor behind his head. As he welcomed the pleasurable wave of unconsciousness that was enveloping him like a liquid darkness, and coming to lead him to his death, he saw a familiar face peer over the meat counter.

It was the White Oriental.

Eight
A Conspiracy Exposed

Apparite opened his eyes; his vision was blurry and uncertain, and his chest ached horribly. Each breath he took felt as if a fire was being stoked within his right lung, and when he tried to move his left arm, a stabbing pain shot through it. He stared at the winch and chain that swayed gently from the ceiling above him, trying to recall who he was, and why that ceiling looked so familiar to him, when a smiling face came into his view above him, and he remembered: he was back at the warehouse, and the face belonged to J.

"Glad to have you back; we've missed you," J said.

Apparite's disorientation briefly returned: have I been *gone?* he wondered. He reflexively took a quick breath, and the fire started again in his right lung; looking down at his chest, he saw a large tube was sticking into it. Exhaling with the pain, he then took another deep breath, and heard the strangest noise—an unusual bubbling sound, like someone blowing out air underwater—and it took a moment to realize that the sound had been caused by *him,* by his breathing. He felt another twinge of pain, and then the rest came back to him: the shop, the mobsters, the bullet to his chest, and the White Oriental. A panicked thought struck him.

"What happened to the million dollars?" he asked in haste.

"Oh, *about* that—there *was* no million dollars," J said, consciously looking away from his colleague. Apparite grabbed J's arm in surprise, his voice assuming a growing anger despite his advanced state of weakness.

"There was *no* money in the case?"

J laughed. "Of course there was *money* in the case: I never said there *wasn't*. But it wasn't no *million dollars* in that case," he added in a staccato, theatrical delivery. "There was sixty-two thousand dollars in the case, but it was arranged to *look* like a million, if they'd asked you to open it."

Apparite was *livid:* after all he had done, and after all that had been done *to* him (three bullet wounds and counting for this mission alone), he was in no mood to play games.

"Why didn't you *tell* me there wasn't a million dollars in that damn case? Couldn't you see how worried I was about it?" Apparite's wrath was rising simultaneously with the discomfort in his chest tube and his leg and arm wounds: all were now throbbing in unison.

J laughed again. "Listen, buddy; it didn't matter that *you* didn't know there was only sixty-two thousand dollars in the case—it only mattered that *I* knew there was only sixty-two thousand dollars in the case!"

"Why?" Apparite queried, somewhat mollified by J's amused demeanor, which was beginning to have its desired effect.

"Lots of reasons. For one, if they'd killed you, the last thing we wanted was a bunch of *Mafiosi* walking around with a million dollars in cash, for reasons that will be made obvious to you shortly. Also, if you had *known* there was only sixty-two grand in the case, you might have *acted* like there was only sixty-two grand in the case, and that might have tipped them that something was wrong. Lastly, and most importantly, there is another reason."

"What's that?" demanded Apparite.

"Because you don't need to know every damn thing about

every mission," J said, all traces of humor having disappeared. "Your job is to follow orders: *period*. You know that. Now," he added, as a grin took its usual place on his face, "let me catch you up on a few things."

"The White Oriental!" shouted Apparite, in a sudden and apparently random exclamation.

"Who the *hell* is the White Oriental?"

"I'm sorry. The man who was my combat instructor; that's what I call him," said Apparite. "When I was lying on the floor of the shop—I saw his face."

"Oh, yes. Your instructor was stationed with a rifle down the street, ready to shoot the guards if they rushed you outside the shop—he is an excellent marksman, as you might have guessed. When the last two mobsters arrived late for the meeting, he ran down the street and into the shop. He took a great chance by getting himself involved, you know."

Apparite interrupted him as a memory burst into his brain.

"I remember lying on the floor, waiting for the end, when I heard yelling and screaming and then I saw his face."

J described what had happened next: the White Oriental had run into the shop holding his rifle, which was useless at such close range. Swinging it like an Okinawan *bo*-stick, he had crushed the nose of the first mobster with the butt of the weapon, and then knocked the revolver out of the man's hand with the barrel.

The second mobster raised his revolver to shoot him, but the White Oriental slammed the butt of the rifle into the gunman's groin; he then brought the barrel of the rifle across the man's face, breaking his jaw. Swiftly pivoting, he brutally crushed the first mobster's left kneecap, felling him; he then put the rifle to the man's head and blew his brains out. The mobster with the broken jaw had fallen to the floor and was screaming and writhing in agony; the White Oriental silenced him with a bullet to the back of the head.

The White Oriental then saw Apparite lying behind the ruins of the counter. Rushing around it, he had knelt down and cradled Apparite's head in his arms, admonishing him, in typical one-word sentences, to *"Live! Live!"*

A rapid succession of questions popped into Apparite's head.

"How did I get out of there? Why aren't I dead? How the hell did I end up *here?*"

"I took you to 'Washington General.' They told me you had a tension pneumothorax, a bullet in the lung, and slugs in your left arm and leg. I gave no explanations to the surgery officer of the day, but a thousand dollars in cash usually does not require one when it is placed in the right hands. All it took was a few hours and a brief surgery and they had you all patched up. By the next morning, when the effects of the bribe had worn off and the police might have arrived, you had already vanished, along with a considerable supply of penicillin. Since then—about three days ago—you have been in this warehouse."

Apparite thought the story hardly credible but was in no position to argue.

"But, who's been taking care of me *here?*" he asked.

"Oh, about that; I have news for you that I think you'll find amusing—*I* have," J said with a broad grin. Apparite's mouth fell open in silent astonishment.

"The chest tube comes with a nicely detailed instruction manual; fascinating reading when you've got the need," J continued. "I've also got a suture removal kit when your wounds have healed over—it's really not as complicated as it looks. The chest tube just takes a bit of practice to get used to, and giving the antibiotic is quite easy: I put your penicillin into this milk bottle, open the stop-cock, and it runs right into a vein in your arm."

Apparite turned his head and was shocked to see what indeed appeared to be a milk bottle—the plain ol' kind of milk bottle that one usually found filled with, well, *milk* on one's doorstep each morning—only this one had a rubber stopper and a tube sticking out of it running into a large blue vein in the bend of his right arm. He could only hope the apparatus had been sterilized.

"A *milk bottle?*" Apparite blurted out in genuine surprise, becoming nostalgic for the three-day coma he had been in: it had been less disturbing than *this* situation. "If you can steal a bunch of penicillin and a chest-tube kit, how come you can't steal a *real bottle* for an intravenous?"

"Hey, I boil those bottles for *twenty minutes*, Apparite!" J retorted, but with a smile. "And I was in a big hurry that night, so gimme a break—how many times do you think I could have bribed the storeroom attendant before anyone caught me? Besides, I've been the one wiping your ass these last three days, *and* doing a hundred other repulsive things you don't even want me to mention, so you could be a little more thankful."

"Sorry—thanks for wiping my ass these last three days," replied Apparite in a smarmy, kidding tone.

J shot him an irritated look and then resumed speaking.

"It's the only way we could do it. The D.C. cops think there was some big Mafia gangland shoot-out, and since you have three unexplained bullet wounds we couldn't leave you anywhere they might find you. We cleaned up Dolci's a bit but left a few bodies lying around—a couple from the New York mob and a couple of the locals from D.C. to give it that good gangland shoot-out flavor—and so far, no one's the wiser."

"What about Dolci? We practically destroyed his shop;

probably did ten thousand dollars damage to it."

"Always worried about money, aren't you? I bet you've already calculated how much each bullet costs the government. Don't worry about Dolci: I left him twenty thousand dollars cash in a package of *capocollo* to get him back on his feet. See—I'm not such a bad guy."

At least someone came out ahead in this deal, Apparite said to himself: Dolci would no longer be bothered by mobsters, and his remodeled shop might even increase its business with the publicity. Fatigued by this brief but heated exchange, he soon fell asleep. He had no dreams—at least none that he could remember—but that was swell by him.

Many hours later, Apparite awoke to the sound of footsteps approaching: soft, little shuffling footsteps that seemed so familiar to him from a time long ago. He raised his head and saw the White Oriental coming toward him; the little man's hands were clasped, fist into palm, and he stopped and bowed in respect to Apparite. Apparite bowed his head as best he could in return, and when the White Oriental was within reach, he clasped his hands around his instructor's.

"I'm sorry you had to get involved," was all Apparite could say before his eyes welled with tears—he didn't want to release what he was feeling inside, but it was no use. Despite the years of burying his emotions behind a demeanor of impenetrable competence, and avoiding any real human connection for fear that death might break it—as it had with his parents—Apparite could no longer deny it: he was beginning to feel human again, and he was letting it show. Sometimes a man must be brought close to death to bring him closer to life.

Apparite turned his head away from the White Oriental and composed himself for a few moments; the emotions he was expressing in front of another man seemed an unbearable humiliation. When he felt able to continue, Apparite looked him straight in the eye and spoke, steadying his voice with a conscious effort.

"I tried to kill them all myself, but when the last two gunmen came in . . ." His voice began to fail, but the right words weren't coming to him, anyway.

"Honor to save," the White Oriental interjected. "Finest student. You—fine man."

It was the longest string of words Apparite had ever heard the little man speak, and the sentiment tugged at his emotions even further. Fortunately for Apparite, J soon returned and interrupted them, saving the emotional Superagent from another potentially tearful display.

"Okay; it's time for him to go. Ever since he ran down the street and into that shop we've been worried someone will ID him—he *is* rather distinctive in appearance—so we'll have to send him away for a while."

The White Oriental let go of Apparite's hands, took one step backwards, bowed deeply once more in respect, and was gone. They would meet again, however, although under very different circumstances and well into the future.

"He is a remarkable man; someday, if it is allowed, I will tell you his story, but I cannot say more at present." J said. "There *is* one problem, though: since we have to hide him out for six months, it looks like my four weeks of combat re-training will have to be put on hold." He paused. "Shame, huh?"

Apparite laughed.

"Yeah, too damn bad," he responded. "I suppose with my luck, *I'm* probably stuck with you for the next four weeks, right?"

"Yes, you are," said another voice, familiar in its harsh

and serious tone: the Director had arrived. Apparite and J both turned their heads toward their chief as he walked determinedly into the warehouse.

"Mission accomplished, Apparite, though not without some trouble and worry," he said.

Some trouble and worry? Three bullet-holes and a chest-tube was more than just trouble to Apparite, and a man who had been a hair's-breadth from dying didn't qualify the experience with words like "some."

"It might have been better, of course, if your instructor hadn't needed to interfere, but I am pleased with the result. We now have the photographs and negatives of Hoover in our possession, and the D.C. and New York mob connection has been severed."

"Are you going to send the negatives to Hoover?" asked Apparite.

"Yes, *some* of them; anonymously, of course. And some I will keep for myself; as an insurance policy, if you will, if the FBI gets too close. The important thing is that they are out of the hands of those who would use them against us; against the United States. It was a small price to pay, Apparite, to have been wounded for them. Believe me."

Apparite weighed it all in the balance and reluctantly agreed: it had been worth it, if not only for the sake of his country, then for the reputation of his old agency and its legendary director. In his heart, Apparite would always retain a fondness for the FBI and its agents.

"We found some other important items in the shop, and that is why I am here now," the Director said. He turned toward his liaison.

"Get a chair, J; we might be here a while."

As J went off in search of another chair, the Director examined Apparite's various wounds with hands more skilled than the Superagent would have guessed—he's had some medical training, Apparite deduced.

"They're healing nicely," the Director noted, "no permanent damage. One thing is for certain," he said as he lifted the bandage covering Apparite's chest-tube site, "you *do* have some identifying marks now. When all is said and done, I may have a surgeon work on those; minimize them."

Apparite didn't know what to say: *Thank you? Sorry?* He saw J walking toward them, dragging a chair behind him, and thought he'd chance one quick question of the Director.

"One thing I'd like to know," Apparite whispered, expecting a sharp rebuke for what he was about to ask, "is how the 'Nats' have done since I've been out."

"Won two in a row over Cleveland: four-one and three-two," the Director said softly but quickly. "Minor miracle," he added, looking ready to add another comment and halting only when J pulled up his chair.

Apparite was surprised at the answer; not only had the Director *not* rebuked him, he had even *known the scores*. The conclusion was inescapable: the Director, the most nothing-man of them all, the man whose very life depended on being an enigma, being anonymous, having no past, and having no outside interests, had decided to let Apparite know something about him.

He was a fellow Senators fan!

Why is he letting me know this? Apparite asked himself, although his thoughts were soon dispelled by the Director's stern voice.

"The information we took from the mobsters at Dolci's points towards a conspiracy of a most critical importance. The Mafia and the Soviets were going to combine forces in a plot which might have irreparably damaged the government and security of the United States."

"It's hard to believe the Russians and the Mafia would ever work together," Apparite said, his eyes wide open in interest.

"You can get people to do almost anything for money—your experience with the Hoover photos was proof of that. But this is not a new alliance, Apparite: you may not be aware of it, but in the past the Soviets have used the Mafia to perform assassinations in the United States. In nineteen forty-three, for instance, the KGB paid Carmine Galante of the New York mob fifty thousand dollars to kill an American Communist Party leader with whom the Soviets had become displeased. Few persons missed the dead man, and even fewer cared—who in the United States is going to protest the death of a communist? Until now, the Mafia had eliminated only undesirables, and those with no connection with our government, but no longer. The Mob has decided, in its present cash-poor state, that it would be agreeably profitable to kill whomever the Soviets directed for the right price, no matter their importance or function in our government.

"Believe it or not, Apparite, the Soviets had made an offer to pay the Mafia two hundred fifty thousand dollars to kill certain high-ranking United States government officials—and that's two hundred fifty thousand dollars *each*. It might interest you to know that J. Edgar Hoover was among their targets."

"That's the reason the Mob was willing to risk losing the pictures!" Apparite blurted out.

"Correct: they thought they would profit from the pictures, kill Hoover, and then release the negatives publicly to embarrass the FBI."

"Who else had they targeted besides Hoover?" J asked.

"Secretary of State John Foster Dulles, Secretary of Defense Charles E. Wilson, and one man Apparite knows personally—Director of Central Intelligence Allen Dulles—were all to be assassinated. But their plan was not limited only to members of our government; they were also planning the simultaneous assassinations of members of the English Cabinet, and possible even Royals. Fortunately, with the recent change in the British government—Anthony Eden replacing Churchill as Prime Minister—their plans for U.K. assassinations seem to have been put on hold."

"It's hard to believe that Khrushchev would have approved this," said J. "The killing of U.S. and British government officials would escalate tensions to the point of war."

"The plot is almost certainly unknown to the First Secretary, and probably at KGB headquarters in Lubyanka Square as well," the Director answered. "No one connected with the legitimate Soviet government would have the audacity to pay for such assassinations. But there are hard-liners in the Kremlin who would welcome such an escalation, and have many pawns to play their game. In my opinion, the plan belongs to SMERSH; only a powerful man in that agency would be bold enough to order the killing of government officials, yet wield the authority to recruit rank-and-file members of the KGB to aid him. And only after its successful completion would SMERSH have revealed their involvement in the plot, when no one could be second-guessed."

"Do you suspect anyone in particular?" J asked.

"Yes. 'Viktor,' a top SMERSH agent, is almost certainly the architect of the plot. Agent G became aware of him in London, but too late; by the time he had recognized the threat, 'Viktor' had eliminated him."

"G was the agent I replaced," said Apparite.

"Correct," said the Director. "One of our best, but he was up against a mighty opponent; one of the most ruthless and dangerous men in the world."

"Could they have done it?" Apparite asked with urgency.

"Perhaps," said the Director. "The President would have been an obvious target of any major assassination program, but he has Secret Service protection, and is difficult to kill without exposure, which is why I believe they elected not to target him. The others—well, they're on their own aren't they? Anyone could get within five feet of them on a D.C. street, or in a park."

He paused, taking the time to ponder Apparite's question further.

"Yes. I think they could have done it. It's not a pretty thought. But the story gets worse: the Mafia has also been in contact with an important American scientist—a man named Robert Kramer—to arrange his defection to the Soviets. Kramer is involved in critical work to develop portable solid rocket fuel; the kind that could be used to fire nuclear warheads from submarines—just think what that would mean to our national security; to the security of every American living within fifteen hundred miles of our coasts. The Soviets would pay just about anything to have him."

The Director let the significance of this sink in. With such a man, Apparite reasoned, the Soviets could develop a portable nuclear warhead that, with essentially no warning, could be fired into the bedrooms of most of the U.S. population—it could change the balance of nuclear supremacy! The Director continued.

"The Mafia was going to use half of the money from the Hoover photographs to pay off the engineer to defect to the Soviets; five hundred thousand dollars was his price. He was then to be removed to the United Kingdom, where he would rendezvous with Viktor and his KGB agents in London. After providing calculations, plus a sample of the fuel mixture to guarantee that he was on the up-and-up, the mob was to receive an additional million dollar finder's fee, giving them a profit of five hundred thousand dollars on the deal. In combination with the remaining Hoover photograph money, it would have been the biggest score in Mob history."

"But now that Kramer's Mafia contacts are dead, the deal must be off," said J. "It was a damned close call."

"Yes; a little *too* close. But I fear we may not have heard the last of Robert Kramer. Since this information has become known to me, I have been in contact with many intelligence agencies around the globe and have come to one important conclusion: the plan has not yet been exposed. With Kramer's Mob contacts dead, I believe that only Viktor, his men in the London KGB, Robert Kramer, and the three of us know of it.

"This secrecy can be turned to great advantage for us: I believe we can counter them with an equally diabolical plot without them realizing it. I will tell you more tomorrow when my plans are finalized. Until then, J, you need to get Apparite up and around; we have to get him back into shape. Since your combat instructor is no longer available," he said, looking very pointedly at his liaison, "and we cannot move you to a place where you can get your retraining, I will have to put you to other uses."

The Director stood up and walked out of the room, closing the double delivery doors with a force that echoed in the warehouse.

Apparite had started chuckling at the Director's closing remarks, but when J said, "Laugh while you can, pal—I'm getting you up and around no matter how much it hurts!" the laughter died on his lips: Apparite knew that he was in for plenty of discomfort.

J helped the wounded agent up from the cot, although the effort was apparent in the straining faces of both men.

Damn, does my leg and chest hurt, Apparite said to himself as he started walking unsteadily.

"Not laughin' *now*, are ya?" said J.

"You wouldn't laugh if you knew how much this hurt," Apparite responded, holding the chest tube apparatus with his uninjured right arm as he limped with a few cautious steps.

They walked in tandem around the warehouse, and Apparite was surprised that some measure of his strength had returned; much of what he had been feeling was simply the stiffness of joints that had not been moved for three days. They paused along the way to test the chest tube: Apparite took some deep breaths while J glanced back and forth between the chest-tube apparatus and some notes he had jotted down on its instructions.

"You're pretty close to getting this thing out: the leak's almost closed up," J concluded. "You're a quick healer."

Apparite instinctively looked down at his wound and, for the first time, noticed that the chest tube—which was as thick as a finger—was sticking into a site *next* to the bullet-hole and *not* through it.

"You made *another* hole to put the tube in?" Apparite said with sudden anger. "You didn't go *through* the bullet-hole?"

"Hey, don't look at me—I didn't do it!" J answered, his voice rising in pitch and intensity in defense. "I was too busy bribing half the hospital to keep the wrong questions from being asked. In my many years' experience with these things, I've gathered that they can't put the tube through the bullet-hole, but don't ask me why. Quit makin' such a big deal about it."

Apparite faltered briefly on his injured leg; J put his arm around him, holding him up so he could regain his balance.

"Don't worry," J said, "you'll probably just get shot there

again anyway, someday, so whether it's one hole or two doesn't matter much, now *does* it?"

Despite his discomfort Apparite could not stifle a painful laugh.

"Well, when I do, can you tell the doctors to go through the same damn hole next time?"

After another fifteen minutes of walking, Apparite found that his strength had once again left him; his face was ashen and his legs felt like rubber. J had him lie back down on the cot and then brought him a couple of pills.

"Take these. You'll feel a lot stronger tomorrow; I'd expect you to be back to top form in about a month. I'll stop back later and we'll do some more walking."

Apparite nodded in agreement and took the pills, the sleep overtaking him before they had begun to dissolve in his stomach.

"Man, did I sleep well," Apparite said when he awoke nearly twenty hours later; it took him a few more seconds to shake off the effects of his unnaturally long repose, but when he had, he thought he felt pretty good. "What time is it?"

"About nine a.m.; I gave you a sleeper as well as the usual pain pill so you'd get a nice long rest."

"It must have worked. I feel great; feel like I could run a mile."

"Well, don't get your hopes up," J said, "because you may not think the same way in a few minutes."

"What does that mean?" Apparite asked, suspicious of the remark. "Don't tell me we're going to take the tube out today."

"*Oh yes!*" J said emphatically.

"Terrific," Apparite answered with sarcasm; he could tell that J *loved* this. "I wonder how much it'll hurt," he added (and not out of concern for discomfort as much as curiosity—or so he was telling himself).

"What's that?" J asked. "Speak up, Apparite."

"Will it *hurt?*" Apparite repeated loudly. J walked slowly over to Apparite and looked him straight in the eye.

"You bet it will," he said, enjoying himself in his mischief.

J disappeared into another room; he returned holding a small scissors in one hand and some opened sterile packages in the other. He peeled the bandage away from the chest-tube site, adjusted the chest-tube apparatus—an advanced type of water-lock that Apparite had been pleased to note had *not* been made out of discarded milk bottles—and made Apparite take a deep breath.

"Good. Ready for it to come out? You're all sealed up—I think."

"I'm ready if you are," Apparite said, in as steady a voice as possible given J's usage of the words *"I think."*

J cut the sutures holding the tube in place. Apparite could see it sticking out between two of his ribs on the lateral side of his left chest, and the wound from it struck him as kind of funny; like a little mouth that had sprung from his flank. It fascinated him, as if he was seeing it in a sideshow on someone else's body and not his own. He almost expected it to begin *talking* to him.

J placed his hand around the tube to steady it, with a petrolatum-soaked gauze ready to place over the wound after the tube was removed. He grasped the tube firmly between his thumb and forefinger and—

"Wait!" Apparite said, holding his right hand up to stop him, having realized that it was his own chest that this thing had been shoved into—suddenly, he wasn't sure he wanted it out, and if he did, he certainly didn't want *this* untrained maniac doing it!

"How many times have you *done* this before?" Apparite asked, still holding his hand in the air.

Not waiting to give an answer, J tugged on the tube very briskly, pulling it out with blood clots and secretions hanging off it like lichen from an old tree branch. For Apparite, the sensation was that of his testicles being pulled up through his throat.

"Once!" J said as the tube came free, quickly applying the petrolatum gauze over the hole to seal it. Apparite winced and tears formed involuntarily in the corners of his eyes from the pain.

"Someone should take away your license to practice medicine, you crazy bastard," groaned Apparite.

"Well, *that* wasn't so bad, was it? I can take that intravenous out and give you antibiotic shots in the buttocks from now on—no comments, *please*—so you're not tied to anything at all anymore."

Not *tied* to anything? Physically he might not be, sure, but Apparite bet he was the only person in the United States who had his life-threatening bullet wound taken care of by an amateur nurse in a grungy warehouse, and it was all *because* he was tied to something—the Director and his all-secret, all-powerful agency.

But though his wound was throbbing all over again, he could not deny this truth: if they could stop the Soviets from getting Robert Kramer's missile secrets, and if they could stop SMERSH from assassinating Hoover, Dulles and company, then getting shot and nearly dying was a small price to pay. It was, after all, just another part of his duty; albeit a painful one.

Just then the Director entered, his rapid, loud steps foreshadowing the important nature of the business to be conducted.

"Alright," he said, "let's get to work."

Nine
Raising Cane

The Director led the two men out to his familiar, beat-up 1952 De Soto Firedome. After Apparite had climbed into the front seat, with J getting into the back, the Director began driving toward central D.C. in the direction of the Mall, the tip of the Washington Monument visible in the distance rising above the morning mist. After a few minutes, the Director spoke.

"Our target is Robert Kramer, age twenty-eight; an upper-level chemical engineer working as a government contractor for the U.S. Navy. He was educated at the Massachusetts Institute of Technology, achieving top honors in school and a position of importance despite his young age. On the downside, he has a lovely wife cuckolding him with a colleague; fortunately, they have no children. He lives in the Georgetown area of D.C., but in one of the more modest of row houses; he makes barely average pay, despite the critical nature of his work."

The Director stopped talking for a moment to make a left turn but then resumed, looking occasionally at Apparite or in the rear view mirror at J while he drove.

"Kramer is an unhappy man. He feels unappreciated at his job and his wife is having an affair; he has begun to drink heavily. He is very bitter about his meager salary, and fears he will meet a similar fate as his parents, who died penniless in their forties. His colleagues think him a hard worker, but hopelessly humorless and dour."

Apparite laughed to himself: if there was *anyone* who was humorless and dour it was the Director, and the young agent tried not to show his amusement at the thought. The Director continued the briefing as he turned left onto Seventh Street, going south toward the Mall.

"It is fortunate that Kramer was unusually cautious in his dealings. He never allowed himself to be photographed by the Mob, never met the Russians in person, and insisted they know him by an alias: he was only going to reveal his true identity after he had left for London. The death of Kramer's mob contacts has therefore bought some time for us to act, but it will only be a short while before SMERSH learns who he is and how to contact him, and formulates another plan for his defection. We need to eliminate Kramer before this occurs—I estimate we have no longer than seventy-two hours."

"How are we going to kill an important scientist without creating publicity—or suspicion of foul play?" J asked.

"When we reach our destination, I will show you. I believe it will be an interesting demonstration."

Apparite didn't really like the sound of that, but was reserving judgment for the time being. He hated all of this mystery and innuendo, but it served the Director's purpose: Apparite's curiosity was becoming quite intense. The Director made another turn and then continued his briefing.

"Robert Kramer is the most dangerous of persons to our nation: the treasonous betrayal of our scientific secrets is one of the greatest threats the United States faces today; it should, therefore, carry the most severe of penalties, which is death. I am reinforcing this to you, Apparite, because you will be the one who will eliminate Kramer and, knowing you as I do, I fear you may find the method distasteful."

Apparite did not know what to say; he considered telling

the Director in no uncertain terms that he wouldn't care how he killed this Kramer fellow, only that the man would be dead, but then again, given his recently surfacing emotions, it seemed possible that this might not necessarily be true. He had no choice, he concluded, but to keep quiet and wait and see what the Director had in mind, much as he disliked the suspense that this would create.

"I'm going to stop the car and show you something," the Director said. He pulled the car to a halt at Mount Vernon Square, which was nearly deserted. The three men got out of the De Soto and the Director led Apparite to the car's trunk, opening it.

"Tell me what you see."

"It's a cane; a wooden cane," Apparite answered, wondering what its significance might be.

"Take it out; hold it. What do you think of it?"

Apparite took out the walnut-stained, highly varnished cane—just the right length for him to use given his leg wound, now that he thought about it.

"Try it out," the Director told him.

Apparite walked around the park about fifteen or twenty feet, limping slightly as he favored his wounded left leg. His steps were in little lurches, but the pain was bearable and he made decent progress and speed despite his recent injuries.

"Thanks," he said, "but I don't think I'll even need it in a week, I'm—"

The Director cut him off.

"It's not just for walking," he said. "Here, hand it to me."

Apparite limped over to the Director and gave him the cane.

"Begin walking away from me; not too fast." Apparite did so; he heard the Director catching up to him and then felt a sharp jab in his left calf. It was not very painful—just a little annoyance, he thought, like the bite of a gnat.

"Oh, pardon me, sir; I'm so sorry," the Director said in a very obsequious tone. For his part, Apparite smiled: the Director was a *terrible* actor, and he was tempted to say so (but did not, thinking it unwise). The little sore spot on his calf began to throb a bit and Apparite rubbed it briskly, still wondering at the significance of this odd little display.

"I have just killed you," the Director said. "You would have died in the next forty-eight to seventy-two hours. Follow me."

The Director walked over to the car with Apparite a short distance behind; he opened the passenger's-side door and sat down sideways on the seat so he faced the park, resting his legs on the curb. Apparite knelt down on the grass next to the car as the Director held out the cane.

"Looks like a normal cane; like any elderly person or lame man might use, correct?"

Apparite nodded in agreement.

"Look at the tip: see how it is hollow?" the Director said. There was a very small hollow tube embedded inside the tip of the cane; Apparite estimated it was about two millimeters in diameter.

"When I press this hidden lever," the Director said, showing Apparite a nearly invisible depression on the underside of the cane's handle, "a miniscule, almost needle-like barrel extends from the cane—do you see it?"

Apparite leaned forward—yes, there it was. A tiny steel tube about the size of a toothpick had extended from the tip of the cane a quarter of an inch.

"Pull up your trousers and show us where I jabbed you with the cane."

Apparite did so, and to his amazement there was a tiny red spot on his calf.

"You shot something into my calf!" he exclaimed. "What was it?"

"If you press the lever a second time with the barrel extended, a minute sphere, smaller than the head of a pin, is fired using a powerful compressed-air apparatus built inside the body of the cane. The projectile is partially hollowed-out, creating a tiny well that can carry a lethal poison."

"What kind of poison would you use? It would have to be unbelievably potent to kill in such a small amount." Apparite had been told of similar devices while training at CI—the Russians were particularly expert at them—but he had never seen a working model, nor did he have much experience with poisons. The Director handed the cane to him so Apparite could examine it more closely, and resumed speaking.

"During the processing of Castor beans from the plant *Ricinus communis*—the same plant used to make Castor oil, that wonderful purgative you may remember from your youth—a deadly by-product can be produced. The chemist Stillmark discovered that this by-product was lethal in trace amounts; a mere milligram will kill an adult. The poison is virtually undetectable; even after injection with a highly lethal dose. It is also incurable—there is no antidote or treatment."

"How quickly does it kill?" Apparite asked, expecting an answer in the seconds to minutes.

"If you were paying full attention earlier, you might have remembered me saying the victim would die in two to three days. The beauty of this poison is that it kills in a manner that will be mistaken for a natural death. The victim becomes nauseated and develops a flu-like illness, followed by abdominal pain and diarrhea. Over the next two days, these symptoms progress to multiple organ failures, hypotension, and eventually cardiac arrest. The cause of death will almost certainly be attributed to a virulent infection, or a series of fatal embolic events. This is the method you will use to kill Robert Kramer."

Apparite could not contain his displeasure at this slow, inhumane means of ending a fellow human's life: it was one thing to kill a man with a shot to the heart, or even a knife to the throat or chest, but to do it like *this*—it didn't seem right to him.

"Couldn't we just kill him outright?" he asked, handing the cane back to the Director.

"No," the Director answered with force. "I feared you would be repelled by this method, but there is a vital reason for it: Robert Kramer will die in a few days in a hospital in D.C., and no one will take notice of it. His wife will be on a week-long trip to her mother's in Virginia—at least that's what she *told* Kramer, though certainly she will be with her lover during that week—and when she has returned, he will have been dead four days. He has no other relatives nearby to interfere, and after death his body will rapidly be cremated to prevent the spread of the 'infection' that killed him. Hospital officials, not wishing to panic the summer D.C. tourist crowd, will be pressured into keeping the virulent nature of his death under wraps, and I will contact the newspapers to insure that the name Robert Kramer does not appear in print. In short, we have the perfect method for eliminating him."

Apparite knew the Director was correct, and was embarrassed by his own weakness and stupidity. Obviously the man could not be killed by the usual means and, in the end, it wouldn't matter, anyway—dead is dead, plain as that. And after it was done, Robert Kramer, a budding traitor the likes of which the nation had not seen since the Rosenbergs and Klaus Fuchs sold out the A-bomb, would be eliminated; his traitorous threat unfulfilled: that was the critical, essential point.

"I can do it: don't worry about that," Apparite said in an effort to reassure the Director.

"I know," the Director replied, "I've *always* known that you could, and would. You may not know it yourself, Apparite, but when the anvil is in front of you, you do not hesitate to bring the hammer down onto it. It's one of the reasons I chose you."

"After Kramer is dead, what do we do then?" J asked.

"Get back in the car; I will tell you more along the way," the Director answered.

Along the way *where?* Apparite hoped it was not yet to his fatal rendezvous with Robert Kramer; for that, he would need time to get his head straightened out; to get rid of these intrusive feelings. *After all these years of going about his business without the bother of human emotions, where the hell had they come from all of a sudden?*

The Director started the car again; he drove in the direction of Georgetown as the sun rose behind them, the morning mist dissipating and revealing a sky that was clear and blue.

"After we eliminate Kramer, Apparite will assume his identity and meet with the Soviets in London; beyond that point in time, I cannot yet elaborate."

"Sounds alright by me," Apparite said, relieved to have something else to think about besides Kramer's impending death. The Director continued.

"At present, the Soviets only know Kramer by the alias 'Catalyst,' but we will reveal his name to them after you leave for London. Given what Robert Kramer can offer them, this is an opportunity I do not think they will pass up."

"I'm looking forward to it," Apparite said, projecting as much confidence as he could.

"Good. I am going to drive by Kramer's town house, where you will find him tomorrow night; like many scientists, his habits are fortunately quite firm. Every evening after returning from work, he usually takes a long walk—probably talking himself through his defection or, just as likely, cursing his wife and her lover under his breath."

The Director stopped speaking; a black and white spotted dog was crossing in front of the car and he slowed and swerved to miss it. He drove the car through another turn, and Apparite soon saw the brick town houses of Georgetown start to pass them by as they turned onto Wisconsin Avenue going north. The Director resumed speaking.

"Kramer walks briskly, but not so fast that you cannot catch him up. When you reach a comfortable distance behind and slightly to the right of him, discreetly press the cane tip to the back of his trousers at the calf, and fire the projectile into his leg. You should act as if you stumbled and clumsily struck him, but be sure you apologize politely, though in a natural tone. Do *not* engage him in conversation, and for goodness sake do not let him engage you in one, either. I doubt there is much danger of that happening, as his mind will almost certainly be occupied elsewhere at this critical juncture in his life. Walk in his direction at least another block or two, but then leave by a side street. You must not arouse any suspicion on his part; not when you are approaching him, firing the projectile, or leaving him."

"I can do it," Apparite said.

"It's a job that requires more subtlety and finesse than you have had to show so far, although I believe you'll get it done all the same. Be aware, however, that we have only *one chance* to do this right. If you miss or arouse his suspicions, we will have to do it the old fashioned way: a murder made to look like an interrupted burglary. I do not want to have to resort to such an untidy and inelegant method."

Apparite shuddered at the term "inelegant": did that mean that the fatal, painful three-day poisoning of an unsuspecting man was somehow *more* "elegant?" Or was *less* "untidy?" Apparite kept reminding himself that Kramer was a traitor, and the penalty for high treason has traditionally been death, and always will be.

You've just got to get the job done, Apparite told himself. *Nothing else matters.*

"Here is Kramer's town house," the Director said, gesturing toward one of a dozen identical row houses. It seemed incongruous to Apparite that the man who posed the greatest threat to the security of the United States lived in this tidy little house, and in a very decent section of town.

"You can pick him up *there*," the Director said, pointing at an intersection up the street. Driving past it a few blocks, he gestured toward a small side street. "After it's done, you can leave him *here*," he said. "J will park the car . . ." he added, pausing as he drove onward, searching for a good spot, "J will park the car *there*, and wait for you to return," he said, slowing the car briefly to show them a nearly invisible alley. "You will then be taken back to the warehouse. When Kramer is dead, I will tell you of the next phase of the plan."

It all sounded so clinical to Apparite: pick him up *here*, walk with him down *there*, jab him with your cane *here*, leave him right *there*, and the car will be waiting for you *here*. Killing Robert Kramer, thought Apparite, sounded almost *too* easy, *too* safe; particularly when compared to his previous mission in the butcher shop. And yet, for the first time since he had joined the Director's agency, Apparite felt a real touch of butterflies in his gut about doing what he knew he must.

Ten
The Slow Death

The next twenty-four hours ticked by slowly and deliberately, as if some force was resisting the passage of time, and Apparite spent the rest of the long day exercising and working out the kinks he had acquired having been laid-up for the better part of five days. The night before he had slept uneasily, and when he awoke, he still felt out of sorts: he was barely rested and, importantly, sensed no coiling of his inner spring like he had before his previous missions.

Perhaps things were different because he would not be in any personal danger during the assassination, or perhaps it was because he did not believe the event would be terribly physically taxing to him. But he noticed it, and it bothered him. If the Director had allowed Apparite to believe in omens, Apparite would not have thought it a good one.

Physically, he was coming along, despite his many wounds. When taking a deep breath he felt a twinge in his right lung and cracked ribs, and it hurt like hell to cough out his secretions, which he had to do after lying on his back for any length of time, or awakening from sleep, but his breathing came fairly easy. And although his leg ached some and he walked with a slight limp—the mission's use of a cane would not merely be a cosmetic one—his strength was reasonably intact. He was recovering more quickly than any of them had hoped.

But mentally, he was struggling. Apparite thought it interesting that the tasks that entailed the most danger to his own life, or those that required him to maim or kill multiple victims, came easily to him. Once that first shot had been fired, or the first punch thrown, the rest seemed automatic. In that slowed motion typical of his battles, it was almost as if the actions had been scripted for him to perform, and as long as he adhered to the script, everything would turn out fine. Even during that first meeting with the Director, when Apparite had been asked to shoot the driver in cold blood, he had been able to perform the task without emotion, imagining the man a buck in hunting season. If the pistol had indeed fired, the driver's death would not have been difficult to live with— once Apparite had the pistol pointed at the man's heart it had been easy and automatic to pull the trigger.

But how could Apparite rationalize the way he would end Robert Kramer's life? To what experience could he possibly compare it? He had shot plenty of game over the years to be sure, but had always killed quickly, hunting mainly to stretch his food, and not for sport. And as a youngster he had never been the type to torture animals, like those backwoods sociopaths who set fire to stray cats or hacked up live raccoons for their juvenile amusement. In fact, Apparite could not stand the sight of an animal being abused, resorting to force if needed to stop such shenanigans (he once beat an older kid senseless when he caught him disemboweling a mutt, and had wept when he had to put the cur out of its misery).

And now he was condemning Robert Kramer to a slow torture in which death would be a relief when it finally came—even an insect that gets squashed under a man's shoe has a quick, painless exit from this world, he thought. Apparite could find nothing in his past that he could use to temper the anxiety he was feeling; if anything, his reflections on the innocent days of his childhood only added to his misery. But the "event," as these things were sometimes called, had to be done one way or another, and Apparite knew *he* was going to be the one to do it.

J entered the warehouse, drawing Apparite's attention away from his thoughts.

"Let's go; Kramer should be getting home from work at about five-thirty. He always takes his walk between five-thirty and six and then eats dinner—usually at home, occasionally at a cafeteria—at six-thirty. We'll drive to Georgetown and wait for him; it shouldn't be too long."

"Good," Apparite answered, but it sure didn't *feel* good to him.

The two men walked out of the warehouse. Neither spoke as they climbed into the black Nash Rambler they would use for the event, and J started the car and pulled out into the street. It was an unusually sunny day, noted Apparite; almost harsh in its brightness. Apparite would have given anything for clouds and rain; the extreme sun made him feel naked, as if his blackening, rotting soul was exposed for the world to see.

"The cane has been preloaded with the sphere," said J. "It's a difficult procedure and takes a bit of time, so there will be no second chance if your shot goes amiss."

"Right," Apparite said, knowing that it would not.

J drove on, the two of them sitting quietly as block after block passed them by; they were approaching Kramer's town house from the northeast, taking a different route than before to keep anyone from getting too familiar with them.

"Make certain Kramer does not suspect anything unusual is occurring," J said. "We can't have him showing up at the hospital with a microscopic, deadly poison-filled sphere in his leg, can we?"

"No," replied Apparite, missing J's attempt to lighten the mood.

"If he figures you out and runs, you'll have to kill him right then and there—use one of your knives and do it as silently as possible, and then get the hell out of there."

Apparite nodded. In truth, he would rather kill him by those means, anyway.

They were now on Kramer's street; his town house was visible about fifty feet away. Apparite could feel the bile rising in his throat; he could feel his pulse in his ears, and neck; and sweat began to rise under his shirt collar. The air that he breathed seemed recycled, as if a bag had been thrust over his head and the world was closing in around him.

"Jesus, it's hot in here—can I open a window?" Apparite said.

"Sure; just don't say anything a passerby might overhear."

They sat silently and waited. Apparite nervously began swallowing; he could feel his Adam's apple rubbing against his tight shirt collar and tie. He tried not to swallow, but found that to think about it caused it to happen even *more*. His tie was constricting him and getting tighter by the second; man, I gotta' loosen this thing, he thought.

Apparite unbuttoned his collar and casually slipped his tie off over his head (like so many young men, he always saved the knots rather than retying them each day). The heat in the car was building as it cooked under the hot sun, and his legs began to itch under his trousers. When he breathed, his shirt felt uncomfortably tight in the shoulders and chest, as if he was being surrounded and compressed by an external force— he now knew, he guessed, what it was like being encased in an "iron-lung."

"Can I get out of the car and walk around a while?" he asked.

"For crying out loud, Apparite: *no*. We can't have anyone

see you in this neighborhood before the event. You'll have to sit tight."

"No problem," Apparite said, though he knew that it was becoming a problem.

"He's here; I saw him go into the house. He'll be out in a few seconds. Are you ready?"

"Yes," Apparite said, "I'm ready," a true statement in that he was damn ready to get out of this car and get it over with. He took the cane in his left hand, unlatched the car door, and prepared to get out of it as soon as Kramer reappeared.

"J, have you ever done anything like this? I mean, like *this?*"

J's retort was immediate and sharp.

"*God damn it,* Apparite: I can't answer that! And keep your voice down."

"Sorry; I know you can't. But to kill a man like this; it seems," he said, searching for the right word, "so *cold.*" He was struggling to maintain his calm, and he feared he was about to lose that struggle.

"I know; but it's the only way. Now is not the time to get all philosophical on me; now is the time to *act.* And you've got to stop asking me things like that—it endangers your life when you do."

Apparite nodded. J was right, of course, in all of his assessments. Now was not the time to look for comfort or understanding; it was the time to kill a man who was going to betray his country. Apparite opened the door a bit further and put his feet firmly on the pavement—he wasn't going to stumble out of the car and fall on his face, regardless of what else happened.

"His door's opening. Get ready," J said.

Apparite opened the door another foot and watched Kramer step out onto the stoop. The paunchy scientist took a couple of steps and then bent over and retied one of his shoes; Apparite noted that he was wearing a conservative gray suit and a black hat.

"When he starts down the street, out you go," J said.

"Right," answered Apparite, feeling his pulse quicken.

Kramer stood up and began walking down the street, away from the Rambler. Apparite opened the door fully and stepped out onto the sidewalk.

"Apparite," J said, breaking the young agent's concentration and stopping his egress from the car.

"What?"

"I shouldn't tell you this, but no; I've never had to do anything like this."

"Thanks," Apparite answered. "But don't worry: I'll get it done."

J leaned over and held out his right hand.

"Good luck," he said, giving Apparite a firm though warm handshake.

"I won't need it, but thanks all the same. See you in the alley."

Apparite then turned and walked down the street, a bit more briskly than was comfortable given his leg wound. He held the cane in his left hand and, although he was limping slightly, he was also rapidly catching up to his intended victim. He figured that in about one block he would be right on target.

Apparite kept walking, faster and faster: thirty feet behind Kramer, now twenty feet behind him, and now fifteen. He was sweating profusely and noticing the first touches of nausea in his gut. His heart was pounding and, if he had taken the time to check it, he would have found his usual pulse rate had doubled; he could feel it *thump-thump-thumping* in his temples.

Ten feet behind him; Apparite slowed to avoid attracting the man's attention and to compose himself: his pulse was racing and the sweat was hanging in little beads off his nose and chin. He hoped like hell that Kramer didn't turn around, because the way Apparite looked right now, the scientist would probably ask *him* if he needed medical assistance.

Eight feet away, when Apparite's shoe suddenly made contact with a pebble; it flew down the walk and struck Kramer in the shoe: damn it! *Please don't turn around,* Apparite silently pleaded, *for God's sake, please don't turn around.* He mentally prepared himself to go for his knife.

Kramer suddenly stopped; Apparite's heart was in his throat and his breath was coming in halts as if something was stopping-up his windpipe. The scientist looked down at his feet: was he looking at the little pebble I kicked-up? wondered Apparite. Was *his* danger-sense making him suspicious? Apparite slowed and awkwardly stopped as well, now only five feet away. *Don't you turn around; don't you notice I'm here,* he said to himself. Apparite feigned knocking some dirt off his shoes with the tip of the cane and, with his free hand, he felt for the switch-blade he had hidden in his belt: if Kramer turned around, he would have to use it. Apparite was in an exposed position and he knew it: anyone watching them would certainly have wondered why that quiet man with the cane was patiently standing so close behind the intellectual-looking, overweight man in the gray suit, but fortunately, they were alone on the quiet street.

To his relief, the scientist then knelt. His other shoe's come untied, Apparite realized; that's all it was. The man whipped the laces into a bow, stood up, and began walking again, as did Apparite, who was now only about four feet behind him. The two men walked along as if connected by a string: step, step, step, step; the only break in the rhythm being the syncopated beat created by Apparite's limp as he began to increasingly favor his aching left leg: step-*step*, step-*step*, step-*step*.

He was now only a couple of feet behind Kramer and slightly to his right, which is just where he was supposed to be. Apparite couldn't believe the noise his heavy steel-tipped shoes were making—surely Kramer must know the threat just a few step-*steps* behind him by now? Apparite's leg was beginning to absolutely *kill* him, and he had to favor it considerably, placing the cane firmly on the ground with each halting step—using it was no ruse—making the sound step-*step*-tap, step-*step*-tap, when he had a worried thought: what if I've plugged the barrel of the cane walking down the street? What if it doesn't fire properly? What if it's gotten plugged with dirt and the sphere can't come out? His heart was pounding in his ears and he was getting increasingly nauseated and light-headed; sweat had wetted his collar and a visible red line had appeared on his neck from its chafing. He was now only a foot behind Kramer and it was time.

He stumbled and pressed the tip of the cane deftly against the mid-part of Kramer's left trouser leg, simultaneously squeezing the trigger twice as instructed. Apparite made a little groan; just a little *ooh* to cover the noise of the powerful compressed air mechanism firing the lethal sphere. The cane shook a touch, and the scientist stiffened.

"Hey! *Ouch!*" Kramer said, reaching down to the back of his left calf and rubbing it.

Apparite looked at him innocently with assumed and actual horror mixing on his perspiration-drenched face.

"Oh, I'm sorry! Excuse me, I tripped: are you okay?"

"Yes, I'm fine, thank you," said Kramer, and he resumed walking.

That was it, Apparite thought. The poor bastard is dead

and he doesn't even know it. Then the nausea rose and rose and his stomach heaved, and Apparite, waiting to find a good place to peel away from Kramer as nonchalantly as possible, found himself forced to duck awkwardly behind a hedge—he could have shot himself for having lost control of the situation—and he vomited and vomited, his chest wound and injured ribs screaming out in pain as he retched until what came out was only bile and then bitter foam.

It was as if his body was expelling all traces of the evil deed, even if his mind could not; made all the worse by the man's lack of anger at what Apparite had done to him. "Yes, I'm fine, thank you," was all that the scientist had said, and in a tone that sounded almost as if *he* was the one at fault. Maybe by betraying his country he *was*, rationalized Apparite, but all the puking in the world could never rid the young agent of the guilt of knowing what he had just done.

Apparite wiped the vomitus away from the corners of his mouth, checked his shirt front, and readjusted his collar. He took a few deep breaths, ignoring the pain in his leg and chest as he did so and, after a few more seconds, he felt normal again.

He stepped back on the sidewalk and proceeded to the rendezvous point in the alley, where J was waiting for him in the Rambler. Only about five minutes had passed, he thought, but so much can happen in five minutes: five minutes ago, Robert Kramer had a future, and now, the man was a walking corpse.

"Is it done?" J asked.

"Yes," Apparite answered, "he barely even noticed it."

"Are you sure it fired?"

"I'm sure—he was rubbing the back of his calf."

"Good. Remember, he deserves everything that is coming to him."

"I know it," Apparite said, although what he was thinking was, *he didn't even get mad at me when I did it. It would have made it easier if he'd called me a f——g asshole.*

They drove back to the warehouse in silence. Apparite had spent the last eight years trying to forget the deaths of his parents, hiding his memories of them in some deep, dark crevasse in the depths of his mind, but he could not help but wonder what they would have thought of this. They were as patriotic as anyone—his father had even volunteered to join the Army during the war—but could they have understood what the man now named John Apparite had to do for his country? Could anyone with a sense of decency *really* have understood it, besides the Director and his liaison, J?

Apparite knew the answer was *no:* his parents would not have understood it; *could* not have understood it. He did not know to what faraway place they might have gone after they'd been killed, but he only hoped it was someplace where they'd never know what vile deeds their son had perpetrated. In Apparite's first three months as a Superagent he had killed ten men in the name of the United States—the first nine were easy for him, and that alone would have appalled them—but to have snuffed out Robert Kramer like this was beyond anything they might have imagined.

His parents would have never forgiven him, Apparite concluded, no matter what the reasons were for doing it; of that he felt certain and it was a torture to him. The nausea was rising once again; Apparite opened the window to get some fresh air and spent the trip back to the warehouse trying not to puke.

The next forty-eight hours were as tough as any he had experienced, rivaling even those following the deaths of his parents, and in one way, they were even worse: Apparite had not caused his parents' deaths, but he sure as hell had caused Robert Kramer's, and this interminable wait, he knew, was of his own doing. The depressed agent tried to keep his mind off his worries, spending those two long days doing calisthenics and reviewing his combat manual, but he could not clear his conscience, no matter how he tried.

Two long days after the event, the Director entered the warehouse with news on the victim.

"Kramer's condition is critical," he said without emotion. "The doctors believe he has a raging infection; he is in isolation and nearly comatose. His blood pressure is low, his heart is racing, and he has not produced any urine for over a day. He'll die in the next twenty-four hours and then we have to act."

"Right," Apparite responded, hoping Kramer's end would be quick and relatively painless, but believing the opposite more likely.

"I know you well enough to see you were repulsed by the method we used to kill him. Remember what I told you at our first meeting: 'We must protect the interests of the United States using whatever means necessary.' By killing Kramer and stopping his treachery, we might save hundreds of thousands of lives if a missile strike on U.S. soil can be prevented. Look at it this way: is the painful death of *one man* so repellant that you might sacrifice an entire city to avoid it?"

It was a rhetorical question and Apparite did not have to think about the answer: obviously it had been his duty to eliminate a man like Kramer, no matter how inhumane the method; it had been his duty not to question the order as well. Apparite had made a choice to join this agency knowing he would perform countless unforgivable and repugnant acts, and now he had to live with that choice. Much in the same way he had forced himself to kill Robert Kramer, he would now have to force himself to reconcile with the conscience that had *allowed* him to kill Robert Kramer.

"I'm satisfied with what I did: I'd do it again, if I had to," Apparite said after a few moments of reflection. He was speaking the words the Director wanted to hear, even if he was not saying them with full conviction.

"I know you would; if I thought you would not, I might have killed you that first day. But I am not as unfeeling as I appear. I know you need a diversion right now and I am willing to give you one. I have brought a radio so you may listen to the Senators tonight; they are playing Cleveland, and Early Wynn is pitching."

Like a breeze that clears the air of stagnancy, the idea of listening to a "Nats" game brightened Apparite's mood: it would be just what he needed, and he could scarcely contain his joy at the prospect.

"Thanks, but it might be kind of tough listening to Wynn beat us again," he said, anticipating another Senators loss at the hands of a superior hurler. Truthfully, he really wouldn't care if they won or lost; it would be enough for the baseball-starved Apparite just to hear the names of his favorite players as they came to bat; especially Vernon, Sievers, and Yost (if he was back in the line-up from an episode of tonsillitis, that is—the craziest problems always seemed to plague the "Nats").

"We should have never traded Wynn to the Indians after the forty-eight season; those guys always come back to haunt you," the Director said.

Apparite took note of the Director's use of *"we"* when referring to the "Nats," but was uncertain as to its significance. Clearly the Director was a fan—but just how fanatic *was* he? Thinking he might learn something by engaging the Director in further baseball talk—and relieved that his own mind was

being taken off Robert Kramer—Apparite probed deeper into the subject with a tailor-made reply.

"It's hard to believe we traded Vernon to them at the same time—lucky we got *him* back though, huh? I'd hate to face *both* Wynn and Vernon today."

The Director, to Apparite's immense satisfaction, answered him without hesitation.

"Has there ever been a more ill-conceived trade? Think about it: they get Wynn and Vernon, and we get Klieman, Haynes, and Robinson! Have we *ever* made a deal that the other team came out on the short end of? Like getting rid of Busby back in June: foolish! The man was the anchor of the outfield." The Director's voice was gaining urgency and emotion with each word. "I've been following this godforsaken team for over thirty years, and—"

The Director halted and his face turned a stark white: he had said too much. Apparite could sense the man's rising anger—directed at himself, and not the young agent—for having given something away, although Apparite had thought the comment fairly innocuous.

"Is it true that Yost is still out with tonsillitis?" Apparite said, remaining hopeful he could get more information about the Director through his apparent weak spot.

"Yes—but I've no time for baseball. I will stop back when Kramer is dead and then go over the next phase of the plan."

The Director left in a rush of footsteps, and Apparite heard the De Soto start almost as soon as the double delivery doors had shut. The car then pulled away with a loud roar of its engine, mimicking the mood of the man driving it, thought Apparite.

Well, that *was an interesting conversation,* he said to himself. *The Director obviously has some strong tie with the "Nats," and I'm going to figure out what it is.*

He walked over to the Motorola radio and turned the dial until he heard the unmistakable sound of a crowded ball-park—the fans always come out for the defending champs, he thought. The Senators typically wilted against tough competition—the Indians had won 111 games last season, and were always tough on them—but Apparite, like all true fans of a mediocre team, would remain optimistic. His hopes stayed high as the innings raced on and the Senators held a slim 2-1 lead after the seventh but, as always seemed to happen, there was a late-inning collapse: Vic Wertz hit a double with the bases loaded in the eighth and they lost, 4-2.

Despite the fact that Early Wynn had pitched a three-hitter for the Indians and gotten his sixteenth win, and the Senators had suffered yet another close loss (and one that put them at forty-one games under five hundred), it had been a glorious night all the same for the young Superagent. And, interestingly, not once did the name "Robert Kramer" enter Apparite's well-occupied mind during that entire evening.

Eleven
Discovery

The ballgame had removed much of the despair Apparite was feeling, so when he arose and took a few steps the next day his mood was pretty tolerable, and his gait had returned to normal except for a very slight favoring of his left leg. He did some early morning calisthenics, testing his weakened muscles and probing the limits of his lung capacity, and was pleased to note that he felt loose for the first time since his injuries; even with his cracked ribs and chest wound he had only a mild discomfort with breathing. But the Director interrupted Apparite's quiet exercising in the late afternoon, bursting through the doors in a flurry of activity that shattered the tomb-like silence of the warehouse.

"Kramer's dead," he boomed.

"When?"

"This morning: at oh-five thirty-four. I have sent word to the appropriate channels to keep his name out of the papers. And I have had these made for you."

He handed Apparite an envelope; inside it were a United States passport, a State of Maryland driver's license, and a U.S. Military Service card. All bore the name "Robert Kramer," with the photograph on the passport being of Apparite. After the Superagent had taken a moment to review the papers, the Director spoke again.

"You are now officially Robert Kramer, an American missile-fuel scientist working for the Department of the Navy

163

as a civilian contractor. You are defecting to the Soviet Union for two hundred fifty thousand dollars cash to be paid in London, plus another two hundred fifty thousand dollars the Soviets are prepared to give you on your arrival in Russia. You are then to live comfortably on a country estate outside Leningrad, near Lake Ladoga—a cold climate but pleasant and peaceful—where you will be doted upon through the generosity of the Soviet government in thanks for your service to 'Mother Russia.'

"The mobsters who were your contacts in the United States have clumsily gotten themselves involved in a gang shoot-out and have reneged on the deal, having to concentrate on more immediate troubles—or so the Soviets now believe. The British MI Six intelligence service has learned, through one of their agents who has infiltrated KGB operations in London, that the Soviets are comfortable dealing with Kramer directly on arrival to England, as we—or should I say *he*—has proposed. None of these agencies, however, are aware that the real Robert Kramer is dead, and it should be kept that way as long as possible. The British have offered an MI Five agent's services to aid us, although they do not know the details of the mission and believe we are operating for the CIA. I would advise you not to fill their agent in on the particulars until you have to."

He handed Apparite a rather thick attaché case filled with notes but, as Apparite perused them, the information they contained seemed to concern the examination of diamonds more than any other subject. He did not understand their purpose.

"Diamond examinations for the Amsterdam cartels?" he asked.

"Simply a cover for your trip. On the surface, the dossier appears to concern the precious stone trade; if you read it carefully, you will learn much about the examination and grading of diamonds, and the instruments used to perform such examinations. However, imprinted on the title page of the dossier is a collection of 'microdots' that contain all the information you need to know about solid ballistic missile-fuels or, at least, enough to be passable in conversation about the topic. They also contain a significant amount of classified material on the KGB operatives stationed in London, and as much information as we have on Viktor.

"After you have read it, this information *must* be safely disposed of. I suggest you tear off the corner of the paper that contains the microdots and burn or eat it on arrival to the United Kingdom. I will also give you an apparatus that will magnify the microdots so you may comfortably read them on the flight. It is disguised as a powerful diamond magnifier that, if asked, you will say you are delivering to Amsterdam, via London, for approval by the diamond cartels.

"In the bottom of the dossier is a puncture-proof fifty-milliliter tube containing a solid-fuel sample that will be the main enticement for the KGB to make the deal; it is disguised as a tube of gem polish. The tube also contains documents that outline the fuel formula, making it a very valuable commodity, indeed. Do not lose it, and do not let the Soviets take it from you without literally begging for it, but when they do, you may give it to them."

"Why? Is it the missing piece to their fuel puzzle?" Apparite asked. "If so, why would I let them have it?"

"It is an imperfect fuel sample—I'm not a fool, Apparite. It will take them down a long and expensive road to nowhere before they discover this particular formulation is a non-starter. If you give it up too willingly, they may suspect something; make them work for it," the Director said.

"I understand. Sounds easy enough."

"It's more complicated than you know, as usual. I am hopeful that the presence of Robert Kramer will draw out two key Soviets: Viktor, the SMERSH agent that I believe killed your predecessor; and also a leading Soviet rocket scientist named Nikolai, a protégé of Sergei Korolev, the rocket genius the Soviets call the "Chief Designer." Nikolai is the driving force behind their development of portable, solid missile-fuels, and Korolev would not be able to make up for his loss.

"Your mission is to identify these men and assassinate them, making certain that the fuel sample and calculations will be found on the body of the Soviet scientist to complete the ruse."

The Director stopped speaking to let Apparite digest the body of the plan. After a few tense, nearly silent moments—the only sound being the gentle creaking of the winches and chains of the warehouse ceiling swaying above them—he continued.

"Remember that Viktor not only killed Agent G, but had also planned to assassinate at least four high-ranking United States government officials; he is dangerous, as are all SMERSH agents, and will act without mercy. Do not let him get ahead of you in this game—you will pay for it with your life. Do not hesitate if you have to act—you would pay for that with your life as well."

"How do I arrange the meeting?" Apparite asked.

"I sent J to London shortly after your fatal encounter with Kramer; he will meet you at the airport when your flight lands tomorrow morning and brief you on the details of the mission. Your plane leaves from Baltimore in under two hours; I will take you to Friendship Airport myself. After that, you will have no contact with me until the mission is completed."

"I understand," said Apparite. Oddly, he found he might actually miss the Director while he was in London, although

166

he would *not* miss his mind-games.

"Mission success depends on many variables," the Director continued, "but the critical points are these: kill the Soviet scientist, as I estimate this would deal their submarine ballistic missile program a near-fatal blow for at least the next three years; insure that the bogus fuel sample and calculations will be found on the Soviet scientist after his death; and kill Viktor—or, at the least, disable his ability to operate effectively in the United Kingdom. As always, do not forget the program's directives: Maintenance of Secrecy. Mission completion. Minimization of Civilian Casualties. Minimization of Property Destruction." He had assumed a look of utmost severity, and his laser-like stare was turned on full-force.

"Operate at all times under their guidance, and do not let the fact that you will be three thousand miles from D.C. make you believe they are any less important. Remember also that your Shadow-agent will be near. He will not hesitate to act if you ignore them; *that* I can personally guarantee."

"Right: I will follow them—to the letter," Apparite said, in answer to what he perceived was a challenge on the Director's part; he felt confident he would meet it to his chief's satisfaction, no matter what was thrown at him in London.

"I will return in twenty minutes to take you to the airport, and will give you your luggage and weapons at that time. Bring with you your new identification documents and passport, the dossier, and the clothes on your back. That's all you'll need."

Nineteen minutes later, the Director returned to the warehouse driving the familiar black De Soto; Apparite did not inquire into the purpose of his apparent last-minute errand. The drive to the airport was done with a minimum of conversation for the first thirty minutes, except for another quick rundown of the objectives of the mission and the final confirmation of the meeting with J (the Oceanic terminal of London-Heathrow Airport at noon, London time).

During the silences, Apparite was running things over in his mind: the extreme importance of the mission; his need to impress the Director, especially after his near-fiasco during his brief encounter with Robert Kramer; and lastly, his wish, becoming almost a compulsion, to learn more about his mysterious boss. He was aware that it was foolish and possibly even dangerous to do so, but he would chance it: he was leaving on a possibly fatal mission to England, and he might never get another opportunity. Besides, he thought, it took his mind off other, more deadly matters.

"Even though Wynn pitched a three-hitter, I thought we had them right up until that Wertz double," Apparite ventured gamely.

Silence; the Director hadn't taken the bait but, then again, he hadn't told Apparite to clam up, either. Apparite baited another hook.

"Lucky we weren't up against Feller, huh? If there's been a faster pitcher than Feller in the history of this league, *I* haven't heard of him. Ya know, they timed Feller once, using a military speed-gun: ninety-eight point six miles per hour! How can you hit something like that?" Apparite felt the Director stir next to him; maybe he'd hit nearer the mark. He'd fish some more.

"Virgil Trucks is *damn* fast—remember when he no-hit us in fifty-two? I think Feller's got him on speed, though, plus his curve is simply *wicked*. If the 'Nats' had someone like him back in forty-five, I think we might've won the pennant. Boy, Feller's just about the best there ever was." There was an uncomfortable pause, and then the Director suddenly shifted in his seat: the hook had been taken.

"*Walter Johnson* was the greatest pitcher in the history of baseball and don't you forget it." The Director had finally spoken and his loud pronouncement caused Apparite to almost crap his drawers in surprise. After Apparite had settled down from the shock of the Director's emphatic response, he thought he would egg him on a bit more; maybe practice *his* interrogation techniques, for once. What did I have to lose other than my life? he mused.

"Oh, absolutely Barney was one of the best," Apparite responded, using one of Johnson's many popular nicknames. "Look at the record: thirty-six and seven in nineteen-thirteen; four hundred-sixteen wins; a hundred and thirteen shutouts. But I'd bet that Feller was *faster*. I mean, the man threw a baseball *ninety-eight point six miles per hour!*"

The Director stirred again; he was trying to hold something back, but obviously felt compelled to continue the debate as he answered Apparite after only a brief pause.

"I know for a *fact* that Johnson was faster." This was said in a tone that conveyed something as obvious and indisputable as "the earth is round," or "the sun rises in the east." There was, in the Director's apparent opinion, no room for debate on the issue. But Apparite's curiosity had not been satiated. He decided to probe further; luckily, traffic was light and he was able to hold the Director's full attention as he cast yet another line.

"Well, how could anyone *really* know? No one ever timed the 'Big Train,' so we can never really know," Apparite said in a light, flippant tone.

"Walter was faster," was the Director's curt response—he apparently wasn't going to waste words on an explanation.

"I dunno; I've seen the newsreels, and he didn't seem to be throwing too hard to me."

The Director slammed on the brakes and pulled the car

abruptly over to the curb, receiving honks and obscene gestures from the drivers of the cars that had, in the process, nearly rear-ended the De Soto. The Director held up the forefinger of his left hand for Apparite to see: it was crooked.

"See this finger? Barney busted it with a fastball that was harder than any pitch I've seen Feller make in the last fifteen years. So don't try and tell me that Walter Johnson wasn't the fastest pitcher in history." The Director pulled back out onto the road, face reddened and sweaty, only to be greeted by more honks and gestures as another set of cars swerved to avoid them.

Apparite immediately knew he had gone too far: like a curious boy who wondered at a magician's trick and then was told the solution, Apparite would never be able to look at the Director with the same sense of mystery and awe again. The great man's secret was out, and Apparite figured he was the only person in the world that knew it: the human enigma who directed the most powerful espionage agency in the world—*a man to whom secrecy and anonymity meant everything*—had once been a catcher for the Washington Senators.

With even a minimal amount of digging—an hour in the *Washington Post* archives is all it would take—he might know the Director's true name. Apparite realized just how devastating this discovery would be to his superior, and also how foolish it had been to pursue this line of questioning.

Apparite didn't know what to do next; he sat in complete silence, wondering what the consequences of his careless action would be. Would the Director kill him for having disclosed information Apparite could use to discover his true identity? Had their unusual relationship, which was in some ways approaching that of father and son, been irrevocably destroyed in an unthinking instant? Before Apparite had a chance to fully gather his thoughts, the Director spoke.

"I should not have told you that. It was a mistake which, under the usual circumstances, might have led to one of our deaths. But I will take a chance and trust you; I trust you will take what I stupidly said in a moment of weakness to the grave, or until I am deep in mine."

"I'm sorry," Apparite responded, "I couldn't help but notice you were a 'Nats' fan; I pushed my curiosity too far. I'll leave this where it stands."

"Now that you know, I will tell you something else that may have meaning to you. Walter was a close friend, and one of the finest men I ever knew; when he died of that brain tumor in forty-six, it was as if I had lost a brother. I see some of his qualities in you, Apparite, in your exceptional physical skills and intelligence. All you lack is experience and a certain emotional maturity, but I believe with time you will learn to use your gifts to their full potential; like Walter, you, too, might someday become the greatest in the history of your profession. Perhaps this explains why I have been so tough in challenging and testing you: it is because a man of your potential *deserves* it; he *needs* it to become great."

The Director's face remained rigid as he spoke, but his voice was noticeably softening, gathering warmth to it in a way that Apparite had not thought possible.

"Thanks for saying so," Apparite answered, deeply affected by the remarks. "If it means anything to you, I would die to protect your secret—as I would for all our secrets."

"I expect nothing less from you. As you well know, I would kill you to protect the program if I had to. I'm sure you would do the same to me, if need arose."

"Yes, I would; if need arose," Apparite said. And in that instant, he finally understood why, at his initial interview, he'd felt relief that the Director would've killed him if he'd failed that first test: to have let Apparite live would have been against their faith; the religion of espionage and secret agency. This faith, which Apparite had joined willingly, had its commandments and rituals just like any other religion, but it also had its penances which, by necessity, were the most severe.

It all came down to this: for the secret agent, to kill or be killed in the obeisance of the commandments of this religion was more important, perhaps, than the actual missions themselves. Whether one was an American Superagent, or MI6, or SMERSH, each man's duty was to bow down at the same altar, and with the same reverence. It was one of the reasons why the Director had spoken of Viktor with such respect: the man was a damned good disciple of the church of espionage, even if he was an enemy. And as long as the believers followed its commandants, friend and enemy alike, their religion remained pure and holy, and one's death would be honorable.

But it was never that easy or simple. Like any religion, this one had its heretics: the traitorous double-agents who had renounced the tenets of their faith. Double-crossing and deception was an essential and respected part of the espionage game, but to renounce your country to work for its enemies was unholy, and the most unforgivable of sins. Even the KGB defectors who had sought refuge in the West refused to actively spy on their old Soviet colleagues—it just wasn't done. A working double-agent was therefore despised by both sides—even those who had helped the double to "turn" recognized the stench of the Judas—and could never fully be trusted by either friend or foe. Apparite had never met a traitorous double-agent but, if he ever did; well, he would personally demonstrate the meaning of the phrase "Hell on Earth" to that man.

"We're here," the Director said as the car slowed to a halt in front of Friendship Airport.

"Right; I'd better get going." Apparite got out of the car, removed his luggage from the trunk, and walked over to the driver's-side window. A thought had come into his mind; one last order of business to settle before he left.

"Joe Judge, huh?" Apparite said.

"What's that?" the Director answered, unsure if he had heard Apparite correctly.

"*Joseph Judge:* the false identification I used at Butch's Place and Dolci's. He was first baseman for the Senators for fifteen years; played for the Series champs of twenty-four."

The Director smiled as if a pleasant memory had bubbled up to the surface.

"Joe was a good man, even though he swung at too many high fastballs. He wouldn't have minded you using his name. Good luck, Apparite."

Before Apparite could answer, having been ready to say, "Luck won't be needed," the Director drove away. Apparite walked briskly into the airport in wonderment at what had occurred: although he had in essence discovered the Director's identity, his ruthless, ultra-secretive supervisor had elected *not* to kill him for it.

Twelve
Destination: London

At 1830, Apparite boarded the Boeing 377 Stratocruiser that would fly him non-stop to London; as far as he knew, it was not only the first time he had ever been on an airplane, it was also the first time *anyone* in his family or personal experience had ever flown on an airplane. The marvel of a non-stop trans-Atlantic flight was one of those technological feats of engineering which Apparite had always loved—like the workings of a semi-automatic pistol, or the "bug" they had used at Dolci's—first inspired by his father's dramatic telling of pilot Charles Lindbergh's *Spirit of St. Louis* landing in Paris. When Apparite was a child, this tale had practically defined the word "hero" for him.

He had seen the great aviator in a D.C. parade long ago, and had never forgotten it. Lindbergh really looked the part that day, waving at the adoring crowd with a regal bearing usually reserved for dashing European princes. Apparite had always thought it a shame that the man's isolationist, debatably pro-Nazi leanings had tarnished his great legacy at the start of World War II, but no matter what, no one could ever take the magic of that solo trans-Atlantic flight away from him. Apparite could have listened to his father tell that story a thousand times.

And like Lindbergh, he too would now be flying over the Atlantic Ocean, though in much more comfortable surroundings than "Lucky Lindy": the Boeing 377 Stratocruiser was infinitely more spacious, comfortable, safer, and, most importantly, unlike the *Spirit of St. Louis*, it had toilet facilities.

Apparite had always thought the 377 an uncommonly handsome aircraft—it had a pleasing duel-bubble fuselage and an attractive blue, silver, and white color scheme—and he was excited to fly in one. The Director had initially offered him a first class ticket, but Apparite had talked him out of it. "I might stick out too much," was his weak excuse—the Director did not argue the point—although the true reason was based more on Apparite's inherent frugal nature than anything else: he thought it simply cost too damned much! He also knew, even if the Director didn't, that he would be much more relaxed sitting with the "peons" back in coach than with the "bluebloods" up front.

He looked around the cabin with anticipation. The prim, almost "WAC"-like attire of the stewardesses dissipated any sense of danger that one might try to inject into such a journey, as did their expressions, which could not hide the monotonous and repetitive nature of their duties. Apparite settled in for the flight and, when asked the immortal question, "Coffee, tea, or milk?" had chosen coffee: black.

There were quite a few empty seats on the plane—it was well short of its capacity of eighty-one passengers—though there were plenty of businessmen wearing black or gray suits near him, as well as a few small families which he deduced were either "Brits" returning home or Americans going on holiday. Most noticeably there was a sizable group of young, boisterous merry-makers; probably wealthy jet-setters or college kids on trust-fund sprees, Apparite figured. Many of his flight-mates looked bored as the crew made their final preparations (some of the businessmen and children were already sleeping), but a state of extreme excitement had seized the jet-setters—they apparently had downed a few too many cocktails before boarding and were singing college fight songs (the last rendition was of "On Iowa!" by a lone, off-key Hawkeye alumnus). Apparite wondered if they would eventually tackle the University of Maryland fight song—as an ex-Terp, he could perhaps hum along with that one (discreetly, of course).

Until then, he would review the materials the Director had given him regarding the mission. He opened the dossier and took out the sheet that contained the microdots. In the upper left corner was an emblem consisting of the words "International Gem Importers, Limited: Amsterdam, London, New York," surrounding a rendition of the earth. The microdots, he recalled, were hidden inside this rendition.

Out of a pocket in the case, Apparite removed a complicated-looking silver apparatus about six inches high. It consisted of a series of finely cut lenses that were set inside cylinders of various diameters and crowned by an eyepiece; a set of dials on the side were used to bring the powerful lenses into focus. Apparite placed it over one of the dots in the emblem—a black spot about one millimeter in size to the naked eye—and moved the dials back and forth as he looked in the eyepiece.

The blurry dot turned not only into words, but an entire *page* of words that came into an unbelievably clear focus given its microscopic size—it was a very powerful instrument (worth over fifteen thousand dollars—it was probably for the best that Apparite was unaware of that fact). Each group of dots, Apparite noted, contained a different file: "Viktor," "Solid and Liquid Rocket-Fuel Principles," "Soviet Ballistic Missile Program," "Soviet Presence in London," and "U.K. Agent Considerations." It was enough information to fill a decent-sized book, he thought.

"What's that you've got there?" said an attractive brunette

stewardess, taking notice of Apparite's unusual contraption.

Apparite put down the magnifier and said, matter-of-factly, "Oh, it's a new magnifier for examining precious stones: very advanced; the latest prototype. I'm taking it to London for some adjustments, then on to Amsterdam. I've got some test patterns on this paper."

"Really? That's interesting. What can you see with it?"

"You'd be *surprised*," Apparite said, in a voice that hinted at mystery.

"Well, if I can ever get my boyfriend to propose, I'm going to have *you* check out the diamond!" she replied with a delightful laugh.

Apparite laughed in return.

"Sure," he answered, as naturally as possible, "but until then, keep up the pressure on him!"

She laughed again and walked up the aisle. Apparite, relieved at how well this exchange had gone—as well as the fact that no one else seemed to care what he was doing—put the apparatus back on the paper and refocused on the first file, "Viktor."

The stewardess made an announcement.

"We are preparing for takeoff; please remain in your seats and fasten your safety belts. Our flying time will be ten hours and thirty minutes; we will land at London-Heathrow Airport at approximately eleven-thirty a.m., London time. Thank you for flying Pan-American World Airways, and have an enjoyable flight."

Apparite placed the apparatus back into its case. As he was the only one in his row—which he thought was fortunate, as he did not wish to engage in time-wasting or identity-probing conversation with anyone—he moved to the window seat, anxious to get a look at the ground as they took off. He heard the sound of the cabin door being closed, and then felt a slight fullness in his eardrums as the airplane was pressurized. This should be a very interesting experience, he thought; I'll finally get to see what the ground looks like from a thousand feet.

The aircraft shuddered as the engines increased in power and lurched ahead, the thrust overcoming the craft's inertia as it slowly began moving down the tarmac to the start of the long runway. The whine of the engines increased in pitch and intensity, and then the aircraft began to rapidly accelerate. Apparite marveled at the speed that the plane had already attained as it hurtled down the runway. *We must be doing almost ninety miles per hour and we haven't even left the ground yet*, he said to himself.

The pitch of the engines rose rapidly almost to a scream, and though it was muffled by the insulation and skin of the craft, it still took Apparite by surprise. The aircraft began to pitch right and then left, and the shuddering changed into a shaking that grew increasingly violent—was this *supposed* to happen, wondered Apparite?—as the plane raced down the runway with frightening speed. It finally became airborne, loosening itself from the bonds of the earth, and just as suddenly as it had begun, the shaking ceased.

Apparite felt, well, *odd;* his pulse had risen rapidly and his mouth was unusually dry—very strange, he thought. He looked out of the window. The runway shrank below him, and then the whole of Friendship Airport had begun to shrink, and then even the entire city of Baltimore started to pull away until it looked like a tiny but incredibly realistic model. He could make out miniature but picture-perfect renditions of Pimlico Racetrack, Memorial Stadium, and even Johns Hopkins Hospital getting smaller and smaller as the aircraft rose ever higher into the air.

His curiously odd feeling was accelerating into one of impending panic: we are *way* up in the air in this thousand ton machine in defiance of the laws of gravity, he thought, and when you do that, something *terrible* is bound to happen (after all, there's a *reason* why they're called the *laws* of gravity). Gravity is immutable and inexorable; never-ceasing in its effort to pull us back down to earth—wouldn't it just be a matter of time, he thought in his panic, before gravity finally had its way and this giant hulk crashed into the ground and pulverized his body into a thousand pieces? His heart was racing and he was light-headed; he felt exactly as he had when he had killed Robert Kramer, only this time he was not in control of the situation in any way. He was simply human cargo in this law-of-gravity-defying contraption, and about to go crazy.

A thought forced its way through his panic: surely he must not be the *only one* who felt like this? He loosened his collar and looked around him. The jet-setters had merrily moved to "On Wisconsin!" having just polished-off "Hail to the Victors" on an apparent tour of the Big Ten, and the businessmen were all asleep, having cocktails, or reading the papers. Oh my God, thought Apparite, I *am* the only one who feels this way! What's *wrong* with these people? Don't they know the stresses that *four* Pratt and Whitney engines put on the metal skeleton of a craft like this? Don't they know about the *immutable laws of gravity?*

He felt sick. Hc had to close his eyes, to think of something else, something pleasant—like opening day 1954. Mickey Vernon had hit a home run to beat the Yankees and Allie Reynolds in extra innings, and it turned out to be the best game of the entire season. President Eisenhower had been at that one, and the roar of the crowd when Vernon's shot cleared the fence was as loud as Apparite could remember at Griffith Stadium.

A wave of calm slowly washed over him as he dissected his

remembrance of that wonderful day, reliving every detail in an effort to distract himself from his inexplicable panic. After a minute of reminiscing he felt his pulse slow; taking a few deep breaths, he waved the top of his shirt in and out to cool his neck and chest—he was finally settling down.

He opened his eyes again to see if anyone had noticed and, to his relief, no one was looking his way. He motioned to the pretty brunette stewardess with a wave of his hand.

"Excuse me, Miss; may I have a glass of ice water?"

"Certainly; are you okay? You look a little pale," she replied.

"I'm fine; just a touch of the flu. Seems like I always get sick when I travel." Apparite hoped she hadn't seen through his lie. He was embarrassed, of course, about his weakness—how could John Apparite, a highly educated secret agent who had fearlessly fought and killed nine dangerous mobsters have an illogical fear of flying?—but he was more worried about something else. After his unexpected anxiety reaction during his encounter with Robert Kramer, and his panic attack with the takeoff of the airplane, what *other* Achilles heels might show themselves in his uncertain future? He never had these kinds of problems *before*, so why are they happening *now?* And why have they only begun since I joined this agency? he wondered.

And then another disturbing, though wryly humorous thought intruded into his brain: *Someday, after the mission in London is over, I'm going to have to get on an airplane and fly* back!

He let out a sigh—maybe the Director would let him take the *Queen Elizabeth* liner home. The stewardess returned with his ice water a moment later.

"Thank you; I'm feeling much better already," said Apparite.

"Don't worry: flying is the safest form of transportation," she replied, putting a comforting hand on his shoulder.

Apparite smiled weakly in return—she had known all along what had happened, of course. He felt drained and his old wounds were throbbing as he thought of the long hours of flying time that awaited him. He attached the dossier case securely to his belt and closed his eyes to take a nap, still not one hundred percent certain he would ever awaken, but hoping that he could spend the next few hours in as unconscious a state as possible.

Apparite awoke with a start: he had been asleep about three hours. He still had an echo of his panic episode in his head, but the fact that he had indeed awoken—the Stratocruiser had *not* yet plummeted to earth in a fiery heap, he was pleased to note—reassured him that he stood at least a fighting chance of surviving the flight to London. Thinking it best to get the whole episode behind him as soon as possible, he returned to the distraction of his work. Apparite unhooked the attaché case and removed a file; he then took the microdot reader from its case and put his left eye down onto the eyepiece. Bringing a microdot into focus, he began reading the file labeled "Viktor." What he found was some of the most fascinating material he had ever read.

Viktor was born in 1921 or 1922 in Leningrad. His true name is unknown. His parents died in 1942 during the 'Nine Hundred Days' siege of that city, and their frozen bodies were not discovered until after the spring thaw. Viktor has since despised the West for not coming to the aid of those trapped in Leningrad during the blockade, fueling an already acute anti-Western passion.

He was trained by the Soviet military agency GRU, and then SMERSH near the end of the war. He first served at Lubyanka

Square KGB headquarters in Moscow, where he became expert in the torture of captured German officials, extracting vital information on the Third Reich. Since the end of the war he has killed over a dozen West German, U.S., and U.K. agents or officials in his capacity as a SMERSH assassin. He is only an average marksman, but is deadly in hand-to-hand fighting.

He has often been used to demonstrate lethal SAMBO techniques on captured prisoners or Soviet dissidents, unhesitating to kill even in these exhibitions. He plans his assassinations carefully, and in spite of his average marksmanship, has never failed. He often kills his targets after capture and aggressive interrogation.

His psychological profile fits that of the classic sadist. He feeds on the pain of his subjects, sometimes causing him to impulsively lose control and kill them, even in defiance of orders to keep them alive. For this he has been punished on numerous occasions, though most of his superiors feel he is incorrigible in this regard. In many ways Viktor is emotionally stunted and immature, and displays narcissistic tendencies.

There is only one known photograph of Viktor.

Apparite looked at the grainy, miniaturized photograph—taken on a Moscow street, he surmised—showing a tall, thin man with brown hair sticking out from under a typical Russian military cap; he was wearing a heavy woolen coat. The man's expression was not clear enough to read, but Apparite was struck by the vivid brightness of his eyes, which looked almost as if they had been painted directly onto the photograph.

He uses an alias of an Eastern European émigré while traveling in the West, as his command of the English language is barely adequate. He is therefore not the point-man in negotiations and meetings, although he generally attends them, remaining silent. His is an imposing presence, according to those who have met him in person. Despite his psychological faults he is highly intelligent and shows a surprising amount of ingenuity and imagination in his plots. However, he is a novice in political affairs, and has run afoul of the Soviet party line in the past.

Viktor was a fanatical supporter of Stalin, whom he believes was poisoned by one of his guards. It is rumored that this guard, a man named Sergei Khrustalev, was acting on the orders of Lavrenty Beria, the former head of Soviet intelligence. Khrustalev was forced to flee from Moscow under threat of death by Viktor, and in some circles is believed to have been killed by him or his associates. Beria was arrested in June 1953, and executed after a post-Stalin power struggle. It is believed that Viktor had personally obtained by torture much of the information used to discredit Beria.

Since Stalin's death, Viktor has allied himself with Vyacheslav Molotov, the most radical of those at the head of the Soviet government. Molotov is a ruthless politician who is very aggressive in his stance towards the West. He has given Viktor free reign to pursue whatever means he needs to disrupt the governments of the United States or the United Kingdom. Soviet First Secretary Nikita Khrushchev is not fully aware of Molotov's aims, nor would he necessarily agree with them. Until recently, Khrushchev's ear belonged to Georgii Malenkov, a man who has taken a pacifist approach to Soviet relations to the West in regard to the development and use of atomic weapons. But the situation has changed in recent months.

With recent KGB defections, Khrushchev would now embrace any espionage coups no matter how politically charged. Further, with the pacifist Malenkov now discredited, the First Secretary would welcome the bargaining chip of Soviet submarine ballistic nuclear missile capability. It should be noted that if Molotov was ever to attain a position of ultimate authority in the Soviet govern-

ment, and the Soviets were to have such a capability, the West would be in imminent danger of a devastating nuclear first-strike at his hand.

Apparite now understood why Viktor was so feared: the man had the power and influence to alter the entire course of U.S.-Soviet relations, if only given the opportunity. But though the SMERSH agent was cunning and ruthless, thought Apparite, he was still only a man, and had his weaknesses. For one, if Viktor had interrogated Agent G rather than killing him, which Apparite guessed he had probably done for his own amusement, he might have learned much about the Director's program—it was fortunate that he hadn't. The episode reinforced for Apparite the reason why he had an "L-pill" stitched into his right sock: the United States and the Director could ill-afford the destruction a captured Superagent's confession might wreak.

Apparite put down the folder marked "Viktor" and picked up the one marked "Solid and Liquid Rocket-Fuels." He took a quick glance around the cabin, and noting that no one was paying the least amount of attention to him, he began reading once again.

Ballistic missiles entered the modern age with Nazi Germany's V2 rocket in the Second World War. Flying faster than the speed of sound it was virtually indefensible and could destroy an entire city block on impact. The capability of firing a powerful missile from any major oceanic body of water—from a submarine or destroyer, for example—would be a powerful, unstoppable weapon.

Such missiles travel with the use of liquid or solid fuels. There are great disadvantages for liquid fuel-based rockets as opposed to those powered by solid fuels. Liquid fuels, for example, are more volatile and dangerous, less portable, and become unstable in a shorter period of time. Liquid-fueled missiles are also ideally fired from permanent, stationary structures, but these immobile structures are, by their very nature, more prone to destruction by an enemy. Solid fuels, in contrast, may be transported and stored for future use, as in a submarine or mobile rocket-carrier, which would provide a great advantage to the nation that possessed them.

Many nations have the means to fire ballistic missiles with liquid fuels. For example, the United States Ajax rocket uses the following formula for its propellant fuel: 83% JP-4 turbine engine fuel, 17% Unsymmetrical Dimethylhydrazine (UDMH), Inhibited Red Fuming Nitric Acid as an oxidizer, with a starting fluid of 99% UDMH. Although it is a reliable mixture and serves its purpose adequately, it has the limitations of all liquid fuels, as previously stated.

The Soviets have developed a similar liquid fuel for their R7 rocket, although it has not yet replaced a liquid oxygen-kerosene mixture at the present time. In the development of solid rocket-fuels, however, they lag far behind the Unites States, and their capability of firing ballistic missiles from submarines or portable launchers is significantly less. This situation is beginning to cause extreme anxiety in Soviet military circles.

Intelligence suggests that the Soviets even staged, unbeknownst to First Secretary Khrushchev, a falsified submarine ballistic missile test. A Soviet submarine was positioned in front of a floating barge that carried a small ballistic missile launcher, hiding the barge completely from view. At Khrushchev's command, with his ceremonial pressing of the launch button, the barge fired its rocket, which appeared to come from the submarine itself. This bizarre episode is a strong testament to the desperation of their military and scientists, providing an illuminating glimpse into an unattractive side of the Soviet military/political mindset.

That's interesting and not just a little funny, thought Apparite—to think that the Soviets would deceive their leader with such a crude trick made him laugh under his breath. The comic nature of it—a hidden barge firing a missile!—was in contrast to the tales of Soviet rocket superiority he had been told in the past. He had to remind himself that while some Soviets were desperate and incompetent, there were others—such as Viktor—who were nearly machine-like in their efficiency. Apparite knew it would be a mistake to underestimate any of them.

Khrushchev pronounced the experiment a success, but those aware of the deception have had to become even more desperate in their race to succeed. They are now under extreme pressure to obtain the needed fuel formula to make such an experiment a reality for the Soviet Union submarine fleet. It is believed that the one who does so will receive the "Order of Lenin," and be given the title of "Hero of the Soviet Union."

For the United States, a working, portable solid rocket-fuel is in its final developmental phases. In the near future, the United States government will start testing its new Hercules solid fuel-powered rocket, which will carry a payload of 1,000 pounds, or greater than three times what the Ajax may presently deliver. If successful, the solid fuel-mixture can then be adapted for submarine ballistic missile use. It is anticipated that within five years, the United States should have a reliable solid fuel-mixture to fire submarine-based ballistic nuclear missiles.

The solid fuel being developed by the United States Navy uses an asphalt compound with fuel and binding capacities as the primary propellant, with potassium perchlorate serving as an oxidizer. It is estimated that the Soviets would be willing to pay an individual greater than two million U.S. dollars to obtain the exact formula for this fuel. In practical terms, its value to them cannot be overstated.

Dry stuff to be sure, but the lesson had been driven home: the Soviets would do anything to get their hands on this fuel-mixture; they would kill, without question, anyone who would stand in their way. *No wonder the Director wanted Robert Kramer to suffer for his impending treachery,* thought Apparite, and although the knowledge did not fully relieve his guilt for the method of the man's assassination, he had been fully convinced that the world was a better and safer place with Robert Kramer no longer in it.

He perused the rest of the documents: humorless and dull material on the inner workings of the Soviet Union's Central Committee, the KGB's London bureau (stocked with either old, reliable agents past their primes, or new, untested ones felt to be immune from defection to the West), and long dissertations on the intricacies of rocket fuels. He skimmed page after page of endless calculations showing why liquid oxygen was undesirable (low flash-point, and temperature concerns), ozone and fluorine were inadvisable (stability concerns), and then a whole list of available commercial fuels—jet fuels, automobile fuels, diesel fuels, and alcohol—with detailed and soporific explanations on which ones worked (JP-4 jet fuel), and which ones didn't (just about everything else).

Although Apparite had been an excellent student, he had not taken what one would call an excess of chemistry classes in college (sticking mainly with human and applied biology, and the Romance languages), and he quickly tired of this material. He knew it was useless for him to try and memorize it—any attempt by him to use technical terms when he met with the Soviets would probably just expose him as a pretender, which would be disastrous. His best option would be to keep his mouth shut and let the sample fuel and calculations do the talking for him. A real traitor would probably be more inter-ested in the money anyway, so if asked anything, he would stick to this point: When will I get my money? That seemed to be the most realistic way for him to act, he thought, if the situ-ation required any speaking at all.

The last file he read regarded the British intelligence ser-vices, MI5 and MI6; now *this* was interesting stuff. There had been some recent setbacks for the British, he noted; most ob-viously in the Philby, Burgess, and McLean episodes of the past few years. And, although it was hard to believe, the British *still* didn't have enough on double-agent Philby to put him in jail, and Burgess and McLean, two of his treacherous allies, had been allowed to defect to the Soviets. These three traitors had operated for the KGB as double-agents for nearly a decade *in the United States and England,* for crying out loud, while everyone futzed-around in a series of extreme embar-rassments to the British and U.S. intelligence communities. No wonder the Director was so paranoid about secrecy and security, thought Apparite.

He paused to take a brief look around the cabin—no one was watching him, he noted with relief—made a slight adjust-ment to the microdot-reader, and read on.

MI5 was the agency in charge of British internal security, with similar responsibilities as the good old FBI back in the U.S. And while MI5 agents were capable and generally salt-of-the-earth, there had been problems; for one thing, they were always playing second fiddle to their international coun-terparts from MI6 in the press and intelligence community, resulting in a distinctive inferiority complex. MI6 agents therefore tended to look down their noses at their MI5 com-patriots, the result being that the two agencies were often *not* on friendly terms.

And there had been morale problems at MI5. Many of

their agents felt like underpaid civil servants, and had been leaving for other, more lucrative areas of employment. The rebuilding of much of southern England after the war had nearly crippled the British economy and, even after leaving MI5, quite a few former agents remained unemployed. With the Soviets' desperation apparent in their willingness to part with a million dollars or more for Robert Kramer, Apparite wondered how much it would take for the Soviets to buy off an underpaid, under-appreciated MI5 agent? The prospect seemed quite plausible, and if the British were going to lend an MI5 agent to help with this mission, as the Director had told him, then Apparite sure hoped that they would get one who was dedicated—and good.

Moving on to MI6, Apparite was much more impressed. This agency might have had the black mark of the Philby affair against it, but their men received top training—almost as intensive as he had undergone, he thought. Their agents were intelligent, resourceful, adept at hand-to-hand combat, and uniformly exceptional marksman. They lived and worked quite comfortably all over the globe, but were particularly effective in the areas of the old pre-war British Empire: India, South Africa, Singapore, and Hong Kong. They had the run of Europe, too, of course, and had done quite well against the Soviets in Austria and East Germany—particularly in Berlin. Their pay was better than those slaving away in MI5, and many of the agents, the file told him, came from highly placed families; some were even in the peerage. No wonder they felt superior to their colleagues at MI5, Apparite thought, although he personally could not condone it.

He remembered the Director telling him of an MI6 agent who had infiltrated the KGB in London, pretending to be a "defector-in-place" working for the Soviets. Apparite hadn't thought of it before, but after reading the files he realized what a truly impressive act of espionage that had been. How on earth had the man done it? Did he understand what would happen to him if a maniac like Viktor found him out? Apparite thought he surely must. *That guy must have balls of iron,* he said to himself, wondering what kind of man could perform at such a high level, and whether he might meet him on this upcoming mission.

He tucked the files away in the attaché case, reattached the handle to his belt, and asked the waitress for a pillow and a glass of water, having become reasonably comfortable with the idea of flying tens of thousands of feet above the earth despite the immutable laws of gravity. He soon nodded off, hoping that when he awoke (feeling *almost* one hundred percent certain he would do so), he would be in the United Kingdom.

At the sound of the pretty brunette stewardess making a loud and very distinctly enunciated announcement, Apparite finally stirred and awoke; he had been asleep for quite some time.

"Please get your passports ready; after deplaning, you will need to proceed through immigration and then through customs. If you have anything to declare on entry to the United Kingdom, I have the appropriate forms and can provide pencils to fill them out. If you are not a citizen of the United Kingdom, then please fill out an immigration form as well."

Apparite looked at his watch, noting that he had been blessed by nearly six hours of uninterrupted sleep. He must have resisted all attempts to awaken him as he had missed the evening meal, but he wasn't hungry anyway, particularly for airline food (he had heard it was worse than K-rations most of the time). He stretched his arms and legs, stifled a yawn, and took out the dossier. He tore off the microdot-infested corner of the cover page and swallowed it as he had been directed, although he felt ridiculous doing it (it was exceedingly dry and drained the saliva from his mouth). He then took his passport out of his attaché case, comparing the picture on it with the name that was attached to it.

"Robert Kramer": that's who he now was. It had been difficult enough getting used to being John Apparite—a name that he still didn't automatically answer to—but the idea of being a dead man was very ghoulish to him, particularly one that *he* had killed. A man's name defines him somewhat, he thought, and if so, then how would the man called Robert Kramer be defined *now?* Robert Kramer the scientist was a budding traitor who was going to sell out his country before he was killed. The new Robert Kramer was a diamond examiner-*cum*-secret agent, and the question had become this: what horrible deeds would *this* version of Robert Kramer do?

He tried not to think about it. Apparite was becoming increasingly concerned by these philosophical questions he was asking himself; these little bits of humanity which were thrusting themselves into the one part of his life that could not accommodate them. These emotions (which he struggled to quell), and these questions (which he could not answer), were frustrating to him, and he knew that in some way they were connected to his episodes of unexpected panic. But, as the Director had said, when the anvil was in front of him, Apparite would not hesitate to bring the hammer down upon it, no matter *what* his budding conscience was trying to tell him. He would remind himself of that over and over again, until it became as much of a fact and a certainty as anything else in the physical world: the earth orbits the sun and John Apparite will do his duty. The second *had* to be as indisputable as the first.

"Thank you for flying Pan American World Airways: you

may now disembark via the gangway," the stewardess said in her delightful voice.

Apparite picked up his leather valise and proceeded down the aisle; the pretty brunette stewardess looked his way as he passed the plane's tiny galley.

"Sorry about your meal!" she told him. "We tried and tried to wake you, but—"

"That's alright," Apparite said. "I was exhausted from the New York to D.C. 'Sunrise Special' yesterday morning. Besides, I needed the sleep much more than *airline* food!"

The stewardess laughed; a bright, bubbly laugh as enticing as the sound of a brook that comes from deep within a wood. For the first time, Apparite noticed what a delightful smile she had: it was perfectly symmetrical, with a row of whiter-than-white teeth poking out from underneath her strawberry-colored lipstick. She stuck the tip of her pink tongue through them ever so slightly as she laughed, and it was charming.

Apparite blushed; his tongue felt paralyzed and he could think of nothing to say. He was exceedingly self-conscious at not only the attention she was giving him, but also in his undeniable and uncontrollable attraction to her. Something was stirring inside him that had not stirred for the longest time and, he thought, it could not stir *now!*

Steeling his visage, and recovering his powers of coherent speech, he rigidly said, "Thank you for the flight, Miss; I must be going." He then walked off the plane as rapidly as he could. As worried as he had become about having further attacks of panic or, God forbid, further attacks of *feelings*, he had just discovered something else which could prey on his anxieties just as devastatingly: a pretty girl.

Thirteen
Land of Hope and Glory

Apparite followed the rest of the flock through the corridors of the new Oceanic terminal of London-Heathrow Airport. Finally reaching the apparent end of the maze, he joined a long, serpentine line of the newly arrived awaiting their passage through immigration and customs. He took out the forms he had been given on the plane, and filled them out as he had been instructed.

Name: ROBERT KRAMER. Nationality: U.S.A. Occupation: SCIENTIST. Nature of Visit: ON HOLIDAY. Residence while in the United Kingdom: ROYAL AMBASSADOR HOTEL, LONDON. Date of Departure from the United Kingdom: DECEMBER 1, 1955. The document told a simple enough tale, he thought, although the full story of Robert Kramer's trip to Britain might have shocked (or impressed, perhaps) even Lucrezia Borgia.

The queue thinned and eventually Apparite was second in line; the immigration officer appeared to be in a heated discussion with the Dutch couple who had been in front of him. Five minutes; ten minutes of arguing went on between the three of them until finally the immigration officer put out his palm in a forceful gesture—like one who has suddenly decided to halt a long line of traffic—and called for reinforcements. The Dutch woman was audibly weeping, and both she and her husband were visibly shaking. Three identically dressed immigration officers came out of a small interrogation room, as if summoned by an invisible bell, and led the frightened couple away.

"Next in the queue, please," cried out the immigration man as he looked in Apparite's general direction. Apparite approached the tall, stern-looking Brit, who was dressed in a heavy and formal blue uniform with yellow piping on the sleeves and trousers. His pinched face was formed into an off-putting sneer, which was made all the worse by a little moustache that reminded Apparite of Adolf Hitler's.

"Good morning," the man said curtly, taking Apparite's documents in hand.

"Good morning," Apparite responded in a brusque tone, echoing the immigration agent's words and demeanor.

"Come here on holiday, have you?" the man said as he perused Apparite's papers, glancing only briefly at him.

"Yes; I'm sightseeing in London."

"Staying long?" He glanced up briefly, took in the young American's face for a moment, and then refocused onto the passport.

"No; just a little over a month," Apparite responded, "and then it's back to D.C. and the grind of my job."

"American scientist, are you?" he said, his voice rising slightly; the immigration agent sounded unusually suspicious, thought Apparite, who had hoped he would not be asked such questions, although he had been prepared for them.

"Yes, I'm working for the U.S. Navy right now: tough job, so I'm glad to get away for a while."

"Not going to cause any trouble while you're in the United Kingdom, are you?"

Apparite was put off by the man's question: did he *look* like a troublemaker to him? He recovered after a moment.

"Not unless it finds me *first!*" Apparite said with a grin, letting out a playful but forced little laugh (*God, this is uncomfortable,* he said to himself).

The unsmiling immigration officer looked at Apparite with probing eyes as he searched the young American's face for untruths or weakness of character or tale. Apparite was concerned by the man's severe stare and increasingly invasive questions—if he was taken into custody, the particulars of his name and point of origin might be investigated, and he would risk discovery. At best, it would prove an uncomfortable and annoying delay. At worst, if the immigration officers were unusually aggressive, putting him in real danger of exposure (*Directive number one: Maintenance of Secrecy,* he remembered), he might have to make use of the "L-pill" sewn into his sock. After a very long pause, the stern Brit spoke.

"Right. Make sure you visit St. Paul's, Mr. Kramer—it's a long climb to the top but the view is breathtaking. Welcome to England."

And that was it. The official stamped Apparite's passport and handed it back to him. It had been a very strange interaction, Apparite thought; one minute, he was weighing the possibility that he would have to end his life with a lethal poison, and the next, he was being exhorted to visit a famous London landmark.

He went to the baggage claim area and retrieved his two black suitcases. Following the others from his flight he passed into customs, only to join another long, winding queue. When his turn arrived, he approached the customs agent with trepidation, fearing another grilling like he had undergone at the hands of the immigration officer. Apparite relaxed, however, when he saw the smiling, heavy-set customs agent's friendly, full face and rosy complexion, and unlike the grim immigration man, he seemed to be fairly overflowing with good cheer. He held out his hand for Apparite's passport.

"Coming from the U.S. are you, Mr.—Kramer?" he said, opening the document, smiling broadly.

"Yes," Apparite answered.

"Are you bringing any plants or animals with you to our lovely country?" he asked.

"No. Nothing like that."

"We have lengthy rabies quarantines for animals brought into the United Kingdom, which is why we have to ask," he said, as if he was apologizing for some imagined offense.

"I understand; no, I don't have any animals," answered Apparite.

"Fan-*tastic*," the jovial man said with enthusiasm, flashing another smile. "Enjoy your stay in England, Mr. Kramer."

"Thank you." Apparite took back the passport and walked out to collect his bags. No, he thought to himself, he had not brought any plants or animals with him, but what the jolly officer hadn't realized was that Apparite had smuggled in much more deadly cargo right under his nose. He imagined what other questions might have been asked by the friendly agent, if only he'd known.

"Have you got any weapons, Mr. Kramer?" the man might ask.

"Oh yes. I've got a thirty-eight caliber nine-shot Colt Super Automatic pistol, and a forty-five caliber seven-shot Colt M nineteen-eleven, along with a hundred rounds of ammunition."

"*Super.* Which do you prefer, by the way?"

"I like the balance of the Super Automatic, and the extra two shots in the clip sure come in handy in a tight spot."

"Yes, they might at that!" the amused customs man would say, laughing. "You don't want to be short two plates at supper, do you? How about knives—are you set there?"

"I've got five: three all-metal throwing-knives, a combination slashing or throwing switchblade, and a Peskett close-combat weapon—you know, the kind with a combination dagger, garrote, and cosh for bludgeoning."

"Yes; they're bloody *brilliant,* aren't they?" he would say, impressed by the effectiveness and utility of such a device. "That bloke Peskett was dead clever: nothing like having a variety of options in a pinch."

"Absolutely," Apparite would respond, "I've got to cover every possible base."

"Well, seems you're ready for just about anything. What else have you got?"

"Oh, just a few minor gadgets: tie-clip Minox camera, wireless 'bug,' key impression kit, hypodermic pen that injects a highly lethal poison, that sort of thing."

"Well, we don't want to waste your valuable time cataloguing all that. Let's just put that under 'miscellaneous spy gear,' shall we? Right—off you go!" he would say, in wonderment at the variety of tools at Apparite's disposal.

Apparite smiled at the imagined exchange as he tucked his passport back into his suit's right inside pocket, his enthusiasm returning as his duty as a secret agent beckoned to him. He was ready to get at it.

"Mr. Kramer!" shouted a familiar voice. Apparite turned in the direction of the sound—though having to make the conscious connection between himself and the name "Kramer"—and saw J waiting for him near the exit. After a firm handshake and a few friendly slaps on the back, J took Apparite's luggage in hand. The bags were significantly heavier than they appeared, and he grunted audibly when lifting them: despite their limited size, they had been stuffed to near-bursting with weapons, trousers, shirts, boxershorts, socks, and toilet articles. But there was more, of course: hidden in a multitude of hidden pockets was a sizable cache of U.S. dollars, English pounds, and gold bullion as well—just in case (the care of such large amounts of cash would have given Apparite the shivers a few weeks ago, but as long as it remained in his sight, he was not overly concerned).

And yet, despite having over fifty thousand dollars worth of cash and equipment in the bags, perhaps Apparite's most valuable possession in them remained his signed Walter Johnson tobacco card. He could survive the loss of almost all of that other stuff, he thought, but to lose that card might very well kill him. Although he figured he would not be able carry it on him for security reasons, he'd feel better knowing it, too, had made the trip.

They got into J's car; a green, 1951 Morris Minor two-door that made the Director's beat-up Nash look like a Rolls-Royce in comparison. J turned the ignition key and the engine hiccupped to a hesitant and shaky start, and when he pushed on the accelerator, it added various wheezes and coughs to its repertoire of sounds. He let out the clutch and gave it some gas; the car leapt forward, stopping and starting like a gear missing a substantial number of teeth. He aimed it in the general direction of the road leading out of the airport, although Apparite doubted it would ever get to London, lurching about as spastically as it was.

"First thing you've got to learn, Apparite, is that the English make very dubious automobiles and they drive them ass-backwards, on the left: left turns are therefore right turns, and vicey-versy."

Apparite chuckled at the remark, but was cut-off by J.

"Don't laugh! Driving this way is harder than it looks."

As J himself looked quite comfortable with the driving situation (aside from the horrible car he had obtained goodness-knows-how), Apparite surmised that he had previously spent some time in England. He knew better than to ask about it, of course.

"It's more than being cautious when driving," J added. "*You*'ll be lucky not to get run down simply crossing the street. When you step into an intersection, look *right*, not left; then *left*, not right—savvy?"

Apparite took a second to untwist the remark, but eventually was able to pull it into some semblance of understanding. He chuckled again when he had it figured out.

"I'm *not* kidding, Apparite," J added. "Winston Churchill nearly got killed in New York when he looked the wrong direction crossing the street and was hit by a cab. You can't imagine the consequences if you got run-down by a London taxi and ended up in St. Bart's Hospital. Take a drive if you have the chance, but it's more important that you practice walking while you're here. I know it sounds crazy, but you've got to do it."

"Right—I will. Don't worry—I know how to *walk*," Apparite added in irritation. He felt it his duty to come to the defense of his ability to cross the street without remedial course work, for Chrissakes.

However, his curiosity about the matter had risen considerably, so he decided to pay more attention to the road ahead and, by God, the traffic in England *was* disorienting! As if the left-right reversal wasn't confusing enough, the English had these wild roundabouts where four, five, or even six streets met in a circle surrounding an island of grass or flowers. The cars spun round and round, finally tailing off to their left when the desired street came upon them, and he found it dizzying. As hairy as D.C. traffic might get, *this* was absolute chaos. Apparite thought it best he *not* take a drive in this backwards-land: a failed practice session might put him "in hospital," as the Brits said, easy as one-two-three.

But the practiced J didn't seem to be having any problems. Mile after mile of brick apartment and row houses passed, broken by the occasional bombed-out block that hadn't yet been rebuilt after the war, as the Morris made its uncertain, hiccupping and coughing way toward central London. After a time, the buildings thinned and Apparite saw a huge expanse of green ahead.

"Kensington Park," J said as they turned onto Kensington Road.

Kensington Palace soon came into view, followed by the tall, gothic-inspired Albert Memorial on the left and the famous Albert Hall to the right. Apparite had lived in D.C. for some time, and had always looked upon that city's monuments and Federal buildings with some measure of awe, but he could hardly hide his glee at the sight of these famous London edifices. To the young American, London seemed *entirely* to consist of large, ornate, imposing buildings; as if the materials they were made of came from a land where everything naturally grew bigger and more beautiful than anywhere else, and all it took was to find some giant to simply fit them together.

"Yes, it's quite a neighborhood, isn't it?" said J, amused by his young colleague's expression, which showed a combination of innocence and delight. "You look like you're seeing a naked lady for the first time!" he said laughing, and bringing a flush to Apparite's face. "Nearly everything around here was built by Prince Albert and Queen Victoria after the Great Exhibition of eighteen fifty-one, or in memoriam *for* him— she never did get over his death, you know, even after forty years. Shows what determination *and* the fruits of two centuries of colonialism can do, eh?"

The car sped down Exhibition Road, where more architectural wonders lay ahead for the embarrassingly wide-eyed young agent. The huge, Romanesque, terra-cotta Natural History Museum soon passed on his right with the cupola-topped Victoria & Albert Museum on his left, and all the while Apparite's awed expression never wavered: it was stuck there like that of a child who'd just seen an unusually large present awaiting him under the Christmas tree.

After a few more seconds, J turned the car into a neighborhood which seemed to consist solely of beautiful stucco-fronted nineteenth century townhouses and hotels, giving Apparite the impression of being in a living postcard sent by someone on a high-class London holiday. J made a quick turn into a little back-alley mews; he slowed the car and then stopped in front of an old stable door that had been converted into a garage. They had arrived at their safe house.

"It's nearly overwhelming," Apparite said, "especially for someone like me who—"

He stopped and composed himself, having nearly said, "grew up in the Maryland panhandle."

"For someone who's never been here before, I mean," he quickly added.

"Sure, but it'll wear off sooner than you'll like," J said, trying to stifle Apparite's sense of wonder and bring him back into the fold of reality. "London is a lot like an overripe fruit: beautiful and soft on the outside, but on biting into it you may find that the center is rotten. Don't be fooled by her exterior; in many ways, it's an illusion."

J took the key out of the ignition; the Morris, having finally gotten used to the idea of moving, resisted stopping its engine and sputtered on for another full five seconds before it finally gave up the fight and silenced itself.

"This flat will be our safe house: the owner is on an extended trip to India, so we've got the place for three months if needed," said J. "I understand he wanted to go one more time

before 'those damned Indians ruin the whole bloody place,' "
he added in a mock-English accent. "Apparently, he's a little
bitter about it being given back to them after the war, though
in my opinion, both countries are somewhat the lesser for it."

They climbed out of the Morris and J took Apparite's bags
from the boot of the vehicle.

"We're fortunate to have found a place in such a nice,
quiet neighborhood. It's very well located for us, and everybody minds their own business. Let's take those bags inside
and I'll catch you up on a few things." They walked to a door
next to the garage; J took a small, brass key out of his trouser
pocket.

"I'm particularly expert at lock-picking and key-making
on the fly," he said immodestly, inserting the key in the lock
and effortlessly unlocking the door. After opening it, he
jerked his thumb in the direction of a sizable pile of twisted
brass in a wastebasket in the foyer—in it were the remains of
countless, ill-fitting forged-key attempts. J flashed a sheepish
grin.

"Hell, you did eventually get *one* to work didn't you?" said
Apparite.

"*Damn* right," responded J as the two men walked into the
flat. "But I always bring along plastic explosive just in case!"
he added, slapping Apparite in the back and laughing.

The apartment was tastefully furnished in a very literal
British Colonial style: there was wicker furniture mingled
with richly detailed teak and mahogany pieces; manicured
potted palms placed in the corners; ornate Indian rugs covering nearly every inch of the floor; and prints from India,
South Africa, and Singapore gracing the walls. Oddly, there
was nothing from England itself, lending the room an air
which unmistakably shouted, "The Sun Never Sets on the
British Empire." Apparite sat down in a comfortable wicker

chair; J took a seat on a richly decorated sofa of Indonesian mahogany.

"Alright Apparite, here's where we stand. The KGB isn't ready to meet with you; they need more time to get Nikolai, their fuels expert, into England. But when they do, I think they will deal with you on the up-and-up; otherwise, they wouldn't bother bringing him here. I have a photograph of him so we can confirm his presence before the event."

"What about Viktor?" Apparite asked.

"Viktor is here but laying low. I'm sure he does not wish to arouse suspicions or play his hand before he is ready to deal." J's face suddenly got very serious. "He's the real thing, Apparite. Despite his maniacal personality, Viktor's probably the most dangerous man in the world in a face-off. When the time comes, you'll only get the one chance of dealing with him."

"I know; it wasn't difficult to read between the lines of his dossier."

"Then we have our new colleague from MI Five to worry about: Clive Hitch. Frankly, he seems a little shaky to me. Nice enough guy, but he's been through a lot recently: had a messy divorce and then some money troubles. I have a feeling the British have not exactly sent us their best man—you'll see what I mean when you meet him."

"That's not good news," Apparite said. "I've read enough on MI Five to know about their troubles. The last thing we need is a sub-par English agent dragging us down."

"Unfortunately we're stuck with him, and in some ways, we'll need him: it's always handy to have a native on board when you're operating on foreign soil. I've met with him twice in person; the second time I had to let him in on our fuel ruse, but only told him that a man from CI was coming to impersonate Kramer and dupe the Soviets. I'm not telling him anywhere near the complete picture; at least not until I get to know him a bit more and we're closer to the date of the event. He can never know the *full* particulars of our situation, obviously."

"Obviously," Apparite repeated. No one, not even the closest ally, could ever be told of the Director's secret program.

"Hitch has been in contact with an MI Six agent who has infiltrated the KGB; name of William Standerton. He's a near-legend for that feat; probably MI Six's best man: Cambridge-educated, wealthy family, and with an uncle who's in the House of Lords. Served in the Desert Rats in the war for Montgomery, and then was on Horrocks' staff in Operation 'Market Garden' in Holland before joining MI Six. Hitch tells me Standerton has gotten himself situated high enough in the KGB that he should be there when we do the deal. Do you understand what that means for us?"

Apparite understood immediately: it meant everything. With Standerton present, it was practically a sure thing: Hitch could watch the back door and Standerton the front, leaving Apparite with the run of the house, so to speak. The only variables would be the scientist and Viktor, but three agents versus one agent and a scientist sounded good odds indeed.

"When is the event?" Apparite asked.

"We have at least two, three weeks delay. We'll be lucky if their fuel engineer is here in ten days, and knowing the Soviets as I do, it could be even longer—Christ, they're so God damn slow it drives you out of your mind. You know, I doubt we'll have to kill communism, Apparite—it'll just get slower and slower and slower until it simply just *stops!*" He chuckled at his own remark and continued.

"Even after their engineer gets here, we'll have to convince the Soviets with another packet of calculations that you are who you say you are. When the time comes, it'd be best if we let the Soviets select the meeting place—it'll give them confidence that they're not being hoodwinked into anything, especially since this'll be the first time they'll have met Kramer—meaning you, of course—in person. At the earliest, I'd look at October.

"Unfortunately," he added with an amused expression, "that leaves you little to do but to loaf around and see a bit of London. You'll be on your own; you need to avoid being seen in public with either me or Hitch until the last minute, aside from the occasional planning session. Please note that this lovely neighborhood is the home of many consulates, not all of whom are our friends. Learn where they are and avoid them; some have surveillance cameras that photograph anyone who comes near. I would be particularly careful to steer clear of the Bulgarian consulate: the KGB is in and out of there all the time."

"I understand; I will," Apparite said.

"The break will give you a chance to fully recover from your wounds and get back into shape—not that you have fallen much out of it, from what I can tell. But whatever you decide to do with your time, do it *discreetly*. Do not get noticed and do not make noise; blend in with the natives as best you can." J laid a hand warmly on Apparite's shoulder and looked at him with mock-sorrow in his eyes.

"I really hate to say it, but I think it might be best if you spent the next few weeks quietly drinking ale in pubs."

Fourteen
Signal Intrepidity

When Apparite awoke the next morning, he was alone in the flat; with KGB and SMERSH agents roaming around, the two Americans might risk discovery if they stayed in the same place, so J had decided to relocate to another safe house in Chelsea for the time being. The result was that, for the first time in ages, Apparite was his own boss, and he planned to relax and enjoy himself as much as possible. He decided to first take a walk around Hyde Park to start getting back in shape, and then spend some time visiting some of London's famous sights: it sounded to him the perfect way to become acquainted with the city.

After a quick though satisfying breakfast, he took the homemade key, locked the flat, and began walking toward Cromwell Road. His legs felt loose and there was no pain as he strolled down the street; his lungs inflated fully and easily and his arm had no ill-effects from its wound. Nevertheless, he felt he was probably deconditioned from his recovery period—a long, brisk daily walk would be a necessity.

Apparite walked up Cromwell and then turned onto Exhibition Road; when he reached Hyde Park he turned right along its southern edge. More than a few persons were already meandering about the park: mothers pushing prams; students of the London universities studying for their exams (though months away, it was never too early to start, he gathered); and quite a few tourists. The tourists, identifiable by the silver cameras hanging from leather straps around their necks, were taking pictures of nearly anything of even the remotest interest: pigeons, squirrels, London taxis, the famous red double-decker buses, horse riders, and even London "bobbies." Apparite wondered only that they didn't take pictures of each other taking pictures.

The air was crisp, with only a hint of the industrial pollution that Apparite knew was an increasing problem for the city, and the sky was a striking bright blue—an unusual sight in England for any significant time—and he was glad he could enjoy it; he was having quite a nice little stroll. He passed the Duke of Wellington's old house and then on to the Wellington Arch. Pausing to find a break in the increasing traffic, he crossed the road and started up Constitution Hill, noting Buckingham Palace in the distance.

When he reached the sprawling palace, he saw that the Royal Standard was not flying, meaning the Queen was not in residence at the moment: good. If Viktor had any assassination plans, better that the Sovereign be unavailable for a while, although she would eventually have to return for the State Opening of Parliament and Remembrance Day in November. Apparite figured that their problem with Viktor and the Soviets would be cleared up by then.

He wondered if her absence and Viktor's arrival was not mere coincidence: might it have been ordered by MI5 given the recent events and intelligence? He would have to ask Hitch about it when he saw him. It made Apparite realize what high degree of responsibility they had—*one word from people like us and the Queen of England hops the next train for Balmoral*, he thought.

Apparite walked on, though unlike most tourists he did not turn right when he reached the front of the palace, fearing he might end up in a surveillance-photo dossier if he got too near the main gate. Instead, he waited for traffic to thin once again and then crossed the street to the large traffic island on which sat the Victoria Memorial.

Walking around the Memorial, he recrossed the street and proceeded down the Mall, with St. James's Park on his right. *The Mall in D.C. is impressive, but it's not half as classy as what they have here,* he said to himself. Feeling a strange compulsion to wander, he jumped a short iron fence and began walking down one of the park's many paths. He took in its large, inviting emerald lawn, accented by the slow, gentle swaying of trees in the cooling breeze—most noticeably in the willows, whose branches hung like stray locks of long, green hair—and the reflection of the crystalline, clear blue sky in the still water of the pond. He thought it as peaceful a time as he had spent in years.

After a few minutes of contemplation, he turned to his left, walking back onto the Mall until he saw something that stopped him in his tracks: it was the Royal Artillery Memorial; the place where Agent G had been murdered. The memorial was larger than he had expected, consisting of a forty-foot curved wall in front of which was a large pedestal bearing a black statue of Winged Victory and a large stallion. An inscription had been carved into the wall, memorializing the Artillerymen of the South African war of 1899–1902, he noted—interesting, but that had not been the reason he had stopped. Apparite had really wanted to see the rear of the memorial; the place where his colleague had been murdered. He casually walked around it.

Standing behind the memorial, he would never have guessed a man had been killed here: there were no signs of a struggle, or blood; no traces of a life having been taken even vaguely scented the air. And yet Apparite knew it had happened. He stood in a break between two large, mature shrubs: *here,* he thought, was where G would have been, waiting to meet—*who?* Why had he been here that fateful night? What had occurred here?

From where he stood, Apparite realized how vulnerable G had been—anyone could have crept around the edge of the monument and he would have been defenseless. Why would G have put himself in such a vulnerable position? The answer came to him immediately: G hadn't expected an enemy! G had come here to meet someone he had thought was an ally, and had paid for that assumption with his life. But who could have done it? The possibilities flooded into his head: a rogue KGB agent using himself as bait; a SMERSH assassin, posing as a double-agent or friendly contact; an informant turned hostile from the London underworld; or, though he hardly wanted to admit it, even a traitor from CI, MI5, or MI6 who had gained G's trust.

Apparite was sickened at the thought of his fellow Superagent having been killed in such a treacherous fashion, and without a chance to defend himself. He got down on his hands and knees, searching for any kind of clue, but there was nothing—simply the bare ground where Agent G's life had poured out that May night. It didn't seem right that G had lost his life behind a monument honoring brave men who had died doing their duty, and yet there would be no memorial to mark his own sacrifice.

He would visit the memorial many times—discreetly, of course, and varying his route—and each time, he became angrier and angrier at what had passed there. No matter how long it took, Apparite would see that the man who had turned on G and watched him die would follow him to the grave (and by his hand, too, if he had any say in it). And if he survived his mission, he would somehow find a way of remembering Agent G in this very spot—it only seemed right to him.

He made his way back home again in near-silence of voice

and mind, thinking only of what he would tell J about the possible traitor in their midst.

J stopped by the flat that evening; when Apparite told him of his discovery, the liaison arose from his usual place on the sofa and began pacing the room.

"Yes, it all makes sense; I'm only embarrassed that I hadn't figured it out first." J paused for a moment, thinking of the possibilities, and then continued.

"My first thought is that the KGB or SMERSH lured him with the promise of information or defection—even a veteran agent would have been tempted by that. I'm doubtful G would have trusted the London underworld enough to involve them in his activities, or that a British agent would 'turn,' but we need to keep our minds open about any possibility, distasteful as some may be. G was the kind of man who worked alone and confided in few, so we may never know the whole story. In fact, we hadn't had any contact with him for over two weeks before his death, which was usually a good sign from him—he never called unless there was trouble."

"What was he like?" Apparite asked, compelled to learn something about the dead man he had replaced.

"He had a difficult personality and could be rather unpleasant—I have to admit that—but he really knew his stuff. Never complained; could kill a man as soon as look at him, if he had to. Not the type to be fooled by just anyone, or take unnecessary chances unless it was critical. Knowing him as I did, I think the person he was meeting was someone he had a strong degree of trust in. It makes it all the harder knowing he was betrayed by that same man."

"I know I shouldn't ask," Apparite said, "but can you tell me anything about his background, now that he's dead?"

"I can't tell you much, of course, for security reasons, but

I'll say this: he was the type to have worked his way to the top without any help." J paused to catch Apparite's eye. "Remind you of anyone?"

Apparite appreciated the remark, although he found it a little embarrassing to be complimented so directly.

"Thanks for saying so," he answered. "I'll admit that some things have happened recently that have shaken my confidence." Apparite regretted he had said as much as soon as the words had left his mouth.

"Don't worry about what happened at Dolci's," J said, apparently unaware that Apparite had been referring to his anxiety attacks and not his near-death in the butcher shop. "In fact, don't worry about anything except getting the job done." J stopped speaking and looked at Apparite in a reflective manner before continuing.

"Maybe I shouldn't tell you this, but I'd give anything to have your talents, Apparite; *any* of us would. I expect that sometimes you wish you had a normal life—a nice girl; friends to go to the movies with; parties until midnight. Sometimes I do, too, you know—to have a dull, safe, normal life like everyone else. But that's not for us."

"Not if we want to do our duty," Apparite said, hiding his surprise at his colleague's sudden candor.

J sat up straight before speaking.

"That's right," he said forcefully. "Our duty comes first— it *has* to come first. To men like us, nothing else matters, and any way we can get the job done is the right way, no matter the consequences. Sometimes we have to make tough decisions, but in our business the ends *do* justify the means."

Apparite nodded his head in agreement. And yet he was puzzled by J's openness—why was the liaison speaking as if something terrible was about to happen? Or as if Apparite would someday regret joining the Director's agency—or was

211

already regretting it? But he was relieved that J apparently remained unaware of his growing anxiety problem—this mission was too important to take any chances, and Apparite knew he could ill-afford a panic during the event. Nevertheless, the upshot of what J had said reassured him: do your duty and worry about everything else later. The liaison had a tendency to tease him and pull practical jokes, maybe, but he also had a way of putting everything into perspective when it counted.

"Get a good night's rest," J added, "and tomorrow, explore the rest of London and relax. You may learn something along the way—like you did today—so keep your eyes open. I can tell that you're itching to get into a scrape now that you're about healed up, but be patient—you'll have plenty of chances to avenge G before this is over. The less contact we have from now on the better, so I'm going to stay at the safe house in Chelsea until I've worked out our plan. At this point, I don't want to leave a number or address, or have any contact with you. You'll just have to wait to hear from me." He opened the door, but paused to make one last comment.

"Oh—and if your new pink spy shoes come in, I'll let you know right away." J smiled and winked, and Apparite flashed an amused grin back at him. Giving Apparite a friendly and encouraging grip on the shoulder, J walked out of the little flat; a moment later, Apparite heard the bronchial-like coughs and sputters of the Morris' engine flare and then gradually fade into the far reaches of his hearing as J drove the wheezing machine out of the mews.

He lay down in bed and was soon asleep, unusually free from his cares. In some manner, Apparite felt he was discovering his true place in the world, even if it meant hastening the exit of others from it. His only worry was that he might not feel the same way after he had killed again.

★ ★ ★ ★ ★

The next morning found Apparite standing in front of the Gloucester Road underground station's map, trying to find his way to St. Paul's Cathedral (while he hadn't taken to the immigration officer on a personal level, Apparite thought that he could at least follow his advice and see the great cathedral). Although the Tube was reputed to be the best subway system in the world, its famous route map was usually undecipherable to the first-time observer: each line weaved and over-lapped like strands of multi-colored spaghetti with the stations interspersed like meatballs. Most tourists found themselves staring at it interminably while they traced their routes with uncertainty, but Apparite spied his right away: the Piccadilly line to Holborn, and then the Central line to St. Paul's should do it, he thought. Despite the critical nature of his visit, Apparite had really taken a liking to London, and could see himself living there someday (*if* he survived his time as a Superagent, and *if* he collected the five million dollars as promised by the Director, that is).

Stepping off the carriage at St. Paul's station twenty minutes later, Apparite opened the indispensable little London guidebook he had bought at a street side newsstand: the *Geographia Visitors' Guide to London*. He was glad to have found it, but had been sorely disappointed to have come up empty-handed in obtaining something else he had needed even more desperately: the latest American League baseball scores (when he had asked the newsstand operator about them, all he had received was a blank stare). To Apparite's astonishment, there did not appear to be a single Washington or even New York paper for sale in the city, so the disconsolate American had been forced to accept—with great difficulty—a baseball-free existence while he was abroad. It was going to be a long four weeks, he thought.

Still trying to come to grips with this news, he took a cursory look to the right before crossing the street, saw that it was clear, and hurriedly stepped out into the road. A loud horn blared to Apparite's left: a London taxi was fast bearing down on him. Apparite jumped back instinctively and, although the taxi swerved to avoid running him down, its side mirror clipped his left arm, dumping him unceremoniously back onto the curb. Apparite stood up, his face flushed with embarrassment, briskly rubbing his sore arm.

God damn it! he said to himself, upset at his uncharacteristic carelessness, *I need to remember what J said about these ass-backward traffic rules.* He stepped back onto the curb, slowly and deliberately; he looked right then left, and then crossed the street. He felt like a child, but at least he felt like a child that wasn't going to be run over by a London taxi.

He turned a corner and was surprised to see the towering bulk of the cathedral right before him—the buildings surrounding it seemed surprisingly close for such a monumental structure. He strolled along the northern side of the cathedral, turned the corner, stepped inside the west entrance, and stopped: the long, high-ceilinged nave was before him. He bought his admission ticket and resumed walking, albeit slowly, as he quietly, almost reverently made his way down the length of the nave until he was under the dome. He felt unusually serene, as if in a dream where any sudden movement might awaken him and make it all disappear.

He had never been a religious man—his father and mother were Catholic and Episcopalian respectively, and had found a compromise by not raising their son in any denomination at all—but Apparite felt the presence of, well, *something* inside the huge expanse of the cathedral. If it wasn't God, then it was at least the idea that there was a force beyond this world that had united the men who had built this place—mere mor-

214

tals acting on their own could not have done it, he thought.

It was still quite early in the morning and the cathedral was practically deserted; only a few tourists and church employees were present. He craned his neck to look at the ornately decorated ceiling of the dome, described by his guidebook as depicting the great acts of St. Paul. It defied his long-seated cynicism about the world he lived in—the world that had taken his parents away from him—to see what beauty could be created by his fellow man, and the sight affected him deeply. If Apparite had not believed in God until this moment, then afterwards he would at least believe in that indefinable *something;* the vague presence of a force which was felt but could not be touched; was heard but could not be listened to.

He ventured into the North aisle and transept, walking past the huge Wellington Monument until he reached the Regimental Chapel of Middlesex. Looking around him he saw numerous smaller memorials; monuments for brave men who had fought in the Napoleonic Wars, often at the loss of their lives. Many of the men had died quite young—such as Captain Robert Faulknor, just thirty-two years old—and Apparite found what was written on them unusually stirring. He read one softly aloud.

"The circumstances of determined bravery that distinguished this action, which lasted five hours, deserve to be recorded." He quietly read the rest of the account of the battle, ending for Captain Faulknor with his untimely though heroic death. "Soon after this bold and daring maneuver he was shot through the heart," Apparite intoned in conclusion. He could not help but be moved by those final words, etched as they were in this solemn place. He moved on to another.

"Andrew Hay," he began in a whisper as he read the inscription to himself, though speaking the last sentence aloud:

"Closing a military life marked by zeal, prompt decision and signal intrepidity." He wondered what Hay was like: did he dote on his wife? Did he bounce his laughing children on his knee when he returned from his campaigns? Did he feel conflicted about killing so many men, for so many years? Did *he* ever have episodes of panic or self-doubt?

Still walking slowly and in silence, Apparite descended a set of stairs and entered the crypt. Two tombs dominated the low-ceilinged room: Lord Nelson, the great naval hero, shot and killed at Trafalgar, his greatest victory; and Wellington, the "Iron Duke," mastermind of Napoleon's final defeat at Waterloo. Great men, he thought, and impressive tombs, but everyone knows about *them;* pupils in English schools probably take entire courses about them. It was the less celebrated heroes that intrigued Apparite: men like Hay and Faulknor; Thomas Dundas and Charles Napier. Great enough to warrant their place in this massive edifice, but forgotten as *men* by all in modern times.

He went back upstairs after completing his tour of the memorials and tombs in the crypt. Like Agent G, whose name had remained undiscovered by British officials even after his death, John Apparite, J, and even the Director would also probably die forgotten, if not anonymous. And in some ways, he figured, they were already dead: his freshly carved headstone in a Maryland cemetery, courtesy of the Director, attested to that. The deeds of all the brave men in the Director's agency, though done in service to their country, would never be celebrated in great cathedrals like this.

To the rest of the world, their lives were as invisible and shapeless as the presence that he had felt in the nave of the cathedral—yet they existed, all the same. The millions whom Apparite and the Director served would never learn of the men who had fought and died for them; yet perhaps they might know, somehow, that they had. Their deeds would not be writ in any book or carved into any slab, but those they protected would feel their efforts and presence in their lives, if only in their comfort and safety. And it would be best, perhaps, that they would never know of the unspeakable acts Apparite and company would do to keep them so—almost assuredly it would be better that way.

Apparite walked over to the steps leading to the Whispering Gallery, profoundly moved by what he had read and felt in the cathedral and crypt. He might have to break every Biblical commandment to do his duty, most particularly the one that said "Thou shalt not kill," but if done in duty and for a higher purpose—well, he could live with that. Even if John Apparite had doubts about his actions; even if his heart occasionally fled into panic; the inscriptions that he had read in the cathedral ("a military life marked by zeal, prompt decision, and signal intrepidity," "the circumstances of determined bravery that distinguished this action") inspired him, and allowed him some measure of forgiveness for the cruel nature of his profession.

Leaving the nave, he climbed the many shallow steps—all two hundred and fifty-nine of them—that led to the famous Whispering Gallery. The ascent took nearly ten minutes—Apparite moving more slowly than usual in his current contemplative state—but he reached the gallery without tiring. He stepped out onto the balcony and leaned against the chest-high inwardly curving iron rail, looking down at the cathedral floor below.

"*Whew,*" he whistled; it was a long way down but, fortunately, acrophobia was not one of his weaknesses and the sight did not bother him. Looking around, Apparite realized he was alone in the gallery—he had no whispering "partner" to test the unusual sound-effect (usually, two people would walk into the gallery and go to opposite sides of it to whisper against the wall; the sound would be quite audible to the other). He thought he would go to the point of the gallery opposite the stairs; perhaps he could motion the next person entering the gallery into whispering for his benefit.

He walked to the appropriate spot and sat down; unfortunately, no one else had yet entered the gallery. While quietly waiting, Apparite began to reflect on his life to date: he thought of his parents, the Director, his duty to the United States, the men he had killed, Kramer's widowed, cheating wife, his childhood friends, and the pretty brunette stewardess from the flight. He leaned his head slightly to the side and, resting for a moment in deep thought, put his ear against the wall.

And then he heard it; a distinct whisper.

"Apparite."

"Apparite."

"*K——!*"

At the sound of his true name—which now existed only on a cemetery in Maryland—Apparite whipped his head around to look at the opposite side of the gallery. No one was there, but a wave of panic came over him: had it been real, or had it been imagined? Who in all of England could have known his true name? Why hadn't he turned his head when he had first heard the voice say, "Apparite"? It was as if he had been hypnotized and rendered immobile; carved in stone like the statues on the memorials below. He ran across the gallery, raced down the stairs, and saw—no one.

It must have been my imagination, he said to himself; it *must* have been. He left the cathedral shaken and, in some ways, a changed man. He would visit St. Paul's countless times during the course of his life—it would become a point of pilgrimage for him, the one place where he might find a measure of understanding about the nature of his duty, and the horrible deeds his nation would require of him—but it would be the only time he would ever climb those two hundred fifty-nine steps to the Whispering Gallery. It would also be the last time he would hear his true name again, real or imagined, for many years.

Apparite settled into a daily routine as many long weeks passed while awaiting the arrival of the Soviet engineer: each day he had a light breakfast, did calisthenics in the safety of the flat in the mews (five hundred sit-ups, three hundred push-ups, one hundred deep knee bends, thirty minutes of rope jumping, and thirty minutes of *Isshin-Ryu* karate exercises), followed by his daily, vigorous walk through Hyde Park.

He might then catch a famous London attraction in the afternoon—the National Gallery one day, and then the British Museum or the Victoria & Albert the next—but none of them impacted him quite like his emotional experience at St. Paul's. Even Madame Tussaud's famous wax figures left him unmoved, except in the disturbing sense that they reminded him of very freshly minted corpses, and he spent only a few minutes wandering amongst the famous (Queen Victoria and George Washington), and the infamous (Jean-Paul Marat, the Frenchman whose tableau depicting his assassination in his bath had left an especially vivid, macabre taste in his mouth, given Apparite's recent experiences with stabbings and death), before seeking the refuge of the living in the bustle of Marylebone Road outside.

Unmoved by such popular tourist sights, the contemplative Apparite often sought refuge in the usually dark, though rarely quiet London pubs; now, *they* were places he took to right off the bat. The Director had warned Apparite that he had a tendency to drink too much beer—though it was "not felt to be a risk," he had said—so Apparite only partook in a pint or two each evening, but in J's continued absence, that Imperial Pint glass became one of Apparite's closest friends. Young's Brewery will miss *me* when I'm gone, he mused, as he drained the bottom of yet another perfect pint of bitter pulled from the cellar of The George.

Apparite even ventured, against his better judgment, a few discussions with the locals. He always concentrated on the differences between England and America—a sure-fired conversation starter if there was one—though he never let out any personal information, of course. He would usually begin by asking the difference between baseball and cricket, which always initiated a round of good-natured insults from the Brits ("Baseball? Oh, you mean *'Rounders'*—you Yanks have the most bloody awful sort of games; it's nothing like the gentlemanly sport of cricket; it's as dull as the city on a Sunday afternoon; etcetera).

But the young American relished these arguments; they brought back fond memories of hot summer days spent in Griffith Stadium; a National Bo in one hand and a "red-hot" in the other. If he couldn't get news of the "Nats" in London, at least he could remember them by defending the sport they played.

One spirited debate (in the Northumberland Arms, a pretty little pub just off Trafalgar Square) stood above all the others: in it, Apparite not only had to admit but *defend* the notion that the mighty New York Yankees were the greatest sports team in the world—oh, the humiliation of it!—to a pack of boisterous North Londoners. The naïve Brits had been under the misapprehension that a football club called the Spurs could not be topped in the area of world-class athletes (Apparite tried to locate their town, which he believed they called "Hotspur," on a map, but found no such place), and he had felt it his patriotic duty as an American to set them straight, much though it pained him to do so. In its own way, even this exchange was pleasurable to him, despite the heresy of a "Nats" fan admitting the New York Yankees' superiority in *anything*.

After one such evening of pubbing, concluding with a discussion at The Salisbury as to whether Vivien Leigh was the better Blanche in *A Streetcar Named Desire* than Jessica Tandy (though he'd seen only the film version himself), Apparite received a pleasant surprise when he opened the door to his flat in the mews: sitting in his familiar place on the sofa, and having been absent for over a month, was the ever-smiling J.

"You're well past your curfew," he said with a laugh, although Apparite could sense the anxious excitement in his colleague's eyes. "I should probably ground you, young man, but there's important work to do."

J then leaned forward as if he was about to whisper a secret.

"We have our plan."

Fifteen
Clive Hitch

J outlined the mission details the next evening with Apparite over supper at a fish and chips house. After the meal, Apparite couldn't decide which had made him feel more uncomfortable, the convoluted audacity of the plan or the fried haddock he had eaten (the newspaper-wrapped fish was a bit too greasy for his taste), but he had to admit that what J had planned was very good, achieving an almost elegant subtlety in places. The first step to be taken was a meeting with British MI5 agent Clive Hitch at the Red Lion pub near Covent Garden. Before the meeting, J cautioned Apparite about the Englishman once more.

"Hitch is an odd duck; he's the kind of guy the English call a bit 'dodgy,' so remember, only the basics for him at the present."

"Right; I'll let you do the talking," Apparite answered.

J broke into a grin.

"That may have been the single most intelligent statement you have ever made," he said, punctuating it with a chuckle.

Apparite shot him a dirty look—and not entirely in jest, as he could not tell if J had truly been kidding or not—but then a laugh escaped him, too. It wasn't worth arguing over; especially with J, with whom he could never seem to get in the last word.

The two men took the Tube to Leicester Square station; after walking for a few minutes past the brick storefronts and restaurants that populated the theater district, they turned down a little brick-paved alley. Apparite saw the tavern in the distance: a large painted sign of a red lion on its haunches hung over the door of an ancient three story building a short jog ahead. The roar of conversation inside the busy pub greeted them as they entered the open saloon-bar door.

"Hitch is going to save us a booth in the back, for privacy," said J. "The Red Lion is one of the oldest pubs in London, with quite a history behind it: some believe that Blood's plot to steal the Crown Jewels may have been hatched in one of its snugs. Plus—and you'll love this part—the beer's terrific."

They walked inside and saw the pub was indeed as crowded as the noise had hinted. Nearly every cocktail table and booth was full, and there were a considerable number of persons standing about on the bare floorboards.

"Oi!" shouted a voice from one of the dark, wooded booths in the back. J turned to Apparite, motioning in the direction of the voice.

"That's Hitch. As he cannot know our true names, he'll be calling me 'Jack,' and you, 'Robert Kramer,' since that's the part you're playing in the ruse. He's been told we're agents from CI, so we need to act like it."

Apparite nodded in agreement as they walked toward the booth, forcing themselves through a crush of patrons watching a tense football "friendly" between England and Holland on a small, black and white television behind the bar. A televised football match was a rarity and a functioning pub television even more so, so an unusually large and noisy crowd had been drawn to the Red Lion. Apparite thought that Hitch had chosen an opportune time for them to meet: the football match provided good cover, making the pub loud enough to cover their conversation and crowded enough for them to remain inconspicuous. *Maybe Hitch* does *know what he's doing,* he said to himself.

The pub crowd's roar rose audibly as an English midfielder made a run into the penalty area, waned as he was dispossessed of the ball, and then roared again when an England corner-kick was declared. It's almost as intense as a Yankees–Red Sox game, thought Apparite, pushing his way through the throng.

Upon reaching the booth, he turned his attentions to the British agent waiting for them, but was not impressed—the MI5 man's appearance was one that did not radiate much confidence. He was unusually gaunt and had unkempt black hair that needed a trim. His eyes had dark shadows and bags beneath them as if he hadn't slept in a month, and he had an impressively large, protruding Adam's apple, giving Apparite the impression that something was trying to escape from inside his throat. The Englishman rose and held out a somewhat shaky hand; he looked very, very nervous.

"Clive Hitch: happy to meet you, Kramer," the Englishman said, revealing a working-class accent and a slight tremor in his voice. Apparite shook his hand; Hitch had one of those weak, damp handshakes that he had always likened to grabbing hold of a cold hunk of meat. He also noted that Hitch had not greeted J or shaken *his* hand—what might *that* mean? Apparite wondered, sitting down in the booth opposite Hitch.

"Shall I get us a couple of pints?" Hitch asked, rising and walking quickly to the bar before waiting for an answer.

J sat down in the booth next to Apparite.

"See what I mean?" J said. "He's a real live-wire; seems to be powered solely by nervous energy." The crowd roared as a shot from an England striker was a near-miss, causing Apparite to reflexively turn his head toward the television.

Hitch soon reappeared, carefully carrying three pints; they

apparently had been sloshed about considerably, as more than a couple of inches of ale were missing from the top of each.

"Sorry; had a bit of a spill on the way back. A free-kick off the cross-bar—causes a commotion, you know."

Apparite took a sip of the ale Hitch had handed him; it was a bit warm and flat, but delicious and smooth. It would be an effort, he thought, to only have one or two.

"Right," Hitch said, "what's the plan?"

"The mission's objectives are four-fold," J replied in a business-like manner. "One: we kill the Soviet fuel engineer, Nikolai. Two: we plant the phony fuel sample and calculations. Three: we kill as many KGB and SMERSH agents as possible, including Viktor. Four: we do not compromise the security of our own agencies in the completion of the plan. The Soviets have requested that the meeting take place in the British Museum's Reading Room—agreed?"

The noise of the football-watching crowd rose to a shout as a penalty-kick was called against Holland—keeping the three men from speaking aloud for a moment—so Apparite was reduced to silently nodding in agreement. When the noise lessened enough to resume normal conversation, Hitch rose up in his seat and leaned purposefully toward the two Americans with a shocked look on his face.

"What the *bloody hell* do you think you're playing at?"

Apparite glanced at J after Hitch's surprising outburst; the liaison's face wore a mix of shock and disgust that said to Apparite, *this guy is unbelievable.*

The pro-England crowd yelled in surprise and disappointment as the penalty kick was blocked by the Dutch keeper, keeping the three men silent a few seconds longer. When the noise had died down, J spoke.

"I'm sorry," he said to Hitch, with a quiet but rising anger in his voice. "I don't understand what you mean." The subtext was obvious: *That was no way to talk to a fellow agent, Hitch.*

"Well, it's clear to me you're over-reaching," Hitch answered. "No one can do all of that and survive, or avoid exposure. And to do it in the Reading Room! Do you have the slightest idea what the place is like? No wonder the Soviets chose it—it affords them every advantage."

Apparite could see J's mind at work: the wheels were grinding and turning inside so rapidly he could almost hear them.

"Listen, Hitch," J spat out, "we've come four thousand God damn miles, so we're going to do the job just as I've described it—and then some, if we can get away with it. You don't have to worry about losing your skin: Kramer and I will do nearly all of the real work. Your role is going to be a supporting one at most."

Hitch's face abruptly dissembled and he seemed on the verge of tears; it was as if he had changed into an entirely different man right in front of Apparite's eyes, and it was pathetic.

"It's just that," Hitch said, halting between almost every word, "that things haven't been well for me recently. The missus left me; I've got bills to pay . . ." His voice trailed off, as if the effort to complete the sentence would have proved more taxing then it was worth: the man was clearly beaten.

Apparite could not believe this display of weakness: could they really work with this guy? Hitch was a *wreck;* he seemed terribly desperate and just this side of unbalanced. *Christ,* thought Apparite, if the KGB ever got hold of him, he'd turn like a flapjack in the heat of their skillet. Even though J had told him not to open his mouth, Apparite felt compelled to say something.

"Listen, Hitch, we all know how difficult this job will be," he said. "But we've got to do it—it's our *duty* to do it. And if we get through this alive, I'll make it worth your while—if you know what I mean," Apparite added, thinking of the cache of money and bullion hidden in his suitcase. "But you've got to get your mental ducks in a row, or you'll get us all killed."

Hitch composed himself. Pushing a stray lock of hair out of his eyes he sat up rigidly in his chair and took a few deep breaths, shamed by the concern this young American agent was showing him. He looked Apparite directly in the eye.

"You're right, of course; thank you. Please don't mention this to anyone; it won't happen again."

The football-watching crowd roared to an almost in-human level as an English forward made a long run and put a cannon-shot into the back of the net past the stunned Dutch keeper. Barely able to hear himself think in the din, J glanced impatiently at Apparite, the look on his face apparently asking, *can we trust this man with our lives?* Apparite, guessing the intent of his expression, nodded at him as if to answer, *yes, we can; you can leave him to me.* The crowd settled down and J began speaking once again.

"Fine. Now that *that's* settled," he said with distaste, "here are the particulars. In the name of Robert Kramer, I have arranged a dead-drop for the KGB tomorrow to give them fuel calculations and our meeting demands; it'll be at oh-eight hundred near the cottage in Soho Park. The daylight drop gives us the opportunity to tail their courier and locate their safe house so I can do surveillance on them the day of the meeting. Its location changes often, but I think it'll be stable until the event."

"Right; I can tail them easily," Hitch said, confidence returning to his voice although his hands were still trembling.

"The Soviets, as far as I can tell, have no motive other than to get the fuel formula, although they might take the opportunity to kill any of us that are exposed as agents; especially you, Kramer," J said, looking at Apparite. "They must never find out who we really are, or what we mean to do."

Both Hitch and Apparite nodded in the affirmative, and J continued.

"If we are exposed before the meeting we'll have abort the whole operation, so *we*," he said, looking pointedly at Hitch, who reddened at the not-too-subtle hint, "need to make sure we don't slip up."

Hitch looked back at J with annoyance: it was obvious that the MI5 agent couldn't *stand* him. The idea that someone might actually dislike the generally easy-going and likable liaison amused Apparite tremendously; he couldn't wait to needle J about it.

"Also," J said to Hitch, "can you get in touch with your KGB-mole—the man from MI Six, Standerton?"

Hitch blanched visibly at his colleague's name: *Did the two of* them *not get along?* Apparite wondered. Hitch answered after a brief pause.

"No; it's too risky for his cover—if I tried to reach him it might place him in jeopardy. Even though my last contact with him was about two months ago, I'm confident he'd be there for this type of deal. All of the signs point to it."

"What's Standerton like, Hitch?" Apparite asked, trying to defuse the situation by changing the subject. "I'd love to meet the man who infiltrated the KGB."

"You know the type. Family in the peerage, top-drawer marks in school, highest recommendations in every course, chest full of decorations from the war. A bit posh for my taste, but—"

Apparite could see there was more, and guessed at it: Hitch did not like the man *at all;* Apparite figured that

Standerton's overwhelming competence, wealth, and breeding really grated on him. He also guessed that Hitch, who had come from the working class and never had wealth or privilege, had become even more embittered after his own recent misfortunes. Apparite might have felt sorry for him if he hadn't had the feeling that, under the right circumstances, the MI5 man might be ripe to betray them all.

The conclusion of the football match came, closing the books on a one-nil victory for England. A loud roar erupted from the supporters in the pub, breaking the rising tension between the three agents and forcing them to halt their conversation for another moment. When the noise receded, J spoke.

"If we cannot risk exposing Standerton, then it's impossible to count on him being involved in the killings; still, his presence will give us another ally if all hell breaks loose. As long as everything goes to plan, I think he'll be able to continue his mole operations even after mission completion. But be careful: do not do *anything* that might expose him to the Soviets; let him 'escape' after the event."

Apparite and Hitch nodded in agreement; Apparite vigorously, though Hitch begrudgingly.

"Despite your reservations, Hitch, I believe the Reading Room of the British Museum is the perfect location for us—I don't have any problems with it at all," J continued. "From what I understand, it takes a 'Reader's Ticket' to get in, which limits the number of people present at the engagement—and that's always desirable for us. You can obtain one of those tickets for yourself through MI Five, correct?"

Hitch nodded in agreement.

"Yes, they can get one for me. As for the Soviets, I'm guessing their consulate is providing theirs."

"I figured that, too," answered J. "In a couple of days, I'll send an intermediary to pick up Kramer's ticket—the Soviets are mailing it to a post office box. As for how many they'll bring to the meeting, I'm guessing there'll be three: Nikolai, Viktor, and—we all hope—Standerton. Since they chose the meeting place, we're going to insist on setting the time of the event—we can't roll over and let them take charge of *everything* or they might get suspicious. But the Soviets *have* requested that Kramer sit at Reader's Desk A-seven and seem firm on that—do you have any idea where that is, Hitch? I only had a quick look around the room yesterday before the attendants ejected me."

"I do, actually," Hitch answered. "It's been about a year since I've been there, but I think that seat is in the back of the room, near the north exit. I don't see that as a problem. As far as a meeting time is concerned, I'd think that as late in the day as possible might be best, especially on a Monday—with any luck, the room might be nearly deserted. I'd recommend a sixteen-thirty meeting since it closes at seventeen hundred."

"Fine," J said as the tension between them appeared to dissipate. Apparite saw that J, despite his misgivings about the MI5 agent, was making the effort to involve him and boost his confidence. "Whatever we do in there, it must be done discreetly and, most important, *quietly.* We cannot attract the attention of the attendants or the other readers—is that possible, Hitch?"

"If seat A-seven is where I remember, then yes, I suppose so. They've rearranged the front desk and card catalogues so that area is in a bit of a blind spot—it's clear on the other side of the room from the main entrance. I'm sure that's the reason the Soviets chose it." Apparite could see Hitch's confidence rising as he spoke, and thought it a very good sign. "As far as remaining quiet, I think that even a quick stabbing or garroting would probably draw just a vigorous shushing from other readers; at least until they figured out what was happening. Also, the volumes of books surrounding you tend to dampen the noise; especially in those seats, which are quite close to the stacks."

Hitch stopped speaking to think on it for a moment.

"Yes, I think it could be done without attracting undue attention," he continued after a few seconds. "But if anyone did cry out, the exit is close by; it leads past the British Library stacks that surround the Reading Room and then out onto Montague Place—as nice a route for a quick escape as anyone could ask for."

"Good," said J. "The Soviets won't want to attract attention either, and that's to our advantage as well. Kramer," he said, indicating Apparite, "will sit at the Reader's Desks with the Soviets and do what has to be done. Hitch, you should position yourself nearby, but not within their line of sight."

"There's a small coat closet near the north exit that I can slip into if need be," Hitch replied. "Otherwise, I'll stand just outside the room and browse through books in the library stacks."

"There's one last item, Hitch," added J.

"What's that?" he asked, a bit peeved at a tone he had perceived in J's voice.

"Are you *absolutely* sure Standerton will be at the meeting? Only he can provide us with the numbers we need to guarantee the assassinations of Viktor and the scientist go off smoothly. With Standerton at our side, success is almost a sure thing. Without him, it's less than a fifty-fifty proposition in my estimation."

"Yes; Standerton will be there. I'm really quite certain of that," said Hitch, his confidence palpably plummeting to its previous depths at the mention of his MI6 colleague. It was apparent that Hitch was displeased at the respect the two Americans were giving Standerton; a man that, unbeknownst to them, Hitch had not only disliked but *despised* for years with an absolute, jealous passion.

"We'll include our demands for the meeting particulars in tomorrow's dead-drop material," said J. "If they show at the Reading Room at sixteen-thirty on Monday, we'll know they've bought into our ruse."

J paused, and looked pointedly at Hitch.

"I *cannot* overestimate the importance of Standerton being at this deal," he said, inadvertently tipping his hand and revealing his rather underwhelming faith in the MI5 agent.

"I'm sure of it," Hitch replied with a nervous insolence in his voice. "I'm sure of it."

Sixteen
The Tail

Apparite was waiting for Hitch outside Leicester Square Station at 0730 before the dead-drop the next morning, anxious to gauge the MI5 agent's mood after the events of the day before (J would be the one to leave the package itself, consisting of pages and pages of bogus fuel calculations and theory, plus the details for the final meeting the next Monday: "1630, Reader's Desk A7, Reading Room, British Museum").

Hitch saw Apparite standing outside the station and waved to him; even at a glance the MI5 agent seemed more relaxed and settled to the Superagent, in contrast to his bizarre and disturbing behavior at the Red Lion. Was he getting comfortable with the plan and the players? Or had he made some decision about his future? If so, Apparite hoped it was retirement from MI5 rather than recruitment into the KGB, but either way, he knew he would have to watch him very carefully. Hitch spoke as Apparite reached him, his voice sounding more confident than Apparite had heard before.

"It was my idea to make the drop in Soho Square, you know. We believe the KGB safe house is near, and by dropping the package between Underground stops their courier will probably walk or take a taxi. Makes it easier for us to tail him that way, rather than chasing him around the Tube, eh?"

Apparite nodded, smiling; Hitch was seeking his approval and he would be good enough to give it to him. On the inside, however, he remained as vigilant as ever for signs of impending betrayal or cowardice.

"It's a good plan," Apparite replied with good cheer in an effort to bolster Hitch's optimism. "As long as we keep him in our sights, it should be easy enough to follow him to their safe house, barring a wild goose chase. Do you think we'll see Viktor or the engineer?"

"No," Hitch answered. "Viktor would never get involved with lowly work like this; he'll assign it to his KGB minions. And they'll keep the engineer sequestered until the meeting—he's too valuable a commodity to let walk around in public. I don't think we'll have too much trouble today; from what I've seen of the London KGB, their agents look young and freshly trained, and I'm betting their courier will be a bit careless. I think he'll make a token effort to circle around a few blocks, but I doubt he'll be able to lose us. As long as he stays out of the Underground, we'll be fine. Besides, I have a secret weapon."

"What's that?" Apparite asked.

"Wait here."

Hitch jogged toward Leicester Square, just out of sight. Apparite then heard the sound of a car starting; not the Morris's horrible coughs and wheezes, but the smooth, firm hum of a highly capable machine. The sound came closer and closer, and then he heard the honking of a car horn and a shout.

"Over here!"

Apparite turned and saw a sight that released a guffaw of unrestrained laughter from him: Hitch, wearing the complete vestments of a London taxi driver, was sitting behind the wheel of one of the famous and ubiquitous black London taxis. It was a brilliant stroke; even the KGB would have difficulty detecting and losing a tail by a London cab! Apparite walked up to the vehicle.

"Perfect, Hitch; absolutely 'spot-on.' "

Hitch smiled in acknowledgement to the compliment.

"Thanks. Pop-on in the rear seat, and happy hunting to us."

After Apparite climbed into the cab, Hitch drove down Coventry Street toward Piccadilly. No matter what Apparite had thought of Hitch's abilities as an agent, the Englishman was a terrific driver. As Hitch smoothly glided the large car through congested and confusing Piccadilly Circus (a half-dozen chaotic streets that seemed to lead into the Circus but not out of it!) and then up Regent, Apparite was impressed: the MI5 man knew his way around London. He'd be sure to tell J how Hitch had risen to the occasion; perhaps he could thaw the "cold war" that existed between the two of them.

Hitch parked the cab a block from Soho Square; the drop site was obscured somewhat by tall shrubs, but Apparite's unusually good eyesight could discern it reasonably well.

"I don't want to get too close until it's almost time," Hitch said. "But I doubt we'll have to wait much past eight: the Russians won't let a package like that sit for long."

Apparite nodded in agreement, carefully examining Hitch's expression and demeanor, but there was absolutely no trace of the anxiety and tremulousness that he had exhibited yesterday. Hitch *had* made a decision about himself, he thought.

"I noticed that you and 'Jack' don't get along very well," Apparite said, referring to the discomfort apparent between Hitch and J.

"He doesn't trust me—would you want a bloke like that to be a mate?"

"Jack's a good man; he's just very cautious, Clive," Apparite replied, hoping the use of the Englishman's Christian name might open him up. But Hitch did not respond; he continued sitting in silence as if the conversation had ended.

Apparite did not have the luxury of time: he needed to find out what was on the MI5 agent's mind, and soon. He decided to provoke Hitch, even at the risk of alienating him, thinking he might divine something from his reaction.

"I'm concerned about you. It's obvious you're unhappy, and if you can forgive me for saying so, it's the disgruntled agents that become ripe for the picking."

Dead silence. Unexpectedly, Hitch hadn't reacted at all to Apparite's probing statement; he continued to sit mute in the front seat of the cab, staring off into space. Is he oblivious to what I'm saying? thought Apparite.

Suddenly, Hitch turned his body in order to face the rear seat and spoke in anger.

"Don't talk rubbish: I may be many things, but a traitor isn't one of them. Even though I've given MI Five over a decade of service, my superiors want to be rid of me just as much as your mate Jack does; that's why they lent me to you in the first place. And I'm ready to give them exactly what they want—I'm getting out as soon as I can."

His outburst destroyed Apparite's budding faith in the Englishman. A cynic reading into Hitch's statement might guess that he was either going to deep-six the mission and quit, or possibly defect to another agency that would better appreciate his talents. And yet it wasn't that simple, thought Apparite: Hitch *had* come up with the details of the drop, plus the brilliant idea of the London taxi, and that admittedly stood well for him.

Confused and deciding not to confront him further, Apparite thought he would place Hitch's statements in a mental file that he would open for J the next time he saw him. The two of them would put the pieces together in private at that time, and figure out what to make of everything.

"Let's keep our minds on the task at hand, Hitch; you can worry about quitting later."

Apparite looked at his watch; it was 0748.

"I'm going to pull a little closer," said Hitch. He put the cab into gear and drove another half-block nearer the square: Apparite could plainly see the dark-timbered outline of the small cottage behind a statue of King Charles II; J, he knew, had placed the package in a decorative concrete planter on the west side. They waited for fifteen and then thirty minutes, but there was still no sign of the courier.

"Are you sure they'll bite?" asked Hitch; it was almost 0820.

"They'll bite," answered Apparite. "They're desperate for that fuel formula; they'd pay millions for it." He immediately wished he hadn't said that—he didn't need to give Hitch any ideas on how to make a quick million pounds.

"Wait—over there!" Apparite added, spying a man walking a little too nonchalantly toward the cottage, eventually stopping next to one of the concrete planters on the west side of the square. The man clumsily bent over to tie his shoes—he's being much too obvious, thought Apparite, immediately pegging him as an inexperienced agent—and on standing reached into the concrete planter. He surreptitiously placed the small black tube he had found into his trench coat's pocket, and walked northward at a brisk but inconspicuous pace.

Hitch pressed on the accelerator and followed the Russian, keeping the cab about one hundred feet behind him. The KGB agent made a couple of turns through which Hitch was easily able to follow, but eventually the Soviet turned down Charing Cross Road, and Hitch had to alter his route: Charing Cross was a high traffic, one-way street at this point, and they were facing the wrong direction. Hitch crossed

Charing Cross, turned the taxi down a side street to the right, and then doubled-back again, recrossing Charing Cross with another abrupt right turn. Apparite was becoming worried: how could they *possibly* pick-up the KGM man after this sudden detour?

"Gerrard!" Hitch shouted. "He's gone down a one-way street he knows a tail can't follow, and then he'll cut across and go through the crowds on Gerrard Street into Soho." Apparite had no idea how Hitch could have guessed this, but deferred to the MI5 agent's superior knowledge of London.

Hitch turned sharply to the right and drove another block. He then took a left, stopping at the western end of Gerrard Street, which was becoming London's new Chinatown (the prior one in the East End having been leveled in the Blitz); it was lined with busy restaurants and shops. Through the crowd they could see the KGB agent: he was about one hundred fifty feet behind them but was now walking *toward* them, still moving at a brisk pace.

"Amazing," Apparite said in admiration of the MI5 agent's instincts. "How did you know?"

Hitch looked in the rear-view mirror and smiled at Apparite, but didn't answer. Looking at the KGB man, Apparite could see that he was oblivious of the tail: his gait, which had been brisk but stiff and cautious, now had the discernible cocksure swagger of one who believes he has gotten away with something.

The KGB man turned up Wardour, taking no notice of the two men in the London taxi parked less than ten feet away as he sauntered past them. Hitch followed the man from a discreet distance as he eventually turned left onto Broadwick, and then disappeared into a small side street. Hitch sped up the cab, just in time for Apparite to see the KGB agent slip into a small door a short distance down an alley. They had him.

"He went into a door in the alley—that must be the place," Apparite said. "We should probably make sure he's not going to pass through the building and keep walking."

Hitch nodded; whipping the cab expertly in a turn he drove around the block. He slowed at the point opposite where the agent had entered the building from the alley, but no one appeared. Hitch drove around the block a few more times and, as there was still no sign of the agent, he made a turn and began to drive toward the starting point at Leicester Square. He was beaming with pride, like a traditionally sub-par schoolboy who had unexpectedly received top marks.

"Looks like that was the place," Apparite said. "That was damn fine work, Hitch; congratulations. I bet even Standerton would have been impressed." Apparite saw Hitch stiffen in the front seat, and regretted having invoked the MI6 agent's name.

"Please don't mention him to me again," said Hitch in disgust. He took the taxi out of gear, put on the brakes, and let it idle at the curb.

"I'm sorry, Clive. Is there something between the two of you that I should know about?"

"He's been 'taking the piss' out of me for ten years," Hitch answered, his voice tight and strained. "Ever since we went through training together after the war. I'm sure you've been around blokes like him: if there was a bird I fancied, he'd get off with her; if there was an exercise, he'd make damn sure I 'bollocks'd' it." He looked downward, averting his eyes from Apparite's gaze in an unconscious gesture of embarrassment.

"There was an instructor at my Academy; taught karate," Apparite said. "He made my life a living hell for an entire year; the SOB even insulted my mother. I doubt there's ever been a man I hated as much."

"What did you do?" Hitch asked.

"I beat the living s—t out of him after the course was over," said Apparite, a broad smile forming on his face in remembrance. "Man, it felt good."

"There's no way of doing that with Standerton. He's the best hand-to-hand man in MI Six. Studied SAMBO; highest degree *Shotokan* karate black belt."

"Maybe you can even the score by getting this mission done and then quitting—leave on a high note," Apparite said, injecting as much encouragement as he could.

"Maybe. Or I could—" Hitch said, muttering a few more soft, inaudible words before cutting himself off. But Apparite knew Hitch was leaving something important unsaid, and it worried him.

Hitch revved the taxi's motor, pressed the accelerator, and drove off down the street with a lurch. The Englishman spoke once again, though in a more firm tone of voice and with an obvious change of subject in mind.

"I'll drop you off at Leicester Square Station. I'll see you on the day of the event."

Apparite wondered what Hitch had meant to say that moment before and, after a little reflection, he had a good guess: after the deal, *Hitch was going to kill Standerton.* And when that evil deed was done, concluded Apparite, what choice would Hitch have but to defect? Apparite tried to convince himself that he must be wrong, but it was the only way he could put it all together and have it make sense.

He would have to tell J, but what could they do—kill Hitch? Tell his superiors? The rest of the drive was done in complete silence, and when he was let off at the station Apparite did not even bother saying good-bye. The cold war between Hitch and J was about to become hot—*very* hot—and Apparite, who had been warming up to the MI5 agent, now felt the need to keep his distance from him: the man's days, he feared, might just be numbered.

The rest of his day was spent figuring what he would tell J about Clive Hitch, although he knew he had to be careful: if he was too harsh on the unfortunate MI5 agent, J might recommend termination without a second thought, and Apparite didn't want to be the one to have condemned Hitch without adequate proof. But if he under-painted the scene, glossing over his suspicions, then J might ignore what Apparite had discovered about Hitch, and the meeting could explode in his face come Monday. And yet despite his suspicions, Apparite had to admit that Hitch, though the very picture of an agent vulnerable for KGB recruitment, had not said or done anything solidly incriminating enough to convict him in his mind as a traitor.

And given what Hitch had said about Standerton, there was now a second question for Apparite to consider as well: if Clive Hitch could kill a decorated MI6 agent like William Standerton, could he also have killed a Superagent like G? Apparite thought and thought on the question, and came to this conclusion: he did not believe the Clive Hitch he knew could have done it.

The man who had lured G to his death must have been cool and calculating to have gained the experienced Superagent's trust, he thought, whereas Hitch was desperate, burned-out, and skittish. But even if he wasn't, perhaps, the man to have murdered G, Apparite could not dispel the notion that Hitch had the means and impetus to kill Standerton, whom the MI5 agent had long viewed as his personal enemy. Apparite knew that he could not stand by and wait for MI6's most talented agent to possibly be assassinated by a British colleague. What course to take, however, continued to elude his reasoning.

★ ★ ★ ★ ★

Apparite slept uneasily that night. He did not usually remember his dreams, but an especially vivid one had persisted into the morning: he was in a field, hiding from unseen enemies; it was raining and cold. Just as Apparite was to escape to safety, a bright klieg light found him, though he was unable to see the operator's face. A dozen KGB agents ran toward him, guns drawn, each holding an iron shackle to bind him; he turned to flee but saw another man walking in his direction: the klieg light operator. The man's bright light remained fixed on Apparite as he approached, his face still shielded from view, until finally the light was removed and he revealed himself to the captured Superagent: it was Hitch.

Apparite awoke with the dream still foremost in his memory; the clock read 0415. He pushed whatever significance the dream held for him out of his mind and fell back asleep once more. When he awoke for good, two hours later, most of the dream had disappeared into the cool English night, except for one image: the disturbing sight of Clive Hitch pointing him out to the KGB. He knew this image could not easily be dismissed as anxious fantasy, especially since he feared it might prove to be true.

After a poor imitation of an English fry-up, he heard a knock on the door; it was J. Apparite took a last sip of coffee—the one part of breakfast he *could* make better than any Englishman or London eatery—poured a cup of it for the liaison, and let him inside.

"From my perspective, the drop went well," J said with his trademark grin. "I dropped off the goods a little after seven, took the Tube all over London, and then did some sightseeing for a few hours afterwards. I'm confident I lost anyone trying to tail me."

Apparite thought the extreme precautions typical of J,

whose forte was in secrecy and planning.

"Our part went well, too," responded Apparite. "Hitch really came through in the clutch on this one." He told of Hitch's brilliance with the taxi, his expert driving, and his full command of the situation. He would test J's reaction before springing his suspicions about the British MI5 agent on him.

"Well, I *am* surprised," J said. "I didn't think the man had it in him—after the meeting at the Red Lion I was frankly pretty worried. I thought we might have to go to his supervisors, at the risk of exposure, or even terminate him. Our situation is difficult enough as it is without problems like this: it's frowned-upon for American agents to operate in the U.K. in the first place, so we're basically on our own."

And then Apparite let loose his bombshell.

"I think Hitch might be planning to kill Standerton."

In his astonishment J nearly dropped the cup of coffee Apparite had drawn for him.

"How do you know?" J said; his eyes were narrowed and his voice hurried in extreme concern.

"He nearly said as much during the tail. Hitch *despises* him; practically blames him for every misfortune he's had in MI Five. Unless I'm reading him all wrong, I don't think Hitch was the man who killed G, but I believe he could kill Standerton. What I don't know is if he can be trusted to go through with our deal first."

J thought for quite some time before speaking.

"With the event less than a week away, and the invitations already in the mail, it's too late for us to get rid of him and find a replacement from MI Five. We have two choices, then, as I see it: you could kill him and I'd take over his part, but the risk would be unacceptable; for security reasons, you and I can never be together in the presence of the enemy. Or—and I hate to say it—we can take our chances with him."

"Couldn't I just do it alone? Standerton will be there; even odds at least," Apparite said.

"No, we need better than even odds for this deal, especially with Viktor being a part of it." J paused in thought; he then made a serious face.

"Tell me what you think of Standerton: would Hitch *really* kill him? How sure can you be of it?"

Apparite thought for a minute to find the right words.

"Call it a hunch, but there's something about Standerton that feels a little too perfect to me, even though I've never met him. Maybe it's because of my own upbringing, from humble origins like Hitch, but I understand some of why he feels the way he does. What Hitch said about Standerton had *realness* to it; it struck me as the truth and not just the sour grapes of an unhinged agent. He might hate Standerton with a passion but, if you need an answer, I'm betting he *won't* kill him. I can't be even reasonably certain of that, but there you have it." Apparite stopped to think on it further, and then continued.

"I hope to God I'm right, because if Hitch *were* to kill Standerton, where else could he go but to the Soviets? And that would be a disaster for all of us."

J gave Apparite a long, hard look: he was making damn sure Apparite was holding nothing back from him; that he was getting the straight poop. Satisfied at last, after a full, agonizing minute of staring at him—like the Director used to, Apparite noted—J breathed out deeply and visibly relaxed.

"If I'm reading the situation right—and after your story, I think I am—we've come to this: we've gone too far to flush this deal down the toilet because an unhappy MI Five agent hates one of his colleagues. We'll have to go with our plan as is, but you'll have to watch Hitch as closely as you'll watch Viktor, if you can. If there's any sign he's going to kill

Standerton, if there's any sign he's not on our side, if there's any sign of *anything* you don't like, then *kill* the sorry son of a bitch. I wish I could be more confident Hitch will help us until after the event, but at this point, I think if he's going to kill Standerton—if what you've told me is correct—then it'll be *after* the meeting. To be straight with you, although it would be a shame to lose a man like Standerton, his life doesn't mean nearly as much as the success of the mission. But the final decision, I'll leave up to you: it's your ballgame. What do *you* think we should do?"

Apparite thought again for a moment and found enlightenment in a most unlikely place: the inscriptions he had read so many times at St. Paul's. Like Andrew Hay or Robert Faulknor, John Apparite was going to do his duty for his country, no matter the odds or prospects, bartering with his very life in the process. He was ready to do it even if it meant killing Hitch; he was ready to do it even if it meant dying. Apparite, who had been searching for something to believe in ever since his mother had died, had finally found it: he would believe in his duty to his country; he would place it above all other earthly wants and needs in his life, separate from any human desires, passions, or jealousies he might have.

But had he sensed that same call to duty in Clive Hitch? Was the MI5 agent prepared to sacrifice all for *his* country? Certainly, Hitch had let his foibles and faults get the better of him; had let Standerton's niggling and successes nearly ruin him; and who could say that when the anvil was before him, agent Clive Hitch would bring the hammer down onto it? Yet Apparite had to give him credit for his performance the day before, when he had done so well with the tail. And there was something else that stood in Hitch's favor, but on a more gut level: while Hitch was plenty disgruntled and bitter, the MI5 agent didn't have the grasping, ambitious *feel* of a traitor.

Hitch might not be the best man England had to give, but Apparite believed that underneath that nervous and bitter exterior there did beat the heart of a patriot.

Apparite had his answer: he would trust Hitch just this once, even at the risk of his own life. If his trust proved unfounded and he got killed because of it, Apparite would at least die knowing he had done so in the defense—naïve though it would be—of the man's belief in his duty, and in that he would have no regrets.

"I'm willing to take the chance that Hitch is on the up-and up," Apparite said, his steady voice conveying the firmness of his decision. "But if he makes one wrong move, I'll kill him." His mind had been irrevocably made: Apparite would trust Hitch to show *his* "signal intrepidity" come Monday afternoon, even if he got killed because of it.

Seventeen
Chaos in the British Museum

J wanted the next few days to be spent in quiet preparation for the meeting in the Reading Room, so after briefing Apparite one final time on the details of the plan, at which time he gave him his Reader's Ticket, he told him they must not be seen together until mission completion; Apparite was also to avoid meeting with Hitch as well, unless it was an absolute emergency. Apparite understood J's concern, but had hoped to speak privately with the MI5 agent once more before the critical day—perhaps he could have drawn Hitch out further and learned what he intended to do, or even gotten the Englishman to change his plans if he didn't like what he heard.

Instead, Apparite was left with only an impression of the strange dichotomy of Clive Hitch to reflect upon; a man who, depending on the situation and mood, might assume one of two forms: the jealous, anxious man who might destroy everything, or the highly competent agent who had outwitted the KGB after the dead-drop in Soho Square. Apparite had to believe it was the second, professional version of Hitch who would show up at the meeting in the Reading Room, and not the first—the one that might get them all killed.

The night before the event, he went through the final plan details carefully in his mind: at 1400 the next day, J would station himself near the KGB safe house where he would make visual contact with the Soviets. The liaison would then call Apparite and Hitch—who would be waiting back at the

247

flat in the mews—from a public kiosk phone at 1530 and let them know how many men were in the Soviet party, which ones appeared to be armed, and whether Viktor, Nikolai, and Standerton were among them.

Hitch would carry his old but reliable .25 caliber Webley & Scott semi-automatic pistol and silencer, and would hang back outside the Reading Room's North exit to provide cover and assistance if needed. Apparite, who would be impersonating a presumably unarmed scientist (and who might be searched), would have to remain unarmed for the meeting. Complicating matters, as he was portraying a man about to defect, Apparite would not be able to search the Soviets himself, for fear of raising suspicions—it was, after all, supposed to be a friendly meeting between budding "comrades." J had considered hiding a weapon in the book stacks for Apparite, but had dismissed the idea: if it was discovered by either the Soviets or the Reading Room supervisors, the entire mission would be in jeopardy, not to mention the obvious problem of having Apparite retrieve it without attracting attention. They simply couldn't take that kind of a chance.

Apparite would not be without weapons entirely, however. He would be concealing a switchblade in his belt and, as at Dolci's, the all-metal throwing knives and garrote apparatus in his shoes. The Director had also given him another, more sinister weapon to be used as a last resort: a fountain pen that contained a hypodermic needle which, when pressed against the clothes of the victim and a button was pushed, injected a highly lethal dose of *Ricinus communis* poison; the same chemical that had ended the real Robert Kramer's life. Using the knives, wire, or possibly the poison pen, he would have to assassinate Viktor and Nikolai, and do it in near-silence. Difficult, he thought, but not impossible.

Apparite looked at the diabolical fountain pen apparatus

and asked himself one last, critical question: would he panic when it came time to inject the deadly poison, like he had with Kramer? *No*, he thought; *not this time*. His conscience seemed clear in regard to his obligations to the Director and the needs of his agency: just the day before, he had visited St. Paul's one final time to reconcile himself with the requirements of his deadly duties; to reach the necessary balance between John Apparite the man, and Agent E the assassin. He prayed that this delicate but essential balance would not be upset by what might occur in the coming hours.

He then ran through all of the possible scenarios of the meeting, and was encouraged by his conclusions: as long as Standerton could back him up, and Hitch did not interfere with his MI6 colleague, Apparite felt success was a certainty. The only way disaster might strike would be if Hitch appeared and killed Standerton before Apparite had a chance to deal with Viktor and Nikolai, or if Hitch was indeed the traitor and exposed them all to the Soviets. Both possibilities seemed unlikely to Apparite from what he had guessed about Clive Hitch in the past week.

He could not be sure of it, however, and knew doubt would remain until the mission was completed. But if Hitch indeed rose to the occasion, Apparite remained prepared to give him the cash and bullion hidden in his bags; at least fifty thousand dollars, he guessed. While he thought J and the Director would probably have approved of the measure, it was a subject Apparite was *not* going to bring up with them unless pressed.

J's plan was a good one, and Apparite gave the liaison credit for it. It seemed a lifetime ago the two men had first met—when J had interrogated Apparite at gunpoint in the Director's final test—and yet in truth it had only been about two months. Rather than being envious of J's position of relative safety back at the mews, he was relieved that the liaison would be out of harm's way when the deal went down—at this time in Apparite's life, J was about the only real friend he had.

He undressed for bed and lay down, reciting the inscriptions from St. Paul's in his head; after a time, he had turned them into a sort of mantra that comforted him: he would do his duty; J would do his duty; Hitch would do his duty. They would show their "signal intrepidity," and then the job would be done. His conscience and mind felt clear after a few repetitions, and he fell asleep to another night of unremembered dreams. When he awoke the next morning, he was ready.

He spent the bulk of the meeting day stretching, exercising, and going over the plan in his mind: the time for philosophizing was over. When Hitch came to the mews at 1500, Apparite tried to gauge the Englishman's mood. Dressed smartly in a heavy black suit and looking more composed than usual, Hitch seemed to have more of the competent MI5 agent in him than the other variety: good, thought Apparite. Over a cup of tea expertly made by the Englishman, they went through the plan together, discussing every detail: Hitch was to remain out of sight but within earshot; he was not to involve himself in any of the dealings unless it was of the strictest urgency; and he was not to approach Standerton for fear of exposing him unless there was a critical need.

Apparite continued to read Hitch's demeanor during these discussions, but was unable to discern anything unusual: the MI5 agent's expression remained a complete blank, betraying not an ounce of excitement or anxiety—even at the sound of Standerton's name—and Apparite thought that a good sign as well. They then checked over their weapons, discussed their escape routes, and silently sat and waited for J's telephone call.

Fifteen anxious minutes turned into thirty, and then forty-five; still no word from J. Apparite remained calm but, despite his efforts at emotional detachment, small slivers of anxieties were slipping through his guards: had J been discovered? Had the Soviets not taken the bait? He pushed these intruding thoughts aside and focused on his weapons: the knives in his shoes; the garrote wire; the switchblade; the poison pen. He might need to use them all.

The phone rang; Apparite let it ring twice more and then picked it up. It was J.

"I'm fine," he heard J say in a pleasant, casual tone. "Everything is going just as we thought. We're having three for supper; the usual crowd, as expected. I'm not sure if they're bringing anything; we'll just have to see when they arrive. I think we'll have a good time; I'll see you later back at the house." He hung up.

Apparite was relieved at the news. Three men were coming, J had said, and they would be Viktor, Standerton, and Nikolai. He could not tell if they were armed, but Apparite assumed that probably Viktor and Standerton would be carrying guns. Everything was according to plan: good. Apparite was disappointed that J hadn't ended the call with a joke or—more typically—an insult for him, but he understood that in some situations the usually jovial J could be all business. There'd be time for joking around after it's all over, he thought, with plenty of ale to be downed as well.

"Let's go," Apparite said. The two men left the little flat and walked to the Gloucester Road station in silence. To anyone else on the Tube, neither of the men would have seemed to be in conscious thought—each one quietly staring straight ahead on his journey—nor would they have connected the two of them in any way, right up to their final stop at Tottenham Court Road. They left the station together—and yet apart, to a casual observer—without speaking, and walked up Great Russell Street, Apparite about ten feet ahead of Hitch, until the imposing columned façade of the British Museum came into view.

They continued to walk toward the museum gates; Apparite twenty feet ahead of Hitch. Hitch slowed and slipped into a nearby telephone booth, pretending he needed to make a call. Apparite, now thirty feet ahead of Hitch, turned left through the gates and started to walk across the spacious plaza that led to the museum's front steps. When Apparite began skipping up the steps to the main entrance, Hitch put the phone back on its rest, to all appearances having just completed his call.

But instead of leaving the phone booth and continuing his walk up Great Russell Street, he pulled a small pewter flask from his shirt's left breast pocket. He drained the flask of its contents—an ounce of blended Scotch whisky—placed the flask back into the pocket, and then opened the door to the phone booth. Taking a couple of deep breaths to steady his nerves—he had hidden them well in front of the young American, but now they were coming out again—he started walking up the street once again. When he reached Montague Street, he turned left; his plan was to circle the museum and then go inside through the rear entrance off Montague Place.

Apparite entered the museum and looked at his watch; he had seven minutes to spend until he was due at the meeting. He walked through some of the exhibits to pass the time—the Elgin Marbles, and examples of Greek and Roman statuary—before deciding it was time to head in the direction of the Reading Room. He had been on a brief tour of the museum a few days after arriving in London, but the room itself had not been explored ("The world famous Reading Room," the guide had said, going only as far as pointing toward the British Library before launching into the rest of her spiel).

But he did recall the guide saying that the Reading Room was where Karl Marx had researched and wrote *Das Kapital*. It was also interesting, she had said, that Lenin and Trotsky had had Reader's Tickets earlier in the century, and had used the room as well. Funny, Apparite thought, that in the very birthplace of communist thought, a modern, deadly battle of competing capitalist and communist nations was going to occur in a scant few minutes. He did *not* think Marx would have approved of it, however.

Although Hitch had briefed him in detail on the Reading Room's layout, Apparite wished he had been able to visit it himself. Much would depend on the subtleties of the room's anatomy (a place where he could seek cover being one of his biggest concerns), but J had felt it too risky for Apparite to personally explore it in the days before the meeting. Apparite would therefore be forced to make some very critical decisions on the fly, and he didn't like it. He didn't mind improvising with thugs in a bar, or even mobsters in a butcher shop, but this was SMERSH. This was a different and much more dangerous animal.

He reached into his pocket and took out his Reader's Ticket:

"This ticket admits ROBERT KRAMER to the READING ROOM of the British Library and the Reading Room of the Newspaper Library For the Term of One Month From October 15, 1955 to November 15, 1955."

He passed out of the British Museum and into the British Library, which was located in a large courtyard in the center of the museum. Showing his pass to an attendant, he walked down a corridor and entered the main book stacks of the library. What he saw looked uncannily like an iron web wound around the exterior of the large dome of the Reading Room, embedded in which were thousands; no, *millions* of books, giving the library the appearance of a book-covered insect with an iron exoskeleton. Impressive and functional, thought Apparite, but there was no denying that it was also ugly as s—t.

He reached the main entrance to the Reading Room and showed his ticket to a severe-appearing middle-aged attendant, who took a long, hard look at it with an inquisitive eye. Before admitting the young American, he gave him a stern warning.

"Please, Mr. Kramer, we beg you to remember the consideration of the other Readers, and we ask that you do not remove any books or materials from the room."

"Thank you; I'll remember that," Apparite said, managing a weak smile as he walked in.

The sight that greeted Apparite was one he would always remember. In contrast to the unattractive functionality of the "Iron Library" surrounding it, the Reading Room was an example of Victorian grandeur at its splendid best. It was a huge, perfectly circular room 150 feet in diameter, and to take in its lofty dome, which rose 100 feet in the air, Apparite was forced to crane his neck considerably. The ribs of the dome, he noted, were painted metallic gold in striking contrast to its bright white walls; handsome, curved windows between the bases of each rib of the dome let in a cool natural light, and under each was the name of a famous figure in British literary history: Dickens, Thackeray, and Macaulay, among others.

Three tall book stacks lined the circular room along its circumference, and radiating from the center of it, much like the spokes on a wheel, were eighteen long tables, each with seven or eight Reader's Desks to a side. A tall partition down the middle of each long table separated the two sides, providing some measure of privacy from the readers on the opposite side of the table, but not from those to the left or the right—no barriers separated the Reader's Desks on the same side. Fluorescent lights topped each table's central partition, and the seats and desks were covered in a black leather that looked comfortable, if not a little worn.

The effect was akin to being inside the top half of a magnificently decorated Easter egg; like a Faberge-egg designed for a bibliophilistic Royal. Apparite believed it perhaps to be the single most beautiful room he had ever seen, and the knowledge that he was going to have to kill two people in it jarred him. He took a moment to recover from his initial awe at the unexpected elegance of the location—it was time to be an agent, not a tourist, he realized—and then took a formal, clinical, *spy's* look around.

The first thing that struck him was the quiet: that was obvious; it surrounded him. This was the most preternaturally quiet room he had ever set foot in; even the occasional cough or sneeze sounded muffled, almost *squeezed* within it so stifling was the silence. Whether it was the soundproofing of the tens of thousands of books lining the walls, or the stiff personalities of the few readers within it, the room had a claustrophobic, automatic quiet that was off-putting. To break it, it seemed, might cause enough of a shock to make the roof cave in.

And then there was the lack of cover: that was also obvious, and disturbing. The Reader's Desks were short and well below eye level; if anyone stood up, they would see *everything*. Card catalogue cabinets and files blocked the view of the back of the room from the main entrance, but if other readers got wind of what was happening they might get involved. Apparite would have to show extreme prejudice in his actions.

Hitch had told Apparite that seat A7 was to the right of the clock at the far end of the room: good. While the room itself offered little cover, this seemed by far to be the best location for one to remain concealed; plus, the exit leading to Montague Place was only a short corridor away through the iron stacks of the British Library. As Apparite walked purposefully around the circumference of the room, he counted only eight readers sitting at the long desks, but that was still eight too many for his taste. Fortunately, the closest ones were five rows away from where his seat would be and, with any luck, more of them would leave as closing time approached. Hitch had done well: the timing of the meeting was perfect.

The clock on the north wall read four twenty-eight. Nearing his seat, and still walking along the room's periphery, he passed through the doorways of two small, separate enclosed areas near the north exit—each similar to a butler's pantry in appearance—where there were shelves, drawers, and little cubby holes. The second of these contained the small coat closet Hitch had mentioned; cover might be found there if chaos erupts, Apparite noted. Walking past it at a deliberate pace, he could now see the meeting place a few feet away: row A, Reader's Desk seven.

Three men were seated at the near end of the table, occupying seats A6, A8, and A9; at this particular table, Apparite noted, the central partition did not separate the two seats at the very end, A7 and A8. The man in A6, the seat second from the end of the table, and facing the north exit, was obviously the engineer, Nikolai. He was wearing a gray suit and had small, round black glasses and a short beard, and he looked nervous—his hands were shaking and he had forgotten to take off his hat. The other two men had their backs to Apparite as he walked toward the table, seated as they were on the opposite side of it from the engineer. Both men were tall, although the man in A9 was a shade taller and slighter of build than the other in A8. They were dressed in suits as black as pitch.

Apparite made eye contact with Nikolai and gave him a slight nod; the other two men turned their heads to see who was nearing their row. "I'm Kramer," Apparite said in a hushed voice.

Nikolai stood up and proffered a handshake as Apparite came near. Apparite walked past the end of the desk and shook the engineer's sweaty hand; the other men did not extend theirs, nor did they stand. They remained as silent and rigid as statues; all except for their eyes, that is, which were poring over Apparite as intently as a diamond cutter's over a stone before he makes his first critical stroke.

Apparite looked at the man seated in A8: this one must be Standerton, he thought. The MI6 man was tall, tanned, and well built, and he had that slight overbite so common to the English upper class. His was admittedly a handsome face, but Apparite sensed a rugged cruelness deep inside him that the Englishman seemed to be repressing; Apparite understood why Hitch had found him so intimidating.

The man sitting next to Standerton in seat A9 was obviously Viktor: there could be no mistaking those eyes. Although the only picture Apparite had seen of the SMERSH assassin had been grainy and blurred, and the Russian's expression hidden and difficult to read, his eyes had burned through with an intense clarity. Viktor immediately reminded Apparite of a Slavic, younger version of the Director; he saw in him that same, unnaturally intense expression and white-hot laser-like gaze that seemed as if it might melt everything in its path. A face like his left a lasting impression and Apparite would not soon forget it.

Standerton looked up at the still-standing Apparite and spoke.

"Your passport, if you don't mind."

Apparite took his passport from his left front trouser pocket and handed it to the Englishman. Standerton looked at it with a discriminating eye, showed it to Viktor and Nikolai, and then gave it back to Apparite.

"Thank you, Mr. Kramer. Since I speak English, I'll do the talking. Have a seat."

Apparite knew that if he was to succeed in his ruse, he had to truly *be* Robert Kramer: he had to become the embodiment of the bitter, touchy, and grasping man the Soviets would expect. He sat down at the end of the table in seat A7—directly across from Standerton and to the right of Nikolai—and immediately proceeded to put the Soviets on the defensive.

"So *you* speak English? Fine," Apparite said with bite. "Then maybe you can tell me why I've been kept waiting over a month since I left the U.S., paying for everything myself. I got better treatment from the Navy."

"I'm so sorry, but these things cannot be rushed, Mr. Kramer," Standerton replied, in what seemed to be a sincerely apologetic tone. "If it's any consolation, we will reimburse you for your expenses to date."

"I just don't like waiting around while I spend what's left of my own money."

"Once again, I apologize," Standerton said as polite as can be, but Apparite sensed a growing annoyance underneath this formal and deferential exterior. "Now, let's move on to more important matters, shall we? We have reviewed the materials you gave us; the engineer is impressed at how far the Americans have come. How long before they have transportable solid fuel?"

"About two years, I think," Apparite said. "But the sample I've brought might get you there sooner than them—I managed to 'lose' some critical material before I left D.C."

Apparite was pleased with how it had gone so far. He realized he was not going to be searched, and took it as a sign that they did not feel threatened by him, or believed he was anything but an unhappy and greedy scientist. *After all,* he said to himself, *I am only five-six and about one-forty, so I probably look a helluva lot more like a scientist than a secret agent, anyway!*

"Give sample now," the engineer spat out in broken English; he began pulling small glass petri dishes and vials from his suit-coat with the apparent intention of testing the fuel sample "Kramer" had promised.

"Not until I'm satisfied I'm getting my money and leaving here alive," Apparite said in an irritated and defensive tone.

He heard a noise from across the table and saw Viktor shifting in his chair: the SMERSH agent was leaning slightly to his left to watch Apparite more closely from around the end of the central partition of the desk. Apparite made eye contact with him, noting that the well of white-hot power in Viktor's gaze had not been extinguished: those burning eyes remained uncomfortably and firmly fixed on him. Apparite knew that to look away or betray fear might show weakness and spell disaster: he held Viktor's intense gaze for a second longer and then continued speaking.

"Where's my five hundred thousand?"

A man across the room coughed loudly; the engineer jumped but Viktor remained stone-still.

"You get, when we get sample." Viktor had spoken, and his voice was like the rumblings of a train that crashed and clanged along poorly laid tracks. Apparite found it unsettling, even at a whisper.

Apparite thought he had played with them enough; he would press his point only one more time. "Okay; I've got the sample. But you get it on one condition: after you test it and okay it, you leave the room and bring me back a down payment on the five hundred thousand right now. I also want to be put up in a five-star hotel before we leave for Russia."

Viktor laughed—a low, guttural sound which, like his voice, had a quality similar to a locomotive—but it was Standerton who answered, although it was obvious the Englishman's patience was wearing thin.

"Certainly, Mr. Kramer. But if you're going to deal with us, you have to trust us," he said in his BBC-perfect English accent. "We have no reason to harm you as long as the sample is genuine. When you get to Leningrad, you will have the thanks of a great nation plus all the money you can spend. You have nothing to worry about."

This guy is good, thought Apparite. He marveled at Standerton's coolness, especially in the presence of Viktor, whom he was certain could ignite kindling with an angry look. No wonder MI6 considered Standerton their best man.

Apparite reached into his shirt's breast pocket, pulling out the small packet he had removed from the tube of "gem polish" that he'd smuggled in at Heathrow. He handed it to the engineer—who seemed to have calmed, now that he had work to do—and the scientist put small dabs of it into the two petri dishes and five test tubes he had taken out of his coat.

Apparite was fascinated by the performance: the engineer had taken so much stuff out of his coat, it reminded him of a Harpo Marx routine. (*Animal Crackers*? wondered Apparite, or was it more like *Duck Soup*?) Suppressing the humor he was unexpectedly finding in the situation, he looked over at Standerton to gauge his reaction, but the Englishman remained unsmiling; if anything, he looked bored and impatient. A second later, Standerton stood up from the desk.

"I have to go to the toilet; I'll return in a few moments," he announced.

Apparite turned his attention back to Nikolai. From somewhere in his remarkably accommodating coat, the engineer had pulled out a cache of small, stoppered vials. Concentrating intensely—to Apparite's continued amusement and amazement—the engineer put various drops of liquid from the vials into each test tube or petri dish. He mixed some, sniffed others, and then added reagents to yet more of them that changed them into various colors: yellow, red, and blue.

But despite his fascination with the goings-on at his table, Apparite was beginning to champ at the bit to carry out the final part of the mission: as soon as the engineer had okayed and taken the sample, Apparite was to begin the assassinations. And although he hated waiting, he knew it would be prudent to do so until Standerton returned: Apparite had decided to kill Viktor with a throwing knife to the chest, followed by a choke-hold with silent throat cutting for Nikolai, and either would be more certain to be successful and silent if the MI6 agent were present—for instance, Standerton could hold his hand over Viktor's mouth if the Russian moaned or screamed. One long minute stretched into two, and Apparite's anxiety was mounting—where could the Englishman be? What was taking him so damned long?

The engineer took out the materials J had dead-dropped in Soho Square; using a slide-rule, he made some calculations. He then put the test tubes, vials, petri dishes, and the remaining fuel sample into an apparently puncture-proof and spill-proof bag, found a surprisingly large inside coat pocket that he slipped the bag into, and looked at Viktor with a wry smile.

"The fuel is good, even if the American is an imbecile," the engineer said in Russian, unaware that Apparite could speak the language and would understand him.

"We will wait for the Englishman and leave together," Viktor answered.

Suddenly, the reason for the delay struck Apparite like a thunderbolt: Standerton has run into Hitch, and there's been a confrontation—perhaps Hitch has even killed him. What else could it be? A man like Standerton would have rushed back to the meeting as soon as possible, and the fact that he *hadn't* assuredly meant that something had gone very seriously wrong. Apparite realized he was going to pay dearly for having trusted Clive Hitch. Faced with the disappearance of his immediate back-up, he decided to count backwards from five, and if Standerton had not yet returned, he would have to do the killings alone, silent or not.

Five: no sign of Standerton; Viktor sat staring straight ahead without any sign of emotion. *Four:* a couple of coughs from the front of the large room; a sneeze from row F; but that was all. *Three:* a side door opened and closed; still no Standerton. *Two:* a book dropped loudly onto the floor, causing *"shusssh's"* from the readers in row P. *One.* It was time.

Just as Apparite began to reach for his hidden switchblade, Standerton appeared in the doorway of the small butler's pantry about six feet away, his face looking slightly flushed. He walked to the table and looked pointedly at Apparite; he then whispered into Viktor's left ear for a full five seconds, slipping him something under the table.

Viktor's countenance did not change with what Standerton told him, but when the Englishman had sat back down again into his seat, Viktor said, in his broken English, "Mr. Kramer; fuel sample is good, but I ask question: *why* English MI Five agent be here?"

Apparite's eyes widened in surprise, and although he tried

to suppress his racing emotions, his pulse rose dramatically and he began to sweat: he'd just had an epiphany as dramatic as a husband who'd caught his wife in bed with another man and realized she'd been unfaithful all along.

Standerton was the traitor.

Of course; how stupid they'd all been! There'd been a reason why Standerton had rubbed Hitch wrong all those years, but Apparite hadn't listened to the MI5 agent with the right kind of ears to put the pieces together, and Hitch had never suspected a decorated colleague. And Apparite realized it could only have been the blue-blooded, multi-talented MI6 agent Standerton who, using his daring "infiltration" of the KGB as bait, might have lured the cautious G to his death behind the memorial.

Apparite figured he knew what had happened. On his way to the toilet, Standerton had seen the unlucky MI5 agent Clive Hitch, and realized that Robert Kramer was *not* simply a disgruntled scientist who wanted five hundred grand and a ticket to a life of ease in exchange for missile-fuel secrets. And, naturally, Standerton would now be wondering this: if this young American was not the *real* Robert Kramer, then who the blazes *was* he? Apparite would have to string them along until he found a means of escape from this rapidly degenerating situation.

"An MI Five agent? I don't even know what that is—I'm here alone."

Viktor leaned toward him.

"Who *are* you, Mr. Kramer?" he whispered menacingly, pausing briefly between each word.

"You know who I am—you've seen my passport, haven't you? I live in Washington D.C.; in Georgetown; in a red-bricked town house. I work for the U.S. Navy—I can show you my identity card. The fuel sample's good—doesn't that prove it? Didn't you receive the calculations that prove it?" He hoped Hitch might appear and bolster his chances, but then remembered their strong instructions for him to stay put in the library stacks outside the room. *He will not be coming,* Apparite concluded.

Viktor slowly raised his right hand above the table: it held a gun, which he now had pointing at Apparite's head. Apparite saw the .25 caliber Webley and Scott pistol with silencer and another realization hit him, though on a more personal level: *Hitch is dead. Standerton has killed him and taken his weapon; that's* the reason it took him so long to "go to the toilet."

Apparite could not have been certain exactly how it had played out, but he had made a shrewd guess.

"Hitch?" Standerton had said incredulously when he had spied the MI5 agent perusing the book stacks just outside the north exit of the room.

"Let's talk, Standerton," Hitch had said in response, trying to avoid drawing anyone's attention so close to the meeting place. "Follow me."

Hitch had led him discreetly to the one secure location he knew was nearby: the small coat closet in the "butler's pantry"; although it was only a short distance from where Apparite and the Soviets were sitting, it was shielded from their view and quite private. Once they had slipped inside it, Hitch quietly closed the door. No one had seen them enter.

"What the hell are you doing here, Hitch?" Standerton had asked in a tone of surprise mixed with an arrogance Hitch had always disliked.

"'Kramer' is an American agent; he's going to kill the Soviets."

"How can I help?" Standerton had said, trying to learn more.

"Back him up; discreetly. We don't want to risk exposing you to the enemy."

Standerton had smiled at the irony of Hitch's use of the words "exposing," and "enemy."

"Don't worry; you can count on me," Standerton had said, feeling the primal delight of a cat toying with a weaker and completely unsuspecting mouse.

"The American is going to make the deal and then kill Viktor and the engineer, planting the fuel sample," Hitch had then said.

"Hmm," Standerton had replied as he formulated his own plan. "Brilliant. I have vital information for the American. Where is your rendezvous? I need to speak with him in private."

Hitch had told him the details: he was to meet the two American agents back at the flat in the mews of Queen's Gate Place at 1900, and would tell them Standerton was coming.

"Thank you, Hitch," Standerton had said. He then had quickly pulled-out his semi-automatic Beretta—the same pistol with silencer he had used to kill Agent G—placed it firmly on the left side of Hitch's chest, and pulled the trigger. Hitch had jolted backwards, thumping against the wall of the closet, and then slid to the floor: dead. Standerton had then taken the MI5 agent's pistol, slipped out of the closet, and closed the door quietly behind him.

But Standerton had missed one critical point: Hitch was *not* dead. The gun had been pressed very tightly against the MI5 agent's chest, impeding the flow of air out of the barrel; the blast had therefore been diffused and the bullet had left the weapon with less force than usual. And, unbeknownst to Standerton, Hitch had a shield in his left breast pocket: the anxious MI5 agent had brought the small pewter flask of whisky only to steady his nerves, but it had also just saved his life. The bullet—slowed by Standerton's use of a silencer; its force diffused by the muffling of the muzzle against Hitch's clothing; and having to pierce the Englishman's pewter whisky flask—had shattered two ribs and penetrated Hitch's chest, but had only lodged itself into the meat of his left ventricle—it had not pierced it.

Hitch's heart had fluttered for a second and then beaten very rapidly, but it had not yet stopped: Clive Hitch was near death, but not yet *in* death. Despite the bullet that had lodged in his heart, blood continued to flow to his brain and, after a few moments, he'd regained his senses. Hitch then somehow summoned all his energy, reached up and turned the coat closet door handle, and it had opened.

Crawling on his belly, inch by inch and foot by foot, in absolute silence despite the pain of his wound, he made his way in the direction of row A. He could hear the agents in intense conversation, but they remained completely unaware of his presence. Closer and closer he came, his face pale from blood loss and sweat streaming from it in extreme effort, as he crawled on and on until he had reached a point just a few feet away from Standerton and Viktor.

He collapsed, panting softly; he could go no further. But then Hitch heard Standerton speak, and the sound of the voice he had learned to despise reignited something inside him, giving him the will and energy to continue. Using the last of his body's supply of adrenaline he inched yet closer toward them, his life ebbing by the second. He might be almost out of time, but that bastard Standerton would not be rid of him so easily.

"I suggest you tell us who you are, and for whom you are

operating," Standerton said to Apparite.

Apparite looked him dead in the eye.

"I'd die before I told a traitor like you," he answered. He was going to say nothing and he was going to die; of that he was now certain. Apparite's only regret was that Hitch might be blamed for his death—Viktor was going to use the MI5 agent's pistol for that very reason, he figured.

"I will *make* him talk," Victor said in his foul voice.

"*F—- you,*" Apparite replied with disgust. He thought about standing and shouting for help, but knew it would be useless; they would kill him as soon as he did. This way, at least, he was keeping them talking while he figured out how he would carry out his new mission: to kill as many of them as possible before he, too, was dead.

Viktor, for the first time, let emotion come across his face: he was becoming increasingly, uncontrollably angry and impatient with this insolent young American.

"You *will* talk, Mr. Kramer. *Ti u menea budesh' plakat' kak zjershina, Amerikanez,*" he said with a menacing growl. *I will make you weep like a woman, American.*

Viktor's pale face had become very red and tremulous, reminding Apparite of a cornered animal about to lash out.

"You know there's no way I'm leaving this room alive, you Russian son of a bitch," Apparite said, reaching for his hidden switchblade to begin his own murderous plan, but the temperamental Viktor had passed the breaking point and suddenly lost control.

"*Sdohni, Amerikanez!*" he spat out in anger. *Then die, American!*

"Viktor: *no!*" said Standerton in alarm, but it was too late to stop him: the SMERSH agent had already pulled the trigger.

But as the pistol fired, Viktor was suddenly wrenched

backward by an unseen force and spilled from his chair. The bullet missed the ducking Apparite's head, speeding harmlessly into the third tier of books above them, and when Viktor hit the floor, the pistol flew from his hand and landed well away from the table. The gunshot, given the small caliber of the pistol and its attached silencer, hardly made any sound at all: its little *"pheewt!"* was greeted with only one *"shusssh!"* from an annoyed reader ten rows away.

Apparite pulled the poison pen from his shirt pocket; he pushed Nikolai over and out of his chair, simultaneously injecting the engineer's left thigh with the lethal *Ricinus* poison. Nikolai grunted as he hit the ground with a thud, drawing another, louder *"shusssh!"* from row F. Heads were beginning to pop up from the Reader's Desks around the room, but no one had yet localized the ruckus to row A.

Apparite, who had thrown himself to the ground after using the poison pen, saw what the unseen force was that had pulled Viktor backwards and spilled him onto the floor: it was Clive Hitch. Hitch was trapped under Viktor and his chair but, despite his mortal wound and situation, managed to pull a knife from his trousers and thrust it into Viktor's left thigh. Viktor grimaced, but did not betray his pain with noise of any kind.

Like the others, Standerton had thrown himself to the ground at the sound of the shot, but his Beretta was deep inside his suit pocket with its handle wedged in the bottom, and his searching fingers were unable to grasp and remove it. Hitch reached over and grabbed Standerton's suit coat, thrusting his arm deep inside the pocket and preventing the MI6 agent from freeing the pistol, and then he died.

Agitated readers were standing up all around the room. Some were looking for attendants to eject this rabble, while others swiftly packed their belongings to make a hasty exit from the escalating melee. The panicking Soviet engineer had gotten to his feet and was making a mad dash for the north exit, stepping on Apparite in the process.

"Protect Nikolai!" Viktor shouted, his voice breaking the room's sacred silence as dramatically as a cannon-shot in a cathedral. An attendant in the front of the room located the epicenter of the commotion and began walking toward it, his face a picture of disgust. Standerton broke free from his suit coat, which was still in the dead Hitch's grasp, and hustled the engineer through the butler's pantry and out of the North exit.

Apparite could see the injured Viktor slowly getting up on the opposite side of the desk; the Superagent jumped up quickly and found himself facing his enemy across the table. Reacting first, Apparite let loose an *Isshin-Ryu* fist, tensing his entire body as it connected full-force on the upper part of Viktor's right arm, and breaking the SMERSH agent's humerus with a gunshot-loud crack. Viktor flew into the shelves of books behind him, a dozen volumes tumbling loudly from it onto the floor. Apparite reached down and drew out his switchblade, but Viktor had already stumbled in the direction of the exit; he was limping and holding his broken right arm, and Hitch's knife still protruded from his bloodied leg. Apparite threw his blade at the fleeing Russian but it narrowly missed, burying itself deeply into the spine of a large volume on the first level of books.

Viktor limped into the labyrinth of book stacks just outside the Reading Room; he was about fifteen feet in front of Apparite but his injured leg was slowing him, and Apparite was gaining. Apparite knew that if he caught him he could kill him before he left the building. And then, everything changed.

Seemingly from nowhere, a young man appeared between

the two agents: he was an attendant who had been running to the Reading Room to address the chaos within it, and he looked no older than seventeen. Viktor quickly grabbed him by the throat with his uninjured arm and held him in a firm grip. Despite unimaginable pain, the SMERSH agent pulled the bloody knife from his thigh with his broken right arm, his face twisting in silent agony, and held the blade to the boy's neck.

"Stop, *Amerikanez*," he said. Apparite halted ten feet from Viktor and the terrified young man.

"You're wounded, Viktor; you can't run away from me."

"Maybe no. But, I can slow you down." To Apparite's ever-lasting horror, Viktor smiled and made a quick slashing motion with the knife at the young man's throat.

"No!" shouted Apparite, rushing forward toward the two of them. Viktor let the boy loose and the young attendant slumped to the ground. His throat was slit three inches across in a bloody mess, and air bubbled from his partially severed windpipe.

Apparite knew his directives dictated indifference to the young man's plight; that he should pursue the wounded SMERSH agent and finish him off. But *could* he? Could he run and leave this innocent boy to die because *his* duty to the United States commanded it? Apparite had been prepared to kill in the name of duty, and he had been prepared to die in the name of duty, but he had *not* been prepared to let this young man bleed to death in the name of it—in his worst nightmares he had never imagined *this*.

From deep inside him, in a place where even the demands of his duty had not yet penetrated—perhaps that place where his childhood memories and innocence still resided, and his mysterious but comforting dreams found their inspiration—Apparite felt compelled to help this boy: he would defy his directives, and the Director be damned.

As Viktor fled, Apparite ran to the stricken boy's side, cursing himself and the Director in his heart. The flow of blood from the wound was torrential; Apparite pressed firmly on both sides of the boy's neck to staunch the bleeding as best he could. He called out for aid as the blood gushed and gushed.

"Help me!" he shouted, though the paltry noise he created seemed swallowed up by the millions of books in the stacks. Unable to think of anything else he could do, Apparite prayed to God, or whatever name one might give the presence he had felt in St. Paul's, to save this boy. After ten long, agonizing seconds, another library attendant appeared; he turned white at the horrific sight that greeted him.

"Give me your shirt," Apparite said in haste; the shaking attendant quickly complied. Apparite looked down: blood was *everywhere*, dripping even through the iron lattice-work floor and onto the level below. Apparite wrapped the attendant's shirt firmly, though without too much constriction, around the young man's opened neck. The flow of blood seemed to slow some as he did so, although he guessed it was as much from the boy's falling blood pressure as the compression the tightened shirt was providing.

"Hold it just like that until the ambulance comes," Apparite told the attendant. Satisfied at last he had done all he could, he stood—arms coated with blood like a slaughterhouse worker at the end of a long day—and ran in the direction of the museum's exit. Passing yet another attendant, he shouted, "Call an ambulance; there's been a stabbing!"

He ran out of the museum and onto Montague Place, but there was no sign of Viktor. He looked around for a moment, and then he saw them: small, evenly spaced drops of fresh blood on the pavement that tailed off to the left. Following the blood-trail, and running as fast as he could, he turned onto Gower Street. He was running past the dark brown-bricked town houses when he heard a voice down an alley ahead; accelerating his pace, he ran into it. Without warning, a cosh came down onto his head from the shadows of a doorway just past the alley's entrance, and the world turned to black. Before he lost consciousness, Apparite heard a voice; a voice that spoke in Russian.

"Bring him. We will rendezvous with Viktor at the safe house."

Apparite had been taken.

Eighteen
Taken

Apparite awoke, groggy; he had been unconscious for only a few minutes, but as the KGB safe house was just a short distance from the museum, the Russians already had him hustled inside it. Looking around as his head cleared, he saw muted, golden-hued sunlight coming in through the cracks of a boarded-up window across the room, but as he had no idea himself how long he'd been out, he could only guess that it must be about dusk. He sat up and leaned against the wall: oh, how the back of his head ached; he gingerly pressed a finger on the area, feeling for the crepitation or depression of a skull fracture but, fortunately, there was none. Only a mild concussion, he figured.

It was then that he realized the true severity of his plight. He was naked and his hands and legs were tied with cord; the KGB had stripped him of all his clothes and, in the process, all of his weapons. His hair had been mussed and he could feel dampness around his anus, which was sore—he realized, with disgust, that the SOB's had even examined *inside* him for weapons or devices. The room was completely bare and only about ten by ten feet in size, and in the middle of the ceiling there was but a single, bare bulb which gave off a pale light.

But Apparite knew what to do next: get his hands and feet free. The cord was quite tight and his hands were tied behind his back, but the flexible young agent contorted himself and, after a moment of effort, was able to bring his hands around to the front. He focused on the cord binding his hands and was pleased to see it did not look very thick, although he assumed it must be reasonably strong.

I've got to find something firm and yet sharp on one edge to cut these binds, he thought, but looking around, noted that the walls were bare and the door had nothing on it that he might use. But then his gaze landed on the cover of an air-vent and his hopes rose—*hmm*, he said to himself, *that might have possibilities*. He rolled himself over to a floor-vent against the wall.

He looked closely at it; it had a nice, thin metal edge, and looked to be at least ten years old from the dents and scrapes on it. He figured they'd probably been replaced in the forties after the Blitz and, if the carpenters had taken a shortcut and hadn't drilled new holes into the wall (which seemed a likelihood during wartime), he might be able to loosen one. He kicked the edge of the vent sharply with his heel and it came off the wall, *just like that*.

Now we're getting someplace! he thought. He rolled over to the dislodged vent, wedged it against the wall, and began vigorously rubbing the cord that bound his hands against the vent's sharpest edge; after thirty seconds, the cord snapped and his hands were free. He then quickly untied the cord binding his feet and stood, stretching and loosening his limbs. Taking a few more seconds to allow some residual dizziness to subside, he quietly crept over to the solid-appearing door, but as it had no window, or an inside door handle to "jimmy," he saw that he wasn't going to get out that way.

Apparite took a quick account of what had happened and where things stood, and it wasn't pretty. Hitch was dead, and Standerton and Viktor had escaped. The only bright spot was that the scientist had been injected with the poison and would die within three days—at least that part of the mission had been a success. He then thought of the young boy whose throat Viktor had slit: *I hope he makes it,* he said to himself.

He thought of what would happen if he remained locked in this room and, again, the outlook wasn't pretty. *If I don't show at the rendezvous,* he said to himself, *then I will have to contact my Shadow-agent to investigate.* And even *if* I escape, he realized, it probably wouldn't change my prospects, anyway: when my Shadow reaches me he will naturally assume I've been interrogated, and will have to kill me to protect the agency. But being killed by his Shadow seemed infinitely preferable to having Viktor arrive and torture him for information—Apparite didn't even have an "L-pill" on him anymore to end it all. He thought of only one solution: he had to escape before the time of the rendezvous had passed, but he also knew that his time to do so was running out.

He put his ear to the door and was surprised to find he could distinctly hear two men talking in Russian outside the room. They were chattering excitedly and more loudly than a veteran agent would ever have dreamed of doing—they must be newly trained, he thought, and probably assume I can't hear them or, if I could, that I don't speak Russian. His spirits brightened: new agents are naïve agents, and naïve agents make mistakes. It's also probably the most important duty they've ever had, he reasoned, and they'll want to impress their supervisors—especially Viktor, their intimidating SMERSH colleague. Maybe I can use their over-eagerness to my advantage.

But his confidence fell when he heard what the Russians were saying: "Viktor will interrogate the prisoner at nineteen hundred at the American safe house."

They know the time of the rendezvous! Apparite said to himself in alarm. *They know the location of the flat in the mews!* He imagined that Standerton had tricked Hitch into telling him this critical information. Poor Hitch: how it must have burned him to find out he'd been fooled by Standerton all those years! Apparite could not let Hitch's sacrifice be in vain; he was more determined than ever to make the rendezvous.

And Apparite now knew exactly what would happen if he did not: he would be taken by the KGB to the flat in the mews, where he and J would be interrogated and tortured together before inevitably breaking. Viktor would be teeming with curiosity about the young American agent who had nearly fooled them all; had nearly *killed* them all. *Nothing* would stop him from getting the information he needed, and it would be the downfall of everything and everyone: J, Apparite, the Director, and probably even Agent B operating in Eastern Europe—*everything*. Even Apparite, who had defied an interrogator before at gunpoint, knew his chances of holding out indefinitely against a maniac like Viktor were slim.

And when it seemed like it could not get any more desperate, it did. The Russians began speaking very excitedly about their roles in another mission; this one set for tomorrow. Apparite heard fragments of hastily spoken sentences: "provide cover and escape," and "surveillance for the shooter."

Surveillance for the shooter? Apparite said to himself. *It must be an assassination attempt.* But of whom? The Prime Minister's government was new, as were all his ministers; decent targets, but intelligence had suggested they were not in danger any longer. It had to be someone else.

The State Opening of Parliament, Apparite said in a whisper. *That was it. Tomorrow is the State Opening of Parliament.* Every November, he recalled, the Queen leads a procession to the House of Lords, ceremoniously beginning the Parliamentary session with a speech on the state of Britain.

Apparite had forgotten to ask Hitch about her earlier absence, but it didn't matter now: she might have retreated to Balmoral back in September but, as a young, vivacious, and patriotic queen—and one who'd only ascended to the throne three years earlier—she'd almost certainly insist on returning for this important ceremony.

Who would be the shooter? Not Viktor; his dossier had indicated he was only an adequate marksman, and they would not take a chance on missing the mark—not with a target of this importance. They certainly would not use any of these young and inexperienced KGB lackeys he had been listening to through the door; no. For this job, it would have to be a man of experience and talent.

It would be *Standerton*. As a lifelong, innocuous-looking Englishman he could blend into the crowd and do it from short-range or, as perhaps the best shot in MI6 and with a detailed knowledge of London, he could do it from a distance—either way, an ace marksman like him would be unlikely to miss. But could he really kill his queen? The British were raised from birth with an almost automatic deference and respect for the Royals, and Standerton's family was in the peerage—the man had probably even gone to *Eton!* But any way Apparite looked at it, the answer came out *yes*. A man embittered enough to have turned traitor and killed friendly agents in cold blood would almost assuredly have no qualms about killing the young queen. *The cowardly bastard,* Apparite said to himself.

Apparite's emotions were in a rapid crescendo; he took a few deep breaths to clear his mind and diffuse his wrath, and then walked over to the boarded-up window. He tugged on the boards covering it, but found they were nailed on very securely—he'd never be able to remove them. He ran his hands around the window and found something he thought might be important: in the process of hammering the boards into place, the lower edge of the bottom board had loosened the sill and pushed it out slightly, leaving about a quarter-inch gap between the top of the sill and the wall. *Possibly, possibly,* he said to himself.

He took the air vent he had removed and carefully placed it in the gap between the wooden sill and the wall. He softly, though firmly, pounded against the metal vent with his fist, significantly widening the gap between the sill and the wall. He removed the vent from the gap and went to the other side of the sill, where he repeated the process. If I'm lucky, he thought, the sill will have been put in place before the war with great big long nails, and then I'll *really* be "cookin' with gas" (as his father used to say—the saying had always amused him as a child).

Back and forth Apparite went, the gap getting wider and wider, until the board eventually popped off the wall. He bent back one of the long nails that protruded from each end of the board until it was flush with the sill, allowing him to grip the board at that end with his hands. He then walked over to the door and put his ear to it: the KGB agents were still talking a mile a minute, completely unaware of Apparite's doings in the room.

Hallelujah, thought Apparite: he now had a nice, three foot long *bo-stick* with three inches of nail sticking out of one end at his disposal—now all he had to do was get the KGB men to open the door. In his favor was the fact that there was no window or transom in the door: if they got worried or curious they'd have to open it to see what was going on. But how could he get them *curious* enough to do something as unwise as open their prisoner's door?

Faking an illness? A seizure had worked on J back at the warehouse, but that would be hard to pull off behind a closed door. And an illness would be too obvious a ruse: they'd never buy it, and they might not give a s—t anyway, he figured. How about pounding on the door, yelling and shouting? No; nothing overly dramatic would do it, either. It would have to be something *subtle;* something so curious and mysterious that they felt absolutely compelled to know what was going on and simply *had* to open the door. Apparite smiled: an idea had just come to him.

Taking the sill, he began tapping on the door with the nail sticking out of the end; near enough to the hinges so as not to visibly shake the door, yet loud enough to draw attention.

"Tap. Tap. Tap-tap-tap-tap-taptaptaptaptaptaptaptaptap. " He paused to put his ear to the door; nothing from the KGB agents yet. *"Tap. Tap. Tap-tap-tap-tap-taptaptaptaptap-taptaptaptap. "* He paused again.

"What in the devil is that sound?" Apparite heard one of the KGB men say in Russian.

"Nothing," he heard from the other.

"Tap. Tap. Tap-tap-tap-tap-taptaptaptaptaptaptaptap. " He put his ear to the door again.

"I think it's coming from the American. What is he doing?" one of the agents said.

"Nothing; ignore him. We have orders not to open the door for any reason."

"Tap. Tap. Tap-tap-tap-tap-taptaptaptaptaptaptaptap. "

"Tap. Tap. Tap-tap-tap-tap-taptaptaptaptaptaptaptap. "

"He could be trying to escape, Yuri! Do you know what Viktor would do if the American escaped, with us sitting right here outside the door?"

"How can he escape? His hands and legs are tied; the window is boarded; and the American is naked! We will wait for Viktor."

"Tap. Tap. Tap-tap-tap-tap-taptaptaptaptaptaptaptap. "

"Tap. Tap. Tap-tap-tap-tap-taptaptaptaptaptaptaptaptap."

Apparite paused; he heard fidgeting on the other side of the door and, he believed, the cocking of a pistol. Was one of the agents preparing to investigate these strange sounds? One more time, Apparite thought, and I have them.

"Tap. Tap. Tap-tap-tap-tap-taptaptaptaptaptaptaptaptap."

Pause.

"TAP!"

Apparite quietly crept to the door and put himself flush against it, holding the sill in his left hand.

"It stopped, Yuri! Did you hear the loud bang at the end? I thought I heard footsteps: he's out of his binds! He's escaping! Viktor will *kill* us, Yuri!"

"Stop your nonsense! We will wait!"

"And if the American is gone; *we* will be blamed! *We* will be the ones sent to Siberia to labor like dogs!"

There was a lull in their conversation; clearly, Yuri was thinking something over.

"Alright; we will take one look. You open the door and peek in; I will stay here with the pistol ready. We cannot give the American a chance to get our gun, so you will have to take a knife."

They'd taken the bait, and it had been easier than Apparite had expected. If they had any brains at all, he realized, they could have simply gone outside to the alley and made sure the window hadn't been breached: he was glad these two weren't the sharpest knives in the KGB's drawer!

He heard the door unlock; positioning his body a short distance behind it, Apparite backed up as it opened, keeping himself out of view. Holding the sill over his head with both hands, arms tensed in anticipation for the opportune moment, he saw the door open: first four, then six, then eight inches. The battle would soon be upon them.

Now! Apparite brought the board around and caught the nail on the other side of the door. He yanked it open, jumping quickly to the right and out of its way. The KGB agent, who had not yet steeled his nerve to fully poke his head into the room, was standing right in front of him with a look of astonishment locked onto his face. Before he could cry out, Apparite brought the board across the Russian's chest. The nail pierced him just over the heart and embedded itself deeply; the man moaned but uttered no other sound, and Apparite jumped in front of him and grabbed the knife from his hand. Using the still-embedded sill as a support on one side, and his hand cocked under the KGB agent's armpit on the other, Apparite held the dead man up in front of him; a shield from the onslaught to come.

The other KGB agent fired four shots in rapid succession at the two men as they stood in the doorway. Fortunately for Apparite, the weapon was a smaller caliber Tokarev pistol with silencer and the dead man was taller and wider than he: the slugs buried themselves in the body of the Russian but did not pass through. Flinging the dead man aside, Apparite expertly threw with force the knife he had taken, hitting the KGB agent flush in the chest; the Russian fired wildly into the ceiling as he emptied his clip, and then toppled over: dead.

Apparite ran into the anteroom. His clothes were piled neatly on top of a chair, but had been searched; the empty pockets were turned out. Pressed for time, he quickly put on the pants, but his shirt, still covered with the young museum attendant's blood, was useless—it would draw too much attention. He would have to take the shirt off the agent with the knife in his chest; fortunately, the blood stain from the wound was surprisingly small.

But where are my shoes? Apparite asked himself. He frantically searched the room for his "spy- hoes" as J called them—they contained, of course, a small cache of weapons he might need—but the only pair he found was one that, from the looks of them, most likely belonged to the smaller of the two KGB agents. On closer inspection, he noted how shabby they were: the soles had worn almost clear through at the toes and the crooked heels looked to have been tacked on by a Vodka-fortified Russian cobbler.

But Apparite had no choice, and he started to put them on—they were fortuitously a close fit—until he had figured it out: the KGB man had nicked Apparite's shoes! Throwing the Russian's shoes away, he ran over to the lifeless body of the KGB agent with the knife in his chest and, just as he had suspected, *his* shoes were on the Russian's feet. The Russian had stolen and substituted them for his own!

Criminy, Apparite said to himself, *if every Soviet gets such crappy equipment, it's amazing we haven't gotten them* all *to defect!*

Checking his "spy shoes" to make sure the hidden knives and garrote wire apparatus were still inside them—which they were—Apparite took them off the Russian and laced them up on his own feet. He pulled the knife from the dead man's chest and then removed the Russian's shirt, putting it on as soon as he had taken off his own. He may not have looked fashionable, but he was at least reasonably presentable; the small blood stain over his heart excepted.

He looked at the Russian's watch, which he had put on his own wrist, and began to feel the pressure: it was eight minutes until seven, and the time of the rendezvous was nearly upon him. Hurrying, he grabbed his improvised, nail-tipped *bo*-stick and ran out of the door. He rapidly estimated the time to travel by Tube to the flat, but decided that given the distance between stations and the uncertainty of the train's arrivals, it would take too long to arrive in time. He would have to find another way.

He stopped for a moment: perhaps he could call J to warn him. But he soon realized, in an embarrassing oversight, that he did not know the telephone number of the flat in the mews—it had never occurred to him he would ever need to call his *own* flat. But even if he could, there was little J could do about it—the KGB would only intercept him trying to escape from the area, or overwhelm him at the safe house.

Apparite knew what he had to do: he would have to steal or commandeer a car and drive it pell-mell to the flat in South Kensington. If he failed, J would almost certainly die at the hands of the Soviets; he was not combat-tested like Apparite and would never be able to hold off Viktor and his henchmen. But if Apparite got there in time, then perhaps the two of them might stand a chance. He tore out of the KGB safe house and ran out into the street; he now had about seven minutes to drive half-way across London. His blood pressure rose in anticipation of the chaos he knew he was about to cause.

The sun had nearly disappeared below the horizon, and Apparite wasted no time in trying to find an automobile. A dozen cars passed by but none of them stopped, and Apparite realized he would simply have to take the first one that did (although this was not a time to be choosy, he hoped to God it wouldn't be a Minor).

An eternity seemed to pass until a car finally pulled up near him: a black London taxi, its driver having thought Apparite was a fare. Waving at the cabdriver, Apparite ran up to the vehicle, but to the wrong side of it: in an English car, the driver sits on the *right*, and Apparite, ever the American, had run up to its *left*. Swearing under his breath, he quickly realized his error and ran to the other side of the cab—the

English driver's side—and stuck his head through the open window.

"Where to, guv'nor?" the jovial Cockney driver asked.

"Get out!" Apparite yelled at the cabbie; he pulled open the taxi's door and wrenched the startled man out of the driver's seat and onto the pavement. Slamming the door shut, he put the cab into first gear and took off down the street like a man possessed. He had six minutes to go.

"Bloody Yank tourist!" he heard in the cabbie's unmistakable "Bow-Bells" accent as he sped away. Apparite closed the window to try and block out the inevitable curses and horns and sirens to come; he thought it would be harder to concentrate with every Londoner screaming at him. The taxi was reasonably comfortable—maybe not as comfy as the Director's De Soto, he thought, but not too bad—and it had a nice hum to its engine. The pick-up lagged slightly, perhaps, but its top-end power seemed considerable. Not that it mattered: regardless of its strengths or faults, it would have to do.

Looking down the road ahead, he tried to focus on one critical issue: the English drove on the wrong side of the road. *Left is right and right is left,* he said aloud. *Drive on the left, drive on the left, drive on the left,* he kept repeating to himself. Planning his route, he knew he had to stay away from Piccadilly: too many one-way streets; too much traffic even on a Monday evening. He would go to Oxford Street: it might be busy, but at least it provided for four lanes of traffic, counting the bus lanes, where he would be less likely to hit anyone.

Tires squealing, he made a sharp right turn to the north; he swerved to avoid a Daimler in an intersection, but clipped a green Austin-Healy, sending it crashing into the bumper of a little Metropolitan, igniting a firestorm of car horns. *Thank goodness this thing is built like a tank,* he said to himself, *because*

I'm going to be "swapping paint" the whole way. He pressed the accelerator to the floor as if to punctuate the sentiment.

The sturdy cab had built up a tremendous amount of momentum when he saw Oxford Street ahead; it was almost time to turn left. Thinking for a moment that a left turn would be difficult Apparite made a sour face, but then he realized that it was like a *right turn* when made from the left lane, and that was *good!* He hated driving in England, he decided.

He made the turn, his tires shredding their edges under the strain, leaving a trail of freshly laid rubber on the road behind him. Oxford Street, as usual, was busy as hell. Flying down the road going at least forty miles per hour, he was swerving around taxis and buses like cones on a driving course, with one difference: *these* cones were moving, and had live human beings inside them; he could ill-afford to hit one.

He was feeling the pressure: he was driving a taxi on one of the most famous thoroughfares in London—on what instinctively felt like the wrong side of the road—and if he failed, his closest colleague would be killed. He tried not to think about it. He flew through an intersection without slowing, barely missing an elderly English gentleman wearing a traditional black suit and bowler hat; the man shook his fist at the cab as it passed. Sorry for the trouble, thought Apparite.

He saw another crosswalk ahead but the light was red; too bad, I've got to run it. He honked the horn repeatedly as he approached the intersection; a dozen pedestrians suddenly dove for cover, dropping their packages from the famous Oxford Street shops in their panic and haste (Apparite swore he saw one marked "Selfridges" fly up in the air and land in the middle of the road). The light was still red, red, red as Apparite and the speeding cab got closer and closer, and then . . . it turned red and yellow! Red *and* yellow! What the *f*— does that mean, he wondered?

"God damn it, even the traffic signals are screwy!" he said aloud as he flew through the intersection, crushing a Selfridges bag under the right front tire and seeing another labeled "Marks and Spencer" fly over his windshield, little packages bursting from it like confetti. In the rear-view, he saw the light finally turn green, *just* a tick too late for his benefit. Angry pedestrians were shaking fists and umbrellas at him, and their colorful curses penetrated even the closed windows of the cab, stinging him: *Bleeding arse-hole maniac! Bloody wanker!*

The sun was setting and casting long shadows across the road; after a brief, hurried search for the correct knob, Apparite turned on the cab's headlights. He sped through a light at Regent Street—green, thank God—but then saw two red double-decker London Buses moving slowly ahead of him: one in the regular lane, the other pulling out into the bus lane.

Despite his desperate laying on of the cab's horn they remained unmoved: they reminded Apparite of giant deaf dinosaurs, brains as tiny as walnuts, completely oblivious to his presence as they continued lumbering along at their own plodding, infuriating, ignorant pace. Apparite whipped the car into the near right lane—one of the *wrong*-way lanes on this crowded English thoroughfare—and began dodging the vehicles that were now coming at him head-on as he frantically tried to get ahead of the two buses to his left.

Automobile horns were piling on top of one another, creating a multi-layered symphony of cacophonous wails. Apparite nearly clipped a taxi, coming *that* close to its passenger door, but an oncoming blue Sunbeam Talbot tourer swerved away from Apparite's path and ran smack-dab into the right rear of a green Triumph saloon. The Sunbeam tore off the Triumph's bumper and both cars spun wildly in the middle of the street, causing a massive pile-up behind them; the noise of multiple metal crunches permeated the cab, causing Apparite to visibly cringe at the mutilated machines he had left behind.

Apparite passed the two buses and jerked the cab back into the relative safety of the left lane. Mustering the courage to look in the rear-view mirror, all he could see was those two damned dinosaurs lumbering along behind him, *still* apparently unseeing and unhearing of the events around them. Apparite vowed he would *never* ride one.

The cab passed New Bond Street through a green light, but he could see heavy cross traffic ahead at Davies. He thought he could not possibly go through it without running into someone.

"Green! Green! Green! Green!" Apparite shouted aloud in an anxious, commanding tone, but the light did not hear his pleas and remained red, red, red, red. As he passed into the intersection—picking a small, temporary hole between another black taxi and a little yellow Swallow-Doretti—the light turned red *and* yellow (whatever that meant: he still didn't know), and Apparite clipped the rear bumper of a Triumph that had abruptly appeared in front of him, sending it into a light-pole. The force of the blow sent the taxi's rear end skidding sharply to the right; Apparite whipped the wheel to the left and regained control of the vehicle, but barely. He then looked into the rear-view, expecting the worst. The Triumph, he saw, had wrapped itself around the light pole, but the driver had opened his door—good, thought Apparite; at least I haven't killed him.

He glanced at his watch: four minutes to go. Passing Selfridges and Marks & Spencer—they'll be dealing with some unhappy customers tomorrow, he thought—he saw Marble Arch ahead. He'd have to concentrate when he made his left turn there; it would all be over if he cracked up the cab at this speed. Flying through the clear intersection at Portman Street, he saw the arch and . . . and . . . *now!*

He whipped the wheel to his left, causing the rear end of the cab to lurch suddenly to the right; the tires lost their adhesion and the car spun a full 360 degrees with a loud, long screech. Apparite wildly spun the wheel to the right, expecting to hear and feel the shock of a collision with another vehicle but, by some miracle, he had not hit anything or anyone. Flicking the wheel a little more to the right and then to the left, he got pointed in the general southward direction of Park Lane—one of the swankiest boulevards in all the world—and began tearing down it at over seventy miles per hour.

He passed car after car, swerving right and then left, horn blaring and headlights flashing as cars jumped onto the verge to get out of his way and pedestrians on the sidewalk dove for cover at his approach. Grosvenor House passed, then the Dorchester as he floored the accelerator and passed a black Bentley. He braked to avoid a blue Hillman and then accelerated to get around another of those plodding double-decker London Buses he now hated so much.

He was approaching the Hyde Park Corner roundabout; turning right, he cut through the intersection against traffic: he had no time to circle around like a normal person. As a dozen car horns cried out in alarm, he passed the Wellington Arch at top speed, wheels skidding; two cars swerved to avoid him and collided in at least the tenth metal "crunch" Apparite had heard since he'd left the KGB safe house. He was almost there, almost there; turning down Cromwell he passed Harrods, weaving and darting: swerve here, brake there, around here, brake, accelerate, horn, brake, horn, accelerate. There were two minutes to go, and he was close; so close.

The huge Victoria & Albert and Natural History museums approached on his right; accelerating further, their lengthy grounds passed by seemingly in an instant. Slowing slightly, he whipped the car into a right turn toward Queen's Gate. He cut right across the middle of the intersection and side-swiped, of all things, another London taxi, causing it to jump the curb and bury its front deeply into a wrought-iron fence. Apparite kept his foot on the gas as the street that led to the mews came near.

He turned the corner, drove another fifty yards and then braked hard, parking the car on Queen's Gate. He was still half a block away from the north entrance of the mews, but knew it best not to get too close to the safe house—he did not want to tip the Soviets that he was close, nor did he wish to be anywhere near the cab when the Metropolitan Police inevitably caught up with the offending vehicle. Grabbing the sill-weapon and holding the KGB agent's knife, he jumped out of the cab and tore off down the street. Heart pounding and adrenaline surging, he figured he would be late, but hoped to at least interrupt whatever cruel means the Russians would be using to make J talk, and send them all to hell.

Nineteen
The Price of Duty

Apparite ran into the mews leading to the flat, but heard nothing unusual; only the steady, ambient traffic noises from nearby Cromwell Road—the horns, squeals, accelerating engines, and slamming doors the mind automatically filters out—leaking into the little maze of alleys. He rounded a corner, expecting to see armed KGB agents, but the mews was empty; so far, so good. He sped around another corner, this one less than thirty feet from the flat, and picked up speed: he would meet his foes at full force.

He stiffened when he saw his first enemy leaning against a wall near the flat, smoking a cigarette: it was Standerton. At that moment, Apparite knew he had come too late—not only was it past seven, but the relaxed comfort of Standerton's posture indicated it was all over: Apparite assumed J was, at the least, in the throes of interrogation and torture or, at the most, already dead.

The Englishman remained unaware of Apparite's presence as the Superagent rapidly approached; the White Oriental had taught Apparite the art of running full-bore and yet making little if any sound and it was serving him well. He was twenty-five feet away; then twenty; then fifteen, when finally Standerton realized his danger. He threw down the cigarette and whipped a silencer-tipped pistol out of his overcoat and fired. Though an excellent marksman, Standerton's forte was not in the "quick-draw" and Apparite—using more of the

White Oriental's training—instinctively leapt to his right, anticipating that Standerton would be aiming for his left chest. The leap was not in vain: although the bullet hit Apparite, it buried itself in his left thigh. The wound hurt like hell but he was alive, and it would not impede his fighting abilities; *nothing* would impede them right now.

Using his God-given gymnastic ability, Apparite turned his leap into an airborne roll, the nail-tipped wooden sill scraping on the ground. Before Standerton could get off a second shot, Apparite uncurled his body and threw the knife he still held in his left hand, hitting Standerton full in the right chest. The MI6 agent made a noise—like a soft, little *woof!*—as the knife embedded itself deep within his thoracic cavity, pinning the right side of his overcoat to his chest.

Standerton fired once more but, having been put off-balance by Apparite's knife-throw, he missed his target; he quickly pulled the trigger again, but the weapon made only a dull click—it was empty. He dropped the pistol and drew two knives from the inside pockets of his jacket, his thumbs inserted through a central hole in the base of the all-metal weapons so their glistening, four-inch blades protruded between his fore and middle fingers.

Using the wooden sill like a *bo*-stick, Apparite brought a blow across Standerton's left flank; the nail missed the Englishman, but the board knocked him off-balance and had broken a rib. The English agent winced and brought those deadly knives, one after the other, across Apparite's chest; the razor-sharp blades put large rents in Apparite's borrowed shirt and pierced the skin beneath. Apparite threw himself into a protective crouch, fearful that the knives might have penetrated his chest cavity, but found renewed strength when the breaths he took felt true: the wounds were only superficial. Ignoring the many rivulets of blood flowing down his torso, Apparite instinctively and instantly brought the sill around from his crouch, burying the nail deep into the soft back of the MI6 man's left knee; despite the agony of it, Standerton did not utter a cry. *Christ, he's tough,* Apparite said to himself, quickly standing from his crouched position.

Standerton, thrusting with the blade in his left hand, nearly got Apparite in the gut, but the Superagent was just able to knock it away with his right hand. The Englishman immediately followed with the other, and at an awkward angle for Apparite; in order to block it, he would have to let go of the wooden sill, and he let it fall to the ground. Standerton's right hand, with its gleaming blade sticking out four inches past his clenched fingers, came closer and closer to Apparite's exposed midsection. At the last possible moment, Apparite swung his left arm around; he blocked the Englishman's blow but at the expense of a deep slash into the forearm, causing him to grimace in pain.

Standerton brought around a vicious karate kick with his right leg; Apparite threw himself on the ground to duck under it, simultaneously kicking at the inside part of the Englishman's left knee. The MI6 agent cried out softly in pain as the skillfully delivered blow connected, rupturing one of the ligaments and severing the cartilage. Apparite's kick had been off-balance and without its full power, but the result had been devastating to the Englishman: his knee had been rendered unstable and useless.

Standerton, though made practically immobile from his knee injury, freed the blade he had been holding in his left palm from its thumb hole and grabbed it between his right thumb and forefinger. He was separated from Apparite by only four feet, and his knife throw could not miss: Standerton skillfully launched the blade, which traveled the distance so rapidly that no defense was available for the

American other than a quick turn of his body away from the knife's path. With a dull sound it firmly lodged within Apparite's right deltoid, bringing another flash of silent pain to his face.

Though limping and having difficulty standing, Standerton lunged with the blade still in his right hand. Apparite skillfully deflected it with his left, and as Standerton's thrust had left him open to a kick in the midsection, Apparite sent the MI6 agent flying into the wall with a right-footed karate kick, his steel-weighted shoe connecting full-force on the Englishman's exposed torso.

Standerton slumped to the ground, panting and wheezing as the effects of the knife protruding from his chest began to take its toll. He was pale; his lung deflating; his knee useless; and he was dying, but nevertheless, he was not about to leave this world alone: he took his remaining knife and let it fly at the American. As if in slowed-motion, the knife seemed to traverse the seventy-two inches between them very slowly and deliberately, almost one at a time, and as it closed in on Apparite he reached down before him and, whether by luck or design, he saw the wooden sill sitting there at his feet, not unlike a dog awaiting the orders of its master.

He brought it up with lightning speed and the blade embedded itself deep into the wood. Apparite walked up to the panting Standerton to give him the coup de grace, wooden sill in hand. The Englishman looked resigned to his fate: he was breathing very heavily and the color had completely drained from his face; the ground around him was stained red from his many wounds.

And yet, he was still not finished. When Apparite got within a foot of him, the Englishman's right hand expertly brought yet another dagger from his lower left inside overcoat pocket and thrust it at the Superagent's gut. But not fast enough: with even greater speed, Apparite brought the sill down and to the left, expertly blocking the knife-thrust. He grabbed the MI6 agent's right hand and brought the blade it still held up to Standerton's throat.

"We've got your man, you know," Standerton said in a gurgling rasp.

Apparite dropped the wooden sill and used his free hand to slap Standerton full across the face.

"You f——g traitor; you're not worthy to speak of him to me." Apparite pressed the blade further into Standerton's neck until blood began to run down from it in a single and steady stream. He pushed it ever deeper into the Englishman's throat, ready to end it, but then stopped: Apparite had thought of Hitch, and Agent G, and especially J, whom he assumed was already dead or beyond saving, and he flew into a rage.

He violently slapped the Englishman repeatedly with his right hand, the blade he was holding in his left puncturing the soft tissues of Standerton's neck over and over again; countless streams of blood now covered it. His voice rose almost to a yell, creating a din louder than their battle.

"Why did you do it?" Apparite cried out at him. "Why? You had everything, you bastard! Why did you do it?" He stopped, having exhausted his anger and energy, and looked at the Englishman for an answer.

Standerton smiled in defiance at his tormentor.

"Go to hell!" he said, as foaming blood-red saliva spilled from his mouth and his body jerked in its death spasms.

Without hesitation, Apparite thrust the blade fully to the hilt into Standerton's neck; he then quickly withdrew it and plunged it deeply into the dying Englishman's heart. The man had been a ruthless traitor to his agency and to his nation, staining his family's legacy with the blood of at least two friendly agents, and Apparite rejoiced angrily in his demise: he spat in Standerton's face and let him slump into the gutter where he belonged.

He then heard slow footsteps coming from the end of the mews, but in an odd rhythm: the *clip-cloomp, clip-cloomp* of one who limps, favoring a leg. Apparite pulled the knife from Standerton's still chest and, although wounded in the thigh and arm, stood unsteadily, grunting with the effort. He scanned the area for Standerton's gun but in the growing darkness could not see it, and recalled that it was empty, regardless.

Apparite knew the noise did not announce the arrival of the police; they'd come crashing into the mews like stampeding cattle, he thought. Nor was it likely a passer-by; the neighborhood had looked deserted, and there had been no voices. The only other noise—aside from the footsteps—was the random clamor of the traffic from Cromwell Road, which had continued as if nothing of any import at all was occurring in the little mews. *Clip-cloomp, clip-cloomp, clip-cloomp,* he heard, and then the sound of the steps stopped.

"Mr. Kramer," a voice said, unmistakably announcing the presence of Viktor, the SMERSH agent. He stood twenty feet away; out of Apparite's knife-range but not out of *his* pistol-range: he was holding a Tokarev with silencer and it was aimed squarely at his quarry. His thigh was heavily bandaged in the place where Hitch had stabbed him, and when Apparite noted the Russian's broken right arm hanging in a sling across his chest, he could not suppress a smile, taking pleasure in the damage he had caused with his karate thrust in the Reading Room.

"Mr. Kramer," Viktor repeated in his gravelly voice, "it is time to have talk. You may come inside to have, or you may stay here and have."

"I'm saying nothing. You'll have to kill me right here."

"I will kill you, just like the other," he said, although Apparite could not guess whether he was referring to Hitch or J.

Apparite was trapped, and he did the first thing he could think of: he threw his knife as hard as he could at Viktor and catapulted himself into the direction of a nearby doorway, thinking it might afford him at least a minimum of temporary protection. As he did so, he heard the *pheewt!* of a silenced gunshot, and Apparite reflexively tensed, awaiting the inevitable sting and burn of a bullet entering his unprotected body, but it did not occur.

Instead, he heard running footsteps and then another silenced shot. Apparite poked his head out of the doorway, peered around the corner, and saw Viktor running with a limp out of the mews toward Cromwell Road, having been shot in his left arm. A moment later, a car started and drove off; Apparite guessed that Viktor was behind the wheel, although how the SMERSH agent was able to drive with his wounds was beyond his reckoning. Then again, Apparite *had* seen him pull a knife from his own thigh using a broken arm, so anything, he figured, was possible.

But who had chased him off? Aside from Apparite and J, only Hitch and Standerton had known the time and place of the rendezvous, and both of them were dead. There could be only one answer: it had been his Shadow-agent. When Apparite had not showed for the rendezvous, his Shadow would have been alerted and sped to the flat in the mews. Apparite wondered who he would be—and if he would even show himself—when he heard slow, steady footsteps coming toward him, and knew their meeting was inevitable—and, he realized, possibly final. He sat back in the doorway, waiting for the appearance of the man that might have to kill him if their agency had been significantly exposed.

The form of a human shadow made an appearance around the doorway, distorted by the angle of the light which cast it; it looked long and stretched, as if being pulled by the ends. Slowly, as the man came closer, the shadow contracted until the recognizable form of a person appeared; a man with a raised Beretta pistol and silencer aimed directly at Apparite's head. The gunman removed his hat and light fell upon his face, revealing a grave visage Apparite knew all too well.

It was the Director: Apparite realized the operation had been deemed so critically important that his supervisor had personally taken on the role of Shadow-agent. Holding the gun as steady as stone, the Director spoke in that familiar, official tone which Apparite had always found so discomforting.

"We have to go inside, Apparite. We need to see if there has been a breach." Motioning with his weapon for Apparite to rise, the young agent did so, though in a greater effort than it had taken even a few moments before: he was losing blood and strength.

Dragging his injured leg behind him, Apparite knew what was to come: if J had been interrogated, then his own life was in jeopardy. He was unsure if the Director would kill him or not, but knowing the man's fanatical commitment to secrecy, he thought it probable. It pained him to feel so helpless, and his heart was torn as he weighed the possibilities: he prayed that J would still be living, but knew that if it were so, both of their lives might be forfeit. The Director followed Apparite into the flat, steadily holding the Beretta on him from a short distance. But there was nothing for it: Apparite would not fight and he would not try to escape; he knew to do so would be cowardly and sinful to the spy code.

The Director flipped the light switch, revealing that the

flat was in utter disarray: the manicured potted palms were upturned; the elegant mahogany coffee table smashed; and pictures had been ripped from the wall. Three dead KGB agents lay on the floor, each with knife or bullet-wounds, and blood stained nearly every square foot of the carpets beneath them. Lying on the sofa, in his usual place by some bizarre chance, was J: his lips were blue, his eyes were closed, and his chest was not discernibly moving. He had bullet wounds in both thighs, and many slashes about his arms and chest. Apparite realized he had underestimated the liaison's ability to fight when cornered: J might have died, but he had taken three armed KGB agents with him. The White Oriental would have honored him—it had been a "good fight."

"An 'L-pill,' " the Director said in a grave tone. "When he knew he would be taken, he took an 'L-pill' to avoid interrogation."

Apparite walked over to J and placed a forefinger on the left side of his neck, feeling for a carotid pulse. He thought he felt a slight stir, but even if a weak pulse had been present, it was hopeless: taking an "L-pill" was to begin a journey from which there was no return. Apparite could do nothing and his emotions overwhelmed him.

"Didn't you know I'd come?" he said, his voice quavering with emotion. "Didn't you know I'd never let them take you?"

Whether it was from the sound of Apparite's voice, or the touch of the young agent's hand on his neck, J weakly opened his eyes, and although the stricken liaison could not speak, the emotion that emanated from them spoke directly to Apparite as clearly as words.

"*I knew you'd come for me,*" they seemed to be saying, "*but I didn't have a choice.*" A hint of a smile formed across J's face, lifting his cheeks and the corners of his eyes, and Apparite started to weep, his tears falling onto J's forehead and rolling down the liaison's face, giving J the appearance that he, too, was weeping. He looked at Apparite one last time, his eyes expressing the deep affection and respect he had for the young agent, and then he was gone.

Apparite began sobbing, uncaring whether the Director thought him weak, or queer, or anything at all, and he did so without reserve: it was time for him to mourn and the whole world could go to hell. He reached down, gently closed J's eyes, and then embraced him, weeping as if the world itself and everyone in it had died to protect him. He felt a hand on his shoulder; to his amazement, it was the Director's, initiating a human connection with Apparite and comforting him in a manner that would have seemed an impossibility but for the fact that it was happening. Apparite reached up and embraced the man's hand, longing for the touch of another human being; of anyone who might sympathize with him or lessen his pain.

"We have to go, John," the Director said, unexpectedly using Apparite's first name (for one of only three times, it later proved).

Roused from his grief by the unfamiliarity and shock of hearing that name, Apparite stood and nodded his head in reluctant, though resigned agreement. He reached down, gently gripped J's shoulder for a moment (like his colleague had done to him so many times in the past), and left the flat with the Director.

"What will happen to him?" Apparite asked in a whisper.

"Don't worry; I'll make sure he's taken care of. But we need to get out of here. I made a few calls to delay the police, but that won't last forever; they'll be here soon. Someday, Apparite, I'll show you where he'll rest."

The two men walked onto Queen's Gate, to be met by the

two-note musical sound of English police cars; rising in intensity and pitch, it foretold the impending arrival of the Metropolitan Police to the mews. The Director silently led Apparite to a Triumph saloon car parked nearby and they climbed inside.

"You're wounded; I'll take you to a doctor at another safe house."

Apparite nodded in agreement, feeling as weak from the death of his colleague as much as from his many injuries. The Director pulled away from the curb and turned south towards the Thames; out of the corner of his eye, Apparite saw the police turn onto the street which led to the mews.

"Take good care of him," he said as he looked back toward the little flat, speaking to no one in particular.

It was nearly dark, and a thick blanket of clouds obscured what little light was coming from a sun which had long disappeared over the horizon. The Director turned the car right then left, then left and right, as he negotiated the short, maze-like streets which led to Chelsea, and Apparite, who no longer had the strength to remain upright, assumed a nearly supine position in the back seat. As the car made turn after turn toward yet another of the Director's many safe houses, Apparite began to sway from side to side, side to side, until he had been lulled to sleep by the softly rocking motion.

Twenty
Back Amongst the Living

When Apparite awoke, he was in a small, nicely furnished home with cranberry-painted walls and cream trim. A large marble fireplace was in front of him, and he took comfort in the warmth which radiated from the fire within it: this seemed as homey a place as he had been in for many months, or even years, he thought. He looked about him and saw he was alone; the Director was nowhere to be seen.

He was lying on a small though comfortable couch in the center of the room. Looking down, he noted that his wounds had been fully dressed and that he had been nearly fully undressed; he was now wearing only a flannel robe and boxer-style undershorts. He heard someone coming, but his danger-sense remained quiet—although the footsteps sounded unfamiliar, they did not feel threatening to him.

A kindly looking, silver-haired elderly man appeared. He had a well-groomed beard, and was informally dressed in tan corduroy trousers and a gray wool sweater. He gave Apparite a smile and then took the agent's pulse at the wrist.

"Welcome to my little hospital, Mr. Apparite," he said in a slight French-sounding accent. "I am Dr. Hoevenaers; your supervisor brought you here so I may tend your wounds."

Apparite managed a weak, "Thank you."

"You are a lucky man. The bullet in your thigh missed the femoral artery by millimeters; a little nearer to the groin and you would have been dead."

He fished into a traditional black leather doctor's bag and withdrew a syringe, needle, and small vial.

"I need to inject your buttock with a dose of penicillin; please roll over."

Apparite complied and then winced as the man injected quite a few cc's of liquid into the Superagent's left gluteal region.

"I've also given you a small dose of morphia to dull your pain and bring on sleep." He put the syringe and vial back into his bag and smiled at his patient. "Last evening I removed the bullet from your leg and sutured your wounds: I believe they will not trouble you further. You have earned a few more scars, however, as you shall soon see."

Apparite was growing woozy with the morphine; all he could do was nod inaccurately in the doctor's general direction as his head bobbed like a doll's. When the doctor resumed speaking, the morphine had distorted his voice in Apparite's mind, making it sound as if he was underwater.

"I will let you rest, for now. When you awaken in the morning, it is important that you begin walking again—take a few steps at a time, and hold pressure on your leg sutures when you do so. Your supervisor told me to say he will return before noon tomorrow. He will answer your questions at that time."

Although Apparite's mind was swimming, random questions floated past and occasionally one came near enough for his enfeebled mind to latch onto: Who was this French-sounding doctor, this Hoevenaers? What will the British say about Standerton? What will they say about Hitch? Where is Viktor? Is the Queen safe? Where did they take J's body? *Why can't I think straight?* His chin sank to his chest and he was dead to the world for many hours, which was exactly what John Apparite needed to be.

★ ★ ★ ★ ★

He awoke at ten a.m.; bright sunlight was shining through the thin lace curtains, warming and comforting him. He went to the window and peered through the pattern in the lace, but what he saw struck him only in its banality: people walking their dogs, stopping to let them soil the pavement; London taxis delivering *Times*-reading businessmen to their appointments; and delivery trucks bringing goods to houses along this quiet Chelsea street—*as if nothing at all had happened the day before.* The only event which would have marked that day for this quiet neighborhood would have been the sight of a young man being carried into the little townhouse across the street last evening, and all anyone would have thought at the time was, *"Poor soul: he must be ill, or drunk!"*

A door opened; Apparite turned his head and saw the Director enter the room. He had a morning newspaper—the *Daily Mirror*—and held it up for Apparite to see.

Apparite recoiled in anticipation, expecting to see the words "Reading Room Terror," or "Murder at the British Museum" plastered across the top. Instead, and to his astonishment, there appeared only the unremarkable headline, *"Queen Elizabeth to Appear at State Opening of Parliament: Rumours of Illness Unfounded. "*

The Director handed the newspaper to him. Rifling through it, Apparite saw no mention of his frantic drive in the London taxi; no mention of the bloody Reading Room encounter; no mention of the two dead KGB agents at the Soviet safe-house; no mention of the massacre at the mews; and, specifically, no mention of William Standerton or Clive Hitch.

"How did you do it? How did you keep it all hidden?" Apparite asked, baffled (and impressed) by the feat.

"I made three phone calls: one to MI Five, one to MI Six,

and one to CI Director Allen Dulles. They, in turn, contacted the right people to keep it quiet; not as difficult as it sounds, particularly since I chose the right words to convey the importance of their cooperation."

"What will happen with Hitch? And what about Standerton—does MI Six know about him?"

"I told them about Standerton; the silence on the other end of the line was enough to tell me they were ignorant of his treason. Not that it would matter—they would never publicly admit his treachery, particularly since his family is in the peerage. I'm guessing William Standerton will die honorably and in the line of duty at a future date."

The thought that even one person might think Standerton a hero who had died doing his duty appalled Apparite.

"The SOB killed Hitch and G! He might as well have killed J! How can they do that?"

The Director held up his hand in a gesture that silenced the angry agent.

"Someday the truth will come out; his name will be reviled in the end, as it should be. For now, you will have to be content to know that his treachery will not be forgotten in MI Six: *they* know what he did. As for Hitch, I think MI Five will eventually leak his exploits, especially as it will raise the morale of their agency. The public will never know the full details of what happened in the Reading Room, but Hitch will not be forgotten."

Apparite then realized something: the Director had found out what had transpired in the Reading Room, but how? He couldn't have been there—or *could* he? Guessing the nature of the quizzical expression that had formed on Apparite's face, the Director cleared the confusion.

"I wasn't there, of course, but I know what happened. I have many reliable and accurate sources in Scotland Yard, as you should have guessed."

Of course, thought Apparite: he had forgotten the legendary information-gathering capabilities of the Director's agency. How had the man phrased it at that first meeting? *Oh yes,* Apparite said to himself, they had *"infinite intelligence gathering capabilities; as invisible as the microscopic insects that live in our eyebrows and scavenge dead skin for food."*

A mental flash hit Apparite like an iron cosh: he had forgotten someone.

"What happened to the boy?" he asked anxiously. "The boy whose throat Viktor slashed?"

"He's in University College Hospital."

"He didn't die?" Apparite said in disbelief. "He didn't die?"

"No; the ambulance came shortly after you bound his neck. He was rushed to surgery in critical condition, but will survive."

Although Apparite was relieved to hear it, he felt some measure of shame mixing with his joy that the boy's life had been spared: if he had run past him and let him die, perhaps J would now be alive, and perhaps Viktor would be dead. Had he made the right decision? *Was* there even a right decision? Would he ever be able to tell the Director the choice he had faced, and the choice he had made? Or had the Director—who seemed to know *everything* anyway—already guessed it?

"I wonder," Apparite said, thinking of all that had been lost, "if it was worth it." The Director did not hesitate to answer.

"The Soviet fuel engineer is in the hospital and will be dead in forty-eight hours; he cannot be replaced. Viktor has been seriously wounded—in pride and in body—and has been smuggled out of the country; although he is not dead, he has been incapacitated for a time. The KGB's London bureau has been decimated to the point where, at present, there is only a token KGB presence in this city. There is even a chance the Soviets will develop the false fuel formula, wasting valuable time and resources. You tell me if it was worth it."

Apparite thought it over. Everything the Director had said was true, but then again, so was this: Agent J was dead, and he had been Apparite's closest friend and colleague; Clive Hitch, the man who had saved Apparite's life in the Reading Room, had lost his life as well. A frightened teenaged boy lay in a hospital bed, his throat laid open by Viktor's knife, having become involved in this affair by unhappy chance; he might have escaped death, but forever would be scarred.

So many lives had been lost, and so many others had been irrevocably changed, that although much had been accomplished in the name of the United States and of Apparite's duty that day, a part of him would have gladly given it all away to spend a few more moments drinking pints with J and Clive at the Red Lion. But that was not the way the world worked, he knew, and a Superagent could not afford to have regrets.

"I know that J did what had to be done," he said, when he was ready to speak. "Just as you and I would have, if the program was in danger of being breached. And Clive died in the line of duty; I suppose none of us would have it any other way."

The Director, sensing Apparite's melancholy, changed the subject to one which would almost certainly pique his young charge's interest, if not wholly distract him from his troubles.

"Perhaps you'd like to know how the 'Nats' did."

Hell yes, thought Apparite: he'd been exiled to London without any baseball news for almost two months, and suddenly felt starved for it.

"Where did they finish?" he asked with emotion. "Did they put it all together in September?"

The Director sighed: while he knew that Apparite would welcome any news of the Senators, he also knew that the news wasn't good.

"In the cellar," he said. "They finished fifty-three and one-oh-one; even Dressen couldn't save them from themselves"

Apparite's expression became one of shock: the Senators were awful, but they couldn't have been *that* terrible. It had been their lowest finish in half a decade.

"What *happened?*" he asked.

"Injuries for one. Yost out for weeks with that tonsillitis; sore-armed pitchers; plus outfielders that couldn't field, and pinch-hitters that couldn't hit—you name it. There's some hope for next year—a third baseman named Killebrew came on strong with Yost out—but fifty-five was a complete debacle."

The Director could see the crestfallen look on Apparite's face and knew it would only get worse with what else he had to say. He began to regret having changed to this subject.

"But there's more," the Director said, his voice sounding even more serious than the sentence before.

"What?" Apparite asked, sensing something really horrible was coming: had Mickey Vernon wrenched his back again? Had they traded up and coming outfielder Roy Sievers?

"Clark Griffith died five days ago. Calvin is now in charge of the team."

Apparite visibly whitened at the news: the Hall of Fame pitcher and decades-long owner of the Washington Senators; the namesake of the stadium and the heart and soul of the club, was dead.

"And there's been talk of moving the team," added the Director. "Maybe to Minnesota or maybe Los Angeles. I thought you should know."

Apparite felt the room begin to spin: losing the " 'Nats" would be akin to losing a brother. There had always been a deep, unbreakable bond between Apparite and his ball club, especially in the spring when the grass greened and the sound of a bat hitting a baseball eclipsed all others in its beauty. And now the Senators, whom he had depended upon these past eight years to make him feel human when nothing else had, and in whom he had invested all of his emotions, might be gone, and it hurt him worse than a wound. It was beyond the most pessimistic of his imaginings that someday they might be lost to him; the idea had never occurred to him.

He put his hand to his forehead; he was sweating profusely. Move the Senators from Washington? Apparite pictured a lonely Griffith Stadium filled with over-grown weeds and rotting bleachers; a decay so pervasive and inevitable that even the dirt and pebbles that had been trodden upon in triumph and defeat by Walter Johnson, Sam Rice, and Goose Goslin would eventually blow away into oblivion with the passage of time. Soon, he thought, no one would be able to recall the feats of the great players of the Washington Senators Baseball Club at all: there would be just a few yellowing newspaper clippings, some grainy photographs, a few thousand feet of jerky newsreel footage, and the dusty reminiscences of old men to remind the world of the team that once was.

Apparite was nauseated and his heart was pounding; he sensed a panic coming on. He began fighting it as if it was a living thing, but it had gotten its claws too deeply into him and he was losing (and besides, how can you win a battle against yourself?). It was happening full-bore now, completely out of his control, his heart racing just as it had on the airplane, and the nausea rising just like it had when he'd killed Robert Kramer. Most appalling to him was that it was happening in the presence of the Director.

Apparite knelt on the floor; he was hyperventilating. The Director, noting his distress, walked over to him and put his hand kindly on his shoulder.

"There's still hope Calvin won't move them; maybe if fifty-six is a better year and attendance picks up they'll last a bit longer in D.C."

Apparite was comforted by his sentiment, but even more so at the hint of the camaraderie between them. *"We're in this together,"* the Director seemed to be saying, *"even to the very end."* Seeing Apparite's downcast expression, the Director reached into the inside pocket of his black suit and removed a brown envelope.

"Here's something that might make you feel better," he said. Apparite stood up from his kneeling position, having just about regained conscious control of his emotions. He held out his hand and the Director handed him the envelope. Apparite's mood rose visibly, expelling any residual panic, when he opened it and saw what was tucked inside.

It was a first class, one-way ticket to New York on the Cunard liner *Queen Elizabeth*, and it departed in three days— he would *not* have to take an airplane home, after all. He smiled: the Director knew everything, of course; hell, the Director *always* knew everything.

"I have to leave you now," the Director said. "I'll see you back at the warehouse in D.C. Enjoy your voyage home."

The doctor returned that evening; he removed the bandages covering Apparite's wounds and prodded them gently with a sterile metal probe.

"No suppuration or induration; no evidence of infection," he said in a formal though gentle manner. "Very good. You have no fever?" he asked.

"No; I feel fine," Apparite answered. "I wish I could be up and around more; maybe go outside."

The doctor got a concerned look on his face.

"That is not possible; your supervisor wishes you to stay indoors. He feels it is too dangerous for you to be seen in London. It is best to remain here until you take the train to Southampton."

Apparite nodded; he knew it was true. But if he had to stay indoors with this doctor, he at least wanted to know more of *his* story: where had he come from? What was *his* relationship with the Director?

"Am I allowed to ask who you are?" Apparite ventured, too curious to remain silent.

"Probably not," the man answered as expected. "But I will tell you some of it anyway," he added, smiling at Apparite. "I am an old man, and have learned when a person may be trusted and when they may not. I know I may trust you."

He sat down in a chair and lit his pipe; warm, richly scented smoke began to fill the room.

"I have known your supervisor for many years; he once saved the lives of my family, before the war with the Germans. He is a very great man, although he must do many unpleasant things. Even," he said, leaning closer to Apparite as if in fear of being overheard, "even the *killing* of persons. But he is a just man; I do not believe he would kill without reason."

His pipe had gone out. He stopped talking to relight it, extinguishing the lit match by a gentle, elegant shake of his hand.

"Many years ago, I pledged to do whatever I might to help

him," the doctor said warmly, "and the debt has been reduced, though not yet repaid."

He leaned back and looked at Apparite with a curious expression on his face.

"You remind me of someone from long ago; from the war. My memory is not what it used to be, but somehow I feel I have met you before. Have you ever been to Belgium, Mr. Apparite?"

Apparite shook his head. "No; this is my first trip overseas."

"Ah, then I suppose I am thinking of someone else. No matter. I should tell you nothing more, regardless."

Apparite nodded in understanding of the doctor's reticence; he had been amazed to hear him say anything at all about the Director or their past together. And yet this brief and cryptic conversation would be dissected by Apparite over and over again: although he had discovered a few facts and formed a few theories about the Director's past, the doctor's statements had opened up a whole new avenue of questions for him to ponder: *Why did he think he'd met me before? Why did he ask me if I'd ever been to Belgium? Was there some hidden link between himself, the doctor, and the enigmatic Director, perhaps?*

The doctor resumed speaking.

"I should also say that I am sorry for your friend; the one called J. I knew him little, but could tell he was a kind and brave man—and so very humorous! It is interesting: so many homosexuals are unusually kind and humorous, you know."

"*Homosexual?*" Apparite said, his voice rising in disbelief. "*J* was a homosexual?"

"Yes—did you not know? He spoke to me once about it: I believe he felt more comfortable speaking with a stranger, or perhaps it is because I am a doctor. He had the highest regard for you. He spoke of you with the greatest affection."

Of course, thought Apparite; *it explained everything:* J's obsessive need for privacy; his dislike of J. Edgar Hoover; and his willingness to work in the Director's unnamed agency. Apparite figured he knew what had happened: J was an FBI agent who had been discovered to be homosexual and had been drummed out of the agency by Hoover in disgrace. Disowned from the agency he had loved, he had satisfied his need to serve his nation by joining the Director's program.

Had the Director known about him? Absolutely, thought Apparite; the Director left nothing to chance, even taking the trouble to research Apparite's own sexual preferences. Had he cared? No, Apparite decided. J had been highly competent and fiercely loyal, and *that* was all that had mattered to the Director. And who else but J, a man whose FBI career had been ended by exposure, could know the overriding importance of secrecy? Apparite's stoic visage began to crumble as he thought about him: the crushing pain of J's death was returning as acutely as when he had first seen him lying on the couch after taking the "L-pill." He wondered how long it would take to get over it—or if he ever would.

"I must travel to Brussels tonight; my daughter has unfortunately fallen ill," the doctor said, "so you will be on your own until your ship sails. Your supervisor has already departed for the United States; he wished me to tell you that. He has, at your request, downgraded your ship's ticket to tourist Class—did you not want to travel in *style,* Mr. Apparite?"

"Well, I thought the first class ticket was too expensive; a big waste of money. I know I'd feel better being in tourist."

The doctor laughed.

"*Such* an unusual man! So many young people throwing their money away on nothings and you *want* to travel tourist

Class! No wonder he speaks so well of you."

The doctor rose from his chair, went to a cupboard, took out three small pill canisters, and walked over to Apparite.

"If you feel ill, take one of the blue pills; if you wish to sleep, take one of the green pills; if you are in pain, take one of the red pills. If you have a fever, or your wounds turn warm or red, you must give yourself a shot of antibiotic," he said, as he gestured toward three pre-filled metal syringes, "in the muscle of the thigh. Inject it in the thickest part."

Apparite nodded, desperately hoping he would not have a fever for the next seventy-two hours, and that his wounds remained clean: like so many men who do not blanch at even the goriest of wounds, he could not fathom giving himself an injection.

The doctor walked to the front door, opening it quietly. As he walked out of the house, Apparite heard him laughing softly to himself and saying, in French, "Tourist class. Tourist class."

Apparite spent the next two days exercising and keeping himself limber; to his relief, his wounds remained clear of any sign of infection, and the diabolical-appearing metal syringes remained unused. He had found use for one of the blue pills and two of the green ones, but had not had to take any of the red ones. By the afternoon of the second day, however, he had developed a condition that back home in Maryland they called "cabin fever": a sudden urge to rush out of the house and get some fresh air back into his lungs. Unfortunately, the doctor had given him no pill to treat that particular malady.

Although Apparite knew it was unwise to go outside, he felt compelled to make a few visits before he went back to the States: first, he would go to University College Hospital and see the young boy whose throat Viktor had slashed, and then to St. Paul's Cathedral to try and find some measure of peace with his decisions. Following that, and under cloak of darkness, he would return to the Royal Artillery Memorial where he had a final, though important errand to run. He did not doubt that the Russians were searching for him, but hadn't he been sequestered in secret to the town house in Chelsea? And hadn't the Director said the KGB's presence in London had been reduced to a mere token? After all, he would be taking a chance with no one's life but his own, and he would be very cautious.

Apparite, though limping somewhat from his leg wound, made his way to the Fulham Broadway underground station. On his journey to the hospital he listened carefully to the conversations of the persons around him, trying to detect any Slavic intonations or Russian phrases that hinted at an enemy presence, but there were none and his danger-sense remained still. He checked and rechecked his steps many times along the way, looking carefully for tails but, again, nothing suspicious declared itself. By the time he had reached University College Hospital, and despite the fact that his wounded leg was becoming quite uncomfortable, he had relaxed considerably. *Good grief,* he thought, *there are countless people in London, so why do I think I'm going to be discovered so easily, one man among millions?*

Inquiring discreetly at the desk, he learned the unfortunate young man's name: Edward Humphreys; age of seventeen. He took a lift to the floor where the post-surgical unit was located and began walking down the hall with purpose—they never stop someone in a hospital who walks with purpose, he surmised—until he saw a clipboard outside a large ward marked "Post-Operative Care." *This must be it,* he thought.

Taking the clipboard in hand, he found Humphreys' name

and deduced that his bed would be the third from the left in the sizable open ward. As surreptitiously as Apparite could— which was not very, he thought, so he knew he didn't have much time—he lingered just outside the door for a few moments. As he did so, Apparite took a quick glance at the young man in the bed in question: he had a tracheotomy tube protruding through the sizable large yellow and red-stained bandage secured around his neck, but was sitting up and taking sips of water from a cup. Apparite dared to walk a short distance into the room and, taking a closer look at the young man's face, saw that it indeed was the boy from the museum.

Two persons entered the ward, a middle-aged man in working-man's clothes and a woman in a flowered house-dress, and edged past Apparite. They made straight for young Humphreys with urgency in their steps.

"Eddie! Eddie my love!" the woman said, rushing up and embracing the boy: it was the first time young Humphreys' mother had seen him since he had regained consciousness just an hour ago. The man walked toward him as well, though much more slowly, deliberately, and with obvious trepidation.

"Hello, son," he said, trying not to look at the boy's bandaged neck. "Thank God you've made it." He then lost all his composure and rushed up to embrace his son, and the three of them sobbed and held on to each other as if they were one. Although young Humphreys could not yet speak because of his wound, the stream of tears running down his smiling face needed no voice or translation: *I'm alive.*

Apparite had been profoundly moved by the tearful reunion; he could feel his eyes beginning to mist over and his jaw began to tremble, and he had to rush out of the room or risk discovery. But the reunion remained bittersweet for him: young Edward Humphreys was alive, but Apparite could not shake the feeling that somehow he had been to blame for what had happened to him.

The day was getting late, thought Apparite, but if he hurried to the city, he could just slip in a visit to St. Paul's before it closed. Ensuring that he was not being followed, he took the Tube to the cathedral—no need to consult the map now, having made the journey many times—and walked up the steps to the main entrance. Perhaps, he told himself, I can find the answers to my questions here—if there are any answers to be found.

The cathedral closed in less than fifteen minutes, so there were only a dozen persons walking about. Some were staring up at the ceiling in awe of its majesty, others were quietly talking about the architectural features of the building, and a few were reading the inscriptions on the memorials, just as Apparite had done so often before. But despite the tragic events of the preceding days, he still felt that indefinable *something* in the building: he felt it in the silence that seemed to bind the persons in the cathedral like threads of gossamer, and in the expressions of reverential delight which graced the faces of all who entered it.

The organ began to play; a rich, booming sound that drowned out conversation by its volume, though it would have done so anyway—the music falling upon those in the cathedral had the effect of saying, "hush, it's time to be quiet now," and all had naturally fallen silent. Apparite slowly walked over to the memorials he knew so well, hoping to find some inspiration in the familiar names of Hay and Faulknor, whom the young agent had begun to consider his friends and colleagues, in a fashion.

What would they have done in the Reading Room? Apparite asked himself. Could *they* have let innocent, young Humphreys die in the pursuit of their quarry? Would they have faulted him for choosing to aid the young man? He stared at the memorials, struggling to find an answer to these questions.

A small group of persons walked by, necks craned upwards as they stared at the ceiling of the cathedral's dome, and on each of their faces was a rapturous expression. *These* were the kind of people he had been charged to protect, thought Apparite, and seeing the delight they took in Wren's masterpiece made him realize that the Director had been correct in his assessment: despite all of their losses, the mission *had* been worth it.

These people would never know how close their young queen had been to assassination in a rogue SMERSH agent's plan, nor how near the Soviets had been to stealing secrets that would have allowed them to encircle the U.S. and Britain with nuclear missiles, but that was, perhaps, the way it *should* be, Apparite decided. Compared to the millions of Americans and Britons who would sleep more soundly in their beds that night, the sacrifices of men like G, Hitch, and J had not only been worth it; in fact, they had been *expected*. And, he now realized, the taking of the life of an occasional innocent like Edward Humphreys had been expected as well.

Apparite drew a cruel conclusion about the confrontation in the Reading Room: it had been his unfortunate duty to let Humphreys die, but he had let the wounded boy's plight cloud his judgment at the expense of his duty. Apparite left the cathedral cursing his weakness and the conundrums which his profession had thrust upon him, but it had not been a wasted trip: Superagent John Apparite had not only learned the high price of his duty, but also that it must always be paid.

After a pint at the Olde Mitre, he picked up some supplies at a shop and took the Tube to St. James's Park; darkness had descended on the city, and he could now go to the Royal Artillery Memorial to complete his last task of the day. Looking around as he approached it, he saw no one in sight and surreptitiously slipped behind the large, curving memorial; he then walked to the spot where Agent G had been killed and knelt down.

He ran his hands across the smooth concrete of the memorial: it felt as cold as a tombstone, he thought; an apt analogy in the place where his colleague had died. Looking to his left and right, and seeing no one (in fact, Apparite was very well-hidden between two large bushes), he took a small hammer and chisel from his overcoat. Holding the chisel in his right hand and the hammer in his left, he began to chip out small pieces of stone as softly as he could, ignoring the discomfort of his wounded arm.

There were memorials to every conceivable branch and type of military service in the city of London, and Apparite had decided that agents J, G, and Clive Hitch would have theirs. He thought it fitting that it would be hidden from view, discoverable only by chance or by one who had been told of its secret location. And, appropriately, the masses of persons whose lives these dead men had been charged to protect would walk by the spot every day, unaware of the presence of their little memorial, or their sacrifice, or even their existence, just as it had always been.

Apparite quickly carved out their initials in the order of their deaths: first "G," for the Superagent who had been killed here; and then "CH," for Clive Hitch, the MI5 agent who had pushed his personal demons aside and died for his country; and then "J," for Apparite's friend and colleague, who had taken his own life to protect their agency. When the hammering was done, Apparite blew the dust and bits of concrete from the marks, and bowed his head in tribute to his fallen colleagues.

He took his tools back to the little house in Chelsea but did not dispose of them; as long as he lived, he would to return to carve into the memorial the names of future agents who would sacrifice their lives in the line of duty. Even today, if one were to slip unnoticed behind the Royal Artillery Memorial and look close to the ground, sweeping away the detritus from the undergrowth, the marks might still be visible, though many years have passed. If one were to count them, their number would exceed a dozen.

Twenty-one
What Goes Around

The next morning after an early and unsatisfying breakfast of bangers, toast, eggs, and coffee—and only the coffee was any good, he muttered to himself, while he cleaned up afterwards—Apparite boarded the train for Southampton. Rubbing his eyes, he found he had become unexpectedly tired, which was especially surprising since he had felt pretty good physically just the day before. If he could find no physical explanation for his fatigue, then he figured it must be a purely mental exhaustion that was manifesting itself.

And he had plenty to be emotionally exhausted about: he continued to struggle with the deaths of his colleagues, and could not get the sight of the wounded boy out of his mind. Apparite asked the porter for a glass of water, and took one of the doctor's green pills, hoping to sleep the rest of the journey to Southampton and escape the disturbing images in his head.

Some time later, the train lurched to a halt, awakening him; they were in Southampton, Apparite having slept undisturbed for the entire trip. He felt much more rested after his nap, but those distressing thoughts and images were still in his mind, as intrusive as ever. *When am I going to get past those terrible events?* he asked himself in his frustration. But the mind, he knew, was a slippery opponent—how can one actively *not* think of something? It was akin to forcing oneself to go to sleep: the harder one tried, the less likely one would succeed.

Leaving the station, he hired a taxi to drive him to the *Queen Elizabeth*'s berth. Stepping into the cab only brought back more painful memories: the angry Cockney Cabbie; the wild drive through London; and the arrival at the mews, too late to save J. As the taxi neared the port where the passenger vessels berthed, he saw the liner's tall stacks in the distance contrasted against the sky. The cab made a few more turns, and then, through the spaces between the buildings that lined the port, Apparite could see the body of the ship itself, although it was too large to be viewed in its entirety.

The taxi dropped him off at the Cunard terminal entrance; he went inside to use the toilet facilities and drop off his largest bag which, given his arm wound, was becoming a burden to carry. He kept the smaller bag close to him, however; it was into this one he had stuffed the majority of his weapons and the cash and bullion, and he wanted to keep it in his sight. After completing the necessary tasks, he left the terminal via the exit nearest the port, and then had his first full view of the *Elizabeth*.

Up close, the Cunarder looked *immense;* as big as a skyscraper lying on its side, and many, many stories tall; her two large red and black funnels seemed to rise hundreds of feet in the air. Apparite guessed that it was the single largest object he had ever seen; bigger than the Washington Monument, St. Paul's, or even the Capitol building. He had read about the great vessel in *Popular Mechanics* and knew of her huge size and tremendous power—eighty-three thousand tons, making twenty-eight and a half knots while ferrying over two thousand passengers across the Atlantic—but in person, she looked larger than any man-made object he could imagine. Gazing up at her from ground level, it was easy to forget that this monstrous hulk was floating on the water and could *move;* that it could actually sail the breadth of the Atlantic to dock in New York.

The impressive sight took his mind off of his worries, and for a moment, he had forgotten about J and Hitch and the unfortunate young Humphreys. But a boy about Humphreys' age suddenly stepped in front of him, and the sight of his face caused Apparite to flash to a mental image of Viktor drawing his knife slowly across young Humphreys' throat.

Damn it! he thought. *How can I stop this?*

He was unaware of it, but the cure to his frustration was standing only a few feet behind him and in a most unusual and unexpected form: an attractive, trim brunette waiting in the queue to board the liner.

"Hey! Hey!" she said.

Apparite heard the voice; a pleasant, musical sound that immediately attracted his attention. It seemed vaguely familiar to him, but he could not identify it amongst the growing throng waiting to board, nor see to whom it belonged.

There was an increasingly chaotic crush to board the liner—the movement of the crowd reminded him of thoroughbreds jockeying for position as they rounded the final turn at Pimlico—and Apparite was being jostled about considerably: someone stepped on his left foot; a bag banged into his right thigh; he felt a poke behind his knee; he felt a bag smack against his hip; and a handbag hit him in the side of the head. He had always been impressed at the quiet civility of a British queue—what a disappointment to see it all fall apart just as he was leaving their country!

"Hey! Hey!" the voice called out again but, in the increasing confusion and noise, Apparite had barely been able to hear it, and it had hardly registered. As Apparite approached the ship, the queue began to thin (the Cunard porters and attendants were herding people into a more orderly formation up the narrow gangway), and he began to feel some measure of relief. Reaching the front of the queue, he showed his ticket, walked up the rather steep gangway—now limping a bit from his leg wound—and boarded the spacious *Elizabeth*.

Finally, he thought, I've got some breathing room. And then he heard the voice again more clearly, recognizing it immediately as one from his very recent past.

"Hey, Mr. Diamond Examiner!"

Apparite whipped his head around—he knew of no one else who might be referred to by that unusual moniker—and immediately saw that his voyage home would be much different than he had ever imagined: the voice belonged to the pretty brunette stewardess from the trans-Atlantic airplane flight, and she was waving at him excitedly.

Dressed in a stylish, form-fitting light blue outfit with a pink buttoned-down sweater, she looked a dream; like a model from a fashion magazine spread. He felt as transparent and light as tissue paper; the breath from a baby might have bowled him over for the surprise and shock he felt at the moment. More importantly, he had forgotten about J, Hitch, and young Humphreys at the sight of her.

She ran up to him, smiling broadly and laughing—the tip of her little pink tongue stuck out between her front teeth as charmingly as he had remembered—and she planted as warm and affectionate a hug as he had ever experienced on him.

"It's me! From the *plane!*" she said when she had let him loose from her grip.

"I can't believe it!" the stunned Apparite somehow choked out.

She got a funny look on her face, as if she remembered something that had been missing from their previous conversations.

"*Oh,* I should probably tell you my name. It's Peggy Stokes."

"I'm John Apparite," he said, relieved he was allowed to use his "true" identity outside the United States—it made him feel like a real person, unlike his uses of "Robert Kramer," or "Joseph Judge." The fact that it was a name assigned to him by the Director of a super-secret espionage agency seemed immaterial.

"Why are you taking the *Elizabeth* back home?" asked Apparite. "Why aren't you flying?"

"My boyfriend broke up with me, the rat!" she said, a cute little scowl forming on her face, "so you won't have any diamond ring to examine after all!"

"I'm so sorry," Apparite said, disguising his joy at the news.

Her scowl then receded and was replaced by her usual, lovely, white-toothed smile.

"Thanks for saying so. After that, I wanted to take some time for myself before going back home, so I took a couple of weeks off. I've always wanted go back on one of these ships."

For someone who's just broken up with her boyfriend she seems awfully happy, Apparite said to himself. *And maybe,* he added, *it's all because she saw me.* Apparite was feeling all aces right now: everything was changing for the better.

"I won't try to hide why *I'm* going back on a ship," Apparite said with a laugh in return, "because you saw how much I enjoy flying!"

She laughed as well, playfully slapping his right shoulder and arm with her hand.

"How did your diamond machine work out?" she asked.

"Great," Apparite answered, as he consciously (though unsuccessfully) tried to shrink the ridiculously wide smile hanging on his face. "I'm going back to New York with the news and a big order for the company." He was lying, of course, but the way he was feeling made it almost seem true.

Apparite could not remember when he'd had such a delightful conversation; all the intrusive thoughts he'd been having about the tragic events in London had completely disappeared. His mind was his own again and he rejoiced in it, even if the ability to get rid of his ridiculous grin was *not*.

"Are you traveling in first? I'm stuck in lowly tourist myself," she asked.

"No, no," Apparite answered, "I'm in tourist, too!" Having the Director change his ticket from first class to tourist was a godsend, he decided.

There was a brief pause; usually, this was where one or the other would say, "Well, I've got to check in," or "I'd better be going now," but neither of them seemed to want to leave the other—they just held each other's eyes for a few seconds, until Apparite suddenly broke.

"Would you like to meet for lunch?" he asked, trying to hide his anxiety about the invitation, but when she laughed out loud and smiled, his worries were immediately dispelled.

"Of course! Where?"

"How about the Verandah Grill? It's supposed to be swell." Swell? Did he really say that? Thank God the Director isn't witnessing this exchange, he thought.

"Doesn't that cost extra to get into?" she asked.

"Don't worry about that; I'll take care of it. I'll take care of *everything*. I'll see you there at about one-thirty, okay?"

"Great; I can't wait," she said, leaning over and kissing him on the cheek.

She then picked up her smart little pink handbag and walked away with that brisk, confident walk so typical of a stewardess (Apparite had also noticed it in nurses and secretaries, and had always found it *very* sexy and appealing). He smiled as she left him, knowing he would have at least six days to spend with this wonderful little gal. She was so vivacious and full of life—with her lovely, long chestnut hair she reminded Apparite of a fresh Maryland filly—and he marveled at his change in fortune and mood.

The salty sea breeze seemed to be washing away all his worries, and the bright sun above hinted of lazy days to be shared by the pool, or playing shuffleboard (laughing at their shared ineptitude), or just sitting on the Sun Deck and sipping ice cold beer. And then when night fell, they might have a romantic dinner in the restaurant, followed by dancing in the Salon. He would hold her in his arms (had he mentioned that she was the perfect height for him, he being five-six and she about five-four?), his naturally witty nature bringing the laughter bubbling out of her like a spring of pure, crystal clear water: such a delightful sound, and always accompanied by the enchantment of that little pink tongue sticking-out between her white, perfect teeth. Afterwards, when they could dance no more (his leg would be paining him, of course: perhaps we should go out on the deck?), they would lie in a shared chaise-longue, cuddling to keep warm in the cool November evening, sharing a few private jokes—and not just a few private kisses—and then . . . ?

Apparite took his bag in hand. He felt lighter than air and practically floated back to his room, the *Elizabeth*'s grandeur adding to the dream-like quality of his stroll. Along his way he marveled at the beautiful woods and paintings which graced the vessel's lounges (peeking into the Verandah Grill, he thought it the perfect venue for a lunch with "my girl"), and at its elegant Art Deco accents, which were practically everywhere—even the polished floors of the corridors had the unmistakable patina of class. The *Elizabeth* was as swanky as the fanciest D.C. hotel.

An impartial observer might have noted Apparite's limp, but in his current state of euphoria the young agent was feeling no pain: passing into the corridor that led to his cabin, all of his thoughts were on the lovely Peggy Stokes and the romantic adventure on which the two of them were about to embark. He knew it would not, *could* not last beyond the docking of the ship in New York, but he cared little for such practical concerns at the moment: they were insignificant compared to the experiences they would share on this voyage, and the memories he would bring home. And who knows? Maybe someday *after* his duties had been fulfilled—and if he survived them—then something more *could* happen between them.

The ship lurched slightly and he heard cheering from the hundreds of passengers out on deck, indicating that they were leaving port and sailing into the open sea: his journey home had officially begun. Nearing his cabin, he saw the larger of his suitcases awaiting him outside his room. He took it in hand—it now felt as light as champagne bubbles, even though he was lifting it with his injured arm—and went into the room. The cabin was compact but classy and well-appointed: there was a smallish though comfy-appearing bunked-bed; a tidy little closet; a compact but complete washroom; and understated but elegant wall coverings. He was no longer fatigued—not in the least—but he *had* worked up a sweat. He thought it might be best to shower and then get spiffed-up for his big date with Peggy.

He opened up his suitcases and carefully repacked them, insuring that his weapons, his money, and his Walter Johnson tobacco card were well hidden. (He would occasionally have to leave his bags alone on the trip, and then run the gauntlet of U.S. Customs in New York City after arrival, and he was taking no chances of their discovery.) Having done that, he hung up his clothes in the closet, placed his socks, under-shorts, and undershirts in the drawers of the little dresser, and began to disrobe. *What a remarkable day,* he said to himself.

He was thinking about which shirt and tie combination to wear for his date when he first noticed it: a tiny, *tiny* red dot on the back of his right leg. Pressing on it, it was very slightly tender; now, how the hell did I get *that?* he wondered. He looked at the backside of both legs very carefully, but there were none others like it. Not a rash, he thought; an isolated spot isn't really a rash. He was becoming very curious about this little red dot when suddenly he felt a rush from his innate danger-sense: *Where,* he asked himself, *have I seen a mark like that before?*

Suddenly his pulse raced; his palms sweated; his head was spinning; and then he knew. *It was the mark from a poison cane-gun!* He remembered the Director demonstrating the cane apparatus on him back in D.C., and the mark was identical—there could be no mistaking it.

Oh my God, he said out loud. *Oh my God, oh my Christ, oh my God.*

And then he remembered when it had happened: it was in the bustle of the crowd as they waited to board the ship. Someone had stepped on his left foot; a bag had banged into his right thigh; he had felt a bag smack against his hip; a handbag had hit him in the side of the head; *and he had felt a poke behind his knee!*

Apparite grabbed one of his shoes; trying to suppress his rising panic, he removed the highly sharpened throwing knife hidden in the toe. Although his hands were shaking from a surge of adrenaline, he skillfully made a small incision just under the tiny spot on the back of his right leg. Steadying his nerves with a few deep breaths, he gently lifted out a small piece of tissue on the end of the blade. He looked at it carefully, but could see nothing. He'd need more magnification.

He put down the knife, being careful not to jar the little piece of tissue from its resting place on the tip, and took his microdot reader from its case. He smeared the piece of bloody tissue from the knife's tip onto a ten-penny piece and placed it under the apparatus. He focused madly as he moved the coin to and fro, searching for the possible instrument of his death. He began to feel a sense of relief at the lack of findings after a few moments of examination—maybe the dot wasn't the wound from a poison-gun, after all—until he saw something that didn't look like blood, and it didn't look like tissue. He focused the instrument even more finely, and a miniscule silver sphere, much smaller than the head of a pin, came into view.

He searched for a safety pin in his luggage. Finding one, he carefully turned the sphere with the sharp end of it, *and there they were:* two microscopic holes were visible on opposite ends of the sphere. The evidence was irrefutable: he had been poisoned. He washed the sphere down the sink, hid the microdot reader in the larger of his two bags, and lay back onto the bed. Anxious nausea washed over him as he realized his helpless situation, but there was nothing he could do but wait—and think.

Who could have done it? The obvious answer stung him: it had been the *Director.* It was the Director who had a cane gun armed with poison, and it was the Director who had told him to take the *Elizabeth* home. The Director must have decided that Apparite had breached his duty when he'd chosen to save the boy, allowing Viktor to escape. The Director's punishment for such a failure, Apparite now knew, was death.

And whether it was from his anxiety or the effects of the poison, Apparite began to have wilder thoughts: what about

Peggy Stokes? She had been standing right behind him in the boarding line, and wasn't it a little *too* coincidental how they had met in Southampton, two people among tens of millions in England, who just *happened* to be taking the same ship home? And, now that he thought of it, hadn't she been a little *too* inquisitive on the airplane flight about him and his "diamond machine"?

Despite this agonizing realization, Apparite thought he had best concentrate on suppressing his panic and lying still—moving would only accelerate his circulation, drawing more of the deadly poison toward his vulnerable organs. Had they used *Ricinus?* If so, he would be able to tell within hours, and would be dead within days. Cyanide? No, he guessed; he would already be dead, plus death from cyanide might be traceable, and his must be a mysterious demise. A variation of the "L-pill"? Or curare? If so, he knew he'd be dead in seconds to minutes. Whatever it was, Apparite also realized that there would be no antidote to take; no effective treatment to be given: an assassin using a sophisticated poison gun would almost certainly use the most lethal and hopeless poison possible.

As his mind made its transition from panic to resignation, Apparite began to think more logically and critically. Would the Director *really* have thought it best to kill him this way? He laughed out loud: *of course not*—it had been a ludicrous set of suppositions. Hadn't the Director had ample opportunity to kill him without a trace after the battle in the mews? Couldn't he simply have had the Belgian doctor give him an injection that would have done the job in private; nice and clean and without any questions?

And as for Peggy, she was a working stewardess for Pan-American Airlines! How many Pan-Am stewardesses moonlight as assassins, killing super-secret American spies with sophisticated poison guns? Not too many, he figured, an ironic chuckle coming out of him despite the gravity of his situation. The ridiculous thought had its gestation in his panic, and now that his mind was clear he would try to find a more reasonable suspect. After a second, he had one.

It had been SMERSH, of course. Viktor might have left England, and the London KGB might have been decimated, but the Soviets had many allies who would be more than happy to kill an elite American agent. The Bulgarian embassy was quite close to the mews—had they tailed Apparite and the Director, identifying the doctor's safe house? Or had one of the few surviving KGB men, or even another SMERSH agent, followed Apparite on his trip to the hospital, St. Paul's, or the Royal Artillery Memorial? The more he thought about it, the more likely, and even certain, it seemed.

And the technology was not beyond SMERSH's grasp; it was common knowledge that the Soviets had a special talent at developing assassination devices. They had guns disguised as pens, smoking pipes, and cigars; there were pistols, umbrellas, and cigarette packs that discharged poison gas; and they had even invented needle-tipped rings which injected poisons concealed within their stones. SMERSH had the means and the motive—it *must* have been them, Apparite concluded.

Not that it would make a difference: Apparite had been poisoned and would probably die—his only chance was that he had found the pellet and removed it in time. But how much of the poison had leached out of the sphere in the minutes between injection and discovery? The nausea was increasing rapidly and Apparite knew it was the poison taking its deadly effect. He ran to the sink and began retching violently; first bile and foam, and then material that looked like old coffee-grounds began to appear. Exhausted, he fell to the ground and began shaking; not the mild shakes of an evening chill or a breaking fever, but real and true *rigors*—repetitive convulsing movements that left him unable to stand; unable to function. Apparite slowly crawled to the door, thrashing involuntarily, and with some effort was able to fling it open. He threw himself into the corridor and then collapsed.

He felt a liquid substance running down his thighs; he had just involuntarily emptied his rectum, and the urine soon followed. The retching continued, unabated; dark blood had begun coming out of his mouth with each bout of vomiting, creating a small, maroon puddle on the corridor floor. His head was pounding; his body was shaking and contorting; he had a fever; and the sweat was pouring out of him in buckets. The retches were now coming so frequently that he had lost the power of speech; all he could do was gasp, retch, and cough; gasp, retch, and cough. A porter turned the corner and saw him lying in the newly soiled corridor.

"Are you alright, sir?" he asked with concern, bending over him.

Apparite vomited mahogany-colored blood onto the man's polished black shoes.

"Oh my Lord!" he said in alarm. "I'm getting the doctor."

The doctor, Apparite said to himself, *can't do anything for me.* The ship has left port and gone out to sea, and they'll do with me just what they did with Robert Kramer in D.C.: put me in isolation, tell no one, and wait until either I died or the ship docked in New York. *I don't stand a chance,* he concluded.

A few minutes later, a nurse wearing a traditional white uniform and cap ran up to him, carrying a small case; following closely was a middle-aged bespectacled doctor wearing a white lab coat and holding a heavy, brown leather bag. Behind him, and walking briskly, were another two nurses, still adjusting the white caps on their heads.

"Don't get too close!" the doctor cried out. "Wear a mask and gloves." The nurse nearest Apparite stopped, put down the case and opened it, taking a surgical gown, mask, and a pair of rubber gloves from inside it and putting them on. She leaned over and began examining him.

"He has a high fever, doctor: one hundred-four degrees," the nurse said. "And he's lost stool and urine. His pulse is one-ninety; respirations thirty-six per minute."

The doctor also donned a surgical gown, mask, and gloves, and then turned to face the horrified porter standing nearby. "Bring some bleach and a basket of towels. We need to sterilize the floor." He walked to where Apparite lay and knelt over him.

"We have to put you in isolation: you have a severe infection and you might be contagious. Since your cabin is already contaminated, we will put you back inside it to take care of you; I can't take a chance of exposing others by moving you elsewhere. Although we can't treat you in the infirmary, I don't want you to worry—we will bring our medical equipment to your room and we'll give you as much care as we can on board this ship. You'll be fine." He gently rubbed the prostrate agent's head as if to reassure him, but the feel of the doctor's rubber gloves against his bare skin only told the young American, *you look so desperately ill, even* I'm *afraid to touch you.*

The doctor motioned to two fully gowned and masked attendants who had appeared; they carefully carried Apparite back into his cabin and placed him in his bed. As he lay there in agony, the doctor's final words echoed in Apparite's head: "We'll give you as much care as we can on board this ship."

Good luck doc, Apparite said to himself, *because there's not a damn thing you can do for me. You might as well lock the door on your way out and leave me here to die.*

The doctor, satisfied that Apparite was out of immediate harm's way (as far as exposing the other passengers was concerned), began giving orders to the medical staff. Even through his onrushing delirium, Apparite could make out what he was saying.

"Infections like this are usually hopeless: bring me morphine, an intravenous set-up with an 'LR' drip, antibiotics—whatever you've got, bring them all—and a portable heart monitor. The nurses will work in eight-hour shifts; we'll keep him comfortable and well-hydrated, but there is little else we can do. Wear protective clothing at all times, and do not get too close to him if you can help it!

"One last thing: we must *not* spread panic aboard the ship, or alarm the other passengers. If anyone asks, tell them a passenger is ill but insist he is certain to recover, although he is going to miss out on all the fun and excitement of the trip. Do you understand?"

The three nurses nodded in silent agreement. One of them, apparently the head nurse as evident by her age and bearing, spoke to the other two.

"I'll work the first shift; you two get the supplies and bring them here," she told them in a direct tone. She then walked into Apparite's room, closed the door firmly, and sat down in a chair next to him. She watched as the young man gasped and struggled in his fight, looking so alone; so very afraid and alone, she thought. Without medicine or supplies, she did the only thing which she thought could help him: defying the doctor's orders to keep her distance, she put her arms about him and embraced him, rubbing his back, wiping the sweat out of his eyes, reassuring him that he was not alone; that even if he were to die, he would not do it alone. Tears formed in her eyes as she comforted the suffering man as best she could.

Apparite convulsed again and again; the sweat poured down his face, stinging his eyes, and his flesh felt as if someone was flaying it off his bones from inside him. He prayed that *someone*—whether God or man, he cared not— would end his misery, or give his tortured mind a moment of rest. His prayer was quickly answered: as this last conscious thought left him, the world went black and his mind fled to a place of comfort and peace, far away from the tumults of his dying body.

Twenty-two
A Homecoming

Two men were in a dilapidated Victorian-era warehouse in a run-down section of Washington D.C. One of the men, who was wearing a well-tailored black suit and was reading the *Washington Post*, sat in a chair; the other man, who appeared to be asleep, was dressed in Army skivvies and covered by a green, government-issue blanket, and lay on an old WWI Army cot. The man in the chair paid little attention to the man in the cot, other than to occasionally put a foul-smelling liquid down a tube which had been inserted into the sleeping man's nose, and change the intravenous bottles when they ran low. The man in the cot paid little attention to the man in the chair, for one simple reason: he had been comatose for ten days, defying all predictions that he should have died. But if he was not dead, then he was, to all observers, barely alive.

A cough shattered the silence of the room; the man in the chair put down his paper and leaned over the man in the cot: could he really have made that noise? he wondered. It was the first sound that had come from the man in the cot since he had arrived.

"Cough. Cough-cough-cough," went the man in the cot, who blindly began reaching for the tube sticking out of his nose, the catheters in his arms, and even the rubber tube that was draining his bladder. *"Cough-cough-cough,"* he continued, and then he began shouting.

"J! J!" he yelled into the air. The man in the chair ran

336

across the room like a jackrabbit; he jerked a telephone on the far wall off its rest and dialed madly. After he had spoken a few urgent words into it, he ran back to the man in the cot.

"Apparite!" he said with urgency, "Apparite!"

Apparite unexpectedly sat upright and ripped the tube out of his nose. He briefly panicked in disorientation, as if he had suddenly awoken from a nightmare, but after a moment calmed with vague recognition of his location. He had been here before, he thought; a long, long time ago. Yes, he had spent weeks and weeks fighting a curious little man here—it was as if someone was dropping pieces of his memory into a bucket, and when it finally got full, then maybe he would re-member. Random memories then began flooding back to him: of breaking a man's arm in a bar; shooting a man from behind a ruined meat counter; driving very fast in a strange but beautiful city; throwing a knife into a man's chest; and then of a man lying asleep on a sofa. But somehow Apparite knew that the man was not asleep, and then he remembered.

"J! Where's J?"

"J's dead, Apparite," said the other man, who had sat back down into the chair next to the cot.

Of course J was dead; it had come back to him now. He and the Director had entered the mews and found him: J had taken his "L-pill."

"What about Peggy?"

"Peggy Stokes believes you have died, as do the other pas-sengers on the *Queen Elizabeth*. You were barely alive when you reached New York, and died shortly after, as far as anyone needs to know. Even the KGB and SMERSH believe it."

Poor Peggy, he thought. Such a sweet kid; she would have been waiting and waiting for me at the Verandah Grill, and then when she had found out about my illness, she probably tried to visit me, but the doctor would not have allowed it. If only there was a way to let her know I'm alright—but it wouldn't make a difference, he figured. After returning to the U.S. and reassuming my duties, I would have been dead to her anyway.

He looked around and saw the many pieces of medical equipment the Director had somehow smuggled into the warehouse. Man, he thought, the doctor and nurses on that ship must have been stretched to the limit with me. They'd probably spent the entire trip cooling my fevers, dripping every antibiotic they had into my veins, pouring gallons of intravenous fluids into me, and keeping me free from seizures.

It had been a good guess, for that was exactly what they had done, reaching a point where they had induced a barbiturate-coma to protect Apparite's brain from his convulsions and fever as best they could. They had worked night and day to keep their patient alive until they had reached New York, when he could be taken to a "real" hospital. How crestfallen they had been to learn that those long hours and sleepless nights had been in vain, and that their patient had "died" in the hospital shortly after arrival! The only blessing was that no others had been affected by his terrible infection, although the doctor and his nurses had spent many an anxious day worrying if they might not be the next in its deadly path.

They could not have known that their patient had been poisoned, and was the beneficiary of a minor miracle: John Apparite had indeed survived, having removed the deadly sphere from his leg minutes before it would have fully emptied. The *Elizabeth*'s medical team had saved the life of one of the United States' greatest and most secret of agents, but would never know that, either: Apparite's "contaminated" luggage had been left untouched, so his weapons, money, and identity as a spy remained undiscovered. But that was not all of which they would remain ignorant.

They would also never know the identity of the man who had met them at the Cunard pier in New York; the one who had come to accompany their patient to the hospital. They had assumed it was the young man's father—he had such a gentle and caring way with their patient, they thought—and, in some ways, they might have been correct. If they had searched further into that man's identity, however, they would have found nothing; he had no official name or title, although he had been given a nickname by their patient: the "Director."

The doctor and nurses liked this kind, middle-aged man; all the more so when they opened their next bank statements and found that their balances had inexplicably grown by $5,000 each. Despite their many inquiries, everyone at the bank firmly stated that the money was indeed theirs, that they could not say where it had come from, and that *that* was to be the end of it: they would be unable to discuss it further. One of the bank managers—a short, pudgy man with greasy black hair named Peabody—had even gotten a little *huffy* about the matter, and threatened to call the police. After that, the doctor and nurses left the issue alone and took well-earned vacations with their "bonus." They could only guess that it had come from their patient's "father."

A question—an important question—suddenly popped into Apparite's head.

"Who are *you?*" Apparite asked the man in the chair, who looked about thirty-five years old, was at least twenty pounds overweight, and had an unusual number of black moles on his face plus a small goatee that gave him an educated, professorial appearance (even in his weakened condition, Apparite's powers of observation had not been dimmed).

"You may call me 'D'; I'm replacing J as the liaison. I

know you two were close; I want you to know how sorry I am that he died."

His was an unusually warm voice, with more than a touch of an English accent—was one of his parents British, perhaps? D seemed a decent sort, but Apparite desperately wanted to change the subject: he was uncomfortable speaking about J so soon after his death.

"I feel like s—t," Apparite said.

"You should," said D. "When they brought you in here you were *covered* in it."

Despite his low mood Apparite laughed aloud, asking himself, *did the Director always get liaisons who thought they were comedians?*

"Do you know who did this to me?" he then inquired. "Was it SMERSH?"

"We think so. An accomplice of Viktor's—an agent called 'Oleg'—was identified in London after Viktor left the country; we think he tailed you on your journey to Southampton and injected you with the poison. His whereabouts remain unknown, as are Viktor's."

"I let him go," Apparite said, his voice failing him and turning into a whisper. "I had a chance to kill him, but I let him go to save an English boy."

"I know. Let that remain in the past, where it belongs. You may be interested to hear the Soviet engineer died the day after you left London, and they are developing the false fuel formula. Plus, the KGB never did learn your true name—and believes you dead regardless—so your ability to operate in the future has not been compromised. We consider the mission to have been successful—that's all you need to remember."

Apparite thought it was the kind of thing J might have told him, but it did not make him feel any better: J was dead and Viktor was alive, and *that* was all he needed to know about the mission. Apparite could not allow this injustice to remain: only after he had killed that pig Viktor would he consider his conscience clear; cleaned of the stain of the ill-fated mission and the choice he should have made, but could not make.

The double delivery doors opened. A middle-aged man with some gray at the temples appeared; he was wearing an ill-fitting black suit and his expression was severe. He walked purposefully toward the two men and whispered into D's ear. D smiled, rose from the chair next to the cot, and offered it to the other man. The man sat down in the chair and leaned over close to Apparite, revealing his face to the pale and exhausted agent.

It was the Director.

He looked as business-like as ever, thought Apparite, noting the same imperious bearing as when he had first met him but, on closer inspection, something was different. While the Director's body and demeanor had been unaltered, Apparite saw that his eyes no longer emitted the laser-like heat which had so intimidated him at their initial meeting; instead, a gentle warmth was emanating from them. The Director's intense gaze was now as comforting as it had been disconcerting to him only a few months before.

What a change he's undergone, Apparite said to himself. *He's trying to hide it, but I can see it in his eyes; he can't fool me so easily.*

The Director took a few moments to compose himself, and in the silence, Apparite sensed that he was struggling with his emotions in some way. And when the enigmatic man finally spoke, the words came out in a manner that he hadn't planned: he had meant to speak to his young charge in an official tone (especially in front of his new liaison) but, around the edges, a hidden affection would still peek through.

"Welcome home, Apparite," he said, his mouth curling

upward into a slight, involuntary smile.

Apparite smiled in return at the unexpected sentiment: *Welcome home.* It was, perhaps, an odd choice of words for a nineteenth century dilapidated warehouse filled with spies, he thought, but the phrase seemed to fit. The man now named John Apparite might not have had a real home—as the rest of the world would have defined the term—since his mother had died eight years earlier, but the changes he had undergone these past four months had forever altered the word's meaning to him.

Home, Apparite said to himself. If "home" was the place where people knew you best; where your duties were difficult but rewarded with respect; where people watched over you and healed you when you were ill, or comforted you when you were suffering, then he figured this rotting old warehouse would be as close to a home as he would ever have—and better than many in the "real" world would ever have, either. And although Apparite's parents were dead, and his old life had been removed as easily as an annoying spot on a dinner jacket, these past months had given him a new life and, he realized, a new family to replace the one he had lost.

The enigmatic and intensely patriotic Director made for an admittedly strange father, he thought, and his dead colleague, J, as a disgraced, homosexual ex-FBI agent might have been an odd choice for a brother, yet John Apparite would forever consider them his family. But there was more to it than that: Apparite was almost certainly unaware of it, but the Director was beginning to feel the same way in return—as hard as that austere man tried *not* to—which was, perhaps, the most peculiar thing of all.

What a strange world we live in, thought Apparite. Overcome with fatigue, he closed his eyes and let the sleep he so desperately needed overtake him. But when he awoke many hours later from his unremembered dreams, he found that his energy had returned; he had a hum in his head; his inner spring was beginning to coil; and one name burned in his brain: *Viktor.*

Apparite might have finally found his place in the world, but there was unfinished business in it for him to perform. And as soon as he was able, he would see that it was done.

Author's Notes

When writing a book taking place fifty years ago and involving the ins and outs of Cold War espionage, Soviet politics, missile fuels, the Washington Senators, classic semi-automatic pistols, and Italian meats and cheeses, one must give credit where it is due: the Defense Advance Research Projects Agency in the United States Department of Defense. Why them, you ask? Simple—because they developed the wonder that is the Internet, putting much of the esoteric information I needed for this story at my fingertips.

As for others, I must thank my admirably patient editor, Hugh Abramson; John Helfers of Tekno Books; and lastly, the fine mystery author Ed Gorman, for pointing me down a road that led to publication. I also wish to acknowledge a few of the persons who initially read the work and provided many insightful suggestions to make it better; especially Dr. Ronald Sims, Mike Berg, and my wife, Jackie.

While writing this book, I found the works of five authors to be particularly valuable: Tom Deveaux, who has written one of the few comprehensive works on the Washington Senators in existence (entitled, naturally, *The Washington Senators*); H. Keith Melton, whose book *Ultimate Spy* provided much inspiration and factual material regarding the spy game; Michael Rosenbaum, author of *Okinawa's Complete Karate System: Isshin-Ryu*, who brought to life the history and power of this fascinating discipline; Richard C. S. Trahair,

344

whose *Encyclopedia of Cold War Espionage, Spies, and Secret Operations* was an indispensable reference; and Marjorie Caygill, whose short but essential tome entitled *The British Museum Reading Room* is mandatory reading for, um, Reading Room readers, so to speak.

Speaking of the British Museum and its famed Reading Room, I should mention the contribution of their fine staff on my research trip to the great city of London, England: not only did they did *not* eject me when I began to photograph the room with impunity and examine its nooks and crannies like a nosey houseguest, they answered my questions and e-mails with signal promptness and courtesy. The room's recent restoration, I should note, is spectacular, returning it to its original nineteenth-century glory. You must go see it.

While in London, I also urge you to visit St. Paul's Cathedral and take the time to read the memorials in the cathedral and crypt: it truly is a moving experience, especially early in the morning when the crowds have not yet arrived and the cool, damp air in the cathedral is quiet and still. There was a very kind warder in the crypt who patiently answered my many, many queries in the shadow of Wellington's tomb to whom I particularly wish to express my gratitude: I may have forgotten your name, but I have not forgotten your contribution!

Lastly, I must thank my wife for allowing me to visit over a dozen London pubs in search of inspiration during our trip, and though I visited too many to mention each by name, some do appear in this book (the "Northumberland Arms" is now known as the Sherlock Holmes, by the way). Readers searching for the "Red Lion" near Covent Garden, however, might be more successful if they drop by the Lamb and Flag instead. Have a pint of bitter at a back-corner booth and people-watch for a while, but don't wait too long for Clive Hitch to show: MI5 tells me he's notoriously unreliable.

—I. Michael Koontz

About the Author

I. Michael Koontz was born in 1963, and is a medical professional living in the Midwest with his wife and two young daughters. *Under Cloak of Darkness: The Story of John Apparite* is the result of a lifelong, intense interest in Cold War espionage and military history, and is his debut novel. Readers interested in learning more about Superagent John Apparite and Cold War espionage, or who have questions or comments about the book, are encouraged to visit the author's website, www.imkoontz.com.